To save her school,
she needed a miracle.
What she got was a man
who didn't believe in dreams

Until now . . .

SCHOOL

Praise for Patricia Rice
and her novel *Blue Clouds*

A *Romantic Times* Top Pick

"Vastly entertaining . . . A wonderful combination of poignancy and humor."
—*Romantic Times*

"A wickedly luscious novel filled with scintillating dialogue, madcap characters, and a premise that shows what true romance is all about. With her superb talent, Ms. Rice pens remarkable tales that come across the pages in whatever genre she writes."
—*Rendezvous*

"Absolutely stunning . . . Rice gives us *everything* we could want in this 'to keep forever'—love, mystery, and adventure. . . . Fantastic."
—*Bell, Book & Candle*

"[A] romance that snares the reader right from the start."
—*Library Journal*

"You can always count on Patricia Rice for an entertaining story with just the right mix of romance, humor, and emotion."
—*The Romantic Reader*

By Patricia Rice:

PAPER MOON
DENIM AND LACE
WAYWARD ANGEL
GARDEN OF DREAMS*
BLUE CLOUDS*
VOLCANO*
IMPOSSIBLE DREAMS*

*Published by The Ballantine Publishing Group

IMPOSSIBLE DREAMS

Patricia Rice

IVY BOOKS • NEW YORK

This book contains an excerpt from the forthcoming edition of *Nobody's Angel* by Patricia Rice. This excerpt has been set for this edition only and may not reflect the final content of the forthcoming edition.

An Ivy Book
Published by The Ballantine Publishing Group
Copyright © 2000 by Rice Enterprises, Inc.
Excerpt from *Nobody's Angel* by Patricia Rice copyright © 2000 by Rice Enterprises, Inc.

www.randomhouse.com/BB/

Library of Congress Catalog Card Number: 99-91678

ISBN 0-449-00601-8

Manufactured in the United States of America

First Edition: April 2000

10 9 8 7 6 5 4 3 2 1

This book is dedicated to the true teachers of the world—had I the power, I would nominate you for sainthood. Someday, the world will recognize that people like you should be idolized and emulated and rewarded for your talents.

Someday, there will be dragons, too.

And to Elisa Wares, my editor, who let me dream and helped me fight dragons.

Meddle not with dragons
for thou art crunchy and good with catsup.

❧ ONE ❧

i souport publik edekasion.

"If you're a bill collector, all the money we have is in the cash box under the counter. If you take it all, you'll be taking food from the mouths of babes," a musically feminine voice called from behind the long glass counter.

Startled, Axell waited for his eyes to adjust to the murky interior of the New Age gift shop. The chiming bells of the door behind him silenced, and in their place the haunting aria from *Man of La Mancha*: "To dream the impossible dream . . . To fight the unbeatable foe . . ." swelled to a crescendo.

Intrigued despite himself, he wondered if he'd entered some netherworld far from the ordinariness of the Carolina sunshine outside. "Shall I leave the change?" he inquired dryly, searching the narrow shop for the source of the voice. A display case counter stretched along one long wall. Crammed with items too intricate and numerous to identify, it claimed his interest first. The layer of dust and fingerprints on the glass could be the reason most of the objects were unidentifiable. Fastidiously, he dusted a corner over a bumper sticker reading, VERY FUNNY, SCOTTY, NOW BEAM DOWN MY CLOTHES.

"You can have the Canadian pennies and McDonald's tokens," the voice called cheerfully.

"Miss Alyssum?" he inquired, bending to look over the glass for the shop proprietor but captured instead by what appeared to be a crystal ball beneath the spot he'd wiped clean. He ignored the overflowing shelves of commonplace gnomes,

1

dragons, crystals, cards, and dangling beads on the other wall, but the shimmering rainbows of color beneath the glass deserved further examination.

"Still there? Be with you in a minute. Once I'm down here, it's a struggle to get back up."

Intrigued by a telescope on a tripod, Axell used his handkerchief to dust it off, adjusted it to face the dirty shop window, and peeked through the eyeglass. A kaleidoscopic whirl of colors materialized before his eyes, sparkling like jewels through the sunshine, gliding and transforming from the fires of the sun to the tides of the sea in vivid blues and greens.

"Haven't seen one of these in years. They've improved." He'd come in here with a definite purpose, but it slipped his mind as he looked up and fell into eyes the same shade of sea blue and green he'd just admired in the kaleidoscope.

Startled by the unexpected intimacy of her gaze, Axell stepped back. He'd thought that silly nonsense about a man drowning in a woman's eyes a lot of sentimental claptrap. Maybe the air of the shop contained hallucinogenic smoke.

Wryly noting the dusty handkerchief in his hand, she brought him back from his cloud. "Let me guess, Virgo, right? I don't suppose you've come to make order of my universe, by any chance?" She threw her own dusty rag onto the counter. "It's murder cleaning all this junk. Cleo's ideas were always bigger than her ability to carry them out."

Grounded again, Axell blinked and tried to sort out the various impressions conveyed by the extraordinary apparition behind the counter. Once he disentangled himself from the crystal turquoise of long-lashed eyes, he encountered a fiery explosion of dark red wiry curls streaked with—purple? He'd had some interesting clientele in his bar before, but none could equal this eccentricity.

This wouldn't do. He'd come here for a reason. He couldn't allow himself to be distracted—his gaze drifted back to that purple streak. It almost made sense against the blue-green of those eyes.

Taking a deep breath, he gathered his wits again. "Miss Alyssum?"

She nodded, and the curls bobbed vigorously. "Right the first time. And you are . . . ?"

"Axell Holm." Unconsciously, he rearranged the disorderly stack of loose cards on the counter. One fell over, revealing a grinning jokester figure. "Tarot?" he inquired.

"Don't do this to me. I definitely do not need this." She removed the cards from his hands, tapped the deck together, and stacked them with the unopened boxes. "Not only Virgo, but probably Aquarius ascendant. I can't imagine a worse combination. You must have driven your mother crazy."

Unperturbed, Axell opened the cover of a book titled *Messages from Michael*. "I've examined the precepts of astrology and while it has a curiously reassuring effect on certain personalities, it has no scientific basis whatsoever. When looked at as a whole, it is not only improbable, but laughably naive. If this is the kind of thing you teach in your school, then perhaps the mayor is right in wanting it closed. I'm certain the children would benefit from a more scientific direction."

A benevolent smile lit her face, creating the illusion of shimmering mother-of-pearl luminescence in the dusky shop interior, drawing his attention to moist, pink, bow-shaped lips. For a brief—very brief—moment, Axell imagined kissing those lips. Appalled by the kind of lusty image he hadn't experienced since adolescence, he immediately drew back and focused on the details of his surroundings. "The Impossible Dream" changed to a Gaelic lilt, and the angle of the sun shifted to shoot a beam of rainbows through the crystal prisms hanging above the proprietor's head.

"Would you like some tea, Mr. Holm? Whatever my sister's failings, she knows her teas. I have a particularly lovely Chinese green that might soothe your muddy aura sufficiently for us to communicate."

"No, thank you, Miss Alyssum. I have come to discuss the school. The mayor has every intention of closing it."

Panic pierced her, but Maya smiled unblinkingly at the

attractive lion of a man in front of the counter. She'd guess him to be in his mid-thirties, a decade older than she and definitely of a dangerous social status, judging by his excellently tailored dark blue suit and expensive silk tie. She seldom responded physically to men with his cool Nordic looks, especially ones with the arrogant authority of Axell Holm. She preferred her men dark, passionate, and artistic. Good thing, too, because she didn't need those dreamy Aquarian gray eyes messing with her already crazed mind. The way they narrowed as they followed her incited definite palpitations.

"The Impossible Dream is not a public school," she reminded him, removing the carafe of near-boiling water from the hot plate and pouring it over the crinkled green leaves in her sister's prized Yixing teapot. "It's a private school and not within the mayor's realm of power." A brand-new private school with a temporary permit, the germ of all her dreams. She pried her nervous fingers loose from the carafe handle.

"Obviously, you have little experience with government, Miss Alyssum."

"Maya, call me Maya," she replied absently, setting out her own precious porcelain cups and saucers with their intricately painted landscapes of a different world. They didn't match Cleo's brown teapot with its single lotus blossom, but they had the same significance to both of them, so in Maya's mind, they matched perfectly. "And I've had entirely too much experience with government authority, I assure you."

The phone rang, and she ignored it as she carried the delicate porcelain to an old-fashioned ice cream table in the back corner. The Gaelic music changed to a monk's chant, the phone shrieked, and in the back, the steady drip-drip of the bathroom faucet intruded. She really needed to get that fixed, or wait until the utility company turned off the water for nonpayment. That would solve the problem. She'd write it down right after "fix broken lock on back door."

"Your phone is ringing, Miss . . . Maya."

"True Virgo," she muttered as she set down the saucers. "Let the machine get it," she responded airily as he glared at the offending instrument. He vibrated with an acute Virgo intensity that he hid behind catlike wariness, but she'd detected a spasm of some sort as she emerged from behind the counter.

She smoothed the crinkly crepe of her long skirt over her protuberant belly and smiled fetchingly at him. Whoever was on the phone slammed down the receiver as the answering machine kicked on. Bill collector, she concluded. She watched her visitor struggle with his curiosity. Mr. Axell Holm looked like an absentminded professor lost in a particularly disturbing problem instead of the wealthy proprietor of the town's most popular—and only—watering hole. She'd finally placed his face, if not his name. She'd seen it in the local paper several times since she'd returned to Wadeville to take care of her nephew.

Holm was on the city council, she remembered with apprehension.

"I didn't realize you were married, Mrs. Alyssum. I apologize. The way Constance speaks of you, I assumed . . ." He backtracked and asked pointedly, "Is your husband available? Perhaps together we could discuss some arrangement. . . ."

Constance! Of course. The name finally clicked. Holm— Constance's father. Maybe this wasn't entirely about the city council. Maya patted his arm and indicated one of the delicate wrought-iron chairs. "Have a seat, Mr. Holm, and let me pour you some tea. Do you take honey?" She retrieved the pot from the counter, a little too aware of his fascination with her bulging belly. That was the problem with Aquarians, they were too darned nosy. Thank goodness his Virgo sun sign dominated or she might have to dump the tea over his head.

He waited expectantly—not for the tea, she observed. The jasmine fragrance wafted soothingly around them as she poured. "Constance is quite correct; I'm not married. She's an exceptionally intelligent, talented child, and a delight to work with. You should be proud of her."

She took the seat opposite him and sipped the elegant tea with quiet pleasure. Maybe if she concentrated, this would all go away. She really didn't want to hear what new disaster loomed on her horizon. She merely wanted to enjoy her tea and the china and the rainbow of colors through the prisms and the lovely man across from her trying not to frown. And he *was* a lovely man: true golden-blond Nordic hair bleached by the Carolina sun, intelligent gray eyes with thick brown lashes, and a jutting cleft chin that would make Sean Connery proud. His soft southern drawl seemed somehow out of place in a man like this, but it brought back sweet memories from long ago.

Of course, there were those thin lips and the flaring of his aristocratic nose to warn her of a lion king's arrogance behind the knowing expression. . . .

"Umm," he hesitated, looking for a nice way of asking his next question, "perhaps your significant other . . ."

Maya laughed.

Axell watched her features light with the pure joy of her laughter. No weak trill or artificial tinkle for this gypsy. Joy rang out as melodically and soulfully as the musical metal chimes overhead. Definitely high-quality chimes, he observed in wonder, each one perfectly attuned to a note on the scale. He wanted to enjoy it, but the chaos of light, color, sound, and emotion swirling around him proved too distracting.

His gaze followed the prisms of color in her already rainbow-hued hair. The jasmine-scented tea combined with a potpourri of rose petals on the counter, the bouquet of flowers on the table, the pot of golden honey, and the herbal fragrance of the woman herself. The sensual atmosphere was radically different from the sterile environment of his own home.

"You would very definitely not wish to include Stephen in our conversation, even were he here, Mr. Holm. Take my word for it. Do you like the tea?"

He hated tea. From the disorder and dust of this shop, he feared the cleanliness and safety of anything ingested anywhere within a hundred yards of it. Still, in the interest of peace, he lifted the cup to his lips. The fragrance enticed him into sipping.

"Interesting." Calmly, he lowered the cup and sought another approach. The colorful young woman across from him was the antithesis of everything he'd expected. A teacher at the utopian after-school program should be highly intelligent, goal oriented, efficient, independent, and eager to forestall the problems he perceived ahead. She should be grateful for his offer of help.

Instead of the rational, business-suited career woman he'd expected, she was an explosion of femininity. The thick cascade of red curls spilled over delicately boned shoulders draped in a lacy ivory shawl. A satin-trimmed wide collar of a shifting blue-green silky blouse drifted downward in points that clung to high firm breasts resplendent with pregnancy. He didn't dare look any lower. His gaze fastened on unadorned slender white fingers wrapped around the outlandishly decorated burnt-orange teacup.

"I disturb you, Mr. Holm," she said gently, in a voice that whispered above the pulsating tide currently emanating from the speakers. "You do have a first name, don't you? May I use it?"

"Axell, please do," he replied absently as a graceful branch of flowering forsythia dipped and caressed her fingers. The disorderly bouquet of branches, daffodils, and crushed violets reminded him of his purpose. Constance. A thump of panic struck his heart at the thought of his lovely, lost waif of a daughter, and his determination returned.

"The mayor is dead set against the school, Miss . . . Maya." He set the teacup down, adjusted the saucer so the scene of bridges and trees lined up with the edge of the table and the cup's design faced him. "I suspect your liberal principles are anathema to his conservative soul, but mostly, the building occupies acreage the new shopping center needs for parking lot access."

"I have a three-year lease on that building, Mr. . . . . Axell," she imitated him teasingly, the tip of her tongue touching her top lip with mischief. Axell blinked and tried not to wonder if her tongue tasted of tea or honey.

"The shopping center people really should have met dear

Mr. Pfeiffer's selling price if they wanted the land," she continued. "Mr. Pfeiffer grew up in that house. He has no intention of giving it away. My lease specifies he can't sell for three years. I don't see any problem. I trust Constance is happy with the program?"

"It's the only thing that does make her happy," he said bluntly, and therein lay the crux of his concern, although he wouldn't admit it to anyone and certainly not to this pixilated gypsy. "She's very attached to the program." And to the teacher—again, an admission he wouldn't make aloud. Confessions of a personal nature revealed weaknesses that could be used against him, he'd learned long ago. "The location is convenient, and it's a relief knowing she's in capable hands while I'm at work. I don't wish to see that arrangement disturbed, but the mayor is pressuring the department of transportation for a road through there. The state can condemn the property if a road is approved."

A tiny frown wrinkled the delicate bridge of her nose, then disappeared as she took another sip of tea. "Well, just tell the mayor that would be a misplacement of the public trust and a personal use of the taxpayers' money. I have plans to expand to a full-time preschool facility at the beginning of the next school year. As you said, it's an ideal location. The children love the yard, too. We won't be moved."

"You don't understand . . . Maya." Axell hesitated over the preposterous name, wondered briefly what planet she hailed from, then ruthlessly dismissed all his nagging questions in favor of his goal. "A school of your size requires a license. Should the state decide to side with the mayor, you won't receive that license. Unless you're independently wealthy, you won't be able to sustain your lease for long without income. For the sake of Constance and the other children . . ."

She rose and drifted toward the counter where the phone was ringing again. He'd never seen a pregnant woman move with such grace. When Angela was . . .

He shut down that path of thought. "We really must consider some alternatives."

She poured more hot water over the leaves in the pot. A cat

he hadn't noticed earlier leapt from a high shelf to the counter, stretched luxuriously, sniffed the tea, then settled for a cream-filled saucer beside the hot plate.

His gaze fastened on the gauzy red-brown pleats of her jumper as Maya turned. He glanced away as the baby moved. She was definitely making him uncomfortable.

She patted his shoulder reassuringly as she passed by. "Don't fret, Axell. I know you like all your little soldiers in a row, but life isn't like that. I appreciate your concern, but fate will decide whether the school survives or not. You may try to steer the hands of fate, if you like, but I'm afraid I rather have my hands full dealing with more earthly concerns. Fate is out of my realm."

She said this last so dryly, he almost winced. "You're new to the area, I believe?" he asked, determined to get a handle on the situation despite her evasiveness.

"No place like home," she murmured.

"Perhaps you don't understand the local politics," he suggested diplomatically.

"Authority rules for the good of all and the benefit of none." She set her cup down. "I appreciate your concern, Axell, but I'm certain you have better things to do. Constance will always have a place in my program after school, and she's welcome to join our full-time summer classes. I think she might be happier with a little more individual attention, don't you?"

Setting the cup precisely so the handle aligned with the table's edge, Axell rose. "I don't think impossible dreams make a good basis for an education, Miss Alyssum. If Constance needs individual attention, I'll place her in a more traditional private school. Thank you for the tea. It was nice meeting you. Good day."

He strode out, not a wisp of that sunny hair misplaced by the spring breeze, not a speck of dandelion fluff daring to cling to the knife-sharp crease of his gabardine trousers or the broad expanse of his suit-coated shoulders as he passed by the shop window. Tall and sturdy rather than elegantly lean,

Axell Holm strode down the street with the arrogant certainty of his place in the world.

Maya admired the surety of his stride as he passed, then smiled as he stopped on the corner to examine a foil kite displayed outside the corner drugstore. That Aquarian curiosity would be his downfall, she predicted.

Patting the restless stirring inside her abdomen, she relaxed against the chair back, reprogrammed the sound system, and let the aria from *Man of La Mancha* carry her away from this time and place. Music was supposed to inspire the unborn child, increase their intelligence and awareness, and she wanted her child to have all the right advantages. She breathed in the crescendo of "The Impossible Dream." Impossible dreams were the only kind she knew.

She had no money, a stack of bills higher than her sister's inventory, and no real job to speak of, but wherever her heart was, was home. She could pack up and leave anytime she liked—after Cleo got out of jail.

December 1945

> *The night you walked into the bar, I thought you were the most amusing thing that had happened in a long time. The joint stank of beer. Pete had passed out at his usual table. The piano player was more interested in one of the guys at the bar than in what he was playing. Then you walked in with your shiny new church suit and spiffy fedora, trying to look as if you walked into dens of iniquity all the time. You were irresistible.*
>
> *I was halfway to drunk when you looked at me, but I sobered up quick. God, you were one good-looking fellow. Why am I telling you this? You damned well knew it all along. You probably got through the war on your looks and charm. I'll sober up in the morning and rip this letter to shreds, so it doesn't matter what I say anyway.*
>
> *Or maybe I won't. Maybe I'll mail it and hope it poisons your two-timing heart.*

You had eyes that seared the soul and set my jaded heart thumping. Even Pete wasn't amusing anymore. I didn't want you to ignore me, so I walked right up and caught your tie between my fingers and led you straight down the path to hell.

Or maybe I hoped you'd lead me out. I never was very smart.

❧ TWO ❧

Depression is merely anger
without enthusiasm.

"Maya, is that you? We've got problems, girl." The lilting southern accent drifted down the darkened hall through the office doorway, sounding more bemused than worried.

Maya kneeled and hugged the five-year-old clenching her hand. "It's all right, sugar baby. Selene makes jokes. Everything's going to be just fine. Why don't you turn on the lights and check on Mr. Pig?"

The solemn little boy with her sister's bright green eyes nodded his shaggy head. She really needed to get his hair cut. Maya ruffled the dark strands and kissed his forehead. Maybe pregnancy was magnifying her emotions, but his solemnity tore at her heartstrings. Except for his eyes, he didn't even look like Cleo, but she saw her older sister's worried frown in his expression now. He might be only five, but he carried the world's burdens on his shoulders already. And just like Cleo, he frequently rebelled at the weight. He still didn't entirely trust Maya to carry the burden.

"I bet Mr. Pig missed you today. Pat him nicely so he knows you care."

Matty smiled shyly. "I will. Can I have a chocolate milk?"

"May I," she corrected. "Sure thing, sugar dumplin'. Only one, though. We've got to have enough for everyone." Maya bit her lip and watched with a sob in her throat as her nephew ambled down the long hall toward the school's main workroom. That poor child had lived through hell these last few

12

years. She cursed Cleo and turned to find Selene watching her from the doorway.

"That boy will be just fine. Kids bounce back fast. It's you I'm worried about. Get yo'self in here and put your dogs up."

"Don't give me that cotton-mouth, girl," Maya mocked, following Selene into the office to drop onto a shredded couch that was one step ahead of the garbage heap. "I may be white trash, but you've got upbringing."

Selene's grin spread across her face. "You're the one with the education, not me. I'm just here washing floors."

"Scrubbing." Maya arranged her expanded belly comfortably on the sagging cushion and put her feet up. "One scrubs floors and washes dishes. Shows how much you know about real work."

With a more serious expression, Selene inquired, "You heard from that sister of yours yet?"

She sighed. "Going cold turkey hasn't made Cleo any more communicative than before. She won't take my calls." Just the topic of her sister made her nervous. She hadn't seen Cleo in years, had barely exchanged more than a dozen phone calls with her since Cleo had reached the age of eighteen and fled the series of foster homes they'd grown up in.

Still, Maya treasured memories of her street-tough older sister rescuing her from childhood dragons, and she figured she owed Cleo. She just couldn't rely on her. For that, she had her wealthy partner.

Only today, Maya felt dumpy and dowdy beside Selene's tailored ivory linen magnificence. At five-ten and barely a hundred-forty pounds, Selene could scarcely disguise her elegant carriage. Pregnant women weren't supposed to be elegant, Maya reminded herself. Still, it would have been nice if she'd felt a little less like a mushroom around a man like Axell Holm. Not that Norse gods noticed insignificant white trash.

"Earth to Maya, earth to Maya, come in, please." Selene had taken her chair behind the desk and waited patiently for Maya's return to the world. "You get any ditzier, girl, and you'll have that baby and forget where you left it."

Maya grimaced. "Don't remind me. It's one of my nightmares. Now, what fascinating problem do we have besides the mayor's desire to run a highway through our kitchen?"

Selene looked impressed. "My, you do have your signals tuned in for a change. Where did you pick up that one?"

Selene had grown up in the little town of Wadeville, North Carolina. Her father might have started out as the token black in the local bank, but he'd moved up in the corporate world until he currently occupied a spacious corner office high in the bank's uptown Charlotte headquarters. Selene had hated city life, and dropped out of high school to waste several years playing at being a local fashion model before discovering she had an aptitude for investing her earnings.

Few people realized she had inherited her father's financial acumen. She accepted the town's prejudices by hiding behind a shield of silent partnerships and displaying her party-girl charm in public, letting the community believe she lived off her father's generosity. Maya had seen through that disguise the day they met. Geminis could frequently do two things at once. Selene managed three or four.

"A little birdie in the form of a Nordic god told me. It's hard to imagine poor little Constance with a father like that. No wonder she has an inferiority complex." Maya relaxed into the sofa cushions as Selene answered the phone, switched on the computer, scribbled a note, and sent her a glaring look, all at the same time. She couldn't have found a better partner, financially or otherwise.

Selene slammed down the phone and switched on the answering machine before stabbing her pen in Maya's direction. "You talked to Axell Holm? *You?* My stars and garters, heaven help us. What did you say?"

Curling her fingers behind her head, Maya shrugged. "What could I say? I know nothing about it. I just flattered his daughter and offered an invitation for her to join us this summer. I'm not a complete airhead, you realize."

Selene sighed and dropped back in her chair. "I know. You're the one who stuck out the grind and got your teaching certificate. I still don't know how you did that."

"Slept with the teachers."

"Oh, don't get all touchy on me, woman. Get a grip. I just figure you got too much brains to stay with the program. College is for those with no imagination." She waved her hand hastily at Maya's glare. "I know, without the degree, we wouldn't have the school. Don't rub it in. Just tell me everything Holm said. And why the hell did he say it to you?"

"Because I'm the licensed owner and administrator and you're the flunky?" Maya suggested. "He hasn't figured out I'm just the figurehead yet. He said the mayor favors the plan to build that shopping center over the hill. They want Mr. Pfeiffer's land for parking lot access and apparently they're asking the state to condemn the property and pave a highway entrance through here."

"Yeah, that's what I just heard, too. Pfeiffer never said anything about it when he signed our lease." Selene stared gloomily at the blinking phone lines. "Reckon ol' Mayor Arnold heard about me financing this place? Surely the man wouldn't hold a grudge since high school."

Hearing the arrival of cars in the driveway, Maya groaned and lowered her feet to the floor. "I don't know what you and the mayor have to do with each other, but I knew what Pfieffer was doing. His aura was definitely ambiguous. If you'd just let me read your cards, Selene—"

"Oh, hush. I don't know why I got myself mixed up with no honky mind-reader. You must have done a spell on me," Selene mocked as she released the answering machine and jammed her finger on an immediately blinking phone line. Her sculpted features reflected only pleasant concern as she waved her partner out of the room, and her trash talk dissolved into perfectly enunciated accents to the client on the other end of the line.

" 'Cause this honky mind-reader knows a soft touch when she sees one," Maya called as she departed, knowing full well Selene would hear her. Geminis were like that.

With a smile, she turned to greet the first student traipsing in for the day. "Boffo butterflies, sugar. Did your mommy put those in your hair for you?" She hugged the beaming little girl and forgot about all the other problems waiting outside the door.

"Constance, you ought to be dressed by now. You'll be late for school."

Harassed by an early morning call from a constituent, Axell wiped his sleep-blurred eyes and struggled for patience with his eight-year-old daughter. Still in her pajama top, her mousy hair a tangle of snarls, she stood in bewilderment before a closet full of the finest clothes money could buy, arranged in a neat row at a level she could reach. He'd thought organizing her closet and drawers would help her to get ready faster in the mornings. Apparently, the choices only prolonged her indecision.

He couldn't see anything of himself in Constance's dainty features and fragile bone structure. Constance's mother had been petite, but she'd always been elegant. His wife's brown hair had been tipped with golden highlights and her lovely face had been awash with color and life. Axell slammed the door on that memory. Angela's highlights had been artificial and the color, cosmetically applied. Female emotion might forever be a mystery, but he'd learned about feminine artifices the hard way.

There was nothing artificial about his daughter. Her wide-eyed silence tugged at every heartstring he didn't possess. He had no idea how to reach her.

"Let's wear the blue dress today, shall we?" he asked hopefully, pulling out a denim jumper.

Constance regarded the jumper doubtfully but began unbuttoning her pajama top. Wondering if it was healthy for a father to help dress an eight-year-old daughter, Axell turned and searched her drawers for appropriate underwear and socks. He had to crawl under her bed for shoes. Finding only one ballet slipper, a pair of bunny slippers, and an ancient tennis shoe, he combed the closet for a complete pair of anything. A clunky pair of Nikes in hand, he turned to see how far Constance had progressed.

The shoulder straps of the blue jumper hung loosely on her

bony shoulders. It definitely needed a shirt underneath. Frustration mounting, Axell grabbed a red blouse from the closet rack. "Here, put this on—under the dress," he amended, remembering another morning when she'd worn the shirt over the top. Didn't girls automatically know what clothes to wear and how to wear them?

Through it all, Constance remained silent. She never spoke unless absolutely necessary. Some days, he wished she would chatter to fill the silence of their monstrous house. Since Angela's death, it had echoed hollow as any tomb.

He didn't know how to fill the silence any more than he knew how to reach his daughter. She was growing up like one of those forlorn waifs from the hideous velvet paintings his mother used to collect. He wished his mother were here to guide him, but she had died when he was twelve. All the women in his life had died and left him. The knowledge drained Axell's mouth dry as he watched his frail daughter reach for a brush. Should he lose her . . .

Rubbing his face, he stopped those thoughts. Constance was just going through a stage. The new after-school program would bring her out of it. He didn't have time to run her to ballet classes and music lessons and tennis lessons every afternoon as Angela had. The after-school program was just what she needed. He had to find some way of preventing the mayor from shutting down the school, as well as forcing that airheaded school administrator to recognize the seriousness of the situation. Those were things he could accomplish easier than persuading his daughter to talk.

Recalling the auburn-haired gypsy from the New Age shop, Axell wondered if he just shouldn't start shopping for a new school.

Glancing at his lineup of blue phone-message slips, organized in order of priority, Axell crumpled the one he'd just answered, and dropped it neatly in the wastebasket at his feet. He scribbled a corresponding note in his day planner, then sat back in his chair as he recognized the brisk knock at his office door. There was no need to tell the visitor to enter. From long acquaintance, he knew Katherine would enter whether he wished it or not.

His assistant sailed in, impeccably attired, as always. He'd often been told they'd make a good pair: they were both tall and blond with a fashionable sense of style and a similar desire for order in a disorderly world. However, no matter how much he admired Katherine's leggy good looks and sensible attitude, she stirred no interest other than whatever bit of news or information she carried with her. The exchange of gossip was the main basis of their relationship.

Networking, people called it, but in the good old days of his neighborhood bar, it was plain gossip. Axell crossed his hands behind his head and leaned back in his chair as she threw several more message slips on his desk. "You're early," he commented without inflection. His talent for hiring perfect hostesses was half the reason his restaurant was such a success. He certainly didn't possess the necessary bonhomie to greet his clientele.

In a red minidress and high heels that would have the eyes of his male bar patrons popping out and rolling on the floor, Katherine prowled his office, straightening a picture here, dusting invisible specks there, drawing his attention to the spartan furnishings. She'd helped him find the sleek modern furniture, and hired the decorator who'd added the black-and-white engravings to match the ebony lacquered desk and white leather chairs. The splash of red stalking back and forth over the black-and-white interior amused him, and for the first time, Axell wondered if she'd planned it that way.

Remembering the rainbow clutter of the little shop he'd visited yesterday, he sought some pattern between a woman's choice of color and her personality that might aid in his understanding of her behavior. He almost jotted a note to himself to study the matter when Katherine finally spoke.

"The mayor just offered me a position in his office."

On your back? was the first thought that leapt to mind, but Axell had learned long ago to suppress his often irreverent humor. People seldom appreciated it and never expected it. "And you replied?"

She swung around and glared at him from beneath her stack of blond tresses. "You'd let me go without a protest, wouldn't you? My God, Axell, just exactly what are you made of? We've been together from the start."

The start of what? was his next question, again suppressed. Keeping his mouth shut was a habit he'd acquired from his father, but in Katherine's case, one of necessity. She had an unfortunate tendency toward dramatics, and he disliked scenes. Lowering his arms, Axell steepled his fingers across his chest. "Katherine, I value our relationship as much as you do, but if you think the mayor can open doors for you that I can't, then in the interest of friendship, I can't stand in your way."

Her angry expression turned to exasperation. "What doors can the mayor of a two-bit town open? Can't you look beyond the obvious? The two of you are at constant odds. What have you done now, that he's attempting to buy my favors?"

Axell raised his eyebrows, but she'd asked a healthy question. He rocked his chair back and forth, then shrugged. "I objected to his decision to have the state run a highway through the Pfieffer property, but then, I objected to the shopping center development as well. The list could probably go on for months. I don't know where you fit into any of it."

"The Pfeiffer property!" Her eyes lit with recognition. "The old man is second cousin to my uncle or some such. The whole family thinks he's cracked to hang on to that crumbling old mansion."

"He partially restored it while his wife was still alive," Axell reminded her. "And the land itself has been in the family since the beginning of time. I wouldn't be surprised if you found a couple of Cherokees on the family tree and discovered burial mounds or whatever on the grounds. Not many people can hold on to land that long. I don't blame the man for trying to preserve his heritage."

She shrugged the padded shoulders of her bolero jacket and paced the carpet at a more leisurely rate. "The city is expanding in this direction too rapidly for property like that to go undivided. The price of land is skyrocketing. Those may have been rural roads ten years ago, but the Pfieffer property stands directly between two major traffic arteries now. A connector road through there is inevitable."

"I live out there," he reminded her dryly. "I'm well aware of what's happening. I just don't agree that we must allow wall-to-wall housing from the city outward. I thought the whole point of the town zoning laws was to prevent Wadeville from becoming just another suburb of Charlotte. We're a rural town and we should acknowledge that."

"It's part of our southern charm," she said waspishly. "We could all take to wearing straw hats and muddy boots."

Since he could remember when his father owned the local grill on this corner and the patrons who'd indeed dressed that way, Axell didn't comment. He'd learned more about human nature and running a business while polishing the counter downstairs than he'd ever learned at the university. Unfortunately, he'd never had his father's talent for being one of the "good ol' boys."

He dismissed that thought and applied his knowledge of human nature to the current situation. "Let me guess: Pfieffer is in ill health, doesn't have a will, and the whole family is counting the dollars that property could add to the coffers."

Katherine shot him a hooded look. "I doubt there would be enough to trickle down to me, if that's what you're aiming at. No, I'm looking for the connection between me and the mayor, and the Pfieffer property has to be it."

"Not to mention that the governor and probably half the department of transportation likes looking at gorgeous blondes," he added dryly. "You really don't want to hear the reaction of the city council when you show up for one of our meetings wearing a miniskirt."

"Holm, you have ice water for blood." She swung on her high heels and started for the door. "Headley is downstairs, said he'd like to talk to you when you get a chance. Shall I send him up?"

Vaguely perplexed by her reaction but not particularly concerned, Axell nodded. One of these days he'd calculate the pattern that guided female emotion. Until then, he just accepted that he would seldom understand what set them off.

He'd straightened out an order with the New York wine merchant and decided on the best bid for new restaurant linen by the time Headley ambled upstairs. Axell liked taking care of material details. It was people like Headley he had difficulty keeping in line.

Spreading his gray suit–jacketed arms across the back of the leather sofa, the newspaper reporter swung his gaze around the room in fascination. "So, this is the lion's lair, is it? Far cry from the old days."

"We all have our little rebellions," Axell replied mildly. His father's office had been windowless, stuffy, and cluttered with files that hadn't been opened since his first year of business.

Headley had almost single-handedly made Holm's Grill a success. Three decades ago, before the law allowed liquor sales by the drink, the reporter had adopted a seat at the corner of the restaurant counter, where he could pull the flask of bourbon from his coat pocket and view the comings and goings of the town from the front window. A decade later, when the liquor law changed and the new mahogany bar was installed, Headley was their first customer. Every neighborhood bar needed at least one eccentric character to meet and greet regular patrons, and to provide a stability they could count on in their ever-changing worlds, and Headley was Holm's.

The front window and the tavern had long ago fallen beneath the treads of a bulldozer, but Headley lingered on, fifty pounds heavier than his youthful self, his full head of hair now a distinguished white. His nose for gossip hadn't deteriorated a bit.

"I can see that." The reporter focused his sharp blue gaze in Axell's direction. "Did you know the ABC board is investigating your liquor license?"

Oh, shit. Axell rolled his eyes skyward as he remembered the altercation the police had to break up last month. A perfectly harmless catfight between two country-club matrons over a man not worth either of their time had deteriorated into a brawl among the other patrons after a particularly drunken evening of race-car watching in the bar. On top of the robbery in the parking lot the month before, he could see the train of the law enforcement mind, especially if egged on by a concerned citizen, like the mayor. If they took his license, he'd be ruined. The mayor's campaign against him seemed to be taking a particularly nasty turn. Should he reconsider his vote against the parking lot access?

"Was there some reason I ever agreed to serve on the town council?" he asked of the ceiling.

"Besides your civic duty?" Headley inquired with a touch of irony. "How about that zoning change you wanted, to stop that seedy hotel down your way from reopening?"

"Yeah, the one the mayor owns." Axell sighed and returned his gaze to Headley. "Maybe I should run for mayor next time."

Headley whistled in appreciation. "Good idea. Hometown boy makes good with squeaky-clean record. Marry that ice maiden you keep as hostess, parade her to church on your arm with your little girl, and you're a shoo-in."

Headley had all but the marriage part right. Axell had learned the hard way that marriage wreaked a havoc in his life that he wasn't properly qualified to cope with, and no amount of civic duty would reconcile him to making that mistake again.

Besides, his daughter hated Katherine and would sooner accompany a salamander to church.

Remembering the light in his daughter's eyes as she mentioned her after-school teacher, Axell grimaced and rubbed his hand over his face. He had some recollection of the prior owner of that junk shop being arrested on drug charges. Had the gypsy woman mentioned something about a sister?

Maybe he better investigate his daughter's after-school teacher a little further. The astrology mumbo-jumbo was bad enough. He didn't need Constance becoming enraptured with drug dealers.

He dropped his head in his hands. His life would become a fishbowl if he ran for mayor. Constance had enough problems without that kind of scrutiny.

They'd both have worse problems if he lost his alcohol license and his business.

Hell, maybe he ought to close the school.

Except—for the first time in two years—Constance was talking again, and the blamed schoolteacher was the reason.

❧ THREE ❧

If—a two letter word for futility.

"Look, girl, if Axell Holm offered to help us, we'd be fools to turn him away. Do you want the school to close?"

Maya huddled the phone receiver against her ear and stroked Matty's hair. He'd had a nightmare, and she'd carried him into the big water bed with her a little while ago. He'd fallen directly to sleep once he was beside her, so she couldn't complain. His learning disabilities caused some frustration—mostly for her because she blamed Cleo for the stress that caused his lack of attention—but for the most part, he was the soul of sweetness. Matty seldom gave her reason for complaint.

Life, on the other hand, was a real roller coaster ride.

She stared up at the cracked ceiling of her sister's shop apartment. The tiny salary the school partnership paid was the only shoestring keeping her off welfare. Cleo's shop was in such financial ruin, it scarcely earned enough to cover outstanding debts, although the free apartment was a boon. No, she couldn't afford to see the school close.

"Why can't you talk to him? You know more about this town and running a business than I do. He's a *Virgo*, Selene. We don't even speak the same language."

"Honey, I hate to tell you, but you don't talk the same language as *anybody* around here. I don't know what they taught you out there in California, but it flat out has nothing to do with the Carolinas. If you want to make it in this town, you'd better learn to talk the talk."

24

If. Maya closed her eyes and wrinkled her nose. That was a mighty big if. She and Cleo had spent the better part of their lives drifting from town to town, house to house, like tumbleweeds, never knowing the meaning of roots. Unlike the Axell Holms of this world, they had no place to call their own and no reason to stay anywhere.

She'd always figured wherever she slept was home. Glancing down at the sleeping five-year-old beside her warned her that she had a different responsibility now. Until Cleo was free, Wadeville was home. By then, the dream of a school would probably be in ruins, and she could move on. Maybe Stephen would have won a Grammy by then, and she could hit him up for child support. She could always hitch a ride on dreams.

Grimacing, she dropped back to reality. "All right. I'll talk to him, but I think he's looking for a compromise, and I'm warning you now, Selene, I don't do compromise. If you're going to make me swim upstream, baby, I swim hard."

Selene sighed into the phone. "Heaven forbid I should understand what that means. If you're going to be a partner in this business, you have to do what's best for all. I'm holding you to that."

Maya wrinkled her nose as she hung up the phone a few minutes later. Her Pisces nature really preferred going with the flow over swimming upstream, but she had others to think of besides herself now. For Matty and the baby, she'd jump waterfalls and dams. Talking to a stuck-up yuppie couldn't be that difficult.

"Axell, dear, I know you try, but it's quite obvious Constance is unhappy. You have your hands full running a *business*"— the word quivered with disapproval—"and with the town council, and besides, you're a *man*. You can't possibly understand the needs of a little girl. She needs a mother."

His mother-in-law patted the gray silk cushion beside her, offering him a seat, but Axell preferred his distance. He was certain Sandra was a very nice woman. He'd never seen evidence otherwise, although admittedly, since she'd moved to

Texas, he hadn't seen much of her at all. That she'd traveled all the way back here to have this confrontation aroused his suspicions.

"You haven't worried about Constance in the last two years. What brings you back here now?" He didn't mean to sound impolite, but he hadn't the patience to work around to her motives. He'd had his fill of game playing with Angela.

"I've always worried about her," Sandra protested, tapping her beringed fingers on the cushion. "I had just hoped she'd recover from Angela's death by now." She hesitated, obviously looking for the right words for her next attack.

Axell supplied them for her. "But obviously my cold, uncaring nature isn't what Constance needs." Fighting the guilt and pain that washed over him every time he thought of his late wife, Axell braced his hand on the marble mantel Angela had chosen when they'd built this palace. "Angela made the complaint more than once. I haven't forgotten."

"Angela loved you," Sandra said placatingly. "But you were so busy all the time . . ."

Damn, but it was as if the last two years hadn't happened, and he was slammed right back into one of those ever-running arguments Angela had hit him with every night when he came home. He didn't need this. Angela was dead. She'd died two years ago driving too fast on a rain-slick highway. She'd been furious with him at the time. He hadn't understood her fury then any more than he did now. He just knew the guilt she'd left behind.

"Look, Sandra, Constance is my daughter. She's lost one parent. I'll be damned if she'll lose another. I know you mean well. . . ."

Beneath her professionally styled blond coif, Sandra frowned. "Axell, I'm prepared to get tough about this. Constance is my only grandchild. I'll never have another. I want what's best for her, and I can provide it. She's not happy here; anyone can see that. I don't see that there's any room for argument."

Axell clenched his fists. He wasn't a man who lost control

of his emotions. If his late wife were to be believed, he didn't have emotions.

"I don't know who you've been talking to, but they cannot possibly know everything that goes on in this household. I've found her a very good after-school program, and she's opening up nicely. Her teacher says she's quite talented." He didn't need to mention that the teacher was a space cadet.

Sandra looked disbelieving. "When even your neighbors notice a child's unhappiness, there has to be something wrong. We could just do this on a trial basis."

Maybe she was right. Maybe Constance did need a mother figure. She was only eight, but Axell recognized that little girls wanted someone to paint their fingernails and braid their hair and hear their secrets, and he was no damned good at it. Even if she'd been a tomboy who loved climbing trees and fishing, he wouldn't be of much use. He'd spent his life between books and the bar. The only time he'd ever been fishing was at Boy Scout camp as a kid. He'd fallen in the lake and never bothered again. The principles of fishing were as illogical as women, and he didn't have the patience for either.

Damn Angela for dying and leaving him helpless.

Hating the feeling of inadequacy, Axell rubbed his hand over his face and nodded. "Give me time to think about it. I want to talk to Constance first. How long do you plan to stay? I can arrange someone to come in and fix meals. . . ."

Sandra rose from the couch. "I'll be staying with Elizabeth Arnold. I wouldn't wish to put you out, dear. Whatever do you do for meals when I'm not here?"

Elizabeth Arnold, the mayor's mother. The last piece of puzzle plunked in place. Axell gritted his teeth and forced a polite smile. "We eat at the bar."

He really shouldn't have said that. Sandra's artfully made-up face dropped two inches. People never knew when he was kidding. The bar's opening twenty years ago had been so scandalous, everyone still referred to it as such, even though he'd expanded into the biggest restaurant in the county. Suddenly anxious to be rid of her, Axell didn't bother erasing her impression of Constance snacking on peanuts while whirling on bar stools.

As soon as his mother-in-law scurried into the night, Axell switched off the lights and walked upstairs.

His heart plummeted as he saw the spectral blur of a white nightgown darting into Constance's bedroom. The click of the door lock fastening echoed down the hall.

She'd heard everything. And he had no words to explain.

"Well, did you talk with him?" Selene hissed as Maya entered the school in the company of a trio of chirping new arrivals.

"No, I haven't," Maya hissed back, removing school backpacks and tucking them into their appropriate lockers.

As the children raced to the workroom, she straightened with a hand to her aching back. "Cleo's social worker arrived to check on Matty's environment and to verify I'm not passed out on drugs or otherwise behaving down to her opinion of me. It's not the very best time of my life to get pregnant." It had been downright stupid, as a matter of fact. She'd known better than to trust Stephen. Next time, she was taking the pill. *Next time?* She'd be old and gray before she trusted another man that way again.

Selene clucked sympathetically. "You had no way of knowing your sister would get put away. Did you tell the worker pretty stories?"

Maya brightened. "I did. Stephen is now a respectable musician who travels a lot in his line of work. His income is sometimes erratic, but we're expecting a large royalty check soon, only I don't think Matty's ready to move from his familiar environment yet. Did I do good?"

"You did good, girl. I can tell you spent time in the system. Did she buy that?"

Maya shrugged and jerked a ribbon from her jumper pocket to tie back her tangle of curls. "She's not happy that Matty doesn't have a male authority figure, and she thinks I should put my teaching certificate to more respectable use. I might *know* the system, but I never fit in it, I'm afraid."

"That's all right. We've got a good thing here and we'll make a mint when we franchise it in a few years. You just hold on till then."

Maya whistled the refrain from "The Impossible Dream" in reply and wandered back to the children.

A few hours later, sitting at the kitchen table with Matty muttering about Big Macs while grudgingly chomping a soy burger, Maya stared at her list of figures and sighed inwardly. She could never break even. Not in a thousand million years. She'd never been any good with money because she'd never had any, and Cleo's finances gave new meaning to the word "bankrupt."

"Maya, can I have new sneakers?" Matty asked through a mouth full of burger.

She didn't bother to correct his grammar. "Can" was actually the operative word here. Considering their budget, new sneakers weren't within the realm of possibility. "What's wrong with the old ones?" she asked absently, running the numbers through her old college hand-calculator again. Maybe she hadn't hit the right keys.

"They got holes in the bottom. Miss Kidd says I need new ones. Dick got some with *lights* on them."

Maya heard the plea and resisted the usual lecture on how poor people couldn't buy what other kids had. She'd heard those lectures from countless foster parents growing up. The speech might be logical but it didn't fulfill a child's need to belong. Besides, they weren't poor. She refused to adopt that mentality. Maybe the wolf was at the door, but she had an education, doggone it. She'd made certain of that. Nobody could take away those degrees. She could make a living and put food on the table. And sneakers on Matty's feet.

Ashamed she hadn't noticed the condition of his shoes, Maya ruffled his straight dark hair. "We'll go to the store after kindergarten tomorrow. Want me to paint smiley faces on your old ones? I bet Dick doesn't have smiley faces."

Matty gave her one of his rare shy smiles. "Can I have dragons instead? Shelly has smiley faces."

"Fire-breathing dragons, coming up," she agreed. She might not be good with numbers, but she could wield a mean paintbrush.

She tucked the memory of Matty's smile into her aching heart as she watched him toddle off to bed. Once upon a time, her practical older sister had been the only buffer between an imaginative little girl and a harsh, cold world of strangers. How could the sister she'd known turn to the escape of drugs and leave her beautiful little boy behind?

Worse yet, what would happen when the system spewed Cleo into the world again, still damaged and helpless and incapable of taking care of herself, much less a child?

The mantle of responsibility didn't fit well on Maya's shoulders, but she wrapped it firmly around her now as she glared at the damning numbers on the sheet of paper in front of her. They blamed well had to turn the Impossible Dream into reality.

The alternative was starvation and living on the street.

Beneath a beautiful Carolina-blue sky, Maya stared at the double wooden doors marking the entrance to the restaurant known only as "Holm's." She had no choice. She'd called the Axell Holm listed in the book and hadn't even reached voice mail. She'd walked Matty to school at eight and had to open the shop at ten. This was the only time she had available.

The restaurant was only a few blocks from the shop. The whole damned town was only a few blocks from the shop. Their mother had apparently grown up in this place but escaped after she married. One of these days she'd try to remember why Cleo had chosen to return, other than she could use foot power for transportation.

Knocking on a restaurant door at nine o'clock in the morning didn't seem reasonable. Figuring she had nothing to lose, Maya shoved at the door, nearly stumbling as it swung open on well-oiled hinges. She should have known Axell Holm would keep his place impeccably maintained, even if it was just a country steak-house.

A man in a cleaning service uniform buffing the floor

looked up and stared at her as she entered. Maya supposed that was better than having a whole barroom full of people staring at her. She'd never been very comfortable in barrooms, even respectable ones attached to small-town restaurants.

Donning the vague persona she used to shield herself from the world, Maya sauntered through the room, waving a greeting at the worker. "Is Axell in this morning?" she called carelessly.

It was a trifle difficult pulling off the carefree bit while pushing a two-ton belly in front of her, Maya thought wryly as the man's eyes widened with interest. He gulped something she took for agreement and pointed toward a door on the far wall. Obviously, she wasn't the suave, urbane Mr. Holm's usual type.

The door in the back wall led to a corridor with a series of doors. She thought she saw one hurriedly close and wondered who else was in here at this hour. She pondered calling out and asking for directions, but the kitchen, rest rooms, and storeroom doors were easily identifiable. That left only the back stairs, and she could find her way from there. Of course, over a month ago her doctor had told her to avoid stairs. Since she lived in an upstairs apartment, she didn't have the option of obeying, so she didn't hesitate now.

Polished hardwood floors, a discreet silver wool carpet matching a sedate striped wallpaper, and a closed paneled door greeted her at the top of the stairs. The narrow reception area had no inviting furniture, no furniture at all. Maya shook her head at the blandness of the decor, pitied poor Mr. Holm his lifeless life in this nowhere town, and tapped at the closed door.

No response.

Frowning, she tapped louder, then deciding she wasn't a supplicant to beg for crumbs, she pushed the door open.

Morning sunlight streaked through bare windows across a glossy black desk where a stylishly shorn head of golden hair bent over a stack of papers. The head barely lifted as she walked in before its owner returned to marking notes in the margins of what appeared to be an invoice. Maya recognized invoices. Cleo had left them, yellowed and stained with tea rings, scattered all over the storeroom.

"Have a seat, Miss Alyssum, I'll be with you in a minute."

Back to the "Miss" business. His cold tone didn't hold much promise for her quest. Raising her eyebrows at the pieces of a clock scattered on one corner of his desk, she decided to stay and take her chances. Daunted by the stiffly upright leather wing chairs in front of the desk, she ignored his command and drifted to the bank of windows overlooking the town's main street. If one counted the old service station converted to a fruit market, Wadeville's business district extended three blocks from the railroad. Cleo's shop was near the tracks and fruit market, difficult to see from this angle.

Most of the town buildings between here and Cleo's had been built in the late 1800s or early 1900s when cotton was still king. Their practical brick facades were now adorned with a century's worth of awnings, painted and aluminum signs, and other atrocities. Holm's Restaurant was of the same brick, but the huge expanse of windows spoke of a later era conceived in air-conditioning. Apparently, Mr. Holm believed in discarding the past in favor of the new and convenient.

A pen clicked as it hit the desk. "How may I help you, Miss Alyssum?"

She swung around, but the sun behind his head prevented her from seeing his expression. Axell Holm exuded the impression of a dangerously successful businessman with no time or patience for sentimentality. Maybe she'd imagined that Aquarian streak. "Perhaps I was a little hasty in dismissing your offer of help the other day," she said as winningly as she knew how. "I've been a trifle overwhelmed by events lately."

He leaned back in the chair and crossed his fingers over his chest. He'd removed his suit jacket, and she noticed he had a very impressive chest and shoulders inside that fitted white shirt. Pity he hid them behind the fussiness of ties and jackets and whatnot. He looked as if he belonged in tight ski clothes. Or in a jungle, with nothing on at all.

Distracted at that wayward thought, she settled her gaze on the business end of a small screwdriver protruding from his shirt pocket. As he talked at her, she studied the little pile of clock innards on the corner of his desk.

"I'm not certain the fate of the school is relevant to me any longer, Miss Alyssum. I'm considering sending Constance to live with her grandmother."

A squeak at the door warned Maya of an eavesdropper even before the door burst open and a miniature whirlwind flew in, wrapping itself around her legs and nearly toppling her.

"Don't make me go, Miss Alyssum! I can go home with you, can't I?"

For one fleeting moment, as she met Axell's gaze, Maya caught a glimpse of the window to his soul and saw despair before he slammed the window shut and glared at her as if this were all her fault.

And so it was. Kneeling, Maya wrapped her arms around the weeping fairy child. "Of course you can, sugar baby. Give me a hug." And she meant it. Defiantly, she knew she'd take this beautiful little girl home with her right now if she could.

As the child wrapped her arms around Maya's throat and practically strangled her, Maya glared at the indifferent man in the desk chair. This was the reason she dreamed of success for her school. All her life, she'd searched for a place that would accept her and offer her love. She was too old to expect it for herself now, but she could offer it to other children, give them the love and acceptance she and Cleo never had.

She'd just never dreamed it would start with a child who had every thing she'd never had.

October 1945

    I met a woman last night, Helen Arnold, the banker's niece. I heard she owned a moonshine joint outside town and wondered what she'd be like, but I never imagined . . . It would be a sin to go back there. I've worked long and hard and survived a war to get where I am. I can't let a

fascination with the Arnold's black sheep ruin my
chances—although, with all that red hair, maybe she
should be called a red sheep? No, there's nothing
sheeplike about Helen. She's a challenge.

 FOUR

Give me ambiguity or give me something else.

Stunned into silence, Axell absorbed the tableau kneeling on his office floor. Had it been a painting, the scene would have been labeled *Madonna and Child*. There was something almost pre-Raphaelite about the glorious spill of fiery red curls down the woman's back, the pure ivory expanse of her curved brow, and the multicolored flow of her gauzy, pleated gown. The striking contrast to Katherine in her tailored red miniskirts struck him vividly.

Constance in her short flowered skirt and padded running shoes demolished the artistic image.

What the hell was Constance doing here? He'd taken her to school well over an hour ago.

Tortured by his daughter's sobs, helpless to cope with them, Axell removed the screwdriver from his pocket and twisted it between his fingers as he groped for some logical means of dealing with this unanticipated problem. The teacher's glare told him it was not the right reaction.

Awkwardly, he emerged from behind the shield of his desk and towered over them. He wasn't the kind of man who sat on floors, but his daughter's brokenhearted cries offered him no choice. Tugging up his trouser leg, he got down on one knee and tried to peel her away from her teacher. "Constance, come here and let me talk with you."

"No!" Angrily, she jerked her little arm away from him.

Constance was never angry.

Frightened by his helplessness, Axell threw the woman a

35

beseeching look. What had she done to his daughter that Constance felt freer to go to her rather than to him?

The teacher's glare relented somewhat as she stroked Constance's long fine hair, gathering the dark strands in her hands and tugging gently. "Hey, sugar baby, look at me a minute, okay? You'll have me crying if you don't stop soon."

Amazingly, Axell heard a smile in her voice. How could the woman sound happy with a weeping, hysterical child in her arms? She didn't reveal any of the desperation he felt. Angela would have been throwing fits and screaming at him by now. This woman looked as serene as the Madonna he'd pictured earlier.

Constance shook her head, but Maya held her so firmly that there was no ferocity to the movement. A grubby hand wiped at a wet eye as his daughter peeked upward.

Frozen in the spell of the moment, Axell continued kneeling, watching. He suddenly understood how women had been cast as witches through the ages. Their spells were inexplicable by any other means but magic.

"Have you told your daddy you don't want to go away?" she asked, still stroking Constance's hair as if gentling a pony.

The little head shook back and forth again, and tear-filled eyes disappeared into Maya's shoulder. Axell wanted to reach out and draw his daughter into his own arms, but he didn't dare. He'd not been able to get a word out of Constance since last night, not that he got much out of her at any other time either.

"Constance, you don't have to go if you don't want," he heard himself say. He'd lain awake all night, agonizing over his decision, unable to avoid the conclusion that Constance needed the guidance of an experienced parent, a mother. He'd tortured himself with the realization that he was a lousy excuse for a father, that he couldn't balance work with his daughter's needs, and that Constance had to come first, that his hollow life in her absence would be a small price to pay to see her smiling again. He threw all those logical conclusions out the window with the fall of a few tears.

The sobs lessened, but his daughter's beautiful innocent

face remained hidden. Axell glanced hopefully at Maya. She caught his look and shrugged, apparently not impressed with his concession.

"Constance, honey, I think your daddy would like to talk with you, and I really need to sit in a chair before I fall over. Why don't you let me get up and let your daddy hold you for a little while? He's got big strong shoulders for crying on. That's what daddies are for."

Appalled at his selfishness in not seeing she must be in some pain from her position on the floor, Axell stood and tugged gently at Maya's elbow to help her rise. She shook her head in refusal, nodding at Constance instead. With reluctance, Axell put his large hands around his elfin daughter and lifted her away. To his astonishment, Constance flung her skinny arms around his neck without protest.

A sopping little face soaked his stiff shirt collar, and the scent of baby shampoo filled his nostrils. He didn't know what to do with her. Axell wondered when he'd held his daughter last. As an infant? A toddler who'd scraped her knee, maybe? Angela had always been there, running interference for scraped knees and childish tantrums.

Axell glanced anxiously at the heavily pregnant woman trying to pull herself upright from the floor. Shifting Constance to one arm, he held out his free hand to haul her up. The schoolteacher's hand curled in his, and he thought he caught the fragrance of sandalwood as she used his strength for leverage, but she drifted away as soon as she stood upright. For a moment, he felt oddly protective toward this unorthodox young woman. She was much more delicately built than he'd realized.

The sympathetic moment dissipated the instant she opened her mouth.

"I believe you and your daughter have a good deal to talk about, Mr. Holm," she snapped in a crisp California accent. "Perhaps you'll reconsider your offer about the school and stop by the shop a little later." Her frosty tone spoke her opinion of his parenting skills.

He almost panicked and begged her to stay, but the little

arms clutching his neck decided the matter. Still completely at a loss, Axell nodded and watched a shaft of sunlight spill over the teacher's fiery cascade of hair. She looked almost as lost as his daughter as she turned her head away and slipped into the hall, gently pulling the door closed.

A woman that pregnant should be tucked comfortably on a soft couch with her feet up, not traipsing up and down stairs and streets, Axell thought irrelevantly, before his attention reverted to his daughter. Holding Constance tightly, he collapsed into the nearest chair and prayed he could pry some answers out of her. How did one know if an eight-year-old's answers were the best ones?

Cuddling his daughter, listening to her heartbroken sobs, Axell experienced pure fear-filled panic.

He'd thought Constance's silence had been a natural reaction to grief, something she would have to get through as he did. What if she couldn't get over it by herself? What if it wasn't just grief? What if it was *he*?

It had to be he. Constance was a different person with Maya. How could he do what Maya did so he could keep Constance?

He panicked again as he realized he hadn't a clue.

The chanting monks greeted Axell as he entered the gift shop. Sunlight sparkled through newly washed windows, but the narrow, crowded interior looked no less musty than before. The wind chimes sang a merry tune in the breeze he let in, and he hastily shut the door while searching for some sign of the red-haired proprietor.

"Anyone home?" he called. He'd like to tell her this was no way to run a business, but he had a sneaking suspicion there wasn't much business to run and she really didn't care.

"Down here."

He leaned over the counter. To his shock, he discovered Maya lying flat on her back, eyes closed, hands covering her distended belly. "Are you all right?" he asked, hearing the panic in his voice. Twice in one day. They'd have him in an insane asylum within the week.

"That's a matter of relativity," she replied in a vague voice. Her eyes popped open, and Axell could see the mischief in them. "But if you're asking if it's time to call the ambulance or get out the forceps, the answer is no. You're safe for now."

Damn, but she'd scared him. He didn't like being scared. Stepping back, Axell stared politely at the black-and-white cat sleeping on the shelf while she righted herself. The cat was probably the only thing in here that wasn't a rainbow of color.

Sunset curls and a wicked smile suddenly blocked his view of the cat. "Well, Mr. Holm, has the domestic crisis been resolved?" she asked cheerily.

"I returned Constance to school," he answered stiffly, uncomfortable beneath her beaming gaze. A woman who lived in this slum had no business being so damned happy. "She wouldn't tell me how she got to the office." He threw her a look of suspicion. "I don't suppose you know anything about that?"

"Sorry, much as I always wished for a fairy godmother, I've never had one and I've never been one. Someone else must have spirited the child there. Or she walked. It's less than a mile, you realize. And Constance is a very resourceful child." She lifted the steaming pot of water from the hot plate and poured it into the teapot she'd prepared.

The idea of his waiflike daughter traipsing a mile of highway through traffic and mud and all the modern-day horrors of civilization boggled his mind so thoroughly that Axell didn't have to be told to take the cups and sit down at the table. Setting the china down, he collapsed into the ugly little chair and propped his head against his hand.

She patted his shoulder as she leaned over to set the teapot on the table. He didn't even *know* this woman, but she was always touching him.

"Did you reassure her that you won't send her away?"

Axell heard the condemnation behind the question. It was none of her damned business. He resisted spilling his guts, but he had no one to confide in. Katherine had no concern for his family life. He had friends like Headley all over town, people he'd grown up with, people who had frequented the restaurant all their adult lives, but he'd been taught to keep his troubles to himself. They no more knew his problems than they knew his bank account. This woman was a near stranger and she already knew more about him than he did himself.

"I can't do that," he announced heavily, leaning back in the chair while she poured the tea. If he came here any more often, he'd have to bring a coffeepot.

She lifted her arched cinnamon-brown eyebrows, and Axell could swear the turquoise of her eyes shot daggers. He winced.

"What kind of father lets an eight-year-old roam a highway?" he demanded. "I can't be there to watch over her all the time. I'm *never* there," he admitted. "She goes from school to your place to whatever baby-sitter I can find in the evenings." Before she could shoot the first verbal bullet, he defended himself. "I pick her up at your place and take her out to dinner, but I own a *bar*. I have to be there in the evening and I can't take her with me."

"Did I say anything?" she asked innocently, sipping at her tea, staring at him with big eyes over the edge of her cup.

His gaze inadvertently dropped to her mouth as she sipped, but he jerked back to his senses at his first reaction to the moistness of her lower lip.

"I didn't notice that your mother-in-law kept Constance from roaming the highway," she continued, as if his attention hadn't strayed. "Did she cook Constance's breakfast? Will she pick her up at school this afternoon? Fix her dinner tonight?"

Axell drew his hand over his face and tried to rearrange his thoughts, but nothing fit. He might as well ask her to gaze into a crystal ball. It couldn't be any more useless than his confused arguments with himself. "Sandra's just visiting. I can't ask her to do those things. I imagine she'll do them when she takes Constance home."

"You *imagine*?" she asked in outrage. "You *imagine* she'll take care of your child? Isn't that the same thing as saying you really don't care? That once she's out of sight, you don't have to worry about her anymore?"

Heat rushed to his head, and Axell almost leapt out of his chair before he realized she'd driven him to rage. He'd spent a lifetime cultivating impassivity. It worked well when tempers flared in the bar. Yet it had taken this California hippie less than five minutes to explode his ironclad control.

He clenched his fists and took a deep breath before meeting her gaze. "I love Constance enough to do what's best for her."

"Which is why you're here," she prodded.

Right, he'd forgotten. He'd had an ulterior motive in coming here. He didn't hold out much hope of achieving it, but desperation led a man to do things he wouldn't do otherwise. He had to at least try to find some means of keeping Constance home. Logic said his mother-in-law would be a much better parent for Constance than he was. But dammit, his daughter belonged with him.

He didn't operate just on protective instinct, though. If Constance's reaction this morning was anything to judge by, she didn't want to go with Sandra any more than he wanted her to go. If Sandra wasn't the best path to Constance's happiness, then he had to find another one.

Axell dropped his gaze to the unappealing cup of tea and forced out his plea. "I don't suppose you would have any interest in taking on the job of nanny?"

A gurgle of laughter reached his ears, and he looked up in suspicion. Maya beamed from ear to ear, presenting him with the picture of soft pink lips and a slightly tilted tooth. She had a mole the size of a speck just on the edge of her delicate chin. Fascinated, his gaze lingered there, blocking out his hearing and probably his brain. He didn't recover until she tapped his hands.

"Don't you think I'm just a trifle overqualified?" she asked in amusement.

Groggy from the spell she cast, he didn't respond immediately. His gaze drifted downward to her creamy skin above the lace-trimmed, collarless pullover she wore beneath her jumper today. He thought maybe it was the same irridescent reddish-brownish-purple dress she'd worn the other day, only with a different blouse, but that didn't lessen her potent feminine allure. A little voice in the back of his mind told him she probably didn't have money for clothes. He clung to that thought as he finally met her gaze again.

"Can you afford to turn down the offer of free room and board and a handsome salary?" he asked blandly.

She blinked, disconcerted. *For a change,* he thought maliciously. The woman had kept him unbalanced since their first meeting. He was older and considerably more experienced. It was time he took charge of matters around here. From the looks of things, she needed someone to take charge. Which made him wonder how she'd formed the school so quickly after arriving here, but that was a matter to be pondered another time.

"As long as the shop makes enough money to pay the rent, I have my own apartment, Mr. Holm. If I'm to pay off my sister's bills, I need to keep the shop open. And the school is a dream of a lifetime. I'll not trade it for the offer of comfort. I'm aware I do not appear to be the most ambitious person in the world, but I'm capable of supporting myself."

He nodded. He hadn't held out much hope that she'd accept his offer. "Then I don't have much choice, do I? Unless you happen to know someone who can give Constance the mother figure she needs, I'll have to send her home with Sandra."

"That child needs *you.*" Rage quivered in her voice again. "Do you have any idea at all how it feels to be abandoned? To feel unloved, unwanted, shoved from place to place, never knowing the rules, never knowing where you belong? It's *hell,* Mr. Holm. I'll do whatever I can to prevent that happening to a child within my reach. Bring her here after dinner in the evenings. I'll be her mother. It's scarcely a palace, but I can offer her a home and the love she needs while you polish your bar and pat the backs of strangers."

She may as well have smacked him. Trembling with fury, Axell stood up. He'd had this or a similar argument once too many times with his wife. He had no good reason to listen to it from this woman who meant nothing to him.

"I'm not abandoning my child, Miss Alyssum. I love her enough to do what's best for her, and dumping her in the arms of a complete stranger is not best for her." In his anger, he ignored his inconsistency. "I think it may have been a mistake to allow her to grow so attached to you. I'm withdrawing her from the school."

The baby kicked hard enough to hurt as Maya watched Axell storm out. She probably deserved the kick, although it should have been a swift one to the rear.

With all his powerful connections, Axell Holm could easily influence the wealthy parents of tuition-paying students to abandon her school, leaving them with only the non–income producing scholarship students.

It looked like her dream of settling in Wadeville was dissolving faster than anticipated.

❧ FIVE ❧

Support bacteria, they're the only culture some people have.

"I would like to buy a gift for my granddaughter."

At after two in the afternoon, Maya had expected the ringing door chime to represent the arrival of her afternoon clerk. She'd considered closing at two to save the expense of salary and taxes, but the teenager Cleo had hired to handle the after-school browsers was desperately proud of her job, and Maya didn't have the heart to lay her off.

Recognizing the haughty, rounded tones of southern aristocracy, Maya sighed and returned her feet to the floor. She'd painted dragons to match Matty's on her own inexpensive Keds. She thought they'd turned out rather fine.

Standing up to the counter, she smiled a greeting at a woman with a helmet of blond hair. "How old is your granddaughter?" she asked cheerfully. Cleo had a lovely assortment of imaginative gifts for children. When not lost in drugs, her sister had a brilliant, creative mind. Admitedly, the whimsy of a New Age shop was out of character, but Cleo would have sold bent nails if it meant the independence she craved.

"She's only eight. I cannot imagine how anything in here could be suitable, but she insists this is her favorite place."

Maya bit her lip and held her tongue—not a pretty sight, she figured, but the best reaction she could summon. Very few children returned here on a regular basis. Even fewer were younger than ten. Constance Holm was one of them.

She studied her customer more carefully, finding little of

elfin Constance in this polished matron. Women like this had to be stamped out with cookie cutters: lacquered coiffures, gleaming lipstick, fashionable designer suits, sensible pumps, and figures maintained by tennis, golf, and private pools. Nothing about her screamed "maternal" or "loving" or even "imaginative." A child with an active mind like Constance needed creative parenting. She should know; she'd been one.

"Children of eight love fantasy," Maya responded quietly. She'd already ticked off Axell today. She didn't need to alienate his mother-in-law. "Most of the ones who come in here love the kaleidoscopes. We have an assortment, of varying artistic quality. The more expensive are handmade. For a child of eight . . ."

"Kaleidoscopes have no purpose." She waved away the suggestion with a manicured hand adorned with a diamond as big as a robin's egg. "Do you have any dolls? Books, perhaps?"

Maya had never known Constance to show any interest in the dolls at school, and this wasn't a toy store. Reining in her impatience, shifting from one aching foot to the other, she clung to her pleasant demeanor. "There's a wonderful children's bookstore just down the street. We don't try to compete with them."

"But Constance says this is her favorite store. Surely you must have something."

The woman seemed genuinely puzzled, as she should be, perhaps. Cleo's shop was cluttered and full of weird objects, some of whose purpose even Maya couldn't discern, which was precisely why children adored it.

This was a small town. Use it to advantage, a small voice whispered in her ear. Maybe Fate had steered this woman in here for a reason. Having been victim of it often enough, Maya had a healthy respect for Fate.

"If you mean Constance Holm, I'm pleased to meet you. I'm Maya Alyssum, her after-school teacher. Constance is a delightful child."

The woman looked startled, then wary as she took in Maya's thrift shop maternity jumper and unfashionable shawl.

"Pleased to meet you," she said uncertainly, not offering her hand.

Accustomed to that reaction, Maya shrugged it off and removed the crystal ball from the counter case. "I wouldn't recommend this for most eight-year-olds, but Constance has her father's carefulness with material things. She adores crystals and this globe fascinates her. I can guarantee hugs in return for this gift."

Instead of looking at the crystal, the woman studied Maya. "You're a teacher?"

Alarm bells clamored at her veiled note of disdain, but Maya merely smiled more brightly. "Masters in early childhood education. I was working forty hours a week at the time so I missed Phi Beta Kappa, but otherwise, my credentials are quite astonishing. The public university didn't require Liz Claiborne suits for a passing grade," she finished dryly in the face of her customer's visible disbelief.

The bell over the door clamored as it swung in on a spring breeze and the healthy shove of an exuberant teenager. "Hey, Maya, Matty's dragons are cool. Could you paint some on my shoes?"

"Even Miss Kidd likes 'em," Matty announced proudly, releasing the teenager's hand and hurrying over to display his red dragon for general inspection. "Shelly says they better 'an smiley faces." He beamed with delight.

Matty's happiness melted Maya into a warm puddle of mush. Not in the months since his mother's arrest and his aunt's arrival had he shown any evidence of pure childhood pleasure. That something so simple as a silly dragon could produce it, a dragon she had created, engulfed her with pride.

"Well, when we get your new sneakers, we'll have to paint even bigger dragons on them," she declared. "We'd better hurry over to the store before we go see Miss Selene."

Daringly deciding Matty's happiness was more important than impressing her condescending customer, Maya handed the crystal ball to her clerk. "Teresa, if you would help Constance's grandmother, I'd appreciate it." Wiping the dust off her hands with a towel she kept for that purpose, she emerged

from behind the counter. Not wishing to encounter the unpleasant sight of her customer's mouth hanging open in
shock, Maya simply took Matty's hand and swept out the
door. Burning bridges was her specialty.

They found a practically new pair of padded athletic shoes
at the Salvation Army store around the corner from the shop.
Matty displayed them proudly to Selene and anyone else who
expressed interest after they arrived at school. At one point
during the afternoon he wore one dragon shoe and one new
shoe. A five-year-old's ability to take pleasure in simple
things warmed Maya's scarred and jaded heart.

It didn't, however, warm her wallet, she thought as they
headed home to an empty refrigerator. She'd spent her last
five-dollar bill on the shoes. She hated to ask Selene for an
advance on her salary. She'd been trying to use the proceeds
from the shop to slowly pay off the mountain of bills in Cleo's
mail, but if it came down to a choice between borrowing from
the till or feeding Matty, she'd have to choose the latter, she
decided as their ride stopped the car at their street corner.

Trying to remember how many eggs remained in the apartment's little refrigerator and wondering if a withered bell
pepper and a piece of onion counted as vegetables, Maya
wearily helped Matty from the backseat and waved farewell
to the mother of one of her students. Living only a few blocks
from the town's main highway into the city had the advantage
of being on the route to almost everyone's home. If Selene
wasn't available, she could usually count on a ride from the
last parent to pick up their child at school.

Her back ached, her feet hurt, and her empty stomach demanded more than an egg for supper. She couldn't deny the
child inside her womb any more than she could deny Matty.
She'd have to raid the day's profits and go to the grocery. If
Teresa had pulled off the crystal ball sale, there should actually be money in the till for a change, but it was probably in
the form of credit card paper. She couldn't count on too many
customers paying cash.

Wishing for the luxury of a decadent Big Mac as they

walked the final block between the highway and home, Maya wrinkled her nose at the flash of blue lights reflecting off store windows and bouncing off brick walls. She had nothing against the police, but the anarchy of her growing-up years had inevitably painted those blue lights as symbols of turmoil in her mind. Matty's hand tightening around her fingers as he huddled closer warned he wasn't immune to them either.

She hated that. She wanted him to grow up secure in his surroundings, not terrified of every new occurrence. Somehow, she would have to teach him to trust in her ability to protect him against the world's unpleasantness.

Glancing down at her distended belly, Maya snorted in derision. Like, right, she'd done such a good job of protecting herself.

Not until they turned the corner did she understand the full extent of the disaster she'd been handed this time.

The entire front facade of Cleo's shop lay in tumbled heaps of old brick spilling across the street and sidewalk. Yellow police tape blocked all access to their home.

If he hadn't been watching for her, Axell might not have noticed Maya between the rows of buildings in the growing dusk. As it was, he caught a glimpse of orange-red in the halo of a street lamp, and hastened to catch up with her. She had a kid with her. He hadn't realized she had a son. Both of them were so pale in the glow of the streetlight he feared they'd faint.

"There's nothing you can do right now." Axell caught Maya's elbow, and felt her shivering through the cloth of her thin blouse. The temperature dropped quickly once the sun set. "They can't let anyone past the police line until inspectors assess the damage. It's just the brick facade that fell, but they don't know if there's underlying structural damage."

"Muldoon?"

For a moment, Axell wondered if her mind had wandered. Her voice trembled, and she hastily bit her bottom lip, but he could see her chin quivering in a battle to fight tears. In a flash of some insane leap of logic, he caught the connection. "The cat?" The black-and-white cat. Muldoon had driven a black-and-white police car in some ancient TV show.

She nodded. The boy merely stared in wide-eyed silence at the remains of his home. Unable to tolerate helplessness, Axell pulled off his suit jacket and wrapped it around Maya's shoulders. She didn't even seem aware that he'd done it.

"The cat's probably fine. Only the bricks collapsed, and they fell outward. I'll have the cops keep an eye out. Do you have anywhere else you can go for the night?"

She stared at him blankly for a minute, then apparently registering the question, nodded. With that nod, he watched her almost visibly discard the shroud of defeat, straighten her shoulders, and don the mantle of blithe vivacity. "We have cots at the school. It's just . . ." She threw a wavering look at the crumbled building and continued bravely, "We'll need transportation."

"You can't sleep on a cot," he said impatiently. "Besides, that place is way out in the country, without security lights. It's not safe for a woman alone. How about family?"

She shot him a wry look that warned she was recovering from the shock and told him of the asininity of his question. Her only family was in jail.

"All right, let's walk over to the restaurant and get a bite to eat and think about it. I left Constance with the kitchen staff. She'll be wondering where I am."

Surprised that she actually acquiesced without protest, Axell steered Maya through the crowd of other shop owners and passersby and warned the policeman in charge to watch for the cat. This was a small town. People looked out for one another. He had confidence someone would take in the cat. He wished he was equally confident about the teacher.

Thinking she looked so frail that he ought to be carrying her, Axell did his best to adjust his steps to hers as they traversed the two blocks to his bar. The lights from the tall narrow windows of the restaurant glowed welcomingly as they approached, but as Axell's step lightened, Maya's grew heavier.

"I can't go in there like this."

Finally, the protest he'd expected. In his experience, women never agreed without argument. Some days, he wondered how women thought the world had survived all these years without them running it. He recognized the chauvinism of the thought, but there were days when he felt conspicuously undervalued.

"Why not?" he demanded. "No one bites."

He couldn't see the look she shot him and probably couldn't interpret it if he could.

"I have dragons on my shoes."

Dragons. On her shoes. Axell closed his eyes and tried not to groan. He'd offered the position of nanny to a lunatic.

"I gots dragons, too," Matty said in what sounded like consolation as he offered up his shoes for inspection.

In the faint glimmering light of a distant street lamp, Axell noted they both wore cheap sneakers and something did look particularly outlandish about the toes.

Well, maybe it was better if he didn't drag her through the expensively dressed crowd of yuppies inside, looking as if she'd just been hit by a train. People would talk.

"We'll go in through the rear door," he said, steering her down the alley.

As they hit the bright lights and bustle of the kitchen, the delicate woman on Axell's arm unfolded like a sunstruck rosebud. The protective armor of her brilliant smile disguised her shattering fragility.

His staff stared as they entered. Axell could hear their minds clicking already. He'd listened to the gossip churning behind these walls for years and knew precisely how it worked. They'd either have Maya labeled as a mistress he'd dumped or as a homeless waif he'd picked up off the street. They'd have him with AIDS next and the mayor really would shut down the bar.

Constance raced to his rescue. Crying "Miss Alyssum!" she practically leapt into Maya's arms.

"Hi, honey bear," she answered softly, crouching to hug the child. "You going to show us where your daddy works?"

That's all it took to get her waited on, hand and foot. The

staff doted on Constance. To make her happy, they would have baked a five-tiered caked and decorated it with diamonds. Fortunately for Axell's budget, Maya only required pasta and a salad. Matty tore into a hamburger as if he hadn't eaten in a week.

That thought gave Axell pause as he slipped into the seat beside his daughter in the staff break room. The boy wasn't precisely skin and bones, but he wasn't sturdy either. The clothes he wore were as neat as could be expected of a five-year-old at the end of the day, but they were a little too small and showed definite signs of wear.

His gaze drifted back to the schoolteacher. She wore the maternity jumper she'd worn every time he'd seen her. Her fine-boned features had a drawn look rather than the maternal glow one would expect, and all the blood had drained from her normally pink lips. Her usual smile had vanished now that she was behind closed doors, leaving her more vulnerable and worried than he'd ever seen her.

"Insurance will take care of it," he suggested, knowing he pried where he had no business, but his insatiable curiosity needed appeasing.

She stabbed a piece of romaine and raised an eyebrow. Checking to be certain Matty still chattered, oblivious to their conversation, she shrugged. "Cleo hadn't paid a bill in months when I arrived. I can almost guarantee insurance isn't an option."

For whatever reason, Axell tried again. "She's just renting that place, isn't she? I'd say most of the damage was to the storefront, not the inventory. You can probably be back in business elsewhere in a few weeks."

She poked the lettuce around some more, then grimaced in a fiasco of a smile. "If I could impose on you for a ride, I think I'd better take Matty back to the school and get him settled in."

Axell tried to take her words at face value. He glanced at her plate and except for the lettuce, she'd eaten everything put before her. She hadn't insulted him by offering payment for the meal, but he had a strong suspicion she couldn't offer him money if she wished.

He didn't want to admit that an educated woman—one whose credentials he'd checked, one who ran a business, taught his daughter, and showed no sign of mental incapacity— could be homeless, hungry, and without visible means of transportation.

❦ SIX ❦

**If everything seems to be going well,
you have obviously overlooked something.**

"Where are we going?" Aroused from the lethargy inspired by glove-soft leather seats, the soft hum of a powerful motor, and the numbness of shock, Maya frowned at the unfamiliar turn off the familiar highway. Tree frogs chirruped in the country quiet.

"Constance's baby-sitter will be waiting."

She didn't know this enigmatic man well enough to interpret his tone, and despite the dim glow of the dash lights, darkness obscured his expression. She ought to be afraid out here with a stranger, with more fields than houses around, but this man was a Virgo to his bones. She suspected he was in full caretaking mode.

She could use a little caretaking right now, she thought from the weary fog she'd retreated into. She would like to gratefully accept Axell Holm's words at face value—if it were not for that rebellious Aquarian nature lurking beneath his surface. "What's your birth date?"

He glanced at her, then returned his attention to the road. "September, but I guarantee you that the planets do not guide my behavior."

She shook her head at his predictable response. "The month only gives your sun sign. I'd need the exact date, year, and place of birth to predict the planets, but I'm not very good at charting. Your Virgo nature is obvious. It's that Aquarian streak worrying me." She knew she was avoiding reality, but life had taught her to take one step at a time. Right now, sidestepping worked best.

"Astrology simply labels basic human behavior in a manner people can easily grasp. If it makes you happy to label my behavior, be my guest, but I'd wager genetics and environment more accurately explain character."

"Since I don't know your environment and can't examine your genes"—she threw his lap a naughty glance he probably didn't catch and couldn't follow since he wasn't wearing jeans—"I'll stick with astrology, thank you." Her mind had taken some warped loops with advanced pregnancy, but wondering what was under the godlike Axell Holm's trousers was loopier than usual.

They pulled into the driveway of a typical suburban Charlotte brick residence, the kind with more gables and outcroppings than she could count. As the car followed the drive around behind the house, Axell flicked a switch on the dash, and a garage door silently opened. As far as Maya was concerned, garages were a waste of money in this mild climate, but she supposed the rich had money to waste.

She didn't know why it bothered her that Axell was rich. He had to be a decade older than she was, and a continent away in terms of life experience. She appreciated his thoughtfulness in offering a meal and a chance to pull herself together, but men of his caliber made her extremely nervous, perhaps because she so desperately craved what he had to offer.

Damn, the shock must be wearing off and her brain must be bubbling with panic if she thought Axell Holm was what she needed.

She couldn't keep on like this. She'd been homeless before, but this time she had a baby on the way and Matty to worry about. How would she keep Matty? As soon as the social worker discovered their plight, she'd shove him into a foster home. Maya shivered as the fear rose in her, fanned by the winds of memory. She had to leave Wadeville, go back to California where she had friends. . . .

How the devil would she get back to California? She'd sold everything she owned, including her car, so she could afford the outrageous cost of a last-minute, one-way, cross-country plane ticket to rescue Matty from foster care. The few dollars she'd possessed over and above the fare had quickly gone to restoring Cleo's utilities, buying groceries, and dressing Matty in something besides rags. She'd never earned enough in her few years as a teacher to build a cushion of savings.

Tears filled her eyes, and she hastily wiped them away as Axell opened the passenger door and held out his hand to her. Matty and Constance were already scurrying out of the backseat.

She curled her fingers into her palms and stalled with the practice of a lifetime of rebelling against handouts. "I'll wait here while you take Constance in."

"Don't be ridiculous. I've got room, and you're exhausted. You can have a room near Constance. In the morning, things will look better."

"I've had a lot of experience with mornings. Generally, they only look worse." She refused his hand. She'd spent most of her life trying to fit into other people's lives. She'd earned her degree so she would never have to take charity or depend on anyone else again.

He withdrew his hand impatiently. "Look, you can sleep in the car if you like. I've got to get back to the restaurant after I see Constance settled, but I can take the Rover."

The "Rover" looked to be a looming utility vehicle of horrendous size on the far side of the garage. Two vehicles and one driver. Conspicuous consumption. She didn't have the energy to sniff her disapproval. Terror had replaced her brain.

As Axell turned away, Maya halted him. "What good is it showing Matty what he cannot have?" she demanded. "It would be much kinder if you'd take us to the school."

He didn't turn as he contemplated her words, leaving Maya a view of his wide shoulders. He'd removed his suit jacket and rolled up his shirtsleeves, but the casual look didn't conceal that he was accustomed to dealing from a position of strength: physical and emotional as well as financial. He had absolutely no concept of what it was like to worry that the roof over his head and the food in his mouth could be stripped away if he said the wrong thing, opened the wrong door, wore the wrong clothes.

The automatic garage lights blinked out and Axell hit the switch restoring them. The action apparently bolstered his decision. He turned and faced her with no expression.

"Children adapt," he snapped. "You're the one with the problem. If you want that school of yours to survive, you'd better learn to start working with others."

This time, he didn't offer a helping hand. He strode into the house, leaving her sitting in the enormously expensive car, staring at a wall of gleaming, unused garden tools. He didn't even tend his own yard.

Well, he'd given her a choice, of sorts. She could sit there until he got tired of looking at her and took her back to the school. She could borrow the money from Selene and go back to California with Matty. It would mean living off friends until the baby was born since she'd never find a job in this condition. Or she could get up and follow Axell Holm into the world of the wealthy, a world she'd never known, frequently despised, often envied, and always feared. In her experience, a helping hand usually meant accepting shackles. She wasn't any good at living within the boundaries of other people's rules.

Maya pinched her eyes closed. Either way, she lost her independence. Why not wait until after she was well rested to decide between a rock and a hard place?

Her irreverent humor bounced back as she shifted her belly out of the car. Maybe she could accept his offer of a position as nanny and be like the TV character who lived in wealth and flirted with her clueless employer.

The dubious charms of a wailing infant would end that career soon enough.

* * *

Removing cash from his pocket to pay off the baby-sitter, Axell curbed his impatience as Maya occupied the woman with chatter, drew Constance into the conversation, and appeared in no particular hurry to accept the shelter and comfort of the room he offered her. As far as he could see, Matty had settled quite comfortably into a fascinated trance in front of the television.

No matter what Maya thought, he wasn't offering charity. He'd simply grabbed the most expedient method available of installing a mother figure in the house for Constance and stalling Sandra awhile longer.

Somewhere on the ride here, his good intention of offering a night's shelter had developed into the insane idea that he'd been handed the golden opportunity to solve all his problems. With the schoolteacher in residence, Constance wouldn't need Sandra. He was a quick study. Maybe he could learn how Maya drew words out of his noncommunicative daughter. He would give anything, do anything, to have the same rapport with his daughter that Maya had. That Maya was a potential disruption to his orderly life was a given he accepted as the price of learning.

He was a desperate man.

So, watch and learn, he told himself as Maya stroked Constance's hair, talked about the video Constance had popped into the VCR, and pried a reluctant smile out of her as Maya compared the dragons on her toes with the one in the movie. A minute later, Constance was begging to have her new Nikes painted and was clinging to Maya's hand as if she wouldn't let go.

He still didn't see how she did it.

Instead of lingering in the family room doorway, Axell strolled in and sat on a massive leather footstool near Constance. He took the unadorned Nike from his daughter's fingers, held it up to the TV dinosaur, and tried to join the conversation. "Purple and green?" he asked facetiously, while Matty ignored them in favor of the video.

Constance drew closer to Maya, whipped her long hair

back and forth, and held out her hand for her shoe. She didn't say a word.

He didn't have time for this. Exasperated, he handed back the shoe. "Will you show Maya and Matty to the room next to yours?"

For a moment, her thin face lit from within. Then it shuttered and she nodded warily. Still, not a sound.

"Give your daddy a hug," Maya whispered in tones he could hear. "He has to go back to look after all your friends in the kitchen."

That was a hell of a way of looking at it, but Constance willingly turned and grabbed his neck for a swift hug before retreating to Maya's side. Maybe it was a female thing. Maybe little girls needed mothers at this age more than they needed fathers. Still, her desertion pained him. He'd worked hard at building the bar and restaurant to fill the void left by the death of his parents, but he'd never had his father's knack for making friends of his customers. Dissatisfied, he'd tried filling his lonely existence with Angela. He'd hoped his daughter's birth would build a strong foundation for his marriage. Instead, his inability to interact with others had cost him his wife, and now he was losing his daughter. Pain seared his heart as he watched Constance cling to a virtual stranger, leaving him more alone than ever. He didn't know why he kept trying, except he didn't know the meaning of the word "quit."

He'd always thought fathers worked to provide food and shelter and earned love and respect in return. What had he done wrong?

He simply didn't possess what she needed. Pained by that realization, Axell rose. "I apologize for my lack of hospitality, but I've got to get back to the bar." At least at the bar he knew where he stood. He provided the executive decisions. His employees provided the friendly atmosphere. "Make yourself at home as best as you can. I think the housekeeper keeps up the guest room, but you can ask Constance for anything you need. She knows where everything is."

"Of course she does." Maya slipped her arm around Constance's shoulder. "She's an excellent hostess. You can leave us safely in her hands."

She threw him a veiled look he couldn't interpret. Axell suspected he was supposed to do or say something now but he didn't know what it was. His father might have punched him in the arm and said, "Come on, tiger, let's you and me go to the bar," but that didn't seem the appropriate response in this case. He patted Constance's head awkwardly. "You look after Miss Alyssum and Matty for me. I'll see you in the morning."

Maya shook her head and watched him hurry away. The poor man didn't have a clue. She could almost sympathize with him. Almost. But years of experience told her that men were a self-centered lot when it came right down to it, and just because Axell was older and wealthier than most she knew, he wasn't any different.

She let both Constance and Matty wind down by watching the video. She doubted if Matty had ever seen a video, or that he had any idea how it operated. Cleo's ancient television didn't have cable and only picked up a couple of local channels, and those faintly. Matty watched a few cartoons on Saturday morning but nothing else. Maya preferred it that way, but she didn't have the heart to tear him away from this fascinating entertainment after seeing his home reduced to a crumbled pile of brick.

Homeless. Maya fought off another slam of panic as the baby kicked.

Matty wasn't the only one who needed diversion. Bubbles of pure fear percolated through her veins. She needed her tea. She should have insisted on rescuing her cups.

After the video ended, Constance led them through the darkened corridors of the house. The unlived-in decor didn't ease her fears. Dining room furniture gleamed with wax, vacant of any hodgepodge of sugar bowls or salt cellars or place mats. The beautifully decorated living room with its plush white rugs could never have seen a child's toy. The lovely apricot walls sported no dirty fingerprints. Against the silver sofa, charming pillows lay in perfectly symmetrical patterns that could never have held a human head.

Maya rolled her eyes and with a spurt of humor imagined what this place would look like if she let Matty and Muldoon and herself loose in it for a few days. Axell would never recover from the shock. Maybe she could round up a pickup and move Cleo's stuff into the upper story of the school in the morning. Selene was out of town, but she might have a better idea when she returned.

Maya shuddered at the first sight of the guest room. It looked like a hotel with its prints of English gardens and its heavy draperies in polite mauve-and-blue pinstripes against a beige background. She supposed the cherry bed was expensively tasteful, but it wasn't the kind of thing one would let a child jump on.

"This was gonna be the baby's room," Constance said matter-of-factly as Matty stared in awe at the big bed with its stacks of pillows.

The baby's room? Maya would rather not get into that one.

Looking around at Axell Holm's ice palace, she could see rules and regulations written all over. No sirree bob, she was out of here first thing in the morning.

Constance tugged shyly at her hand. "I made a picture," she whispered.

Unable to accomplish the feat of crouching again, Maya sank onto an upholstered chair and turned Constance around to face her. "What kind of picture? May I see it?"

Constance nodded, pulled her hand free, and opened a dresser drawer. Maya caught a glimpse of a hidden treasure-trove of childish objects: a battered stuffed rabbit, broken crayons, and chunks of what appeared to be plaster. Constance neatly closed the drawer before Maya could see more.

The child handed her a slightly rumpled sheet of drawing paper. Maya could easily discern a baby's crib, a bassinet swaddled in lace, and a corner full of colorful toys. "How wonderful!" she cried in all honesty. For a child of Constance's age, it was a marvelously accurate piece of workmanship. "Is this what this room used to look like?"

Constance nodded.

The baby inside Maya's womb kicked in approval. Wistfully, she wondered what it would be like to have a sanctuary like this for her child. She'd hang a mobile of fairy-tale creatures over the crib, paint stars on the ceiling, stack wonderful books on the shelves. . . .

Someday. She would do it someday. Smiling, she held the picture up against the cream-colored wall. "I think it would look good hanging right here, don't you?"

Constance's thin dark face beamed with relief. "I got tape." She ran to fetch it.

Matty crept over to hug her knee. "We gonna stay here?" he asked in awe.

She didn't believe in children sleeping with adults, but she didn't see an alternative for tonight. The bed was certainly big enough for two. She ran her fingers through his hair and smiled as bravely as she could. "Looks that way, buster. Do you think that bed's big enough for you?"

He eyed it with some trepidation but nodded slowly. "Can Muldoon sleep with us?" he asked plaintively. The cat had been sleeping in his room ever since she'd brought it with her from California.

How would she explain it to him if Muldoon never came back? How could she explain it to him if the social workers took him away?

She just couldn't deal with the disaster yet. "Muldoon's probably guarding your old room to make certain your toys don't get lonely. You're stuck with me tonight." She hugged his small body close, making mental promises to fix everything in the morning.

She wasn't a fixer by nature. That had been Cleo's role. The ever-present burden of doing everything herself swamped her, and loneliness slipped through all the cracks in her defenses.

She just needed to be strong. She had Cleo's child and the one about to be born to fill the emptiness. A life filled with children would be plenty more than enough.

She didn't need useless men making demands, giving orders, and disrupting her goals. She'd take loneliness over that emotional roller coaster again. Children had to be easier.

Why, then, did tears fill her eyes as she gazed around the antiseptic guest room and wondered how her life had come to this?

❧ SEVEN ❧

I don't suffer from insanity;
I enjoy every minute of it.

Maya stared at the enormous stainless steel double doors of what had to be Axell's refrigerator. It looked as if it belonged in his restaurant. Where were the colorful magnets, the childish drawings, the memos of doctor appointments and whatnot that should clutter this magnificent expanse of empty steel? Her fingers itched to fill the space with color and life almost as much as if the doors were a piece of drawing paper.

All she'd wanted was a glass of milk to stave off the predawn lonelies. Painting a refrigerator wasn't on the agenda. Biting her thumbnail, she eased open the wider of the two doors. A brilliant white light illuminated the gloomy kitchen. She hadn't bothered turning on the overhead fixture because in her experience, with unexpected light creepy crawly things scattered across the floors. She preferred they scurry out of sight before she had to look at them. The refrigerator bulb, however, was almost blinding.

Probably because nothing blocked its glow.

Maya stared in fascination at the shelves of shiny—empty—aluminum. A half gallon of milk, some eggs, and butter hid in the distant corners of the vast interior. It almost reminded her of home. Almost. In Cleo's ancient appliance, just the milk would have filled a shelf, if they'd had any.

"Miss Alyssum, are you fixing breakfast?"

The soft voice nearly startled her into jumping into the refrigerator. She'd probably fit, belly and all, Maya decided with amusement as she peered around the door to see Constance in her flowing nightshirt. The child had crept up quieter than any mouse.

"Well, it's a mite early, and our options look limited. Would you like something?"

"Daddy's other ladies usually fix French toast." She watched Maya cautiously.

Daddy's other ladies. Right. Rolling her eyes and biting her tongue on that one, Maya eyed the refrigerator contents skeptically. "Well, if you know where to find bread and syrup, we could do that. Or maybe even bread and cinnamon. Or jelly?"

"You and Matty slept on my side," Constance replied irrelevantly.

Maya had enough psychology courses to know when a child had something on her mind. She just didn't want to contemplate this particular topic at this hour of the morning in the house of a man she scarcely knew. By "side," she assumed Constance meant her wing of the house. She'd already figured out Axell had a wing all to himself, since she hadn't heard him come home.

"Well, I guess that makes us *your* guests," she replied brightly, closing the refrigerator and opening a cabinet. Dumb move. Now she had no light.

"Sometimes Daddy's ladies don't stay for breakfast."

All right, so the kid had a one-track mind. Deal with it. She'd long ago discovered how difficult it was to shimmer away from an unwanted topic around kids.

"Constance, what are you—" The kitchen exploded with light.

Maya blinked. The sleepy man standing in the doorway did the same, then rubbed his eyes in the glare of the overhead fixture. Fixtures. The kitchen had track lighting all over the blamed room.

Axell Holm stood there in only his pajama bottoms. A soft brown fuzz nicely delineated his rounded pectorals and descended into washboard abs before dropping beneath the elastic falling over lean hips. Maya thought her eyes might pop out. Surely pregnancy prevented hormonal outbursts. Lean, hungry, artistic types did not have chests like that. She didn't think yuppie businessmen should either.

She closed her eyes and pretended she'd imagined the whole thing. "Don't you have anything dimmer?" she pleaded.

Hitting the dimmer switch, Axell lowered the confounded lighting while trying to assimilate the image of his elfin daughter standing beside a hugely pregnant fairy godmother with chaotic auburn curls and . . . He peeked from behind his hand. The shimmering turquoise nightgown nearly blinded him as much as the kitchen lights. He couldn't remember his wife ever wearing that color, but Constance must have shown Maya the closet where he'd stored Angela's things.

Maybe he was dreaming. "What are we doing out here in the middle of the night?" he asked cautiously. Actually, he'd come home in the middle of the night. It must be closer to morning. He blinked again at the vision in turquoise. Why did she remind him of a particularly striking bouquet of fresh flowers as she stood there against his steel and porcelain kitchen?

"*I'm* after warm milk. I believe Constance is checking on my sleeping habits."

Axell heard her humor and didn't want to interpret that remark. He regarded his daughter's innocent expression with suspicion. Maybe his fault lay in believing an eight-year-old hadn't yet developed the twisted mind of all females. "Constance, go back to bed. It's Saturday. You don't have to go to school."

He recognized the rebellious pout of his daughter's lower lip. Warily, Axell glanced at the teacher to see if she'd help. She beamed sunnily as she poured milk into a cup. Following the pattern of her recent behavior, it dawned on him that the gypsy woman didn't believe in confrontation. She had a habit of slipping and sliding out of the most damning tempests with just a smile as her umbrella.

"Did you want warm milk, too?" he asked his daughter. Two could play at the game of No Confrontation.

"French toast," Constance replied stubbornly.

Red warning flags waved all over that one. Axell glanced at the gypsy putting the milk into the microwave. Her smile had grown suspiciously wider. Damn, but her mouth looked rosy and ripe even at this gawdawful hour of the morning.

She was eight months pregnant, dammit! Easily eight months. Nervously contemplating babies popping out on the polished tiles of the kitchen floor, Axell rubbed his unshaven jaw and tried to gather his thoughts. He was standing here half-naked, for chrissake. He wasn't used to having guests.

"When the sun comes up," he agreed. "Now go back to bed and let Miss Alyssum drink her milk in peace."

"I want milk." Constance sat her skinny rear end in a kitchen chair.

Why in the name of heaven had he wanted the child to talk? It was a thousand times more peaceful when she kept her mouth shut. Axell glanced helplessly at the teacher again. How could she look even more innocent than his child?

"I believe Constance is worried about where I'm sleeping," she replied with muffled laughter, removing the cup from the microwave and pouring a portion into a smaller cup for his daughter. "Go back to bed. I'll see her back to her room."

Where she was sleeping? Axell sleepily pondered that one until heat flushed up his jaw. He hadn't realized Constance was aware of the women he occasionally entertained in his wing of the house. He tried to hustle most of them home before his daughter woke, but some had indulged their fantasies of homemaking and insisted on staying. He should have thrown them all out. With a sigh, he nodded in acknowledgment of her warning.

"All right. I'll see you in the morning. Constance, behave yourself and do as Miss Alyssum tells you." To hell with women. Staggering back down the hall, Axell left them to themselves. The one blamed day he could get a little sleep . . .

Chiming laughter exploded in the room he'd left behind. Confounded, know-it-all woman.

Maya wasn't laughing hours later as she cuddled a meowing Muldoon in her arms while a policeman blocked her path. Through tear-filled eyes, she glared at the blue uniform and yellow police tape cutting off her access to Matty and Cleo's home. She was used to losing homes. It really shouldn't hurt so much. But she'd sort of hoped maybe she could have this one for the baby and Matty—at least until Cleo returned. She bit her lip and tilted her chin up to fight sobbing over this latest twist of fate.

"It's for your own safety, miss," the officer insisted. "The place has to be torn down. Fire marshal's orders. It's a death trap. Those walls could fall any minute."

"But there are works of art in there!" she protested, praying she didn't sound whiny. "Handmade, irreplaceable . . . The artisans deserve compensation for their work. If I don't salvage them . . ."

The policeman implacably shook his head. "No can do."

Maya thought of all Matty's clothes and toys, Cleo's motley assortment of furniture, all the accoutrements they'd gathered in years of careful scrounging, and the tears streamed down her cheeks. They'd been displaced so many times. . . . The teapot! And her china cups! A wrecking ball would demolish their whole lives.

Shaking her head in denial, she hugged Muldoon and sought desperately for some argument to sway the officer. Why did authority always get in the way in the guise of helping? She and Cleo had spent their entire lives being shipped from one house to another with little more than a cardboard box of possessions between them. The teapot and cups were all they still owned from the home they barely remembered. She couldn't lose them.

Wiping her eyes with her shirtsleeve, she thought frantically of ways around the catastrophe. She could creep in there in the dead of night. . . . Creep? With her two-ton belly? Fat chance. And she couldn't just haul out the china when Matty needed his rabbit and his pajamas, and the artists who'd built the kaleidoscopes and wind chimes needed the income from their work and . . .

The CD player, with her recordings. Cleo's photographs.

Their whole damned lives were in that building. She bit her lip on another hiccuping sob.

"Trouble, Miss Alyssum?"

Walking from the corner where he'd been talking with a man Maya recognized as the mayor, Axell Holm stopped beside her with that puzzled expression men assumed when confronted with female emotion. Maya glared back at him.

"Of course not, Mr. *Holm*," she said with sarcastic emphasis on the formal name. "Everything my family owns is going to be demolished with that wretched building. That's no trouble at all. It just makes it easier to pick up and move."

A frown knitted the bridge of his nose as he looked at the collapsed facade of the building. "That could be the mayor's intention," he replied thoughtfully.

Startled, Maya jerked her head around to look at him. *"What?"*

He caught her elbow and steered her away from the ears of the interested policeman. "The mayor wants your school closed, remember? If you have nowhere to live and no reason to stay, you'll close the school without his having to make what could conceivably be an unpopular political decision."

"You were just *talking* to the man," she exclaimed. "Did he tell you this?"

"Don't be ridiculous. If Ralph was gloating, he kept it to himself. We were just passing pleasantries about having all these old buildings inspected before someone gets hurt. We seldom agree on anything, but we agreed on that much."

"Well, I should think so." Maya shook off his hand and stalked down the alley next to the building, clinging to her cat. "Maybe they should tear down the whole damned town. But right now, I want inside that building. Those are my *things*. He doesn't have any right to take them away."

"He has every right, if there's a danger to human life. That doesn't mean he's right, and that there is a danger."

She stopped and swirled to look at him. "What does that mean?"

Clean-shaven and garbed in his version of casual wear— blue linen short-sleeved shirt and crisply creased khakis—

Axell raised his hand over his eyes and inspected the roof of the building, then studied the remaining brick walls. "I think we can find an inspector who will say the remainder of the building is safe enough to enter to remove the contents. The brick facade may be weak, but the underlying structure should be sound."

Maya thought she would kiss him. If her belly weren't in the way, she'd throw her arms around this enigmatic Norse god and plant a smacker square in the middle of his chiseled jaw. That ought to shake him straight down to his steadfast toes. Instead, she beamed and patted Axell's tanned arm. The warmth of his skin startled her, and she hastily withdrew the gesture. The expression in his eyes was shuttered as he warily lowered his hand and glanced down at her. Even bigger than she'd ever been in her life, she felt dainty and fragile in his solid presence.

"Where do we find an inspector?" she asked bravely.

The "we" she had so ingenuously uttered knelled as loud as church bells between them. All the multifarious implications of "we" winged through Maya's mind in the face of his silence. She didn't think Axell's astute businessman's mind had missed them either.

"It's Saturday," he slowly responded, finally tearing his gaze from her to study the building. "I won't be able to locate an inspector until Monday, at best. And then there's the question of where you'll transport the items once you're free to move them."

Maya could feel the shark's teeth closing over her silly little Pisces head. She should have known better than to play in dangerous currents instead of placid little ponds. Biting her bottom lip, she let the tide sweep her straight into the deep blue sea.

"Any suggestions?" she asked gaily, as if that "we" hadn't already tolled her doom.

Axell's eyes narrowed as he caught her elbow again and steered her around a pile of crumbling brick. "Let's go to the bar and talk about it."

Every time someone in authority wanted to "talk" about

something, it meant being uprooted again. Abandoning all hope, Maya floated downstream, hopelessly hooked on Axell's bait.

Fish weren't supposed to have nests anyway.

December 1945

I don't remember who seduced whom, but I remember the night you carried me back to my bed and stayed until daybreak. Don't you ever tell me that was just a young man getting his jollies off. It was more than that, for both of us. We made the birds sing at midnight and the doves cry at dawn. No one ever made me feel like that before. No one ever can again. Does she wrap her legs around you until you roar with hunger? If she's got breasts beneath all that binding, I bet you haven't touched them yet.

❧ EIGHT ❧

**If it's dangerous to talk to yourself,
it's probably even dicier to listen.**

Axell knew better than to get involved. He especially knew
better than to get involved with a female with "trouble" written
all over her. Some people lived from one disaster to another,
and Maya Alyssum struck him as that kind of person. Her
vulnerability would eventually expose his deficiencies, and
nothing good could come of either.

But he had an inherent need to help the town of his birth,
and to give back to the community some of the wealth it had
so generously provided him. Angela had claimed he just liked
controlling people, but that wasn't so. Of course, in this case,
helping—or controlling—Maya would ultimately solve his
worst fear: losing Constance.

He sat Maya down in a booth at the back of the restaurant
and signaled his bartender to bring them sweet tea. Matty and
Constance were occupying themselves in the employee break
room, well looked after by his doting staff. He could safely
concentrate on bending this tear-stained waif of a woman to
his will. He'd already noted she bent remarkably easily. He
had experience and determination on his side. Surely he
could keep a safe enough distance between them that emotions wouldn't play a factor in their relationship, even if Maya
was prone to all the usual female complexities.

"If I hire an inspector," Axell paused to let the implication
of her obligation sink in, "and he allows you to move your
things, where will you move them?"

She twisted a red paper napkin between her fingers and

didn't look up. "We haven't remodeled the upper story of the school yet. I thought Matty and I could move our things there. But we really need to keep Cleo's shop open. She has to have somewhere to go when . . ." She hesitated, apparently not wanting to say the word "prison" out loud. "If only the mayor understood the awfulness Cleo went through to get this far, maybe he'd listen?"

Axell had looked up the sister, of course. She'd been busted for chronic possession and shoplifting a teddy bear, not the act of a hardened criminal. Still, selling drugs was usually the logical next step for an addict. He had to be cautious here, but he didn't think a schoolteacher would condone the behavior of junkies, even if one was her sister.

"Besides, the artisans who designed the stuff in there deserve an outlet for their creativity and some reward for their work," Maya continued. "Some of it would sell for a fortune in California. Cleo had a brilliant idea. She just didn't know how to make it work."

Axell sat back as the bartender set the teas in front of them. Crossing his arms on the wooden table, he studied his companion. He'd read her credentials. She had a Masters in childhood education, four years' teaching experience, and an extremely high grade-point average at an excellent state university. He knew nothing of her prior life. He didn't even know where the damned father of her child was. Maybe that was a starting point.

"Do you have any income other than the school?" he asked pointedly. "Child support, alimony?"

She shook her wavy curls, and the purple streak fell forward across her brow with a will of its own. Since she couldn't reclaim her clothes, she wore the same outfit she'd worn the day before. Somehow, the outlandish gauzy pleats and silky shirt looked exotic and expensive, even though he knew damned well she'd bought them at some thrift store.

"Stephen and I aren't married. We were more or less separated when I heard about Cleo . . ." She skipped over that part with a wave of her hand. "I didn't even know for certain I was pregnant when I flew out here. He travels a lot. I've left messages, but he hasn't any money. I can't expect any help from that quarter. I can make it on my own," she said defiantly, "I just need to get my stuff out of that building."

"I've been through the Pfeiffer place." He hadn't blindly sent Constance to a school he knew nothing about. When it had opened, he'd had every aspect of it checked thoroughly, except the finances, which weren't a matter of public record. He wondered if he ought to probe that angle further but decided against it. Selene Blackburn's family had money. They would probably invest in anything to keep their rattle-brained daughter off the streets. "The upper story hasn't been refurbished in decades. You don't even have working plumbing up there. No heat, no air; it's not fit for habitation."

She stirred the sweet tea with her straw and watched the ice cubes swirl. "I've lived in worse. The plumbing downstairs is just fine. We can open the windows upstairs in the summer. By winter, maybe something better will come along."

She'd lived in worse? Axell didn't want to imagine it. Old Man Pfeiffer had pulled the upper story apart in the process of renovation, then lost interest after his wife died. Wallpaper hung in ragged strips. Plaster had been ripped from the lathes. Molding for the unfinished floors above the school lay in jagged lengths full of nails that invited tetanus. The mayor was probably right. The building should be demolished. He shook his head.

"You're not thinking, Miss Alyssum," he admonished. "You not only have a son, but an infant on the way. They can't live like that."

She shot him an angry look. "The name is Maya, Matty is my nephew, and my sister and I lived like that more times than I can count. Not everyone in this world was born with a silver spoon in their mouth."

Back off, Axell. He retreated against the booth seat and signaled for more tea. Don't provoke emotional outbursts, he reminded himself. Matty was her nephew. Cleo's kid. Things were getting clearer now. He'd thought her a bit young to have two kids, but what did he know about how the other half lived? After all, he'd been born with a silver spoon in his mouth.

"Having lived like that, I'm sure you'd prefer Matty and your child to live otherwise." Dumb, he realized as soon as he said it. Now he'd really raise her hackles. How in hell did one go about approaching this topic carefully? Already, his deficiencies were showing.

Maya's brave smile faded, and she shrugged. "There are a lot of things I'd like. Not many of them are attainable. Kids don't really notice their surroundings too much. What they notice is how much they're loved. Just tell me what I have to do to get you to hire the inspector. I have no idea what one costs or how to go about hiring one. I just know I can't afford him."

Amazed at how easily she cut to the chase, Axell raised his glass in salute to her astuteness. She offered a wry grin and a lift of her glass in return. He admired a woman who could speak his language.

"My interest in all this is Constance. I don't want you returning to California. I don't know how you do it, but you're bringing my daughter out of her shell. If you leave, she might regress and give my mother-in-law the means to pry her out of my hands. I'll do whatever it takes to prevent that."

He'd considered offering her a place in his home again, but the incident this morning had given him second thoughts on that. He didn't need wide-eyed waifs in his kitchen at four in the morning. He didn't need women giving birth on his kitchen floor. He had all he could handle already without adding the dangerous complications a female would bring— particularly after Constance's revelations about the other women in his life. He'd never have any privacy. "I own the building next door to this one."

Her head jerked up, her eyes widened, and she stared at him with an awakening hope and fascination that shot Axell's hormones into overdrive. She was pregnant, dammit! She was little better than a helpless child. Just because she looked at him as if he'd handed her the moon didn't mean he was free to lose control.

His libido never had listened to reason. That's how he'd ended up married to Angela. He learned from his mistakes.

Shifting uncomfortably, Axell gulped his iced tea before continuing. "The last tenant left it in fairly reasonable condition. It's not earning any money sitting there empty. Maybe we could make some kind of deal."

"If we can get the inspector's approval to move my stuff," she reminded him. "What kind of a deal did you have in mind?"

Had she not been twenty-months pregnant, all kinds of possibilities would have danced through his lecherous mind. He'd always been a sucker for helpless women, and this one not only appealed to his wretched need to protect, but with that wisp of uncontrollable purple hair and huge, wounded eyes, she appealed to his baser instincts as well.

But her pregnancy ruled out all his low-minded thoughts, simplifying his answer. "You can move into the upstairs apartment, set up shop downstairs, and pay me a percentage of your gross every month. My only stipulation is that you be available to Constance as much as possible. Keep her with you, as you do Matty, while I work. Except on busy nights like Friday and Saturday, I try to get away from the bar around nine or ten. If she's right next door, I might be able to get out to see her more often."

Her eyes lit up like a child with a new toy as she contemplated his promises. He'd never seen anything like it. Grown women should be a damned sight more wary of men offering candy. This one just seemed to slip off into her own little dream world.

"We'll have to move the counter. Do you think I could hire someone to help me dust all that stuff before we put it back out again? Could we go look at the building now? I want to tell Matty. . . ."

She was already across the booth and almost out of her seat before Axell could help her. Had she not been so pregnant, she'd probably be out the door before he could get up. Like quicksilver, she shimmered and glided and disappeared before his eyes. He'd never seen anything like it. His front door closed after her before he could cross the restaurant.

Feeling considerably less burdened now that he had the problem with Constance solved, Axell loped after her, whistling a happy tune.

"This is marvelous! This is *gorgeous*." Maya whirled around in the vast open space of the downstairs shop of the restored old building. "The light from here is heavenly."

"The foot traffic outside is heavier and should draw more customers," Axell added.

Ignoring him, Maya ran her fingers over the mahogany banister to the upstairs. "Someone treated this place with respect. There's a much happier aura in here."

"It's called profit." Axell examined the ceiling tile twelve feet above them. "Heating and cooling is a problem, though."

"There's a ceiling fan. And look at the floor! If I could just have it waxed . . ." Seeing that Axell was counting pennies, Maya slipped up the stairs. She really shouldn't take another place with stairs, but what choice did she have? The baby would come when it was ready. Ignoring a frisson of fear at her lack of preparation for that event, she peeked around the corner at the living quarters. She didn't own a crib or baby clothes. She had no nesting instincts to rely on. So she ignored the future in favor of the present.

"Perfect," she murmured happily as she glimpsed the upstairs. "Look at those windows! I could turn the front room into a gallery if we didn't have to live here." Wrinkling her nose at the thought of Cleo's ugly plaid couch desecrating the marvelous airy space, Maya crossed the wide front room to look out on the street below.

"Streetcars used to go up and down that road on the half hour."

She hadn't heard Axell come up behind her, and she caught her breath at his sudden proximity. His square build seemed so solid and reassuring, she had to resist leaning into him. What would it be like having a man like him to lean on?

Boring, she reminded herself. Just because she was scratching the bottom of the barrel financially and longed for the security he represented didn't mean she'd be happy with riches. She needed a man who understood her dreams, not a stiff Norse god who'd never had a dream in his life.

"Wouldn't it be lovely to have one of those cute little trolley cars going up and down someday? Tourists love trolley cars, and this town would be ideal for an artists' colony. With these huge old windows in most of the stores, we could have art galleries for paintings and pottery and textiles. There's room for antique dealers specializing in the arts. Then in some of those larger places, someone could have flea market and craft items for the less wealthy. An ice cream parlor! Wouldn't that be fabulous?"

"Would I have to serve artichoke hearts and radicchio?"

She heard the sarcasm and shrugged it off. "Men would love your place with the dark paneling and steaks and hearty fare. Someone else would have to open a tea room for the women. And a bakery! With traditional southern desserts—mud pies!" She drooled of dream heaven. "There's room for all kinds."

"I'm glad to know there's still room for me. In the meantime, don't you think you ought to be putting together some kind of business plan? You can't continue operating on a song and a prayer if you expect to make a profit."

Maya wrinkled up her nose. "You and Selene sound just alike. Where's the room for creativity in a business plan?" She turned and nearly bumped her nose into his chest. She looked upward but couldn't read his bland expression.

Axell stepped backward, putting more distance between them. "I'm amazed Selene knows the definition of 'business plan.' Are you going to look at the rest of the place?"

"Selene has vision, which is more than I can say for most people," Maya said pointedly, traipsing across the front room and aiming for the back.

"I don't know a damned thing about art galleries," he called after her, "except they can't possibly be profitable. People have to eat and wear clothes. That's where the money is. You'll have a hell of a time finding a market for the inventory your sister left."

"Admittedly, there are better places to sell enlightened art than this two-bit backwater, but the city is out there. We just have to reach it." Maya peered out the back bedroom windows overlooking an alley. She'd prefer trees and grass, but beggars couldn't be choosers. It was better than Cleo had before.

"The people here are more practical than the dilettantes in the city with more money than sense," Axell argued from behind her.

"And beauty isn't practical." She carried her bulk to the narrow galley and shrugged off the comparison with Axell's enormous state-of-the-art kitchen. Well, at least the place came furnished with a stove, so she wouldn't have to move that abomination from Cleo's home.

"I didn't say that," he answered grumpily. "I just said you'll have a hard time selling it out here."

She was avoiding looking at him. She wasn't much on self-analysis, but generally she didn't avoid looking at people. She didn't usually argue with them either. Maybe some of his distancing technique was rubbing off on her.

Reluctantly, Maya turned and caught Axell's gaze. He seemed startled but this time refrained from backing away, although she saw the wariness behind his eyes.

"Well, I can't sell groceries, and I'm not much of a cook, so I guess I'm stuck with Cleo's inventory for now. I'll just have to make it work."

With this admission of her weaknesses, Axell crossed his arms over his chest and leaned back against the kitchen counter, master of all he surveyed. "I think in your own best interests, we need to form a partnership," he announced.

❦ NINE ❦

Auntie Em: Hate you, hate Kansas.
Taking the dog. Dorothy.

"She's *staying* with you?" Katherine asked incredulously as she escaped the demands of hostess to take a break at the rear of the barroom where Axell surveyed the Saturday night crowd. He knew nearly everyone in this room and had no compelling need to make his presence known unless necessary. People didn't expect it of him.

Axell eyed Headley at the far end of the room regaling some young ingenue with his war stories. Headley had never been in a war. Axell dipped his gaze back to Katherine, who bristled with hostility—for what reason, he couldn't imagine.

"If you mean Maya Alyssum, yes," he stated calmly. "Unless we can rescue her things, she has nowhere else to go. If you're concerned about the proprieties, you might mention that to the mayor. Once we retrieve her furniture, she can move next door."

"You don't get it, do you?" she asked bitterly. "You're so damned blind, you can't see beyond that bar over there. That woman is out to get her hooks in you, and you're helping her shove them in."

Axell raised his eyebrows at his hostess's vehemence. "She's a pregnant schoolteacher, Katherine, not a temptress. If anything, I'm making Constance deliriously happy by entertaining her. I believe they're finger painting right now."

He tried not to remember the happy chaos he'd left after supper—a pizza he'd provided because there was nothing in

79

the refrigerator. Maya had spread thick layers of newspapers over the antique oak kitchen table, but he rather suspected the newspaper might be as bad as the water-logged finger-painting sheets. His housekeeper would have hysterics. His kitchen would soon look like a war zone, given Matty's penchant for red. But he'd left Constance laughing ecstatically, and the almost-forgotten sound decimated all objections. He knew his priorities. Constance was on the top of the list.

"You bought her clothes," Katherine said accusingly, jerking him back to the present.

Axell caught the eye of a waitress and nodded toward a table where a patron had just spilled his drink. He returned his attention to Katherine's nagging. He'd never thought her the type to nag.

"All their clothes are in the building the mayor had condemned," he reminded her. "It's not as if I supplied them with designer outfits. It was all I could do to persuade her to buy at Wal-Mart instead of the Goodwill store."

Actually, he hadn't persuaded her. Taking advantage of her habit of nonconfrontation, he'd simply driven to Wal-Mart instead of Goodwill. She'd speared him with her eyes, but looks couldn't kill, and she hadn't been able to say anything in front of the kids. Axell smiled remembering Matty happily accepting everything he chose for him. The teacher, on the other hand, had insisted she needed only clean underwear and a shirt. Once he'd figured out her size, he'd bought her two new maternity dresses and a big sweater to keep her warm on these cool spring nights.

She'd insisting on writing him an IOU. He'd considered trashing it, but for whatever reason, he'd carefully folded it up and tucked it away in his wallet as a reminder of how far he'd come. The grand sum total of their purchases equaled what he paid to have his cars detailed once a month.

"She's playing innocent," Katherine fumed. "Just you wait. She'll have you caught—hook, line, and sinker—if you don't wake up soon."

She flounced off to her duty of greeting customers, leaving Axell to consider her warning.

True, he'd always had a habit of helping those who couldn't help themselves. Marrying Angela had probably been a result of that, but he'd been much, *much* younger then. Her parents had just divorced and moved away. She'd bombed out of college as a result and taken a job as a waitress at the bar. His father had just died. One thing had led to another and she'd ended up pregnant. Marriage had seemed the best thing to do at the time. Now that he understood the complexities of the wedded state, he'd never make that mistake again. He wasn't cut out for sharing his life. Angela had called him uptight and heartless, but he just didn't see the need to expose his insides for all to see.

He didn't think Maya Alyssum much interested in marriage either, or in him. He occasionally caught her looking at him as if he were some fascinating but particularly repellent bug. There were way too many differences between them to find a common ground. He figured he was safe.

From the schoolteacher, anyway. As he watched Mayor Ralph Arnold enter with the mayor's mother and Sandra on his arms, Axell wasn't at all certain he was safe in anything else that mattered. His mother-in-law and Ralph's mother were old buddies, or biddies, he revised spitefully. Watching the three of them take a table was like watching the enemy occupying his turf.

Feeling like the French Resistance struggling with the German occupiers, Axell ordered his bartender to send over a bottle of wine. He'd yet to lose a battle. He wouldn't start now. Constance was his, if he had to pay the schoolteacher's salary to keep her.

Noting a drunk and disorderly situation building to his left, Axell released some of his frustration by collaring the jerk and hauling him out to the local taxi. The jerk began yelling "Police brutality!" as Axell heaved him into the taxi's backseat. Another night, it might have amused him. With the mayor inside and his license on the line, the comment only seared more acid through his stomach.

Under the guise of retrieving a drink from the bar, the mayor was waiting for him when Axell returned.

"Your bartenders are pushing too many drinks," Ralph said coldly, rattling the ice in his glass. "This is a family town. Drunken disturbances won't be tolerated."

Axell was more than familiar with the southern propensity to hide liquor behind closed doors. The vote to ban all alcohol sales had narrowly lost in the last election. Taking a swig of the mineral water his bartender handed him, Axell bit down on his temper. "You'll not have my license on that flimsy excuse, Ralph, and if you really want that school gone, you'd better find new tactics." Now that he had the schoolteacher in the palm of his hand, maybe he could bluff the mayor into a trade-off.

"That shopping center is more important to this community than any artsy liberal kindergarten," the mayor warned. "I'll do what it takes to take care of the people who elected me."

Axell snorted. "You'll do what it takes to take care of yourself, Ralph. I've got the schoolteacher. If you want my cooperation, you'll leave my bar alone."

"Scratch my back, and I'll scratch yours." Nodding approval, the mayor returned to his table.

Axell squeezed the plastic bottle in his hand until water squirted from the opening. How could he trade a schoolteacher for a liquor license? Cursing silently, he escaped to the orderly chaos of the kitchen.

"You could have moved in with me, you moron," Selene exclaimed over the phone line, "but I can't complain if you're sleeping with the enemy. That goes well beyond the line of duty."

Maya wrinkled her nose at Selene's commentary and watched as Matty proudly taped his creation to the vast barren space of the refrigerator door. He might not be good at letters yet, but he was definitely expressive in paint. "I wouldn't want to cramp your style, girl," she returned her attention to the conversation, "and I'll have you remember 'sleeping' is the only thing a woman in my delicate condition can do."

Selene clucked disapprovingly. "Shows how much you know. Does this mean we have a serious advocate on the city council?"

"For as long as it suits his purposes." Maya eased her weight onto a kitchen stool. If this baby wasn't born soon, her feet would be flatter than Matty's painting. "He's not half-bad, once you get to know him. Just kind of stiff and proper and accustomed to having his way." Remembering the clothes shopping incident, she figured that was the polite way of putting it. "Domineering" was the better word.

"Well, you just keep pouring on the butter, and I'll work my end of it. I've got a party with a DOT board member tonight. Wish me well."

Maya grinned. She'd never seen Selene work one of her "parties," but she could imagine it. "Sweet-talk him good, sugar. We'll have that nasty old shopping center installing underground parking yet."

"I'll not go that far. That's a flood zone out there. But we'll find something."

Selene hung up, leaving Maya to admire the artwork of her two talented charges. Matty was into dragons at the moment. Constance, apparently high on earlier praise, was painting more and more elaborate nurseries.

"Grandmother gave me a baby doll," she replied matter-of-factly when Maya asked about the infant in the picture. "But dolls aren't like real babies, are they?" Big, serious eyes watched Maya expectantly, with a trace of wariness behind them.

Maya felt as if she were on a witness stand, sworn to tell the truth. She didn't like being pinned down, but she couldn't lie to a child. "Dolls are pretend babies." She dodged the question agilely, sending a mental apology to Constance's grandmother. Sandra hadn't bought the crystal ball, after all. Apparently, she'd found a suitable doll elsewhere.

"You've got a real baby in your stomach." Constance pointed at the figure in the painting. "This is a real baby, like my mommy had in her stomach."

Oh dear. Deeper and deeper waters. She wished she'd taken more child psychology courses, but there'd never been enough time, or money. She leaned over and taped the picture to the refrigerator. "I'm sorry you lost your mommy and her baby."

"I didn't want the baby," Constance whispered. "I *hated* the baby."

She slid away, back to the kitchen table and Matty.

Shocked, Maya pretended normalcy by taping the picture in place. Scary little spikes of panic raced through her veins, piercing her heart. Axell needed to be here—*now*. This was his daughter. He knew the score better than she.

Without thinking, she grabbed the kitchen phone and hit the starred code number for the restaurant. She was only an outsider in this precarious little family scene.

Grimly, Axell slammed into the house. He didn't know what was so all-fired important that he had to leave his bar to the mayor and his vipers, but it didn't appear the house was on fire.

He stalked through the mudroom into a brightly lit kitchen no different from the one he'd left a few hours ago. Maybe there was more paint splattered across the newspapers and floor, and his refrigerator looked like a cockeyed pop art gallery, but he didn't see any dead or dying. He watched his daughter decorate Matty's forehead with a sunburst, then turned his glare on the teacher sitting on a stool by the counter, stroking her cat.

"What?" he roared as she met his gaze with a worried frown. She'd scared him half to death over nothing.

"Daddy!" Constance raced to throw her arms around his legs.

Amazed by her reaction, Axell didn't even blink at the smear of yellow paint across his new Perry Ellis trousers. He crouched to stroke her hair and gratefully accepted the paper towel the teacher handed him.

"Can you stay? Me and Matty been painting."

Constance—when she bothered speaking—usually spoke grammatically. Axell threw the teacher another glare.

"Show your daddy your paintings, honey," Maya intervened calmly from her seat.

Axell wondered if she was feeling all right. She usually bounced around as much as the children. That made him wonder if she'd been seeing a doctor, which returned his terror of her having the kid on the kitchen floor. He had to get her out of here—soon. He didn't want anything to do with babies.

Constance seemed oddly reluctant to display her art. Holding her hand, Axell crossed to the refrigerator. Matty's swirls of red with polka-dot nose holes and pointed ears were easily discerned from Constance's carefully detailed scenes. He wasn't entirely certain he understood the subject matter, however.

Crouching beside her, he examined a painting of what appeared to be a room full of furniture. The cat leapt from Maya's lap to curl around his ankles, meowing. He scratched its head with one hand while holding out the picture with the other. "Want to tell me about this one?"

Pink little lips closed firmly, and her fine hair flew around her face as she shook her head.

"That's the nursery," Maya explained from her seat.

The nursery. Axell's heart plummeted to his stomach. He couldn't look at his daughter. His fingers clenched around the wrinkled painting. The nursery, of course. There was the crib his daughter had outgrown, the cradle he'd built himself, and the playpen full of toys they had shopped for every weekend.

Agony shot like fire through his chest. His stomach cramped, nearly bending him in half. Maybe a heart attack would prevent his ever thinking about that time again. Apparently aware of his crippling pain, the cat fled behind the refrigerator.

Carefully, Axell unfolded from the floor, still gripping the painting. "That's a very pretty picture, Constance," he said with what he thought was admirable calm. "I need to talk with your teacher for a moment. Miss Alyssum?" He lifted his eyebrows in expectation and nodded toward the family room.

"You need to talk with your daughter." Refusing his commanding gesture, she remained seated.

He'd fire an employee who ignored his orders. He couldn't fire a guest. Gritting his teeth in frustration, Axell fought the dangerous firecrackers popping behind his eyes. Constance had already returned to the table, but he wasn't ignorant enough to believe she didn't listen to their every word. For two years he'd been pretending she'd forgotten. He couldn't pretend anymore.

Holding the picture, he stormed into the family room. If Maya wanted him to talk to Constance, she'd damned well have to talk to him first. He didn't have any idea how to handle this.

Staring at the childish picture, Axell absently swatted at a dirty tennis shoe in his path. Constance had drawn his son's nursery. The child had been delivered dead after the accident— the accident that had killed Angela instantly. The acid in his stomach spilled through his gut like wildfire, and he kicked another loose shoe in the direction of the first.

The schoolteacher appeared before him without his knowing she'd entered the room. She wore the swinging floral dress he'd bought for her, along with the heavy sweater. The dress was more like summer wear, and the evening had turned cool. He should turn up the furnace. He never noticed the cold, but she was so thin-skinned, she was probably shivering.

Dammit, there he went again. She was a grown woman. She could damned well take care of herself. Avidly seeking lost shoes now, Axell used his toe to pry a slipper from beneath the leather sofa. It took two slams to land it in the pile with the first two.

"Your daughter seems fascinated by nurseries. She made a few revealing comments I can't fully understand. I thought you might prefer to deal with them rather than me."

"What comments?" Axell asked roughly, glaring at the

picture before dropping it on the table as he uncovered a sandal lurking in a corner.

She hesitated, as if afraid to alight anywhere. He pointed at the couch as he swatted the sandal out of its hiding place. "Sit *down*."

She sat. She clasped her hands in her lap. She twiddled her thumbs. She looked everywhere but at him as he stalked the enormous room in search of shoes.

At his growl of exasperation, she finally sighed. "I don't want to get involved in your family problems," she stated baldly.

"Tell me about it," he agreed with venom. He didn't mean to make her flinch, he just couldn't help himself right now. He kicked the sandal until it landed upside down on a sneaker. "Go ahead," he finished a little less irascibly. "We might as well know each other's life stories at this rate."

She threw him a rueful glance. "I don't think so. Comic farce isn't my strong point." She pointed at the discarded picture. "Constance tells me that's a real baby in the crib. That her mommy was going to have a real baby."

Feeling as if a gun had exploded in his face, Axell swayed where he stood. Pain rippled through him, and in a desperate effort to fight it, he dropped to his knees and began systematically searching for the rest of Constance's shoe collection. "I didn't think she remembered," he muttered from the floor. "I had a decorator take the nursery apart and refurnish it right after Angela died. It just seemed simpler."

"No wonder she doesn't talk to you."

He bonked his head on the entertainment center. Rubbing the sore spot, he glared at her as if she were to blame, but he saw no accusation in her eyes. He threw a dusty patent leather shoe into the pile.

"She's only imitating you," she continued remorselessly. "If an adult like you can't tell her how you feel, how can you expect a child to say how she feels?"

Axell cringed and continued prowling the room. "She was so *little*," he protested. "How could I explain? Her mother was dead. That was difficult enough. Damn." He pounced on another sandal. "It was *all* so difficult. Angela and I hadn't been getting along. We'd hoped the baby would cure our differences"—the sandal hit the pile with the first throw—"but it only made things worse. We had a furious fight that morning. I stormed off to my office. She must have decided to follow."

The words poured out, words he'd never told anyone, words that ripped his soul from his gut and tears from his eyes. Men didn't cry, dammit. He jerked a dollhouse away from the wall and located the missing leather shoe. Something wet streamed down his cheek, and standing, he kicked the shoe so hard, it flew past the stack.

In a dead voice, Axell finished the sorry tale. "We'd just had a thunderstorm. The roads were slick, leaves and limbs everywhere. I'd taken the big car because she liked the little convertible. She didn't even fasten her damned seat belt."

"It wasn't your fault," she said softly.

"Hell, I don't know." Wearily, Axell pinched his nose and wiped the tear before turning to face her. Why go over this now? It wouldn't change anything. But she stared at him with those damned open-as-the-sea eyes, and he struggled for words. "Angela died instantly from a blow to the head after she was thrown from the car," he said with a sigh. "The doctors couldn't save the baby. Angela was only five months along."

He. His son. They hadn't even given him a name. He'd just had "Infant Son" inscribed on the gravestone. He hadn't cried. He'd simply stood there at the funeral, holding his young daughter's hand, watching them bury the last of his dreams.

Fighting the tears he hadn't cried then, Axell slammed his foot into the pile of shoes, scattering them across the room again. "What the hell does any of this have to do with the urgent reason I had to come home?"

"Now that I know the story," Maya replied quietly, "I suspect it means that your daughter thinks she's responsible for her little brother's death."

"What?" Axell yelled, swinging to glare at her.

But he already knew. For two years, his beloved daughter had been living the same nightmare hell as he had.

❧ TEN ❦

All generalizations are false.

"What do I *say*?" Collapsing into a chair, Axell covered his eyes.

Maya thought she ought to preserve this moment in her memory. She didn't think it was often that this big, self-assured man crumbled, especially before an audience. If she was any good at this astrology thing, she'd say he had a Scorpio moon—which would make him passionate and profoundly emotional, but for some reason far beyond her ability to understand, he was obsessively disguising it.

She had the nonsensical urge to stroke his hair and pat his cheek and tell him everything would be all right. But Axell Holm wasn't a child.

Glancing at the scattered assortment of shoes, she spoke cautiously. "You tell her you love her, then go from there." When he didn't immediately leap up and kick anything else, she offered, "It's amazing how much children can understand, the untold insecurities we could relieve if adults didn't insist on hiding things. You can't hide things from a child. They always know when something is wrong, and they almost always blame it on themselves."

Lifting his hand from his eyes, he threw her a shrewd glance. "Spoken from experience, I take it?"

"The voice of experience," she agreed grimly.

She saw the sudden look of curiosity in his eyes, that archeology-professor-studying-a-new-hieroglyphic look, "Our parents were divorced, and Cleo and I grew up in foster homes, I'll explain some other time. Go to her now."

He grimaced and threaded his hand through his hair. "I trust you realize I left the mayor and my mother-in-law at the bar, plotting how to take Constance and your school away. Maybe while you're at it, you could wave your wand in that direction."

With that gloomy warning, Axell rose from the sofa and gaining momentum, strode out the door.

Maya had no magic wands. Instead, she lingered where she was, soaking in the ambience of the messy family room—the only room in the house that looked lived in. It looked as if every pair of shoes Constance owned had been under the furniture, and she owned a lot.

This was the kind of room she'd dreamed of as a child—a room where she and Cleo could kick off their shoes and safely sprawl on the floor and watch TV and color pictures and read books to their heart's content. She'd probably painted in a happy mother and father at the time, but she knew better than that now. The happy mother and father was an illusion even in the dreamland of wealth.

The image of a golden Norse god kicking shoes as he writhed in agony wouldn't easily be erased.

She rubbed the tumbling infant in her abdomen. Her limited insurance didn't cover sonograms, so she had no clue whether she carried a boy or girl, and it didn't matter. Maybe she couldn't provide her child or Matty with an expensive room like this one—heck, right now she couldn't give them a roof over their heads—but she could give them love. She had a lifetime of unexpressed love to offer. And she knew a whole lot more about showing it than Axell Holm did.

Matty wandered in and plopped in front of the TV, examining the knobs for the one that would make it work. With a smile, Maya picked up the remote control and switched on the VCR that still contained the dragon tape. Matty's eyes grew wide with wonder, and he threw her one of those magical looks she cherished.

"See, even the TV knows what you like."

He beamed then and relaxed in happy fascination with the movie. He was too easily satisfied to suffer from attention deficit, she'd already decided. Maybe mild dyslexia. She should ask Social Services about testing.

Maya wondered how well Axell was doing with his child. And what plot the mayor schemed to destroy her dreams.

Talking into her cell phone, Selene paced the dusty pine floor of the empty shop with the restless grace of a caged panther. Maya admired her energy but conserved her own as she waited for Axell and the building inspector to return with word on Cleo's shop.

Selene clicked the phone closed and glanced around the empty shell of Axell's building with distaste. "Girl, you got your work cut out for you."

"I've got to do it." Maya wiggled on the high stool she'd found in the back. "Cleo will be home in a few months. What's the chance of anyone hiring her?"

"Zilch," Selene said crudely. "You'd better be praying hard. You got a plan for this place?"

That was a topic she could handle. Maya pointed out the twelve-foot-high barren walls. "I saw an artist at a local art show who had the most amazing paintings. They practically glowed from within. Do you think I could display large oils on that wall?"

"That's not a plan," Selene said with disgust. "That's a dream. Tell me how you're going to make money off those oils, and you've got a plan."

"Selling oils *is* a plan," Maya insisted. "That space would be wasted otherwise. I could take them on consignment so I don't have to shell out money for inventory. I'm not entirely stupid."

"No, just a little batty." Selene swung on her heeled sandals to glare at the walls. "You need to paint them white and add track lighting."

"Sure, and add a crystal chandelier and wine bar, too. I'm not *that* batty."

Selene's cell phone beeped as Axell strode through the front door.

Maya's fingernails dug into her palms, and she wrapped her feet in the stool rungs as she anxiously watched Axell's face for some clue of the inspector's decision. Not a smile, not a wink, not even a frown indicated the results as he walked with lion grace across the bare floor. He held her entire life in his hands, and he didn't say a blamed thing. The tension was killing her. Maybe killing *him* was an alternative. She wanted her teapot back, dammit.

Calmly, Axell handed Maya a wad of official-looking papers. She stared at them, her hands shaking.

"You've got permission to move your things."

Stunned, she just sat there staring at the papers that saved her life, Cleo's life, Matty's future. . . . Tears welled in her eyes and joy spilled from her heart. Unable to jump up and down and squeal with glee, she did the next best thing.

She leaned forward, propped her hands on Axell's shoulders, and kissed him smack on his startled mouth.

Stunned, he stood like a store dummy with his hands at his side.

His mouth woke quickly enough, though, and their lips melted together with incredible ease. He tasted of coffee, and oddly enough, vanilla—all hot and sugary and yummy.

Her turn to be startled, Maya hastily pushed away, flushed, and wrapped her arms around herself instead of him. Axell eyed her warily, with the heat still smoldering in his eyes. She hadn't intended anything sexual with her embrace, but sparks of something electric were suddenly shooting all around them. Maybe the shop had faulty wiring.

The man definitely had a Scorpio moon. *Boy, can you pick 'em, Maya.*

"I take it you appreciate the results," Axell said wryly, retreating a cautious pace.

Entranced by the wild flare in his eyes, Maya couldn't look away. The staid businessman in his pressed suit and conservative tie had real live wires pumping somewhere beneath that deadly attire. The lion king lived. He could roar.

A cough from behind them warned Selene's call had ended. Nervously, Maya glanced at the documents in her hands. At the same time, Axell reached for them. An impromptu tug-of-war ensued until Maya gathered her wits and released them.

"I've called a local mover who's willing to pack and transport everything," he declared. "The building may be safe, but I don't think you should be doing that kind of work. And I've got a cleaning crew coming in to wax the floors and dust your inventory when it arrives. You'll need to be here to tell them where everything goes."

Axell's curt, businesslike tones restored the moment to normal, and Maya breathed a sigh of relief. One of these days she hoped to curb her impetuous behavior. She was about to become a mother; she had to grow up.

She wished she had the papers back just so she had something to do with her hands. "I can't afford all that" was all she managed to whisper.

"We're partners, remember? You're the labor, I'm the capital." Axell neatly folded the stack of documents and inserted them in an inside coat pocket.

"Hold up one minute," Selene intruded, extending her hand. "Partners? You've had an agreement drawn up? Does it specify salary? Profit sharing? Accountability? I've got a vested interest in this woman, too. I'll not have her tied to this place for the rest of her life."

Maya bit back a grin as Axell stared at her friend as if Selene had turned two shades of pink and purple right before his eyes.

"I'll have my lawyer draw something up," he responded cautiously.

"I'll have *my* lawyer go over it," Selene countered.

"I'll just mosey on over and get my clothes," Maya murmured, still grinning as Axell and Selene glared at each other like two gladiators in a ring. She slipped from the stool and edged toward the door.

"You'll damned well not go inside that building!" Axell

shouted, apparently recovering his senses as she reached for the knob.

"If it's safe for the movers, it's safe for me," she called sweetly, marching out without looking back.

Furious at his inability to control the capricious twit, Axell stalked after her.

"She's a Pisces," Selene called after him. "You might as well try to catch a fish with your bare hands!"

Axell shot her a glare of disbelief and strode out. Pisces, his foot and eye. Someone just needed to put a rein and harness on her. And a muzzle.

He found Maya ecstatically polishing her silly teapot and cups and carefully packing them in paper into a box that looked as if it had been carried through Donner Pass on mule back. Three times.

"The movers will bring packing boxes," he reminded her.

Rain clouds had moved in earlier that day, so no sunlight danced through the prisms over her head. Still, her cascade of auburn curls glowed with a light of their own as she shook her head.

"No one moves these but me," she announced firmly.

Since she seldom announced anything, much less acted on it with such determination, Axell resisted arguing. Obviously, he didn't understand the attachment, but he recognized it for what it was. "All right, let me get you a stronger box. Why don't you come over to the restaurant with me and have some tea while I find one?"

She glanced at him mischievously. "You're afraid I'll do something silly if you let me out of your sight. I've been surviving on my own for a lot longer than you realize, you know."

"Yeah, and a hell of a job you've done, too," he said dryly, extending his hand to help her rise from the floor. "Humor an old man and come with me."

Accepting his hand, she glanced at him curiously. "Old man? Have I aged you that quickly?"

Her perceptive look nearly floored him, but Axell tugged

her toward the door without acknowledging it. Her kiss earlier had awakened his awareness of their age difference. She was still young and full of enthusiasm. He was jaded and beyond feeling much of anything, except testosterone surges during mind-bending kisses. Like an alcoholic craving a drink, he wanted another.

"Kids'll do that to you," he replied evasively. She'd have him darting in and out of arguments like a minnow before long.

"Constance seems happier after your talk with her. I notice she even told you what shoes she wanted with her dress this morning."

Axell grimaced. "Yeah, the ones you painted dragons on. Now if she'd just learn to dress herself, we may have accomplished something."

Suspiciously, he watched Maya bite her lower lip as they progressed slowly through the sprinkling mist, toward the restaurant. He recognized that look.

"What?" he demanded. "What are you not telling me now?"

An impish dimple appeared and disappeared at the corner of her mouth as she slanted him a sidelong look. A man could imagine all sorts of things in a look like that. It was a damned good thing she was pregnant, so he knew where he stood.

"Well-l-l," she drew out the word thoughtfully. "You'll not like it, if I tell you."

"I already figured that," he said resignedly. "I've noticed I seldom like anything you tell me." He bit back a groan as he watched his mother-in-law emerge from the restaurant with all her battle armor in place. "You'd better hurry up and say it because this may be the last time you see me alive."

Startled, Maya followed his glance and giggled. Giggled. Axell could scarcely believe his ears. No one giggled at Sandra in full battle mode. Southern ladies might be all sweet and creamy on the outside, but a southern man knew the sugar concealed one hell of a tough pecan beneath.

"The hair looks like a helmet, don't you think? Does she carry a sword?"

"What do you think that ring is on her finger? She can cut a man's throat with that thing."

Maya's gurgle of laughter almost had him grinning. He'd never grinned in Sandra's company before.

"The designer suit is full battle regalia, right?" she whispered as Sandra apparently saw them and waited impatiently, tapping her elegantly shod toe.

"The pearls are her magic shield. They're supposed to blind the enemy with her wealth and protect her from all who couldn't possibly afford them."

"Ooo, you're good." Maya shot him an admiring glance. "I might need you in storytelling class."

Since they were within earshot of Sandra, Axell didn't respond to that remark. He hadn't failed to notice Maya had avoided his earlier question about Constance's dressing habits. He would have to learn to keep the conversation focused around this slippery little fish. Fish! He swung his attention to Constance's grandmother.

"Good morning, Sandra. Have you met Miss Alyssum, Constance's teacher? Maya, Constance's grandmother, Sandra Matthews." He no longer had to introduce her as mother-in-law, Axell realized with an odd feeling of relief. Sandra was nothing to him anymore.

Sandra glared venomously at Maya. "I believe we have something to discuss in *private*, Axell."

"I can't imagine what, Sandra." Skillfully appropriating Maya's elbow with one hand and opening the restaurant door with the other, he nodded for Sandra to precede them. He'd be damned if he let the old biddy walk all over a tenderfoot like Maya. The schoolteacher didn't have the social daggers to protect herself.

"I'm talking to the judge this afternoon," Sandra ground out, apparently through her neatly capped teeth.

"Tell him hello for me," Axell replied insouciantly, although his insides were clenched as tightly as Sandra's teeth as he led the way to a table. Stoicism had its price.

"I've tried to be polite about this, Axell," she said, refusing his gesture toward a booth. "But you've gone out of your way to flaunt your improprieties in public. I won't have an impressionable child like Constance living under the same roof as this . . . this . . ." Words apparently failed her.

Words had never failed Maya, Axell realized with a groan as she flashed one of her brilliant go-to-hell-happily smiles. Curiosity prevented his stopping her.

"Nine-months-pregnant schoolteacher?" she supplied cheerfully. "And you will note, won't you, that I arrived here seven months ago? So Axell has nothing whatsoever to do with my . . . 'interesting condition.' And if you think there's anything else between us but his old-fashioned solicitude and generosity, then you have bacon where your brains should be. Now, if you'll excuse me, I'm after a box from the kitchen."

She swam away, out of the conflagration she'd fueled. Axell could only admire her dexterity as she swept from the room. He'd hate to see how swift she was without the burden of pregnancy holding her back. Like the Cheshire cat, she'd probably leave her smile still spinning in the air behind her.

Popping the top from a water bottle, he leaned against the bar. "Give Judge Tony my regards, will you? And tell him if he wants to make a political case out of this, I'll take it all the way to the Supreme Court. That should thrill him. Constance is mine."

Sandra narrowed her eyes. "Are you certain Constance is yours?" she asked coldly. "My daughter wasn't exactly a one-man woman when you married." She stalked out, spine straight, high heels clicking.

Axell heaved his water bottle across the bar at a row of whiskey tumblers. The sound of shattering glass didn't equal the devastation inside his soul.

October 1945
I've gone back there every night this week. I can't stay away. She's all I can think about. I can scarcely concentrate on the books for seeing her in my head, her red hair sprawled across the pillow, her white skin pale

*in the moonlight. I'm not a poetic man, but she makes me
want to sing songs.*

*I've got to stop going there. I'd be ruined if Dolly's
father found out.*

❧ ELEVEN ❧

I need someone really bad . . .
are you really bad?

Returning from the kitchen with an assortment of boxes, including one filled with freshly baked cinnamon rolls, Maya discovered Axell sitting at his polished bar, sipping an icy drink, a black cloud almost visibly hovering over his golden head. Her insides did a tumbling number as she remembered one of too many incidents in her childhood involving bar stools and alcohol. Then seeing the half-empty bottle of mineral water sitting on the bar, she breathed easier and approached with firmer tread.

"Drowning our sorrows so early in the day?" she teased daringly, taking the stool beside him and opening the box of rolls. After seeing Axell's human side last night, she couldn't view him as an invulnerable paragon any longer. "Sugar is much tastier than water." She helped herself to a steaming soft roll, and with a sigh of ecstasy, sank her teeth into it as she pushed the box in his direction.

Axell took a bun and tore into it like a vicious dog handed a bone. Maya considered that a sacrilege. She adored cinnamon rolls, even the kind from a can—which were the only ones she'd known growing up. One savored cinnamon rolls, not swallowed them whole.

Picking out a plump juicy raisin, she contemplated leaving this obviously angry man to his tantrum and going on about her business. Unfortunately, right now, it looked like he *was* her business. Or Cleo's, anyway.

"Ticked you off, did she?" she asked conversationally, licking a particularly sticky cinnamon-coated finger.

A V wrinkled the bridge of Axell's nose as he glanced over and caught her childish act.

Beaming in response to his frown, Maya popped another raisin into her mouth. "Tell me not to play with my food if it makes you feel better."

Axell managed a smile of sorts. At least his lips turned up briefly at the corners. His eyes, however, remained stony cold. His square jaw had a stuck-out set to it that would have driven Maya into spasms if she thought it aimed at her. For a change, though, she figured she was innocent.

"Carlos makes those rolls for the staff. I don't ever get one unless I go to the kitchen and demand one." He polished off the remainder of the sticky bun, and with a defiant gleam, licked his fingers.

Maya grinned. "You'll notice most of your staff is female," she replied.

Axell squinted at her, followed the track of her thoughts, and finally saw its destination. He snorted in appreciation. "The old billy goat."

Maya snickered. "Shame on you. He's a sweet old man. Shall I go back to packing my boxes or would you care to explain your serious snit?"

"I don't have snits," he snapped, throwing back the water as if it were whiskey.

"Right, and I don't have constipation." She slid off the stool, and leaving the rest of the rolls to sweeten his temper, strolled toward the door with her boxes.

"Where the hell do you think you're going?" he called after her. "Don't you ever sit in one place for three minutes?"

Maya directed a wry look over her shoulder. "Not where I'm not wanted. I'm perfectly aware I'm a hideous intrusion in your life, so I'm doing my best to make myself scarce."

She walked out before Axell could summon a reply. Refusing to consider Sandra's insinuations of Constance's parentage, he distracted himself by staring at the door from which Maya had shot her parting volley. A hideous intrusion?

Was that how the gypsy saw herself? He realized that's probably how she'd felt most of her life. He remembered her mentioning she and Cleo had spent time in foster homes. What must that have felt like to an uninhibited child like Maya, being shoved into a stranger's house, into an established way of life, not knowing the rules or limits or how long she'd be welcome?

And that's just exactly what he'd done to her and Matty—shoved them into a strange situation, and left them to flounder for themselves. She was good at it, he had to admit. He hated having his orderly life turned upside down, hated any break in his routine, but she had slid between all the cracks in his walls and found a niche of her own.

Amazed, Axell poured the rest of the water into his cup, ignoring the shattered glass behind the bar as determinedly as he ignored Sandra's words. Maya and Matty hadn't once set foot in his wing of the house. Actually, if he thought about it, they hadn't set foot anywhere but their bedroom, the kitchen, and the family room, places he didn't particularly consider his turf. They stayed out of sight and sound when he was home. He didn't even know when they ate breakfast or how they got to school. Matty took the bus, presumably.

Damn, but he'd been a blind bastard. Here he'd been thinking of himself as a humanitarian, when all he offered was another substitute foster home. He hadn't thought of either of them as walking, talking human beings with minds and needs of their own.

All right, so he was a piece of shit. Considering he was actually contemplating safeguarding his license by scratching the mayor's back and agreeing to close her school, that was nothing new. Slamming down his glass, Axell stood up. On second thought, he turned and grabbed the box of cinnamon rolls.

Watching Maya eat that roll was an experience he didn't mind repeating. Remembering his reaction to the kiss she'd bestowed upon him earlier, he figured his libido was in sorry need of feeding. He'd have to wait until the teacher moved out before satisfying his hunger.

* * *

"Bosco," Matty declared in satisfaction as he wrapped his arms around the ragged rabbit and literally squeezed the fluffy pink stuffing out of its many holes.

"Let me guess," Axell said dryly from atop a ladder where he was attempting to affix chimes over the door. "It's a chocolate rabbit."

Maya beamed in approval. "I would have opted for 'Nestlé,' myself, but Cleo is into ancient commercials. I think she gets them from the oldies station."

"N-E-S-T-L-É-S, Nestlé's makes the very best . . ." Matty sang almost absently as he rummaged through his box of toys.

"Chaw-w-klet," Constance finished for him in a deeper voice.

Maya erupted in giggles and Axell glowered down at her.

"Clowns! I'm working with clowns. And remind me never to meet your sister. The two of you in the same room is likely to be dangerous to my sanity." He stuck out his hand. "Give me another nail."

Maya sobered as she handed several up to him. "You do realize this is all her stuff, don't you? I'm just a place holder." As Cleo's release date grew closer, her anxiety level climbed. At least Cleo's last curt note had thanked her for sending Matty's artwork.

Axell spoke around the nail he held in his mouth. "Yeah. So call me stupid."

"Stupid," Matty mimicked from below. "S-T-U-P-I-E-D."

"Stew-w-pid," Constance intoned.

Maya broke up all over again.

Grinning, Axell hammered the chimes in place. "Who taught that kid to spell?"

"He's five years old!" Maya protested. "He barely even knows his letters yet."

"He can almost read my Dr. Seuss books," Constance said matter-of-factly, opening another box the movers had left stacked in the middle of the newly waxed shop floor. "Look, the crystal ball!"

"Don't play with that stuff, Constance," Axell warned as he

climbed back down the ladder. "Maya has to tell the cleaning crew where to put it all."

"Actually, I think Matty is memorizing the words," Maya started to say, but the door swung open as soon as Axell moved the ladder from in front of it.

"Headley! What the hell are you doing here?" Axell propped the ladder against the wall and dusted his hands on a rag.

"Hell," Matty repeated idly, removing one of his few tattered books from the box. "Hell, bell, well . . ." He stopped and pondered a new rhyme.

Maya covered her mouth with her hand to hide her laughter since Axell didn't look particularly happy with Headley's presence. She didn't want to tick him off any more. It was generous of him to take time off from his restaurant to spend the evening helping her move in. She eyed the older man warily, knowing who he was by sight. Everyone knew Headley.

The elderly reporter eyed the children and the confusion of boxes as if they might explode in his face at any minute. He shook out his soaked umbrella—the rain had continued all night and through the day—and leaned against it as he observed the contents of the few unpacked boxes. "Same weird paraphernalia, hmm? Not much call for that stuff around here, is there?"

"That's what you tracked me down to tell me?" Axell removed the crystal ball from his daughter's hands, swiped it with his dust cloth, and set it inside the glass counter Maya had cleaned earlier. "There's actually some pretty good stuff in here. It just needs the proper display."

"A clean one," Maya said dryly, not rising from her seat on the packing crate as she set another pot of water on the hot plate. "Would you care for tea? I can't offer a seat. . . ." She gestured at the stacks of boxes burying the table and chairs.

"I'll clear those away for you. The packing crate is making me nervous." Axell crossed the room and shifted a box from one of the ice cream parlor chairs, ignoring the man who had obviously come to see him.

Headley shifted another box and gallantly extended his

hand to help Maya from her awkward seat. "Miss Alyssum? Jason Headley. Your name is familiar. Are you from around here?"

Maya shrugged. "So they say, but I don't remember the days of infancy."

Headley grinned. "Anyway, I've heard a lot about you."

"From Katherine, I suppose," Axell interjected. "She exaggerates."

"*She's* not the one who calls me twenty-months pregnant," Maya pointed out, accepting the reporter's hand and exchanging her seat on the crate for the chair.

"Well, you are, even if you refuse to act like it." Axell glared from her to Headley, than stalked toward the door. "All right, Headley, let's take it to the bar. I'm just getting in the way of the lunatics over here anyway."

Headley hesitated, glancing at the children digging through still another box. Maya caught the hesitation immediately.

"Constance, why don't you help Matty take his things upstairs? Now that we have furniture again, we'll be staying here tonight."

Matty screamed with delight and raced for the stairs. Looking uncertain, Constance glanced back and forth between the adults, then obediently followed with her skinny arms full of toys.

"Does that help, Mr. Headley?" Maya asked as the children disappeared up the stairs.

The reporter lowered his bulk into the other chair and eyed her jasmine-scented tea skeptically. "I'm not certain anything helps, but I thought this might be something you needed to hear, too." He glanced at Axell, who stood with arms crossed, lean hip propped against the glass counter, waiting. Receiving no prompt to continue, Headley shrugged. "The police arrested your busboys for possession and sale, Axell. Rumors are flying that they're just the flunkies and you're the bigger operation. Some people are jealous of the success you've made of that place."

Even through the gloomy twilight, Maya could see Axell's knuckles whiten. She recognized the lines tightening beside his mouth. He had an enormous capacity for restraining his temper, or diverting it in strange ways. She didn't think she wanted to be around when the dam broke this time. To drain off a little of the pressure, she spoke before Axell could. "And why did you think I needed to hear this, Mr. Headley?"

"Just Headley, dear. That's all anyone calls me." He shrugged his gray-suited shoulders again. "The connection is nebulous, but it doesn't take much in a small town. Your sister was busted for drugs, Axell is moving her inventory into his building, and you're living out at his place. Your sister's shop attracted a lot of teenagers. One thing leads to another and tongues are flapping like sheets in the wind."

Shocked, Maya couldn't summon a reply.

"Ralph is after my liquor license," Axell explained wearily. "I take that back, he's killing two birds with one stone with that rumor. Label us both as druggies and he eliminates any chances of my running for his job and kills your business along with mine. He figures you'll pack up and move out, and then I'll leave the Pfeiffer property uncontested. He must have found out that I persuaded one of the other council members to vote against the access road."

"Is that what this is all about?" Headley asked with interest. "I'd wondered."

"He can't do that, can he?" Maya asked with trepidation. She'd lost homes before. Lost parents, dogs, cats, and every valuable possession she'd owned except for the teacups. But she'd never been the cause of someone else losing anything. She watched Axell with growing horror. Surely this was all just a rumor gone out of hand.

"The mayor can't do anything personally, but he can pull strings. I'll have to investigate the financing behind that shopping center. I thought Ralph had kept his hands clean, but he's dumping too much into this to be doing it just for campaign contributions." Axell shrugged and didn't move from his position against the counter. "Thanks for the warning, Headley, but you shouldn't have worried Miss Alyssum. I'll take care of this."

"*You'll* take care of this? Someone is insulting my integrity, threatening my sister's shop and my school, and *you'll* take care of this? Do you have any idea what kind of catastrophe this could be for me? They could take Matty away, take my school away, destroy Cleo's livelihood. . . ." Maya shoved up from her chair. "I'll damned well snatch the mayor bald before that happens."

Axell grabbed her arm as she stalked by. "It's my liquor license and my fight, and you don't have the experience to deal with it. Now go on upstairs with the kids and get some rest. Ralph and I have been battling it out since he switched to a Charlotte football team in high school."

Had she been in any condition to swing a punch, she would have. Instead, Maya smiled sweetly and shrugged off his hold. "Of course, honey bear. You do that. You just look out for little ol' me. You're so good at it." She patted Axell's wide chest, decided immediately touching him was a mistake if the tension shooting up her fingertips was any indication, then pinched his cheek in defiance. "I'll just sashay upstairs and let you big ol' men take care of everything."

Axell's eyes narrowed into stony slits, his jaw muscle twitched, and he crossed his arms again, apparently restraining himself from shaking her. "When I need a woman to fight my battles, I'll let you know."

"Why, sure thing, sugar dumplin'. Isn't that what Ah just said?" She mimicked her mother's drawl. "I'll just go upstairs and call Selene and we'll have us a real nice gossip. You call me if you need anything, y'heah?"

Flowing skirts twirling around her, Maya drifted up the stairs and out of sight.

Headley grunted and shoved up from the awkward parlor chair. "If she's talking about Selene Blackburn, you got your hands full, son. That little witch could scalp an army and leave them grinning. You won't have to worry about poor Ralph, except where to send the flowers for his funeral."

"Selene? She's a pest, but from what I hear, she didn't even graduate high school." Uncomfortably catching himself watching the empty stairs, Axell adjusted his focus. Maya could damned well do whatever she wanted to do. She wasn't any of his concern. He just had to decide the best way of handling this. "Selene will call her daddy and have Ralph's accounts audited or something."

Headley snorted and shook his shaggy head. "You're living in a dreamworld, boy. You need to get out and around women more often." He glanced at the stairway. "And I reckon that one bears watching as well. She might look like an addlepate, but keep in mind: she arrived broke and homeless seven months ago and already she has a school and a shop and a hook in you and one of the richest families around. She's not dumb. She's got an agenda. You might look further into *her* background."

No, Maya wasn't dumb, but agendas weren't precisely her method of operation. Axell glared at Headley, then glared at the far wall after Headley strolled out.

He had to remember why he was doing any of this: Constance.

And she might not even be his own kid.

A wave of emptiness engulfed him, and Axell wearily unfolded from the counter to head back to the restaurant. He'd pick up Constance later, after he got off work. He just couldn't face her again right now. He kept searching for signs of himself in her, and even *he* knew kids were sensitive to things like that.

❧ TWELVE ❧

**Ain't nothin' in the middle of the road
but yellow stripes and dead armadillos.**

The tension headache pounding in the back of his skull matched the churning in his gut as Axell watched Ralph Arnold parade up and down the floor, oozing sincerity. The mayor's office in this tiny town was scarcely a standard of high living, but the polished desk and the flag hanging behind it offered a semblance of southern patriotism. The mayor, with his professionally styled chestnut hair and gym-maintained physique, practiced the role of up-and-coming politician with more arrogance than the office deserved. "Alyssum. That's the name of the woman who owns that shop, isn't it? I'd heard her family was from here, but that name doesn't ring a bell."

"Only ding-a-lings hear bells, Ralph," Axell growled. In a town like this, family name was everything, but he wasn't buying into that tradition. "It doesn't matter who their connections are. The point is, these rumors are bordering on slander, and I want an end to them."

The mayor shrugged. "Where there's smoke, there's usually fire. Charlotte police have been cracking down hard on dealers, but drug use is escalating. Face it, Holm, the dealers are moving out here where they figure we don't have enough police to catch them. And they're probably right."

"They're not using my premises," Axell said irritably. "Let the police do their drug busts elsewhere."

"It's not my venue, Axell, you know that. I have nothing to do with any of it."

Grimly, Axell slapped his hands on the huge desk and

leaned forward. "Don't give me that bull, Ralph. It's got your signature all over it. Those busboys have only been with me a week. In another week, they'd have been gone. Kitchen help comes and goes faster than flies. It was only a matter of time before some of them got busted for something. You just made sure it was on *my* time and that the incident got publicized."

Ralph shrugged his padded shoulders again and stared out the window blinds to the rain-puddled parking lot. "I don't tell the police department what to do."

"You damned well should. That's your job." Axell removed his hands from the desk and swung around, heading for the door. "And if you don't back off, I'm taking that job away from you. That's a promise." He slammed the door after him.

He didn't usually slam doors. Ralph's secretary looked up in surprise, but Axell merely nodded and strode out without greeting. He figured he'd bite off the head of anyone who so much as smiled at him. If he were the kind who snarled, he'd snarl. Instead, he left his car at the curb and dodged raindrops to the rear of the restaurant, releasing what little steam he could in the short walk.

The damage was already done. There wasn't much the mayor could do now unless Ralph called the governor and told him to have the alcohol board back off on the liquor license inquiry. Axell couldn't see that happening. If Axell called a news conference and announced he was filing for the mayor's job, that would only drive Ralph to speed up the license inquiry. The only way out of this trap would be to pacify Ralph by persuading Maya to close her damned school, and that would lower him to the mayor's level of slime.

By the time he reached his office, Axell's brain was steaming full speed ahead. He needed to convince Ralph he had the power to make Maya and Selene change their minds about the Pfieffer property. Maybe he could find them another property. Ralph really didn't care about the bar's liquor license. He wasn't that petty minded. For some reason, he was just determined to have that shopping center road and parking lot and was using the license inquiry as leverage. If he thought Axell could give him what he wanted . . .

"It's about time you got here. The ABC people are crawling all over the kitchen."

Katherine was pacing up and down his office, looking more spectacular than usual with her blond hair cut in some bouncy new way so it swung and danced every time she moved. And she moved a lot. Axell could appreciate the performance, even if he wasn't interested in the play itself.

"You want me to set out mousetraps for them?" he asked, dropping into his chair to jot notes. Last night's dream of redhaired leprechauns had gotten under his skin. He'd actually been hoping he'd come in here and find Maya waiting for him instead of Katherine. She'd promised to stop over and consult him about the shop's grand reopening. The house had echoed emptier than ever last night without her and Matty in it.

"Very funny." Katherine stalked up and down one more time for good effect. Her miniskirt was shorter than usual today, and her legs flashed enticingly above her high-soled shoes.

Axell thought irrelevantly of Maya's dragon-decorated sneakers and bit back a grin wondering if Katherine would dare have her shoes tattooed. That led him to wonder if Maya had ever had anything else but her shoes tattooed, and from there, his mind degenerated into wondering what she looked like naked. He blinked in horror at the wayward path of his thoughts.

Katherine sat on the corner of his desk and her skirt slid to the top of her thigh. She wore shimmering pantyhose that caught the morning light, but Axell's mind traveled rebelliously to a rainbow-prismed purple streak. Maybe he was having some kind of mental breakdown. He should take a vacation.

He slapped his pencil on the desk, leaned back in his chair, and ignoring his assistant's flashing leg, glared up at her. "Did you want something, Katherine?"

He thought she'd explode. Her eyes narrowed dangerously, her lips thinned to half their usual size, and her cheeks pinkened beyond their cosmetically applied blush. "I wanted to *help*, but obviously, your mind is on more important things." She slid off the desk and stormed toward the door before turning for her parting shot. "Judge Tony called me yesterday, making inquiries about how often Constance eats in the kitchen and who takes care of her while you work. I'm thinking of taking up Ralph's offer of a job."

Axell winced as she slammed out. This was not going to be a good day.

Picking up his pencil, he dialed his lawyer.

Sitting at the parlor table, her wrought-iron chair padded with a cushion from the upstairs sofa, Maya polished Cleo's myriad gnomes and dragons while the cleaning crew worked on unpacking and dusting the rest of the inventory. Cleo had always loved playing with the action figures from fast food chains, she remembered. The child in her must have thought this ugly pewter would sell well. Cleo's inventory tended to reflect the toys she'd never had rather than any spiritual interest in New Age mysticism.

She ought to be at school, drawing up lesson plans for summer sessions and their first full-time program. They had several teachers already lined up, and she prayed Cleo would be home in time to take over the store by then. The after-school program worked out nicely for now, in these last months of her pregnancy, but she would be eager to return to the challenge of full-time teaching once the baby was born.

The rain poured down outside. After living these past few years in southern California, she wasn't used to rain. The novelty had worn off in this last day or two of wading through rivers of mud. She wondered if Noah had finished his ark yet.

Or if Axell had recovered from his snit. She'd thought he'd been coming around yesterday until Headley had arrived. He'd even managed a smile or two. She didn't know why it mattered if she dragged a smile or two out of a stuffed turkey like Axell Holm. But he looked at Constance with such pain and suffering and obvious love that her heart went out to him anyway.

She had no business offering her heart to anyone but Matty and the infant in her womb. Arching her aching back, Maya wondered if she'd been working too hard, as Axell had declared. The baby wasn't moving much today. It was due in two weeks, and she still didn't have a crib.

She needed the CD player she'd left for the movers to connect. A good rousing song would lift her spirits. Or a chant, to soothe her nerves. Maybe she should brave the weather and go see Axell. Planning the grand opening had to be more entertaining than polishing gnomes.

But Axell had barely spoken to her last night when he'd arrived to pick up a sleepy Constance. And she didn't have an umbrella or the energy to walk even the few yards over to the restaurant in this downpour. She was restless and jumpy and not much in the mood to deal with her "silent" partner.

Selene had promised to get to the bottom of the drug-possession scam and to stave off the gossip as much as possible, since it affected the school as well as Axell. She just couldn't promise to do more than that. Her influence was more social than political, although she'd promised to give some thought in that arena, too. Maybe Selene could finance Axell's campaign for mayor. . . .

The door chimes rang, and Maya looked up eagerly at this new distraction. A stranger in a dripping raincoat closed his umbrella and looked around. Nobody good ever wore raincoats. Maybe he'd come to repossess Cleo's counter. She didn't think there was much else left of any value.

Wincing at the ache in her back as she stood up, Maya greeted the new arrival. "May I help you?"

The man removed his hat to reveal a balding head and a reasonably jovial expression. "Miss Alyssum? I'm Fred Carpenter, the building inspector."

Maya hid a bolt of anxiety behind a vague smile. "A carpenter to inspect buildings! How lovely. What do you inspect them for? To see if they're buildings?"

He looked a little startled. "For safety, mostly. After the collapse of the facade down the street, the mayor wants to prevent what could be a tragedy next time."

"You're quite right, of course," she agreed with a modicum of relief. Inspections were a good thing. She was turning paranoid. "I was so upset at almost losing everything I owned, I didn't even think of what could have happened. By all means, inspect away. Would you like some tea?"

"Oh, you were the tenant in the old Shafer building? Shame, that." He shook his head at her offer of tea and wandered to inspect the freshly painted plaster walls. "Most of these old buildings have no insulation and weren't meant for modern heating and air-conditioning. The constant expanding and contracting of the joints from heated interiors and cold weather, or vice versa, puts a tension on the materials used back then."

Maya didn't like the sound of that, but in her experience, authority figures always put a bad light on things. Rifling through a box of bumper stickers she'd found in Cleo's storeroom, she giggled over one reading, WEAR SHORT SLEEVES, SUPPORT YOUR RIGHT TO BARE ARMS! and tried to pretend the man didn't exist.

The inspector turned to look at her as if she were crazed, so she held the sticker up for his inspection. He harrumphed and looked a little less jovial. "I'll need to take a look at the wiring. Is the circuit box in the back?"

Maya shrugged helplessly. "If that's where they put those things. I'm sure Axell will have kept it up-to-date. If it were up to me, the wires would have crumbled into dust."

He gave her a look of disbelief and wandered into the back. Slumping back in her chair, Maya sipped her tea. She was trying to keep an upbeat face on things, but she knew better than to expect anything good of people in authority. Still, she couldn't imagine Axell letting his property deteriorate.

Biting her bottom lip, she carefully arranged the bumper stickers by category. Some of them were really pretty funny. Maybe she could get one of those turning kiosks to display them. . . .

She didn't have any money, which was precisely why Cleo hadn't put them out.

Why didn't she just give this up and go put her time in at

the school? At least that had half a chance of becoming a profitable venture, and it was something she was good at. She knew absolutely nothing about the retail business.

If she moved in at the school, she wouldn't have to worry about transportation all the time. The school bus would pick Matty up and drop him off, and she would be at home and at work at the same time. She really should have asked Axell to invest in the school instead of this dead-end proposition.

But Cleo would need the shop when she got home. And the school might be a dead end if the authorities had their way. If Axell invested in the school, she really couldn't be certain he would approve of her dreams for it, and she didn't want any domineering man interfering. She really needed to get in touch with reality. It kept slapping her in the face, after all.

She had all the stickers organized in neat little stacks by the time the inspector returned. She'd taped one proclaiming BEAUTY IS IN THE EYE OF THE BEER HOLDER to the wall above her head, but the inspector didn't seem to see the humor.

"I'm sorry, Miss Alyssum," he proceeded, scribbling notes in his notebook, "but I'm afraid my report will recommend the building be closed until major structural repairs are made. We simply can't take any chances where human life is concerned."

What about *her* life? And Matty's? And Cleo's? Weren't they human?

Probably not. They were just cogs in the wheel. Sighing, she handed him a sticker reading EVER STOP TO THINK, AND FORGET TO START AGAIN?

Startled, he took one look at her face, hastily tucked the sticker into his clipboard, grabbed his hat and umbrella, and hurried out the door into the pouring rain.

Maybe he thought she'd go berserk on him. Maybe she would have.

Watching the cleaning crew industriously arranging the inventory inside the glass counter and on the shelves Axell had built, Maya fought for calm. No building, no store. No apartment, no home. No car. No money. No Matty.

Fighting the panic that always lived within her, Maya gripped the table hard and forced herself to think. She had fair warning this time. She could get her things out. The school would be uncomfortable for a little while, but she could live with uncomfortable. She couldn't live without Matty.

Covering her abdomen with her hand, Maya sent up an impassioned prayer. She couldn't live without this child either. She had to have a home for it.

Panic and tears threatened her control. Choking on them, she grabbed the telephone and dialed Selene's number.

She could do this. She was an adult with responsibility. She wouldn't let the world come crashing down around Matty's head again. Never *ever* again.

December 1945

When you stayed away that week, I thought I'd die. I stayed sober, waiting. I had the bartender throw Pete out and fired the damned piano player. Maloney used to make me laugh but I stubbed my cigarette out on his hand when he tried to pull the stupid coin trick again. He was funnier when I was drunk. You ruined me—in more ways than one.

When you didn't show Saturday night, I got drunk again. I was still half-soused when I got up the next morning. I'm not making excuses. I'm just telling you why I went to church that morning. Probably the only day all week I almost laughed, when I walked in that door wearing my best red dress and saw all those jaws drop.

You were sitting beside her—Miss Butter-Wouldn't-Melt-In-Her-Mouth. Damn you.

❧ THIRTEEN ❦

What happens if you get scared half to death twice?

Tapping his pen against his desk, Axell stared out his office window at the downpour. He'd lived here all his life. He knew the vagaries of North Carolina weather and road conditions. Angela had lost her life on a day like this one, and she'd been driving one of the larger highways and not one of the flood-prone ones. He'd better call Constance's baby-sitter and arrange to have her take care of Constance at the house after school. The road from here out to the house might not be safe later today.

He punched in the buttons, made the arrangements, and one more task taken care of, he contemplated the next. Maya hadn't come over to discuss the store opening. He couldn't blame her for not going out in this weather, but she could have called. He assumed she knew how to work a telephone.

He hoped that old building didn't leak. The previous tenants hadn't complained of it, but they hadn't lived upstairs either. Maybe he should check on her. Business was slow this time of the afternoon, especially in rain like this.

He was making excuses. He knew he was making excuses.

He didn't care. He couldn't focus on anything anyway. It wouldn't hurt to stop next door and see what progress had been made. Matty would be arriving home from kindergarten soon. Maya might need a ride out to the school.

Axell wrinkled his brow at that thought. The road out to the school crossed a creek that rose quickly. With urgent purpose, he took the steps two at a time.

117

Soaked instantly, he ran the few yards to the back of the shop. He should have warned her to keep the door locked, he realized, as he reached for his key at the same time the knob turned beneath his hand. The increase in drug activity lately had led to a string of break-ins.

He shouldn't have to tell a grown woman to keep her doors locked.

Fighting irritation as well as concern, Axell stalked through the unlit storage room. It wasn't as if Maya had anything to store back here, so he didn't expect a flurry of activity until he reached the front, but the place seemed ominously silent without chanting monks or rushing ocean tides.

Not until he reached the echoing emptiness of the front room did he realize something was wrong. There should be cleaning people bustling around, opening all these boxes, stacking ugly gnomes on shelves, and arranging kaleidoscopes on the counter. Maya should be sitting at that empty table, sipping tea. . . .

Axell glared at the empty water carafe and hot plate beside the neat stacks of bumper stickers. ALL THOSE WHO BELIEVE IN PSYCHOKINESIS, RAISE MY HAND. He snorted and almost grinned, reached for another, then caught himself. Maya wasn't here. Neither was anyone else, including Matty or the teenage clerk. Maya's teacups and pot were gone. Something was wrong.

He checked the front door. Locked. Well, at least she had that much sense.

Glancing around, Axell sought some clue for this lack of industry, but his heart was already racing. Maya was a hundred years pregnant. Angela had lost their son on a day like this.

He grabbed the phone and punched in the number for the school. He got an out-of-order message. Nothing new. Damned telephone company couldn't keep the lines up in this weather. He called Selene. They'd argued so much over the partnership contract, he had her number memorized. He almost gasped in relief when she actually answered.

"Have you seen Maya?" he demanded, without preamble.

"She's out at the school, measuring that dump upstairs for curtains," Selene snapped. "What the devil did you think you were doing, moving her into a place the city is condemning? That poor girl had her hopes up so high. . . ."

"What do you mean, condemning? This building is as solid . . ." Axell sputtered to a halt. The mayor, again. He didn't have time for this argument. "How did she get to the school? The phone's out and the water is probably rising right now."

"Well, it's not exactly as if she's going anywhere. Last I heard, she was catching a ride with someone. I think she arranged for that teenager who works for her to bring Matty out there. I had to call off school for the afternoon. Something's got to be done about the damned department of transportation letting those roads get this bad—"

"Selene, do you realize that if school had to be called off because of the roads, Maya could be stranded?" Axell asked impatiently, cutting off the tirade on the transportation board. "Can you get out there and see if she's all right?"

"Look, she's got food, a bed, a roof over her head. She's fine. I've got a meeting with my lawyer in a few minutes. She really can take care of herself, you know."

Axell heard the speculative note in her voice but ignored it. "Did it ever occur to you, Selene, that she's nine months pregnant and doesn't have any transportation?"

He heard hesitation on the other end of the line before Selene replied. "Women know these things in plenty of time, right? She'd have told me if she was in any pain."

"Selene, we're talking about Maya, remember? Have you ever heard her complain? I'm heading out there. You keep calling the school, see if you can reach her. I'll let you know as soon as I get there. Keep your cell phone with you."

"Suit yourself."

Axell heard worry behind Selene's flippant attitude, and assured she'd be on hand if Maya needed her, he hung up.

He wished he'd brought the Rover into town today, but he'd just had it washed and hadn't wanted to get it dirty. Stupid.

Not taking the time to castigate himself properly, Axell

hurried out the front door, locked it, and dodged raindrops until he reached the BMW. He was probably worrying for nothing. She was probably upstairs, dizzily creating palaces out of that trash heap.

She'd do it, too, Axell realized. She would probably scavenge bolts of cloth from Goodwill, decorate the walls with it, and call it home. She'd be sitting there with her teapot, on a toadstool, sipping tea when he arrived.

He needed to reassure himself with those thoughts. He didn't want to accept responsibility for any more women, and certainly not for a comparative stranger.

Maybe not a comparative stranger. He knew her bad habits as well as his own. And there was the matter of that kiss . . . Something else he didn't want to think about.

As he navigated puddles large enough to splash the car's roof, he congratulated himself for not driving one of those low-slung sports cars that Angela had preferred. The Beamer's solidity would get him through.

Axell lost some of that confidence when the heavy car fishtailed in a particularly deep stream of water as he left the main highway. *"Slow down,"* he muttered, easing up on the gas pedal as the rain poured harder, blinding the windshield. He'd driven these roads for decades. He knew every willow oak, every curve around the cotton fields, every skinny creek that rose in bad weather. He'd be all right. He just prayed Maya had the sense to stay where she was. Someone else might not know the roads as well as he.

What the hell was he doing out here? He was being an overprotective ass. Angela had accused him of that often enough. Maya was warm and safe. He was the idiot navigating dangerous roads in flood conditions. Maya would think he was crazy. He ought to turn back right now and go home and check on Constance.

He didn't turn around. Constance was fine. He'd built his home above the flood plain. The rain only threatened the old houses built by rivers and creeks.

He was just being practical, but Selene's words rang in his ears. *What the devil did you think you were doing, moving her*

*into a place the city is condemning? That poor girl had her
hopes up so high. . . .*

How many times could one person be knocked down before they quit getting up?

He wouldn't think like that. Maya was a survivor. She
wasn't like Angela. She wouldn't do anything to hurt Matty
or the baby. Maybe she'd holed up out here so she could cry
her eyes out in private, but she would be fine. By now, she had
that tea ready.

Axell rode high on that confidence until he hit the river of
red muddy water pouring over the road from the new shopping center development, and the car stalled.

Damned planning commission. He ought to sue.

Maya swept the last pile of dirt into a dustpan and dumped
it into a trash bag she'd brought from downstairs. There, she
had two rooms clean. That's all they'd need for now.

She grimaced as the pain in her back lapped in waves
around to her front. Straightening, she clung to a chair until
the ache rolled past. She was overdoing it. The ache had
steadily worsened throughout the day. She eased herself into
the chair.

The telltale burst of water down her thigh hit her with
shock.

Oh, God, not now.

Of course now. That's the way her life worked.

The baby was coming early.

All right, Maya. Let's not panic. First babies took their
time. She really wasn't even having labor pains yet, just the
usual backache.

Clutching the stair rail, she worked her way down to the
lower bathroom. This business of the bathroom and kitchen
on the first floor could be a real pain when the baby arrived,
she realized. Maybe she could adapt one of these lower rooms
for living in and fix up an upper one for school. Be creative,
Maya. There's a solution to every problem.

She washed herself and rinsed the wet dress. She needed to
clean the mess upstairs. She should have kept a change of

clothing here. She'd look real cute with a Pampers taped to her when help arrived.

She clung to the wall while another ache rolled past, then aimed for the office telephone. Who should she call first? Emergency services? She couldn't afford the ambulance bill, but she knew Selene had a meeting this afternoon. Axell? She hated to rely on him. He'd already gone far beyond the call of duty and was paying the price. But even if Teresa picked Matty up after school, the teenager couldn't take care of him for long. Someone would have to take him in tonight. She'd better call Axell.

She hadn't planned this very well. She'd never been real good at planning. Her life was just a series of happenings she couldn't stay ahead of. She'd packed her suitcase for the hospital, but it was back at the apartment, probably buried in an unopened box. Selene had promised to find a sitter for Matty when the time arrived, but she should have remembered Selene wasn't always available.

Things would work out. She just had to take them one at a time. She picked up the telephone and started dialing 911 before she realized the phone wasn't making any noise.

Maya stared at the dead receiver in disbelief.

This just couldn't be happening. Was her name Job? Was God trying to tell her something? Or had Mercury gone retrograde and she hadn't noticed?

Grimacing, she waddled over to the window and looked out. What did one look for when phones went dead? Hanging wires? And what difference did it make? It wasn't as if she could call someone and tell them it was dead.

Summoning curse words she didn't even know she knew, Maya cuddled a quilt around her and paced up and down the front office. Walking was supposed to be good for laboring mothers, she remembered. Maybe walking would clear her head. Or ease the ache. She winced and grabbed her belly as a muscle in her lower abdomen squeezed hard. Well, so much for the backache theory. That was definitely a contraction.

She picked up the phone again. Maybe it had just been a fluke the first time.

Still no dial tone.

Would Selene have left her cell phone?

She rummaged through the desk and found nothing. She glared at the computer. No phone: no E-mail, no fax.

All right, *think, Maya*. She could walk. How far was the nearest house? Or the shopping center they were building over the hill. Would any of the crew still be there? Would they have telephones?

She glanced out the window at the pouring rain. It looked like California during an El Niño winter. Rivers of red mud poured down the gravel drive. The lovely babbling brook through the side yard had turned into an ocean, swamping the azalea garden with a muddy, leaf-strewn pond that seemed to rise as she watched. She couldn't cut across that way.

All right, was it safer to wait in the warmth and safety of the dry house, praying the telephone would come back on and that the baby would wait, or should she risk the weather and mud and floods to seek help?

Instinct said wait. Instinct didn't like getting wet.

At least the electricity worked. She could fix a cup of tea. Selene had hooked her CD player to the intercom. She could find a few good songs and think.

Soaked to the bone, his expensive Johnston & Murphy loafers caked in mud past his ankles, his dry-clean-only linen shirt plastered to transparency against his back, Axell stumbled out of the downpour and onto the wide front porch of the school, panting from the exertion of fighting mud and water and his own anxiety.

He could see lights in all the windows, and relief poured through him. She was here. She was fine. He was the jerk. That was okay. He'd survive.

Throwing open the door, Axell walked into a blast of Aretha Franklin screaming "R-E-S-P-E-C-T" with the thundering power of a class five tornado. They must have wired the entire school with an amplifying system.

Holding on to the door frame, Axell peeled off his shoes and socks. He'd like to peel off the rest of his sopping clothes, too, but striding through the house naked didn't strike him as particularly polite.

Figuring there wasn't much point shouting for Maya over the noise, he padded through the hall and toward the kitchen. Maybe they kept coffeepots there. Surely Selene didn't drink that damned tea.

Axell stumbled into the kitchen and grabbed the doorsill for support at the sight in front of him.

Maya sat wrapped in a quilt, sipping tea from one of her precious cups, and rocking in a chair he remembered had once adorned the schoolroom. Her auburn curls spilled in abandon over shoulders that appeared distinctly naked above the cover of the quilt.

At sight of him, she looked up and her pale face beamed with a tremulous smile that cleaved his heart clear in two.

"Virgo to the rescue!" she breathed happily. "Did you bring your forceps?"

November 1945

She made a spectacle of herself in front of the whole church, nearly cost me my job when she ripped Dolly's hat off and threw it in my face. I explained it all away to the old man, but when I went to tell her this had to stop, I ended up in her bed again.

She makes me laugh. She makes me think there ought to be more to life than twelve-hour days over the mill books. She's the devil in woman's disguise. I want her every minute of every day.

I sent her my mother's teapot today. It doesn't match her mother's teacups, but she'll understand.

❧ FOURTEEN ❧

Make it idiot-proof and someone
will make a better idiot.

"The baby is coming?" Axell shouted.

"I'd offer you a cup of tea, but I think we'd better start for the hospital." She unwrapped her feet from the quilt and stood up. She was barefoot, and her toenails were painted copper brown.

Axell gaped at her shapely feet rather than staring at her shoulders or anywhere between. "Hospital. Right." Stunned, his brain ceased functioning.

The baby was coming. His car was in three feet of water a mile down the road. Maya was naked.

"Axell?" she asked patiently. "Is everything all right?"

He summoned his courage and looked up. She didn't eat enough. Still, her thin face glowed with expectation and her eyes were blue-green lanterns of excitement beneath her mound of auburn hair. Something odd inside him stirred. He figured it was terror.

"Have you called for an ambulance?" he demanded.

"The phone's out," she said. "That's why I've been sitting here waiting for someone to show up. You're my lifeline. I knew God couldn't be so cruel as to not offer me a way out of this. Let me see if my dress has dried yet."

Shakily, Axell reached in his sopping back pocket and retrieved his wet cell phone. "God works in mysterious ways," he reminded her with a sarcasm she didn't deserve as he punched the buttons. "My car died a mile down the road. And the road is washed out."

Her smile froze on her face as she anxiously watched him dial.

The line crackled but he could hear the phone ringing on the other end. Clinging to desperate hope, Axell glanced away as Maya's face stretched taut with pain, and she eased back into the rocker. Fingers gripped into fists, he waited for the emergency operator.

He barked the problem and the directions into the phone as soon as he had the operator on the line. He reminded them the road was washed out. He repeated everything. Twice. The operator seemed enormously slow at grasping the immensity of the problem. Taking a deep breath, Axell fought for calm. Maya bent over in agony and he nearly lost it.

"Hurry, will you?" he shouted into the phone. "She's going to have the baby on the kitchen floor if you don't get here soon!"

Frantically listening to the curt voice on the other end of the line, Axell nodded, then waited until Maya straightened. "Is there a bed in this place?" he demanded.

She grimaced and nodded toward a small room on the right. "The infirmary. I've already made it ready, just in case. Can't they get here?"

Axell clutched the phone as he would a life raft in a raging river, but Maya looked so scared, he lied. "They can always send a helicopter." Grimly, he turned back to the voice on the line. If he was all she had, he'd damned well better do this right.

He'd never done anything right in his life that involved a woman.

"Look, I'm on a cell phone. The lines are down out here. I've got to preserve this battery. Give me basic instructions and get someone here as soon as you can."

He scribbled as fast as he could across a first-grader's alphabet pad. Panic wouldn't help. Screaming at Maya for her boneheadedness might relieve his frustration, but it wouldn't get the baby delivered. If he didn't think about what he had to do, maybe he could get through this. Maybe he could pretend he was talking to a mechanic telling him how to replace a faulty carburetor.

Maya studied him soberly as Axell flung down the pen and closed the phone. "We're stranded, right?"

He took a deep breath. "Pretty much. The water goes down quickly once the rain stops. There might be time. How far apart are the pains?"

"Maybe four minutes." She grimaced at his reaction. "My water broke hours ago. I decided it was safer to deliver the baby myself than try to make it through the flood. I'm sorry. I never meant to get you involved."

"You're nuts. You're completely certifiable. What if the baby is breech? What if you're not big enough? Did you ever think of that?" Axell paced, trying to work off some of his terror. Under his father's tutelage, he'd learned dozens of ways of controlling temper and panic. He hadn't given in to excess emotion in decades. Even when his son had died, he'd managed a stoic calm, probably because he'd already been frozen in shock at the loss of his wife. He had no such buffer this time.

Mechanic. Make like a mechanic. Get the chassis on the ramp.

"All right, let's check out the infirmary. I suppose that means you've got Band-Aids and Tylenol." He strode purposefully toward the room she'd indicated and threw on the overhead light. It had probably been a generous pantry at one time. It was little more than a closet now. The narrow cot filled the interior. She'd piled it high with pillows and stuffed animals.

"Ace bandages, stuff for poison ivy, bacteria preventive, whatnot," she agreed. "I can boil water," she added helpfully, before gasping in pain and bending double.

"On the bed," Axell ordered, throwing open the cabinet door and searching for the alcohol. Sterilize everything, they'd said.

"I'm not ready for this," she stalled, glancing in the direction of the front door. "The baby isn't due for weeks. Couldn't we try—"

"Into bed!" Axell roared as another contraction chopped her sentence short.

"Pisces swim," she choked out, bent double but not obeying orders. "Maybe it would be better to find your car."

He couldn't do this. He couldn't deliver a damned baby. He couldn't even get the friggin' airheaded mother to lie down. "In the bed or I'll carry you there!" he shouted in frustration.

Straightening, Maya glanced at the narrow cot as if it were a spaceship prepared for takeoff.

"Aries," she murmured. "The baby will be an Aries. I'll never survive."

"What?" Terrified by her last words, Axell nearly dropped the alcohol bottle.

She adjusted her bulk onto the cot, settled against the stack of pillows, and cried out as the next contraction caught her by surprise.

Cautiously, Axell set the alcohol bottle down before he crushed it.

Biting back her cries, Maya struggled through the pain. Then wiping the damp curl of purple hair from her eyes, she continued as if she hadn't been interrupted. "Aries can have explosive tempers. And *self-centered*, you wouldn't believe. His father is an Aries. I don't suppose one can divorce children?"

She must be hysterical. Breathing again, Axell washed his hands. Discovering a box of antiseptic gloves, Axell nodded. All good bartenders could handle small talk. "Or trade them in for a different model? I've thought about it. Is the baby going to be a boy?"

She grunted and breathed in short quick bursts before shaking her head. "Don't know. Damn, this *h-u-ur-r-ts*." The last word emerged as a scream.

Faulty carburetors didn't scream.

"I'm supposed to look for the head," he warned. The contractions were coming much too swiftly.

Following instructions helped. If he concentrated on one step at a time and didn't think about what he was doing . . .

He barely had room to bend over. The sight of the woman lying in the bed, adjusting the quilt to hang over her bent knees, terrified the shit out of him. Lifting the quilt terrified the shit out of him, he amended. This was too up close and personal, and he didn't do personal.

"Tell me if you see red hair," she whispered between pants.

Axell managed a sour grin even as his stomach contracted into knots. Okay, he could handle red hair. Maybe they could talk each other through this. He had no difficulty talking to Maya. She didn't seem to care what he said. "Have you reached the baby's father yet?" he asked as he lifted the quilt with his elbow to keep his hands clean.

"His new girlfriend said he's recording in Nashville. She promised to give him word, but I won't hold my breath."

"Nice job of not holding your breath," he said dryly a few minutes later as she screamed the plaster into crumbling. But they were making progress. "I can see his hair!" he called excitedly, caught up in the astonishment of discovery. "He's got a full head of it."

Maya followed his announcement with a screaming curse Axell blithely assumed was for the missing father. Given a chance, he'd issue a few of his own, but his teeth were chattering and he didn't risk speaking. He wasn't a damned doctor. He was a bartender, for chrissake. "Make this one a martini," he could handle, not "deliver red-haired baby."

He checked the notes he'd jotted, wondered how he would dial the phone without contaminating his gloves, and nearly threw up as Maya arched her back, screamed, and soaked the bed pad with a gush of blood and water.

"My God!" Dropping his notes, the quilt, and any semblance of calm, Axell gasped as the infant's head popped out and tiny shoulders slithered into view. This was happening too damned fast. He didn't have time to prepare. . . .

He didn't need instructions to grab the tiny head and shoulders as they slid from Maya's body. Awed, hands shaking, every nerve on edge as Maya moaned and heaved and cursed again, Axell caught the slippery infant and eased him into the world.

Her. Eased *her* into the world.

"A girl, Maya," he whispered in amazement, not having

any idea if she could hear him or not as the tiny creature fell into his hands. "Does she have a name?"

There were things he was supposed to do. Umbilical cord. Afterbirth. Cry. No, the baby was supposed to cry, not him. Hot tears burned his eyes and his hands trembled. Fighting emotions he didn't know he possessed, he cleared the infant's throat, patted her gently to start her breathing, and heard the first faint gasp of air, followed by a weak cry.

She lived. And breathed. Relief so overwhelmed him, Axell nearly collapsed on the bed beside Maya. He'd delivered a living baby. He'd arrived in time to save them. He hadn't lost them this time.

Not stopping to examine that thought, he rubbed his face with his shoulder to wipe away the moisture, and mechanically followed the instructions now clearly imprinted on his brain. The moments after his son had been pronounced dead haunted the back of his mind: the doctor's expression as he'd told him, the wails from Angela's mother, the scream of an ambulance siren. . . . He hadn't been in time, hadn't even been able to hold her hand. . . .

Ambulance siren.

"Let me hold her," Maya whispered, jerking him back to the moment. "I want to hold her before they take her away from me."

Take her away? Over his dead body. The tiny wriggling human form in Axell's hands protested with weak cries and flailing fists as he cautiously wrapped her in a pillowcase. Maybe he should have used one of the Ace bandages. She was small, but her face screwed up pugnaciously as she readied herself for another holler, and her wet hair had a decidedly reddish cast. Axell smiled as he lowered her into Maya's arms.

"Definitely Aries," he said facetiously.

The smile she granted him in return was worth every minute of terror. The knot in his stomach slowly unraveled.

"God, I love you," she murmured, closing her eyes and holding the baby.

And she did. Love filled her heart and overflowed to encompass anyone and everyone: God, her daughter, Axell. . . .

Axell. Holding her daughter tightly, Maya imprinted on her memory the image of his taut face streaked with tears. Those big, capable hands had delivered her daughter—*her daughter*—held her as if she were more precious than gold. The stony gray of his eyes had melted to molten silver for a moment, and she'd seen right through him. Her icy Nordic god had love frozen inside him somewhere. Someone just needed to reach in and lay warm hands on his frostbitten heart.

Constance could. Maybe any child could. She owed him one.

"Alexa," she murmured as the siren screamed louder.

"What?"

She felt Axell leaning over her, and she opened her eyes to smile at him. He really was the handsomest man she'd ever known, even though that square jaw of his scared her half to death. With his hair soaked and the linen shirt plastered to his chest, he looked more like a vengeful sea god than Thor. He definitely looked dangerous—and protective. She wanted to pat his cheek in reassurance, but she had her hands full of beautiful infant. "Alexa," she breathed. "Like Axell, I guess. Close, anyway."

No matter what the future might bring, she would always love this stern-faced man, and as far as she was concerned, this child was his. He'd saved their lives. She dropped into a doze of exhaustion.

Axell stared down at mother and child in confusion.

Alexa.

She was naming the baby Alexa. He heard the paramedics racing through the house with a stretcher, but Axell observed their arrival from a distant plateau. There for a moment, he'd been part of Maya's world, warm and touching and grounded. Now, suddenly, he was on the outside again, with that chilly distance between them.

She'd said she loved him. She must have been hysterical.

Uncertainly, he reached out and brushed Maya's hand where it lay on the stretcher. Sleepily, she wrapped her fingers around his. A warm thrill shot through him. She didn't push him away.

Axell had to let her go as they wheeled her out of the room. One of the female paramedics had appropriated the baby, and he didn't feel qualified to object. But there for one brief second, he'd been part of a spectacular moment in life. He didn't think he'd ever be the same.

For another brief moment, he wondered how he could share that warmth again, how he could be someone other than who he was.

Alexa. Her name was Alexa.

Stupid name. Grumbling, Axell climbed into the paramedic's utility vehicle, beside the stretcher, and propped his head in his hands. He was out of his damned mind.

❧ FIFTEEN ❧

If Barbie is so popular,
why do you have to buy her friends?

"Just where do you think you're going?" a formidable nurse asked as Axell glanced around the hospital corridor, searching for the right room. At the nurse's tone, the flowers in his hand almost wilted.

"To Room 301," he answered cautiously, wondering about the interrogation. Hospitals made him nervous.

"Are you the father?" she demanded.

The temptation was to say yes, but he didn't lie without reason, and he saw no reason here. "Just a friend." He didn't call many people friend.

"Then you can't go in until visiting hours. Come back at eleven."

Stunned, Axell watched her walk off. He'd damned well delivered that kid, and he wasn't going to be put off by any tin general now. Constance and Matty had been bouncing up and down with excitement since he'd come home last night. He'd promised to deliver their artwork to Maya along with the flowers they'd picked from the garden. He'd barely persuaded them to go to school this morning. He deserved some reward for his patience.

Waiting until the nurse had her back turned, Axell strode briskly down the corridor, vowing to tell the next person who asked that he was the father.

With assurance, he located the door and knocked quietly. He didn't want to wake Maya if she was sleeping. Maybe he could just slip in and leave the flowers in a glass of water, with

the artwork beside it, then go down to the nursery and peek at
the infant.

"Come in," Maya's musical voice chimed merrily.

After the ordeal she'd just been through, she still managed
to sound like a damned gypsy queen. Steeling himself, Axell
pushed open the door, and nearly slammed it closed again.
Picturing himself making a Forrest Gump knock-kneed retreat down the hospital corridor, Axell set his jaw and walked
in as if he belonged there. If she didn't mind, he wouldn't
either.

She was sitting up in bed, trying to nurse the infant.
"Trying" being the operative word. Little Alexa sucked and
gulped, then screamed in rage and beat her little fists until
Maya winced. She glanced up at him apologetically.

"I'm sorry, I thought you were the nurse. We're having a
little trouble here, and I was hoping for some advice."

He ought to look away, but he felt as if he'd been poleaxed. He
couldn't tear his gaze from the sight of the infant sucking
frantically at her mother's breast.

Maya was wearing a delicate lace-trimmed nightshirt that
Selene must have brought over with her suitcase last night.
The first few buttons were unfastened, and Axell could see
tiny fingers digging into an ivory curve. The sight nearly un-
manned him, but fascination gripped him stronger. He'd delivered that child. He'd seen far more than the curve of a
breast. That didn't lessen his fascination.

Angela hadn't nursed Constance, so Axell knew less than
nothing about breast-feeding. He should have known Maya
would attempt it. She was the type to nurse even if she could
afford the infant formula and bottles—which she couldn't.
Clearing his throat, Axell filled a water glass with the wilting
flowers and lay the artwork down beside it.

"These things take time, don't they?" he asked cautiously.

Maya sighed and removed the wailing infant from her
breast, fastening her buttons with one hand as she bounced
the baby gently. "I suppose, but the nurse said I may not have
what it takes. I think that means I'm underfed."

She efficiently popped the top of a bottled formula on the

nightstand. "Don't hover. Have a seat. An audience will prevent me from having a temper tantrum."

Put that way, he didn't have much choice, but Axell raised his eyebrows at the idea of Maya having a temper tantrum. "You're both doing well?" He sounded cold even to himself.

"Thanks to you, healthy as pigs, except for this small problem." Now that she had the baby sucking happily on the bottle, she lifted the pink bundle in his direction. "Want to hold her? You've earned the right."

Startled, Axell almost pulled back, but his hands had a mind of their own. Carefully, terrified, he took the infant and bottle in both hands. She was no bigger than his outspread fingers, softer and more limp than a kitten. He could feel her heart beating.

"They don't break. Just hold her head up with your arm. Surely you've had experience at this," Maya instructed briskly.

Axell threw her a suspicious glance but did as she said. Alexa scarcely noticed the transfer. "My wife always fed Constance. Whenever I picked her up, Constance would cry." Amazed, he stared at the tiny fingers now wrapped around his big ones as the baby tugged hungrily at the bottle. She hadn't cried at all.

"She probably wasn't used to having you around. Babies bond with the sound of the parents' voices while they're still in the womb. If you'd kept talking to her, she would have eventually recognized yours."

Maya had pinned her unruly hair in a barrette, her face was scrubbed clean of any hint of cosmetic, but her rosy smile and kaleidoscope eyes added all the color required. She was watching the baby and not him, but he could deal with that. He adjusted the infant more comfortably so she could see Alexa better.

"So while I'm sitting here talking to you, Alexa is absorbing my voice, and she won't scream the next time I pick her up?"

Maya shrugged. "I can't promise that. Babies scream for

lots of reasons. They're still screaming when they're teen-agers." She rolled her eyes. "I did some high school student teaching once. I'm not looking forward to adolescence."

Adolescence. My God, in a few years, Constance would be entering puberty. What the devil would he do with her then? Send her to girls' school somewhere?

"Then the theory isn't much different: give them what they want, and they're happy," Axell said.

Maya beamed in approval. "But what they want isn't al-ways what's good for them. So screaming is just part of the territory. Get used to it."

He didn't have to be afraid if the child cried. Another reve-lation. Angela had jerked Constance out of his hands the in-stant she whimpered, as if he'd been doing something wrong. He'd always felt inadequate and useless. It had been far easier to go to the bar every day and earn money to keep them happy than to stay home and try to figure out what made them tick. But he was older now and had more endurance.

"How's Matty? Did Selene find a baby-sitter for him?"

"I had her pick him up and take him over to the house. Dorothy was already over there looking after Constance, so it just made sense. They play well together."

Maya didn't comment on the fact that he'd ignored her in-structions. "I think she's asleep. Put that pad over your shoulder before you lift her. She spit up earlier."

Little fists lay in complete relaxation even though the rosebud mouth still worked dreamily. The tiny mite may as well have reached through his chest and plucked his heart-strings. He was playing with fire here. Reluctantly, Axell lifted baby Alexa to his shoulder and cautiously rubbed her skinny back.

Perhaps now was the time to get back to business. He could control financial affairs a lot easier than he could control squalling infants and suspicious women. "You want to tell me why the devil you sent the cleaning crew home and decided to move into the school? That's what you were doing, weren't you? You took your teacups."

Baby Alexa squirmed at his tone of voice, and Axell nearly

bit his tongue. A gassy burp scented his shirt collar, and he stared at her in amazement. Recovering, he lifted the small bundle from his shoulder and handed her back to her mother. It wouldn't do to get any more involved than he was.

Who was he kidding? He was already in up to his neck, and unless he cut line soon, he'd be in over his head and going down for the third time.

He didn't want to cut line.

Astounded, Axell watched numbly as Maya cuddled her squirming daughter. He wanted involvement? With the queen of gypsies? Had he lost his pea-picking mind?

"The building inspector said he was ordering the building closed for major structural repairs," she said in reply to his question. "I figured I'd get my things out before the police arrived this time."

Axell let out a curse he seldom used in public, bit back a second one, and in the interest of peace, stood up and stalked to the window. He'd ordered a private room for her so she'd get some rest. He was already overboard.

"There's not a damned thing wrong with that building. I had inspectors crawling all over when I had it renovated. Somebody bought this one off."

"Then I don't have to move?" she asked hopefully.

Axell wanted to bang his head against the window. The rain had stopped, but the clouds hadn't dissipated. The shiny new green leaves of the crape myrtles glistened with raindrops against the dark clouds—bound to be a metaphor for something, but he wasn't a man who dealt in metaphors. "If they put a notice on it, you can't live there," he said heavily, "and we can't open it to the public until I have my lawyers handle it, but you should be able to go in and get your things. It's not in any danger of falling apart."

Her silence told him all he needed to know. She was homeless again.

"Mr. Holm, your intentions are admirable, but the fact remains, Miss Alyssum's nephew is a ward of the state until otherwise released. You know yourself that this department has been under fire for not properly overseeing the children in its protection. I would be neglecting my duties to the child and to the state if I didn't see that he's adequately housed. I've been informed that Miss Alyssum's home has been condemned, and I'm already familiar with her finances. Until she finds a salaried position, she's in no financial condition to provide appropriate housing. I'm afraid I'll have to put him in foster care until further notice."

Axell simmered as he listened to this self-righteousness. This had gone far enough. He might be tough enough to part Maya from the Pfeiffer property, but even he wouldn't dare part her from her home and kids. He didn't care which snitch had reported Maya's temporary housing predicament. They weren't giving her a chance. The next thing they'd do was take Alexa away from her. This was utterly ridiculous.

Axell leaned forward against his desk and glared at the lumpy social worker on the other side. "Her apartment in my building is as structurally sound as it gets. My lawyers are looking into the matter as we speak. In the meantime, she has friends she can count on. She and Matty will not go without a roof over their heads."

The young social worker glared back at him from behind bottle-thick glasses and thin, lifeless bangs. "The state cannot condone a ward living in immoral circumstances, and pardon my putting it bluntly, with people of unsavory reputation. We've done a background check, Mr. Holm. The instance of drug sales in your restaurant, and the imminent loss of your liquor license, do not exactly make you a role model for an impressionable five-year old."

If he hadn't had complete control of his temper, he would have leapt over the desk and throttled her. Soon they'd be trying to take Constance away. This was the next best thing to a police state. Forget running for mayor. He'd go after the governor's job—as soon as he got this mess straightened out.

Is this what Maya had put up with all these years? He was beginning to understand some of her defensiveness. Knock a person down and keep a foot on their neck all their lives, and most people would get a little leery of anyone in authority.

He was amazed that she'd come as far as she had. The gypsy had guts.

"Repeat what you just said in public, and I'll have you sued for slander," he informed her coldly. "Miss Alyssum has no family left, so she relies on friends. I'm a friend. She is part owner of the Impossible Dream day school and my partner in the Curiosity Shoppe. She's a tax-paying citizen and has her rights. You cannot take that child away from her unless you find Matty hungry, unclothed, dirty, and homeless. This is not the case. Until it is, I suggest you stay clear of the Alyssums or expect to have my lawyers slapping a subpoena on you so fast, your head will spin. Is that understood?"

His tirade backed her toward the door. Muttering a few more official imprecations, the social worker spun around and slammed out. Axell collapsed in his chair.

This couldn't go on. The mayor would destroy Maya, the school, the bar, and Axell to have his way. If they took his license, he'd have no means of supporting Constance. With Sandra prompting the judge, and the mayor after his license, he could lose his daughter as easily as Maya could lose hers. Ralph had pushed too far this time. It was time to fight back.

Axell drummed his fingers against the desk. Lawyers took time. While they petitioned the court and wrote subpoenas and did whatever it was they do, three businesses could crumble. And then there was the matter of Constance. While he fought the mayor, Sandra would be fighting for Constance.

He had some decisions to make.

He called his lawyer first. Then he called Judge Tony. He wanted all his facts lined up in a row, then he would storm into this with his eyes wide open and both guns blazing, and the devil take anyone who got in his way.

Maya glanced at the stern man behind the wheel of the BMW. She'd asked Selene to pick her up at the hospital. Axell had appeared instead. He didn't look very happy about it. She'd wanted to be installed in the top rooms of the school before Matty came home. This wasn't the direction of the school.

As he'd promised, the waters had receded as quickly as they'd risen. Tree limbs and leaves littered the road, but there was no reason they couldn't reach the school. She glanced at the infant sleeping in the car cradle in the backseat. Axell had bought a car cradle! Or maybe he already had one. That made her feel better, so she didn't argue the point. Obviously, there were bigger clouds on the horizon than the cost of a car seat.

She turned back and glanced at Axell. His jaw muscle twitched. She didn't think that was a good sign. "Are we just picking up my things at your house?"

The knuckles on the one hand he had on the wheel whitened. He glanced at her through those stony eyes, but her wayward mind thought she saw pain and uncertainty reflected there instead of anger. Had something awful happened and he couldn't find words to tell her? Panic bubbled near the surface all the time now.

"Constance may not be my daughter," he pronounced out of nowhere.

Maya drew a deep breath and held it. Where did she go from there? Watching rain-soaked pines flash by, she gathered her wits, and expelled the air in her lungs. "Does that matter?" she asked calmly.

Axell threw her another one of those looks, then concentrated on his driving. "Maybe it explains why I'm such a lousy father."

All right, take this one slow, Maya. "You're thinking of giving her up to your mother-in-law again?"

"I'm weighing my options. I want Constance to be happy."

Maya nodded as if she had some clue as to where this conversation was going. She noticed her fingers clenched in fists and forcibly unrolled them. "If you wanted to buy a gift for Constance, and she told you Cleo's was her favorite store, what would you do?"

He glared at her and nearly missed the driveway. "Is this some kind of test?"

"Yes," she said firmly. "Keep your eyes on the road and answer the question."

He studied the question for all of half a second and apparently deciding there was no trick to it, shrugged. "I'd probably buy her one of the kaleidoscopes." He hit the garage door opener and waited for the door to lift. "Do I win the prize?"

"Your mother-in-law ignored Constance's preference and bought her the doll instead, a doll that reminded her of her dead baby brother. Now, who do you think is most likely to make Constance happy?"

Pulling the car into the garage and turning it off, Axell slumped in the leather seat. "You," he replied without hesitation. "You are most likely to make Constance happy."

He looked perfectly miserable as he said it.

❧ SIXTEEN ❧

We have enough youth. How about a Fountain of Smart?

"It's damp out here. Let's get the baby inside."

Axell abruptly stepped out of the car and circled around to the back door to unfasten the infant carrier.

Maya swung out of the car more cautiously. Whatever had happened to the good old days of spending five days in the hospital, recuperating from childbirth? She still felt as if a train had run over her, and she hadn't slept well in the damned hospital. She wasn't in any condition for arguing with this domineering man who had decided—for whatever reason— to run her life. She'd known he'd spelled trouble that first day he'd walked into the shop. Virgos were like that.

"I don't suppose I get any explanations?" she asked as she dragged behind Axell into the echoing, empty designer house. He had Alexa. She wasn't likely to let her daughter out of her sight.

"You look like you need rest first. I'll pick up the kids at school, and I have Dorothy coming in to look after them. You get some sleep before the kids decide to entertain you. We can talk tomorrow."

Briskly, he carried Alexa to the room Maya and Matty had slept in before. A lovely hand-carved cradle padded with a pale pink mattress and sheet waited beside the bed. Tears sprang to Maya's eyes at the sight. A cradle. She'd wanted Alexa to have a cradle of her very own. She'd looked at doll cradles, wondering if she could at least afford a toy. It wouldn't have lasted long, but it would have been better than a dresser drawer. And here was the real thing, with flowers and hummingbirds, and daubs of pink and blue paint. She wanted to sit on the floor beside it and sob her heart out.

She didn't think she could get back up if she did.

"Axell, you didn't buy that, did you?" she whispered, praying he'd say no so she wouldn't have to refuse it.

"Made it . . ." his voice broke and he coughed ". . . a few years ago. Will it do?"

She heard his pain even though he kept his back to her as he set the infant seat down and unstrapped the baby. The lion king could entertain governors and run city councils, restaurants, and half the town, but he was terrified of revealing his feelings. Maya shook her head in amazement at this contradiction. Must be a southern thing—real men don't cry.

"It's the most beautiful thing I've ever seen," she admitted tearily.

He turned in alarm at the sob in her voice, and she hastily wiped her eyes with her sleeve. His expression was one of panic, and lower lip trembling, Maya managed a smile. She remembered that look. She'd seen it when she'd told him the baby was coming. Tenderness and longing and an odd feeling of connection welled inside her as she resisted the urge to stroke his clenched jaw. He'd probably run if she did. She was actually beginning to understand the man.

Carefully, she took Alexa from his arms and cuddled her to hide any further outbreak of tears. She didn't think Axell could handle a sobbing woman right now. "Thank you for letting me use the cradle," she whispered. "I've dreamed of having one for her. It's the nicest thing you could have done—except for delivering Alexa," she amended.

Looking a little more sure of himself, Axell nodded curtly. "It was sitting in the attic, going to waste. I'll go get your suitcase. Selene packed up some of your things from the apartment. I just put the boxes in the closet. You'll have to arrange them."

He walked out without any further explanation.

She really would have to learn to argue instead of going all soppy sentimental if she wanted to survive in a partnership with a man like that. But for right now, Axell's decision-making was such a relief, she simply couldn't offer any objections. She hadn't realized how tired she was. Taking care of Alexa in that run-down attic at the school would be hell, especially with dozens of noisy children below. She hoped the substitute teacher they'd hired was working out.

Gently laying Alexa in the cradle and rocking it, Maya did what she did best—swam with the flow. She'd analyze Axell's odd behavior later, when she was stronger.

"Does she sleep *all* the time?" Matty asked in disgust as he entered the bedroom to give Maya a good-bye kiss before school. Last night, he'd refused to sleep in the room Axell offered him but had agreed to a fold-up floor mattress beside Maya's bed. This morning, he was all brash male arrogance again. She was relieved he wasn't retreating into the troubled child she'd found when she'd first arrived.

"Only when she isn't crying," Maya teased. "You grew out of it."

Matty grimaced and gave her a hug. Constance remained standing, fascinated, beside the cradle.

"She's so *tiny*. I didn't know babies were so tiny. She looks just like my doll."

"She won't when she starts crying and spitting up on you, or smiling and pulling your hair. I'll teach you to hold her when you get home, all right?"

Constance looked awed and worried at the same time as she glanced in Maya's direction. Maya held out her arms. "Give me a hug. You're the kind of little girl I want Alexa to be when she grows up."

Constance beamed, hugged her, and towed Matty out of the room with cries of "We're late. Daddy's waiting."

If only they could stay little and so easy forever, instead of growing into impossibly arrogant, stubborn adults, Maya thought whimsically a half hour later when Axell appeared in the bedroom door in all his designer-suited elegance. His tie this morning was a shiny gold and blue silk. His golden hair had been recently barbered, and a drop of moisture on his jaw indicated he'd just shaved.

Instinctively, she shoved her hair behind her ear and wondered if she looked a total wreck. Next to Axell's neatly styled hair, pressed clothes, and self-assured air, she would always resemble a hurricane strike zone.

She wished she could read his expression as his gaze lingered on her for just a second or two longer than it should before he looked down at Alexa, who was beginning to fuss a little. Tentatively, he rocked the cradle with his polished shoe, and the infant settled down. He looked mildly astonished.

"It works. Why do they like movement so much?" There was the curious professor who hooked her every time.

"Because they're used to bobbing around in water all day in the womb? I haven't the foggiest. Cleo used to fall asleep in the car even as a teenager." Maya wound her fingers together and tried to think of some way of relieving the unexpected tension between them. He'd carried in her breakfast earlier—toast and orange juice and hot water with a tea bag—but hadn't lingered for more than an inquiry about how she'd slept. She'd thought he'd forgotten his promise to talk, and hadn't expected him to return here after he took the kids to school.

Still, just attempting breakfast for her was a sweet thing to do, and she rewarded him with a smile, just to see how that would work.

He stiffened like his shirt collar, if that was possible. Nervously, he fingered Constance's artwork on the wall and looked anywhere but at her. She wondered if she had pillow wrinkles on her face.

Absorbed in her college studies and tedious hours of work, she'd never really looked at older, established men as anything more than interesting caricatures as unreachable as the faces on a movie screen. Stephen was the most grown-up lover she'd ever known, and next to Axell, he was positively adolescent. Axell's mature confidence was starting to grow on her. Scary.

She really should apply her mind to looking beyond his

surface polish. That tanned, golden-boy veneer hid a piercingly intelligent mind. Those stony eyes that watched the world so warily disguised a man who couldn't reach out to others. But the lionlike physical grace and Nordic god confidence were bred to the bone. It was a good thing he always wore those suits or she'd be admiring his chest next. Intrigued by his slipping self-assurance but growing as nervous as he, Maya sought another icebreaker.

"You had something you wanted to tell me?" Well, so much for being subtle.

Axell tightened his mouth, lined up the hairbrush and comb on the dresser, and with a decided air of resolution, took the wing chair beside the bed. Against the feminine chair, his shoulders loomed enormous and entirely too masculine.

"We have problems." He steepled his fingers and searched for the next step.

"Tell me something I don't know," Maya said with humor. "I try to tackle them one at a time. You really don't have to solve mine, you know."

He defrosted ever so slightly and shot her a wry look. "They're starting to get a little tangled together, you'll notice."

Maya wrinkled her nose and considered it. "Not really. I can move Cleo's stuff out of your building. You can send Constance to another school. Before long, we're all untangled."

"I'm not certain that's the route I want to take."

He said that so firmly, he startled her. Maya stared at him in incredulity. "Why on earth would you want your problems entangled with mine? I'm a walking disaster area. You don't strike me as the type to handle that kind of chaos well." Actually, Virgos were excellent caretakers. She just didn't know if she wanted to be taken care of.

Axell's steepled fingers slid together until they formed a solid grip across his silk tie. "I'm very good at handling chaos," he replied grimly. "It's Constance I don't manage so well. Sandra has demanded a paternity test, and the judge is considering it. Sandra claims I'm not fit to raise Constance."

Maya's eyes widened. "She can't do that, can she? You've

given Constance everything. Children go through stages. She's already growing out of this one."

Axell shrugged but it wasn't indifference reflected in his determined expression. "Sandra can make life hell for me and Constance. There will be court battles; Constance will have to go to court-appointed psychologists. The lawyers will have a field day."

Maya blinked in disbelief. She'd thought she was the only victim around here, but apparently it didn't matter what end of the socioeconomic ladder one was on when trouble called. In their overeagerness to right all wrongs, the courts hadn't developed a measure for determining good parenting. Money still won more often than love, and women won more often than men. She stared at Axell in dawning horror as she realized his dilemma.

"How can I help?" He'd done so much for her, she owed him more than she could possibly pay in a million years. Besides, he was hurting, and she loved his daughter, and she wanted to help.

"Marry me," Axell demanded, meeting her gaze without flinching.

If sunlight had poured through the roof and Disney bluebirds had started draping pink bunting across the ceiling, Maya couldn't have been more astounded. Actually, a mockingbird burst into song outside and sunlight spilled through the window for the first time in days. In her cradle, Alexa stirred and made sucking sounds.

Alexa. Her daughter. The one she'd sworn to protect with every ounce of her body and soul. She hadn't done a very good job of it so far. This man was offering to take over the responsibility. This man was insane.

"You're kidding, right?" Maya asked nervously, tugging at a strand of hair that had escaped her barrette.

"No, I don't, generally," Axell replied with more thoughtfulness than he'd used in his proposal. "I've talked to my lawyers and the judge. They all agree that Sandra wouldn't have much of a case if I'm married, especially if I'm married to someone with your credentials in child care."

A rebellious giggle formed in Maya's throat. He'd lined up all his soldiers in a row again. He hadn't realized how subversive her form of guerrilla warfare was. She managed a straight face. This was, after all, a serious topic. She thought. "You mean, you're willing to put up with Matty and Alexa and a wife who paints dragons on shoes in return for a live-in baby-sitter for Constance?"

Axell didn't blink a single splendid eyelash. "We can work out any arrangement you prefer. I just know it isn't wise for us to cohabit. Social Services has already threatened to take away Matty if you stay here under 'immoral circumstances.' Since neither of us are his legal parents, my lawyers say they have that right."

He pressed his lips together as he formulated his next argument. So appalled that she was fascinated, Maya held her tongue.

"If I'm to take on a political fight, I need a wife and not a 'significant other,' " he finally continued. "Both our businesses would be on more solid ground if we regularized our relationship, and we would be in better positions to fight the mayor."

Their "relationship"? Did they have one? If so, it was the strangest one she'd ever known. Her heart did drumrolls and the butterflies in her stomach turned to roaring mammoths as she realized his seriousness.

"I hate to point this out," she said tentatively, "but there is a little more to marriage than taking care of kids and making political points."

Axell sketched a nod of agreement, and she thought maybe beneath his hooded gaze she saw a glimmer of warmth.

"I've been married before. I'm not much good at it. I don't like my routine disturbed, and I'm apparently incapable of giving the kind of emotional support women like. I realize I'm not a good candidate for husband. But if you can deal with that, I can offer you and the children the kind of security you would never have otherwise. I can help you with your businesses. I can even help your sister into a rehab program if she needs it. It's a trade-off."

He was serious. Maya stared at him in total disbelief, then turned to gaze around the enormous room he'd brought her to. She could live here in the lap of luxury, give Alexa everything she'd ever dreamed of, protect Matty and Cleo, and never have to worry about Social Services again. She could do it in the blink of an eyelash.

All she had to do was give up any hope of love for herself. The adult kind, at least.

It hurt. It hurt like the very devil. All her life she'd dreamed of finding someone who could actually love her for herself. But she wasn't very lovable. Heaven only knew, she'd been taught that the hard way through numerous foster homes and failed relationships. She had an impossibly eccentric character no one could understand. Could she trade the impossible dream of love in exchange for all the others he could provide?

Could she give up her one shriveled-up bit of hope in return for happiness for Constance and Matty and Alexa? Who was she kidding?

Maya looked Axell straight in the eye. "You've considered all the ramifications of this proposal? Including sex?"

He looked a little taken aback by her bluntness but nodded. "I'd prefer that we keep the vows of faithfulness, for the sake of the children. We'd have to learn to deal with each other on that level."

He carefully avoided looking at her but Maya had a sneaking suspicion that—like most men—his mind had never traveled too far from "that level." A pleasant shiver prickled her skin as she realized that the formidable lion king found her attractive even while calling her twenty-months pregnant. Or the Scorpio passion she was beginning to seriously suspect he possessed had overruled all logic. But physical attraction wasn't enough to keep a relationship alive.

"You haven't disrupted my routine with constant demands as so many other women would," Axell continued. "I think you could adjust to my habits better than most." He hesitated, then apparently decided on frankness. "You're young. You probably want more out of life than someone like me. But you've got a good head on your shoulders. I think you see the wisdom of my suggestion. In return, I'll try to bend as far as I'm capable to make you happy."

Maya bit back another bubble of laughter at his seriousness. He was so right, and so very wrong. And so damned Virgo.

"I adore you," she managed to say with what she thought was enormous equanimity. "Every little girl dreams of a prince on a white horse riding to her rescue, one who will take care of her forever after."

His brow drew down in a frown as he recognized her satire. In his favor, he shut up and waited for her to finish.

"But I can't return the enormous debt I owe you by turning your life into my vision of hell for both of us. I've lived all my life with other people's rules, and I simply can't do it anymore." Maya thought she ought to cut her tongue out right about now, but the words had been building up inside of her for a long time, and they all spilled out at once, with disastrous consequences, she was certain. "As easy as it would be to accept your offer, I've got to make it on my own this time. I'm an adult now; I don't have to take anyone's charity. I may have to live under a leaky roof, but it will be my roof, and I can fly kites from it if I like," she said defiantly. "I can paint on the walls, wear dirty shoes on the carpet, and scream out loud anytime I want—in my own home. This isn't my home."

Axell looked down at his hands. Maya noticed they were shaking. He must have noticed it at the same time. He unclasped them and gripped the chair arms, then looked up at her again. She had never seen so much defiant determination on any person's face.

"Just leave me my wing of the house, and the rest of the place is yours."

December 1945

I've hired a new piano player, one who makes me laugh and doesn't play sad songs. I'm having the walls painted and I'm installing a mirror over the bar. Maybe I'll make the place high-class and invite the ladies.

Maybe I'll start a campaign to legalize liquor, go to church on Sunday, and join your girlfriend's Sunday school class. What do you think Dolly will think of that? Does she know hard liquor has crossed your wicked lips? Does she know where that sinful mouth of yours has been? Should I tell her?

❧ SEVENTEEN ❦

If you ain't making waves,
you ain't kicking hard enough.

Baby Alexa whimpered louder. Axell rocked her cradle with his toe, but she seemed determined to wake this time. He'd have to remember how inconvenient and intrusive children were. Perhaps he should be glad Maya had turned him down flat. Constance and the restaurant kept him busy enough. If he was bored with his orderly life, he could run for mayor.

He wasn't bored. He was lonely.

Leaning over to lift the infant, he grimaced at Alexa's soggy diaper. Another good reason to hope Maya didn't agree to his absurd argument. Babies were dirty and wet and he didn't know what to do with them. He could save his liquor license some other way. Constance might be better off with Sandra.

He wasn't accustomed to rejection, but Maya probably had it right. They'd never work out. What could he have been thinking? He couldn't run for mayor with a wife with purple hair and dragons on her shoes. He should be feeling relief, not this looming shadow of dread, as if the dry sands of the Sahara whispered closer.

Alexa blinked at him with big round eyes and grabbed his finger. The knot in Axell's stomach twisted tighter as they stared at each other.

"Hand her here. I've got dry diapers in the drawer. One of the mothers from the day school gave them to Selene. She would never have remembered on her own." Maya leaned over and produced a disposable diaper and waited patiently for Axell to hand over her daughter.

Her daughter. Just because he'd delivered Alexa and worried about her welfare didn't make Alexa his. Almost reluctantly, Axell handed the whimpering infant to her mother. A tiny fist wouldn't let go of his finger. If Alexa were his, he'd have the right to continue letting her hold it as she nursed. If Maya were his . . . He was doing this for the kid, he reminded himself.

"Infant formula is expensive," he argued, unable to give up without a fight. "The stuff you brought home from the hospital won't last much longer." He'd spent too long studying this issue. It grated on his self-esteem to think he could lose an argument to a twenty-five-year-old gypsy who didn't know where her next meal was coming from.

His mistake had been treating her as one of the empty-headed college students working at his bar for clothes money—like Angela. It was easier to work this out in his head by thinking of Maya as malleable, but that nonconfrontational attitude of hers hid a world of hard-earned wisdom. It would behoove him to remember that.

He watched as Maya efficiently changed the soggy diaper, dropped the soiled one in a trash can beside the bed, and turned her shoulder on him to place the child to her breast. "I haven't given up yet. And there are programs to help children from families of limited income."

Food stamps. She was probably living on food stamps. *My God, a teacher with a master's degree, and she was living on welfare. How in hell did single women with only a high school diploma make it?*

That wasn't his problem. Right now, his problem was providing a mother for Constance, a quality mother, not some socially ambitious, money-hungry female. Maya was the only woman he knew who met the requirements as a mother for Constance, and who might conceivably fit into his life without constant demands and emotional upheaval. And she still wasn't accepting his offer.

"I'll get her bottle—just in case," he added when Maya

threw him an annoyed look. The damned woman didn't know when to give up, but he didn't have a problem with perseverance. He just wasn't going to let the kid starve.

When he returned with the warm infant formula, Alexa was fretting and beating her fists hungrily against Maya's breast. Hot lust shot straight to his groin at just the sight of a full ivory breast.

This was ridiculous. He'd seen women's breasts before. He wasn't a frigging adolescent. This had to be some possessive caveman reaction to the idea of acquiring a wife. But as Maya removed the infant and he caught a glimpse of an engorged nipple, he grew harder than a piling rod. Nervously, Axell dropped back to the chair and hid his lap with a Dr. Spock baby book from her nightstand.

In his experience, a good offense beat a tardy defense every time. Marrying Maya was the best thing for the children. Period. That was enough to make the decision imperative. But their marriage would also force the mayor to realize his dirty tricks wouldn't drive Maya back to California, so he could let up on the building inspections and liquor licenses and whatever other cards he had up his sleeve until he found another outlet. Axell could almost swear there would be an investigation into the day school's license by now. After they were married, if the school lost its license, he wouldn't have to worry about Constance losing Maya.

And with a wife by his side, he'd be more appealing to voters come election time. He was uncertain of Maya as a political wife, but the mayor's job in a small town like Wadeville wasn't precisely as demanding as a governor's. If she stuck to taking care of the kids, he could keep the rest of his life in order.

He'd just have to learn to live with kites flying from his roof and cats in his kitchen and whatever else she demanded. He hadn't really given much thought to that aspect of marriage. He'd been working on the assumption that she'd slip quietly into the empty places in his life as she had thus far. He supposed he could get used to Aretha Franklin roaring through the house.

As Alexa burped contentedly on her mother's shoulder, Axell decided he could manage the material disruptions. He spent most of his time at the office anyway.

He took the infant from Maya and admired her sleepy, wrinkled features. "She doesn't look like she has a temper."

"Give her time. She'll grow into it." She looked at him quizzically. "Don't you have to be at the office or something?"

"Not until we get this settled." He tucked Alexa into her cradle. "You're ignoring my offer."

She regarded him warily. "You're offering me more than I have ever dreamed of, in return for what? A mother for Constance? You could go to the bar on Friday night and choose any woman you like. Why me?"

Startled, Axell raised his eyebrows. "I haven't noticed women falling all over me," he countered. "And I doubt that any of my acquaintances have your credentials for dealing with children. I've watched you at work. You know what you're doing. I'm not walking into this blindly."

She shook her head and leaned back into the pillows. "You're going to wear me down over this, aren't you? Why don't you give me a few days around here and see if you don't change your mind? Admittedly, I'm not up to my usual standards right now, but I think even my brand of low-grade chaos will drive you screaming for the doors."

Axell relaxed a fraction. He had her hooked. He just needed to reel her in. He cringed mentally at the fishing reference. He'd have to remember he was lousy at fishing, and Maya was more intelligent than any fish, but he would win, whatever the cost.

"If you're feeling well enough, we can go down to the courthouse for the license tomorrow." With this suggestion, he called the signals for a touchdown run. She didn't stand a chance against a planned offensive, and he played with a home field advantage.

"It will take a few days to meet the requirements and line up the preacher's time. . . ." Axell glanced at her speculatively. "Constance and I attend church on Sundays. Will that be a problem for you?"

Maya grimaced and tugged at the purple strand of her hair. "And I thought I was the insane one around here."

Axell held his breath, but she fell for his setup.

She shrugged. "Matty and I haven't gone because we have no clothes and no transportation. Church isn't a problem. Don't sweat the small stuff. It's the big stuff that worries me. Isn't a license a little premature?"

"A license isn't a permanent thing. We can always tear it up."

She looked doubtful but didn't argue, as usual.

With the knowledge that he had her trapped, relief flowed through Axell's veins. In celebratory triumph, he leaned over and kissed Maya's worried frown. It felt so right, he let adrenaline overrule caution and transferred the kiss to her lips.

Mistake. Hot blood shot downward so fast his brain bubbled air and all intelligence fled. Taking advantage of the easy access supplied by her surprised intake of breath, Axell indulged in the orange-juice sweetness of Maya's mouth. When her tongue hesitantly caressed his, Axell nearly tumbled into the bed with her. Lust had damned well never steered his course before. Not in years, anyway.

Light-headed, he shoved his hands against the pillow and reluctantly peeled his mouth from hers. He wanted another sample. He didn't have that right yet.

Propping himself up with one hand, Axell brushed the wayward strand of purple from her forehead and watched Maya warily. She seemed more bemused than affronted as she stared back at him.

"I'm sorry, I . . ." Axell halted his automatic apology when Maya's lips quirked upward and her eyes crinkled in the corners. She had the most damnable way of laughing at him. "I take that back. I'm not sorry in the least," he said dryly. "And I don't think I'm ready to hear your comments either."

"You definitely haven't lost your Prince Charming status yet," she admitted. "I've been feeling like one of those bedraggled mice Muldoon presents for my approval. Treating me like Cinderella isn't hurting your cause at all."

Axell nodded, afraid to admit his overwhelming relief. The

next few months would be pure torture, but if she accepted his proposal, he could exist on those amazing kisses for a while. He needed another, just to prove it hadn't been a fluke, but he knew better than to press his luck.

"Just don't paint any fairy tales in your head," he warned, pushing himself upright and out of reach of temptation. "I'm no good at flowers and romantic dinners. I spend twelve- and fourteen-hour days at the restaurant. This is no picnic we're embarking on."

The warning helped. As Maya watched Axell stride out, once more the assertive businessman, she understood her place in this "relationship" a little better. She really and truly would be his live-in convenience, someone to keep the children's schedules organized, to keep his personal life in order, to give him sex on demand. She had a sneaking suspicion she might manage that last, but she already knew she'd be a failure at the rest. Organization was not one of her stronger qualities.

With a tear in her eye from the devastating tenderness of his kiss, she wondered if one out of three would count, because he was offering almost everything she had ever dreamed of, and she had a hard time not believing in her dreams.

❧ EIGHTEEN ❧

Okay, who stopped payment on my reality check?

Curled in a corner of the family room sofa, wrapped in a cotton throw cover, Maya fashioned a sleek version of a paper jet out of construction paper while Matty bounced in the chair on the far end of the room and flung her last model with appropriate roaring noises. Constance preferred the more sedate pastime of rubbing balloons on her sweater to create static electricity and hanging them on the wall so Alexa could admire them. Maya didn't think the infant cared one way or another at this point, but blowing up the balloons kept Constance happily occupied, and her balloon design was quite artistic. Unfortunately, the balloons had captured Muldoon's interest, and he had staked out a place on the floor where he could wait for them to fall. He'd already dug his nails into one, surprising the cat as much as Constance.

Alexa, bless her little heart, slept right through the speakers blaring the sound track from *Pocahontas*. Maya figured the child had to learn to cope with noise if she was spending her days at the school after this week, and if babes in the womb could bond with a mother's voice, then she'd probably bonded with the blare of speakers and screams of children by now, too.

Maya could easily adapt to the illusion that this was really her home, that she could relax in the security of not worrying where the next meal would come from, and that all she had to do was make certain the children were happy and well loved. She didn't often have the luxury of living a dream, so she indulged herself with these few hours of true bliss. Without the fairy dust of magical kisses, the illusion would wear off soon enough.

With surprise, she heard the garage door opening. After his comment about twelve-hour days, she really hadn't expected Axell to return before she had the children in bed. She hadn't deliberately planned to spring her guerrilla warfare on him so soon, but he might as well have a taste of it now that he was here. Carefully folding the last crease into her paper jet, Maya flung it in Matty's direction just as Axell walked through the door wearing his raincoat and juggling a pizza box and a briefcase. It was only sheer coincidence and an amazing amount of her brand of luck that the jet ricocheted off Axell's nose and plummeted toward the balloon-covered wall. Muldoon yowled and struck as two of the balloons bounced in front of him.

Constance cried out and raced to save her creation, Alexa screamed in startlement at the sudden noise, and Matty—apparently needing equal attention—fell off the chair. Axell threw Maya what she could only deem a wry and accepting look as he dropped the briefcase to save the teetering pizza from his startled stumble.

"I don't believe for a minute you're capable of planning this," he stated stoically as he set the box on a table, helped Matty from the floor, and leaned over to kiss Constance on the head as she babbled about her balloons.

Maya stifled a sharp spike of longing as she watched this handsome, elegant man awkwardly patting a sniveling five-year-old on the back, then leaping to retrieve popped balloons from the cat. The man had promise, she'd grant him that, and she shivered a little at the niggling image of all that single-minded determination focused on her.

"Nah," she responded inelegantly, dismissing that stray thought. "If I'd *planned* chaos, Matty would be quietly coloring at the table, Constance would be reading in her room, and Alexa would be sound asleep. I gave up on planning long ago." Maya nodded at the pizza. "I do, however, know how to cook a nutritional meal. I started with something easy, but they'll never eat it now."

Axell had the grace to look embarrassed as he nodded for the children to carry the box into the kitchen. "There's never anything in the refrigerator, and I didn't think you were ready to attempt the grocery store." As the children raced into the other room, he bent over the infant cradle to check on Alexa. "Has she been sleeping through this racket? Constance used to shriek every time I shut a door."

He crouched beside the cradle, still wearing his strikingly tailored raincoat, the one with the caped shoulders that made him look even broader than usual. His square face was pensive as he surrendered his large finger to little grasping ones. Even though that raincoat was a feared symbol of authority to her, Maya knew she was in serious danger of losing her lonely heart to this man. The poor devil instinctively took care of everyone around him, but he had no clue how to accept the same in return.

"It just depends on what they're used to." She shrugged off the topic. "I'm not as good as your chef, but I've got bean soup cooking in the kitchen. Have you eaten?" She tried to dismiss her reaction to him, but she knew it for what it was—the burning desire to have a man's love to fulfill her impossible dream of a family.

She would have to cure Axell of his absurd notion of marriage before she fell any deeper. She knew her nature too well. Without the bonds of love, at the first sign of trouble, she'd be out of here, just as she'd done with Stephen.

He stood and shrugged off his coat. "Bean soup sounds delicious. We actually had beans?" Axell offered his hand to help her from the deep cushions of the sofa.

His fingers were firm and warm and slightly callused as they closed securely over hers. As much as she'd like to, she couldn't dismiss him as one of the effete rich. He was a working man, like all the other men she'd ever known. He just happened to be more successful at what he did.

"In the back of the cabinet. And there were frozen onions and carrots in the freezer. I had to use a ham slice for seasoning, but it looked like it had been in the freezer so long it wouldn't have had much use for anything else. I even found a package of cornmeal without weevils, which is a miracle since I suspect it's been in there since Noah invited them on his ark."

Axell grimaced. "Kitchen cabinets are not high on my priority list, and they're not on the cleaning service's list of chores. Make a grocery list and I'll run in later."

The phone rang before she could reply, and as Axell carried the infant seat into the kitchen, she grabbed the receiver.

"Is Axell there?" a breathless female voice asked from the other end of the line.

"Yes, may I ask who's calling?" Maya had a sneaking suspicion she knew, and throwing a naughty glance over her shoulder, she verified that Axell was caught up in handing out pizza and not paying attention to her. She could tear down walls as fast as he could build them.

"This is Katherine, at the restaurant. I need to speak with him, please."

"He's busy at the moment. Could I take a message?" The man deserved some time to eat his supper. Unless the restaurant was on fire, she couldn't see any reason for interrupting him. Of course, ticking off the miniskirted model he called an assistant was a plus, too. She would have to watch these jealous impulses.

"We have a drunk and unruly at the bar already, and one of the kitchen staff didn't show up. We need him back here, ASAP."

Maya heard the irritation in the woman's voice, but she suspected it was as much at having to leave a message as over the problems arising at the bar. She knew procrastination and dereliction of duty when she saw them. She'd been as guilty of laziness as the next person, in her lifetime. She checked to see if Axell was still occupied—he was watching her suspiciously as he spooned soup into bowls—and lowered her voice.

"He says the bartender can heave out the drunk or call the cops, and you can handle the staff problem in whatever manner you consider most efficient. He'll be down there after he's eaten and put the kids to bed. After all, we wouldn't want him accused of neglecting his daughter, would we?"

The dead silence on the other end indicated a direct hit. With a smile, Maya gently hung up the receiver.

"Problem?" Axell inquired as he set the bowls on the table between the kids.

"Nothing someone else can't handle. I didn't have enough shortening for the corn bread. I hope it turned out all right."

His eyes narrowed suspiciously at her evasion, but he did no more than go for the dishrag as Matty knocked over his glass of milk.

"May I come in?"

The elderly voice quavered, and Maya jerked her head up. She hadn't heard the bells chiming over the door, but then, she'd been feeding Alexa and not paying much attention.

"We're not open," she answered gently, wondering why on earth an old man would even bother with a New Age store like this. The sunlight through the windows behind him cast his face in shadow, but he seemed vaguely familiar.

"That's all right. The girl who worked here before, is she coming back?"

All her protective instincts leapt into gear. Cautiously, Maya leaned her head to one side so she could better see the newcomer. "Mr. Pfeiffer?" she asked incredulously, finally recognizing his silhouette. "You know my sister?"

"We talked sometimes," he answered diffidently. "She's an angry young woman. I hope she's all right."

Maya laid the sleeping infant in the car cradle Axell had carried in for her. He'd objected to her coming to the store, but she'd pointed out that if she could stand in line at the court-house to get a marriage license, she darned well could do the shop books. She couldn't believe she'd actually agreed to the marriage license. Still, she had time to argue him out of going through with a real wedding.

"If being in prison is all right, then I suppose she's just dandy," Maya replied with more sarcasm than she intended.

Mr. Pfeiffer had never done anything to harm her. She had no business taking her irritation out on him. She'd tried calling Cleo with the announcement of Alexa's birth, but Cleo had never returned the call.

"She got that self-destructive streak from your grandmother," Mr. Pfeiffer continued, as if he'd heard her thoughts. "Back then, it was alcohol, though. We didn't have drugs." He hesitated, leaning on his cane more heavily, then glanced at Alexa. "Your daughter?"

The crack about their "grandmother" had nearly stolen Maya's wits. Unscrambling them wasn't easy. "You knew our grandmother?"

"Too well," he admitted wryly in his squeaky voice. "But that's ancient history. Will you be keeping the school open?"

She wanted to hear ancient history. She had vague memories of a yard and a puppy, but she thought maybe they'd been reinforced from Cleo's reminiscences. Cleo was three years older than Maya and remembered their parents much more clearly. But whatever memories Maya had of the Carolinas had been printed over with layers and years of other places, other people, and other traumas.

"We just had to close while the creek was up. Selene is looking into asking the Department of Transportation for a bridge through there, but we seem to be at odds with the prevailing establishment." Maya gestured toward the other chair at her table. "Won't you have a seat? I can fix some tea, if you like. I'd like to hear about our grandmother."

"No, I can't stay. Maybe some other time. My nephew is on the transportation board. He may be part of your problem. I'll talk to him. I hope the other building's collapse didn't hurt anyone. It was tainted and I'm not sorry to see it go, but I worried until I'd heard you'd moved your things here."

Maya was still on the grandmother remark and only half heard this commonplace condolence. The word "tainted" stuck, though. "Why tainted?"

He shuffled uneasily toward the door. "Bought with bad money. Don't ever sell yourself to the devil for money." He halted with his hand on the knob. "Tell your sister I asked after her. I hope her little boy is all right."

"Matty's doing fine." Maya hastily got up as the old man turned the knob. "Please, I'd like to talk with you sometime. Could I call on you?"

She caught a glimpse of the old man's sad smile as he turned away. "They're putting me in a nursing home this afternoon. Said I can't take care of myself properly anymore. Can't say that I ever have, but there's no sense arguing. I'll talk to William."

Maya watched as he gingerly stepped into a battered station wagon waiting at the curb. She caught a glimpse of a woman in a faded cotton dress before the car drove off. He didn't look back.

Old Man Pfeiffer knew her grandmother. Maybe there were other people in the town who knew her family.

Not that it mattered, she decided with a shrug. She could remember various "Aunt Janes" and "Uncle Bobs" through her growing-up years, as they'd traveled from Tennessee to Arkansas to Texas, usually one step ahead of the child welfare services. Nobody had ever bothered explaining the family tree, so she had no recollection if the aunts and uncles were her mother's or her father's relations. She just knew none of them had bothered to fight for two lonely little girls after their parents broke up and they'd ended up cold and hungry and stranded in California.

She didn't have much faith in family. Love wasn't something that arose out of blood relations. It was either in a person's heart or it wasn't. It was just curious seeing Old Man Pfeiffer inquiring about Cleo. His question about Matty made her wonder if he'd been the one who sent the telegram warning of Cleo's conviction. Cleo certainly hadn't had any other friends come forward.

Maya didn't have Axell's curiosity, however. Life happened in strange ways and one just swam with the flow. She'd ask Cleo next time she wrote.

She studied the stairway behind her. It needed painting and additional lighting to look welcoming. She wanted Cleo to come home to something nice. But when Cleo returned, would she want Maya and Alexa cramping that tiny apartment? Their lifestyles had never been particularly similar. Cleo might have imagination, but she liked managing things, and Maya didn't like being managed. The friction might jeopardize Cleo's recovery.

She was making excuses. She could live anywhere, with anyone. She'd proved that for years. She didn't want to do it anymore. She wanted her own home. Axell said she could have his. Axell was insane.

And she loved him for his insanity.

Crossing her arms on the table and lowering her head to rest on them, Maya quit throwing up smoke screens and stared clearly at the facts. She would lose her school if she ran back to California and friends. She could lose Matty if she stayed here. Axell Holm offered her a chance to keep both.

Axell Holm represented the kind of authority figure she loved to hate. But that very same Axell Holm had cried as he delivered her daughter, had suffered anguish so deep it had nearly bent him double at the thought of hurting Constance, had chosen to keep a child possibly not his own without argument, and had surrendered his own peace of mind in the process. That was the kind of man she hated to love, because it could be dangerous and lifelong.

Her teacups were the only thing she'd been able to hold on to for a lifetime. Her heart was more fragile than china.

❧ NINETEEN ❧

Women who seek to be equal to men lack ambition.

"Axell Holm! Have you lost your mind? Gossip is flying all over town! Surely you're not really going to marry that little tart?"

Axell turned away from the new busboy he was teaching to store bar glasses. Thank God Maya didn't come equipped with a mother. "Sandra," he replied without attempting to bite back his fury, "if you were a man, I'd pop you one right now. As it is, I'll just ask you to leave. I won't deny you access to Constance, but I damned well don't have to listen to your insults in my own bar."

Sandra's carefully lipsticked mouth fell open. Maybe he should have yelled at her long before this. Maybe keeping a careful curb on his temper was a mistake. He hadn't the patience to study the problem right now. Grabbing Sandra's elbow, Axell steered her toward the front doors.

"We'll duke it out in court. Judge Tony has already assured me he has no problem with Maya Alyssum in Constance's life. His daughter goes to that after-school program, too. All the kids think she walks on water."

"Her sister is a drug addict and convicted felon!" Sandra cried angrily, shaking off his hold on her. "The woman's had a baby out of wedlock! Who knows what kind of men and diseases . . ."

Axell caught her elbow again and shoved her out the open doors. "Out, Sandra. Go home and find a life." He slammed the door after her and shot the bolt. The restaurant wouldn't open for another hour anyway.

Fury still steaming through his blood, he swung around at the sound of clapping. Axell's kitchen staff and Headley stood in the far doorway, applauding his bad behavior. He really couldn't believe this. All his life he'd tried to be a model of mature control, and these morons were cheering his loss of it.

Not Katherine. She shot him a look full of venom and flounced out without a word. Headley shrugged. The chef—watching Katherine's hips swing in her miniskirt—sighed in regret, and the female staff grinned hugely.

"What the hell are you all staring at?" Axell yelled. "Don't you have anything better to do?"

The staff scattered. Headley remained.

"It takes guts to fight the establishment." Headley wandered back to the bar and helped himself to a bottle of ginger ale from the shelf. "Your father used to smile and keep his thoughts to himself rather than raise a stink, but he got things done. Saw him twist a gun from a madman once, then grin and pat the man on the back. He taught you well. You'll need your fighting gear in shape, though, if you're planning on running for office with a woman like Maya as wife. She'll have every old biddy in town clucking with disapproval. The Garden Club will probably repossess your front lawn."

"Maya would just make a duck pond of the remains." Axell grabbed a bottle of mineral water, contemplated ripping the cap off with his teeth but giving it a vicious twist instead. His father hadn't been any better with women and kids than he was. The old man had worked eighteen-hour days and expected his son to do the same. Axell had once thought his mother had died of loneliness.

"Women!" he growled in frustration, throwing back a gulp of water. "Why the devil am I doing this to myself?"

"Because you need a challenge?" Headley asked dryly.

That could very well be. Axell slumped on a bar stool. Some men climbed the Himalayas. Others sailed around the world in forty-foot boats. Axell Holm married purple-haired gypsies. It made some kind of crazy sense. What else would one do in Wadeville, North Carolina, for a challenge?

"All right, Headley, if I'm gonna do this, you're gonna help me." Axell slammed the bottle down decisively. "Dig out the dirt on that new shopping development. Our mealy-mouthed mayor is up to his ass in it somehow. Two can play at this game."

"Not if one plays fair and the other doesn't," Headley warned. "Politics is an evil business and you're going to get your hands burned before this is all over."

Axell glared at the reporter. "Who said I'm playing fair?"

Headley grinned. "That's right. You've got our own Miss Alyssum on your side. That's definitely stacking the deck."

He walked out, cackling. Axell took another swig of his water. Maya wasn't capable of stacking decks. That would take planning. Maya would simply knock the whole card pile on the floor, kick it under the counter, and bring out her tarot deck.

For some idiot reason, that turned him on so fiercely, he had to swing around and face the bar to hide his arousal.

Damn, but he hoped he wasn't thinking with the part in his pants instead of his head. He'd been down that road before, and it was a dead end. He'd damned well better be certain of what he was doing before he did it this time.

"You're marrying Axell Holm!" Selene repeated, probably for about the third or fourth time, Maya figured. "You're going to live in that brick yuppie house in the middle of yuppie burbs and tool around in a Beamer? You're a cop-out, Maya Alyssum, a real cop-out. I can't believe you're doing this!"

Glumly, Maya couldn't believe she was doing it either— hadn't even realized she'd decided to do it—but the news was all over town. All the parents dropping their kids off at school this afternoon had made it a point to personally stop by the office and congratulate her.

"Well, I probably won't be driving the Beamer after Axell finds out I came back here," she admitted, leaning over to check that Alexa was still sleeping quietly in a curled up little ball. "After we dropped off the kids and went back to town, he gave me the keys so I could go home and nap." Home. She couldn't believe she'd said that. That mansion in the country, home? No way.

Selene wrapped her fingers in her glossy long braids and yanked. "Listen to you! You'll be going to garden parties and PTA meetings and doing lunch with the mayor's mother." She stopped and thought about that. "Maybe that won't be half bad. . . ."

"Get your head right down off that cloud now," Maya warned. "I don't do parties and lunches. My place is here with these kids, and don't you forget it. This school is my dream. We're going to go full-time, sell our concept to banks and factories in a few years, take it nationwide after that. Kids deserve love and attention and can learn a damned sight more than teachers have time to teach in school, and I'm going to see they get every opportunity. If I have to marry Axell Holm to get it, then I'll marry him."

Selene collapsed in the desk chair and stared at her shrewdly. "You're not marrying him to keep this school. I can keep this school together. This is my vision, too, and I'm not about to let those kids down. Maybe if I'd had a teacher like you, I'd have stayed in school." She narrowed her eyes. "You're marrying him because of Alexa, and Matty, and probably Constance. You've got shit for brains, girl."

"Well, no one ever said I was the brightest bulb in the chandelier." Maya tucked the blanket more firmly around Alexa's feet. "Old Man Pfeiffer stopped by the shop this morning. He said he knew my grandmother and Cleo. Do you know anything about that?"

"Why the hell would I know what the old goat knows? Everyone says he went crazy as a coot after his wife died." She frowned at her own thoughts. "If Mayor Arnold knew what a good deal we got on this lease, he'd have the heirs claiming Pfeiffer insane. The mayor sure is pretty, but he's got more devious brains than I do."

Maya worried at a loose strand of her hair. "He said something about his nephew on the transportation board being part of our road problem out here."

Selene jotted a note. "I'll look into it. I didn't know there was a Pfeiffer on the board, but it could be on his wife's side."

Satisfied she wouldn't get any more from Selene, Maya lifted the infant seat and headed for the door. She could hear the shouts of the children enjoying story time in the schoolroom. The substitute teacher was working out just fine. Maybe they could hire her full-time for the summer session.

She felt guilty leaving Constance and Matty in the substitute's hands, but despite her brave words, she did need the rest. And she probably ought to stop by a grocery store. She couldn't feed the kids bean soup every night as if they were living on food stamps.

Or maybe she could. She still didn't have any money.

Maya bounced her forehead off the steering wheel as she cursed her helplessness. She was driving a damned BMW, living in a mansion, and she still didn't have enough money in her pocket to buy beans.

She was very definitely not cut out for this life.

Axell entered the house through the garage door, carrying plastic sacks of groceries, and almost smiled at the sonorous chanting of monks blaring through his expensive sound system. No one had played the damned stereo in months, maybe years. He wasn't even certain he remembered how it worked. Leave it to Maya to figure it out.

His smile slipped as he entered the empty kitchen. He didn't expect supper on the table. Maya had called with the grocery list so he knew she didn't have anything to prepare. He'd just expected the kids or the cat or something to be in here to greet him.

All right, so he wasn't the center of anyone's universe. Leaving the groceries on the table, he wandered into the family room, but they hadn't even turned the lights on. If Maya wasn't in the kitchen or family room, was she still in bed? He'd never seen her so much as glance in any other room of the house.

With a shiver of trepidation, Axell turned down the hall in the direction of Maya's bedroom. Maybe the kids were playing in their rooms. He didn't think Matty had slept in the one he'd been assigned yet, but his toys were beginning to gather in there. The blare of the speakers prevented Axell from hearing the direction of any voices.

A panicky shriek pierced the monks' calm intonations, and Axell broke into a run.

He didn't have to run far. He skidded to a halt outside the formal dining room. The once formal dining room.

He counted heads first. The apparent source of the shriek was Constance, who must have dropped a jar of paint on the plastic sheeting covering the wall-to-wall carpet. Matty watched her in wide-eyed horror. Even baby Alexa appeared to be awake and following the action. Calming his pounding heart, Axell reluctantly dragged his gaze to Maya—his intended wife.

Garbed in loose blue-jean overalls over a bright orange T-shirt, she bent to kiss Constance's head and hug her as she climbed down from her precarious perch on a stool dragged in from the kitchen. The green paint had apparently hit the overalls as much as the sheeting, or Maya had been painting her clothes again.

She was supposed to be resting. Axell's gaze traveled over the rest of the explosion of chaos that had once been his elegant dining room. The heavy formal draperies lay in crumpled heaps across the center of the polished mahogany table. Sunshine flooded the room through the bay windows and the French doors leading onto the deck, reflecting off the crystal of the chandelier and illuminating the cut glass in the display case without need of electricity. His gaze returned to the window. The once neutral ivory wall was now grass green, with what appeared to be a white trellis with purple flowering vines spilling across the green. A lionlike creature crouched in an emerald jungle in the corner.

"This time, it's deliberate, isn't it?" he asked evenly, finally stepping into the room.

Constance shrieked again. From utter silence to shrieks. Maybe he should have been grateful for what he had. As Muldoon purred and wrapped cat hair around his ankles, Axell tried to temper his reaction. He'd promised the house would be hers. Could he live with the result?

Maya tapped his daughter on the head to hush her, then turned her brilliant smile in his direction. Axell felt as if she'd swept his feet out from under him. For a smile like that, he'd *live* in her damned jungle.

"Well, most of it was deliberate," she admitted. "These are the only colors I could find at the school. I've got goop that will take any paint off the carpet, but most of it's on the plastic. What do you think?" She gestured at the rampant vine encaging the lion.

"I'm thinking the draperies will hide it." What was he supposed to say? He figured she expected something, but he'd be damned if he knew what it was. The room had looked fine the way it was. No one ever used it. He gave dinners at the restaurant, where the staff could prepare them. Angela had hated cooking.

Maya aimed her paintbrush at his nose but didn't close in for the kill. "You're supposed to say it makes the room a hundred percent more cheerful. I'll send the draperies out for cleaning, but I don't see any reason to hang them again. It could be a wonderful room with all this sunlight."

Grateful she hadn't chosen enormous red dragons for ornamentation, Axell eyed the huge windows skeptically. "You won't have any privacy."

Maya dropped her brush in the paint can, and wiping off her hands on her overalls, crossed the room and looked up at him. He'd known she wasn't large, but without her big belly in front of her, she was almost delicate. Still, her head reached past his shoulders, and she wasn't afraid to tap his jaw with her long fingers. He liked the contact with those long, slender—paint-splattered—fingers.

"You have an acre of lawn and a field of trees out there.

How much privacy do you need? Lighten up, Holm. You've got kids who will want to play out in that enormous yard. Do you want to watch them play, or eat by candlelight? Or are we changing our minds?" she asked tauntingly.

Her voice shivered up and down his spine as much as her touch. He saw the challenge in her turquoise eyes, and he glared back. "That's what this is all about, isn't it? You're pushing the boundaries, seeing how far you can go before I break."

Axell's composure snapped as Maya's long lashes blinked in disconcertion. The day had been long and frustrating. He deserved a little compensation for his patience. Digging his hands into the wild tangle of Maya's curls, Axell cupped her head and prevented her from looking away. The power of that touch torched a wildfire in his blood, but for the sake of the children, he corraled it.

"I'm not breaking, Maya Alyssum," he whispered so the kids couldn't hear. "Paint posies on the ceiling if you like. Fly kites from the roof. But two months from now, I'll have you in my bed. Want to redecorate it first?"

And then he did what he'd been longing to do since the last time. He kissed her.

December 1945

Helen sent me a frightening letter today. I think she must have been in her cups when she sent it, but I've never seen her drink enough to say such things. I'm worried about her. I need to get her away from that bar and her evil companions. If we married, I could support her, but not in the style of the Arnolds, or even in the style in which she lives now. The old man has promised me a management position, but I'd be lucky to have a job if I marry Helen. I could look elsewhere, but without the backing of a wealthy family, I'd be fortunate to earn as much as Helen's bartender. She'd hate me for taking her away from the bright lights and music.

I'll hate myself if I don't.

❧ TWENTY ❧

Mind like a steel trap—rusty and illegal in 37 states.

The house was dark when Axell drove into the garage. Even for a Friday night, he was unusually late. Katherine's resignation hadn't helped. He'd had to handle host duties while hastily training one of the waitresses for the job. He didn't know what he'd do for an assistant manager. Hire a man, he figured glumly. Women were too unpredictable.

He veered toward the family room to turn off the table lamp and paused at the sight of Maya curled up on the couch, wrapped in the throw as usual, her hair spilling over the edges like part of the tapestry. Axell thought her asleep until he entered the room, and she stared up at him with wide, fathomless eyes. It was those eyes that had held him captive from the first. Like the ocean, they held mysteries that would take a lifetime to explore.

"Can't sleep?" he asked warily. With Maya, he knew better than to expect a simple explanation.

She set aside a paperback with a single rose on the front and wiped her eyes. She'd been crying over a novel, and he wondered if it was one of Angela's romance books.

"You don't have to marry me just to have sex," she announced, but her voice was whispery and not at all as firm as she probably would have liked.

Dropping his briefcase, Axell collapsed on the sofa beside her. "Why not just hit me upside the head with a bat when I come in?"

She sniffed, and he handed her his handkerchief.

Rubbing her nose, she attempted a glare. "I'm a pacifist. I don't believe in violence."

Axell's shoulders shook with laughter. He couldn't believe he was laughing after a day like this. He wanted to howl and roll on the floor, but she'd probably think him insane. Besides, he'd wake the kids. Chuckling anew at the thought of the chaos that could ensue, he shook his head.

"What's so funny about that?" she demanded.

"Passivity." He bit back another chuckle and leaned his head against the sofa. It was kind of nice sitting here in the semi-dark, hearing a human voice instead of the dead emptiness he'd lived through these last few years. "Pacifists are rarely passive, or even peaceful." He turned his head and sought her face in the dim glow of the lamp. His unholy curiosity inspired his next question. "Are you saying you'd go to bed with me without marriage?"

She glowered and tucked the handkerchief somewhere in her lap. She was wearing the lacy blue nightgown Selene had given her, but the cotton throw covered most of it. He'd have to buy her a regular robe. Something green to go with that glorious sunburst of red hair. And a gown to match. Something short and seductive.

"As if you have to ask," she sniffed. "You probably have women waiting in line."

A surge of lust shot Axell's already aroused hormones into overdrive. He really did want to howl with laughter over her jealousy, but the chuckles died in his throat. He looked back over the lonely nights of the past two years, the few furtive couplings, the awkward undressings and whispered questions, and he wondered why the hell he'd bothered at all. His laughter emerged more as a curt bark. "Not so I've noticed."

"Well, there's your problem. You don't notice." She sounded more sure of herself now. "You walk right by women as if they're hat racks. You don't pick up on signals."

His chuckle was a little more real this time. She looked like an outraged gypsy princess wrapped in that shawllike thing with the light illuminating her hair. His gaze fastened on her slender, unadorned fingers. Rings. He'd have to buy rings. He looked up and caught her fascinated gaze. Fascinated. By him. That shot another lightning bolt straight to his groin. He'd need a lap robe of his own.

Something in her narrowing gaze warned this wasn't the time to shrug off her observations, and it was definitely not the time to indulge in *Playboy* fantasies. A challenge, he remembered. Dealing with Maya would be a challenge.

"I don't want to have to pick up on signals," he answered carefully. "I want to know precisely where I stand without interpreting sign language."

She cocked her head like a little bird, studied him carefully, then broke into her beaming gypsy smile. "You're marrying me because I have a mouth and use it?"

His gaze dropped to strawberry-luscious lips and he nodded without thinking. "I sure hope so."

She laughed with clear bell-like chimes that took on a note of wickedness as she finally understood the direction of his tired mind. Leaning over, she kissed his cheek, then boldly, she licked his ear.

His flagpole shot straight up.

"You don't need marriage, you just need a teacher," she whispered tauntingly.

Before Axell could grab her, she twisted away and stood up, leaving him with a handful of cotton throw.

"I've found the teacher," he threw after her departing sway. "I'm just waiting for the lessons."

She shot him an upraised-eyebrow look over her shoulder before disappearing into the darkness of the hall.

Axell remained lying there against the sofa cushions with the cotton throw over his pleasantly throbbing lap and a smile on his face. Definitely a challenge, he decided.

He could spend the next two months planning her seduction. That should certainly give him an incentive to survive the chaos.

"I was managing," Maya whispered as Axell grasped her elbow and nearly dragged her out of the church pew. He'd trapped her into this, damn the man. The instant they'd applied for a marriage license, the whole town heard about it. He'd known she wouldn't fight the whole town.

"So was I," Axell agreed, steering her determinedly toward the back of the church. "But 'managing' isn't the same as living. What are you afraid of?" he demanded. "We're two intelligent adults perfectly capable of rationally talking out any problems. When the kids get older, if it isn't working out, we can get divorced. What do you have to lose?"

He said that so firmly and logically, Maya couldn't help but stare at him with incredulity. She wanted to ask him what the hell kind of household he'd grown up in. She met only curiosity and a glimmer of impatience in his square-jawed expression as he waited for her to follow him. She wondered what he would do if she licked that delicious cleft in his chin or blew in his perfectly symmetrical ears, and bit back a nervous giggle at the thought. He really had absolutely no idea of the devastation the emotional tornado of divorce could wreak. To him, it was just a tactical retreat.

His gray gaze heated as she bit back her disbelieving smirk. All right, so under that logical Virgo mind lurked a boiling cauldron of Scorpio testosterone—she'd got his birthdate from the marriage license and drawn his chart. Definitely Scorpio moon. So, maybe dark, brooding, artistic men didn't have a corner on heat. Maybe security was more rational than love. Maybe she'd just gone without sex too long.

Maya dropped her gaze to Axell's deliriously amazing chest. His shirt was so freshly laundered, she could smell the starch. He wore a three-piece gray suit elegant enough to be a tuxedo. She brushed an imaginary speck from his lapel and straightened his white carnation and absorbed his intoxicating presence. He might be stiff, but he definitely wasn't cold. His question, "What do you have to lose?" still hung in the air. She knew the answer—her heart. Her stupid, illogical, breakable heart.

"You wouldn't understand," she sighed. And he really wouldn't. She was just a means to an end for him. Men understood possession and convenience, but they really didn't grasp the frailty of female emotion. So, this man was more careful than most. What more could she ask?

"You really can't fix my life, Axell," she offered in one final protest. "It isn't broken."

"Mine is," he whispered.

She shouldn't feel his pain, but she did. He had everything she'd never had, he merely wanted to add her to his collection, but that broken plea wiped out all argument.

Surrendering, she followed the familiar path of the current rather than fighting against it. "All right, let's get this over. The kids will be bouncing off the walls by now."

Axell cast her an uncertain look, then offered his hand. He didn't know how to take her lack of enthusiasm. He'd walked Maya all through fashionable SouthPark Mall yesterday, offering her any gown she'd like for the occasion. Instead of excitedly running up his credit cards, she'd spurned all the designer dresses and silk suits and lavish accessories in favor of a simple cream eyelet summer gown from the White House. Admittedly, the fitted bodice and long, flowing skirt looked elegant on her newly slender figure, but it had cost nothing in comparison to what he'd been prepared to pay.

Above the scoop-necked gown, Maya wore her thick curls pinned into an unruly twist. Despite the simple elegance, the soft tendrils spilling down her nape and ears aroused the image of a woman who had just climbed from a tumble in bed, producing an uncomfortable urge Axell couldn't assuage for weeks. Firmly clasping Maya's fingers, he led her toward the preacher's office and the small gathering of friends and family waiting for them. They'd both agreed on a small ceremony. At least they'd found common ground in that.

He didn't like admitting it, but he was as nervous as she was. He knew her credentials as a teacher, had watched her at work, and knew she was an ideal mother. He'd spent the better part of his life honing his people observation skills, and he didn't doubt his instincts. Maya Alyssum was a free spirit completely alien to his nature, but she possessed the pure goodness of heart of a child. He was the villain in this piece.

He was terrified he would destroy her, or that she would leave and destroy him.

Axell shoved his intended bride toward the preacher's office.

This time, it would be different. This time, only his head was involved.

"With this ring, I thee wed."

Maya held her breath as Axell slid the delicately braided gold band on the third finger of her left hand. They'd chosen the rings when they'd bought her gown yesterday. Axell's ring was thicker and more imposing, but they'd both admired the identical gold braiding. She'd wanted no diamonds, no ludicrously expensive platinum, nothing extravagant, but she'd still been appalled at the cost of the simple bands. Axell hadn't blinked an eyelash.

The ring fit solidly on her finger, its weight a reminder of all the responsibilities she assumed with the vows she repeated now. Constance in her shining patent leather, frilled anklets, and rapidly deteriorating pin curls stood solemnly to one side of Axell. Matty bounced impatiently at Selene's side. Garbed in an extravagantly silly lace and eyelet gown that neither of them could resist, Alexa squirmed sleepily in the arms of a motherly Sunday-school teacher who had turned out to be an aunt of Axell's. Maya hadn't even considered the possibility of her husband having relatives.

Her husband. He stood there in the sophisticated gray of his three-piece suit, his shoulders no less rugged for their civilized confines. Her heart dived to her stomach as the preacher pronounced them man and wife, and she made the mistake of meeting Axell's gaze. He wore that solemn businessman's expression she knew so well, but she could swear she saw the impish gleam of professorial curiosity lurking behind his eyes as he leaned over to claim his kiss.

Matty emitted "Ooo, yuck" sounds and Constance instantly abandoned her pretense of obedience to leap between them, yet Axell located Maya's mouth with unerring accuracy, and the explosive shock of his kiss shot clear to her toes before Constance succeeded in pushing them apart.

"Can I hold Alexa now, can I?" she demanded.

Maya could read the amusement dancing in Axell's eyes as he silently handed the responsibility of answering to her. She didn't know whether to smack him for his abdication of duty or love him for trusting her with his daughter.

"I think there are people waiting for us in the reception hall," Maya told her gently, taking Constance's hand. "Don't you want some cake and punch first?"

Satisfied that she'd accomplished what she'd set out to do—separate the two most important adults in her life and focus their attention on her—Constance nodded eagerly, loosening a few more limp strands of hair.

Maya tucked a curl behind her stepdaughter's ear and glanced at Axell to see how he took this. He offered a masculine shrug of indifference, but she could see something smoldering behind his eyes that warned it wouldn't always be this simple. He was a patient man, but every man had his limits.

Well, he wanted her to mother his daughter. Now he had what he wanted—let's see how he liked it.

Smiling as their small audience surged forward to offer congratulations, Maya hung on to Constance as Axell grabbed Matty. Gradually, they pushed their way out of the office and into the reception hall.

For the first time in her life, Maya felt the spotlight of an entire community's attention focused on her as she and Axell entered the room.

She would have panicked and run if Axell hadn't firmly draped his arm across her shoulders and held her at his side, introducing her to one and all as his wife.

When she stumbled in her low-heeled sandals, Axell held her steady.

As the crush of the crowd pressed around them and her heart steadied to a hysterical tattoo, Maya felt the ironclad shackles of Axell's control lock around her, and she finally grasped the term "ball and chain."

She'd sworn to provide her daughter a real home. Now she had one, and the walls were already closing in on her.

Did she have any idea what happened to a fish out of water?

❦ TWENTY-ONE ❦

We are Microsoft. Resistance is futile.
You will be assimilated.

"If you'll sign these papers, my lawyer will start work on your adoption of Constance." Axell shoved another sheet of paper across the broad expanse of his desk. "If you think you can get your sister's agreement, this one will begin proceedings for you to assume legal guardianship of Matty. Once that's done, he'll no longer be a ward of the state, and Social Services will have no more control over him."

Maya stared in dismay at the stack of papers collecting on Axell's desk as he pushed still another legal document in front of her.

"Here's the partnership agreement for the Curiosity Shoppe. I've had it drawn up between us and your sister, since the inventory is hers, and as a married couple, we're assuming joint responsibility. I think the threat of a lawsuit will have the building released by next week."

They'd been married for almost three weeks but they still lived together as they had before—Axell as the man in charge and she as his hapless female boarder—with a few exceptions. She now had a checkbook and credit card in her new name and drove a BMW that terrified her. While Cleo's shop was closed, Maya had her teenage clerk polishing the car after school every day as part of her store duties. She didn't dare do so much as chew a piece of gum in its spotless leather interior.

Maya tried scanning the sheets of legalese crossing the desk. Axell had discussed these things with her in their hurried conversations over breakfast or dinner, and they'd all made sense at the time. She'd rather trust him than argue. Taking a deep breath, she started signing where he indicated.

"You really ought to read those things before you sign them," he admonished.

"I could read them until I'm blue in the face and still not know what they say," she admitted. "Since I don't possess anything anyone could possibly want, I figure I'm pretty safe unless one of these is titled 'Articles of Indenture.' "

He smiled wryly as he arranged the sheets in their proper order and inserted them in their respective envelopes as she returned them to him. "I think that was part of the marriage contract. Didn't you read it?"

Axell so seldom smiled, Maya sat back in his fancy office chair and basked in the moment.

"Was that the part that came after 'love, honor, and accept kitten litters'? I didn't get beyond that." Constance and Matty had just adopted a mama cat and her litter, insisting on bringing them home where they'd be more "comfortable."

"You wouldn't," he agreed dryly, pushing back his chair. "I'm thinking of holding a contest at the bar and the winners get free cats. I almost walked on one when I got home the other night."

He walked around the desk and offered a hand to help her from the chair. Axell's thumb brushed her palm as she accepted his offer, and just that caress of sensitive nerve endings reminded her that this "business arrangement" between them had other aspects. It was just a matter of time before he claimed them. She glanced up to the smoky gray of his eyes and tried to envision his broad shoulders naked and looming over her. She didn't know if it was fear or excitement clutching her insides at the thought.

She'd never so coldly entered into any kind of a relationship with a man. She lacked the innate practicality necessary to look at sex as a physical exercise one did for the sake of good health. She rather suspected that was exactly how Axell looked at it.

That realization always had her backing off whenever the

electric jolt shocked her. Axell's smile slipped away as she pulled free and started for the door, but he acknowledged her reaction in no other way. She'd almost rather he had a tantrum when he walked on stray cats at midnight or found purple blotches on his walls. Going to bed with him would be like going to bed with their friendly neighborhood banker.

"Alexa and Matty both have a doctor's appointment this afternoon, so supper will be late and probably out of the freezer," she warned, choosing not to respond to Axell's earlier banter. It was easier to play the role of teacher than to deal with her conflicting emotions.

"I have to go into Charlotte to talk with the lawyers, so I'll be running late, too. Want me to eat at the bar?"

He didn't have to be so damned *understanding*. Maya brushed his cheek with a kiss and opened the office door. "Just let me know so I won't worry. See you later."

She breezed out as if she hadn't a care in the world—she *shouldn't* have a care in the world. For the first time in her life she had a substantial roof over her head, money in her pocket, and copious amounts of food on the table, and all she had to do in return was love a child she would have loved anyway, and eventually, go to bed with a powerful man she would have only admired from a distance under other circumstances. Why did she feel as if disaster would strike at any minute?

Probably because Cleo hadn't returned her letters, the state had inspectors crawling all over the school, Matty's social worker had it in for Axell, Selene wasn't having any luck pulling strings at DOT to have their access road repaired, and she had an automaton husband who would be expecting sex on demand in a few short weeks. At least Constance's grandmother had gone back to Texas—for the time being.

Besides, she'd never known a day in her life when disaster wasn't imminent. She'd learned to roll with the punches. She'd be getting soft if she didn't watch out.

She'd left Matty playing and Alexa sleeping in the new shop with Teresa while she ran next door to sign Axell's papers. She needed to pick up Constance at school and transport the kids to the Impossible Dream for afternoon classes.

The BMW sedan would have more miles on it in a few weeks than Axell had put on it in a year.

She'd parked it in the alley beside the collapsed building so it wouldn't be in the way of the work crew at the new shop. Knowing it was easier to load up Alexa and Matty if she pulled the car around, she hurried down the street, resisting checking on Alexa and the progress of the cleaning people. Cleo wouldn't recognize her inventory when she returned. If she returned. Would Cleo just walk out of prison and disappear?

Trying not to think about that, Maya focused on a man with a ponytail standing in front of the falling down building, staring up at Cleo's old apartment windows. He seemed vaguely familiar, but from a block away, and in this blinding sunlight, she couldn't discern his features. Why on earth would anyone be studying a condemned building? Was this Cleo's erstwhile landlord? She'd thought the old building belonged to some real estate conglomeration.

Something about the way he held himself made her nervous. Preferring not to find out why, she didn't reach for her sunglasses but aimed for the alley. Before she could escape, however, the man turned in her direction, and the bottom dropped out of her stomach.

Stephen.

Fate had a really cruel sense of humor when it chose disasters for her.

Maybe she should learn Axell's narrow path of duty and responsibility and give up the emotional relationships that made her life hell. Maybe she could grow wings and fly.

"Maya!" Stephen hurried across the broken pavement and past the wilting yellow police tape to greet her. "Damn, you look gorgeous! This is the only address I have for you. Surely you're not living here?"

Before she could manage a sensible thought, he'd crushed her in an exuberant hug.

Why had she once thought Stephen sexy? Only a few inches taller than she, he lacked Axell's strength and breadth and probably couldn't lift her if he tried—not that he'd ever tried anything so romantic. He would probably have written a song about the tribulations of fatherhood while she labored giving birth to Alexa. He had a boyish smile and a lovely voice and no character whatsoever. She smacked his T-shirted chest with both hands and shoved away.

"Swell of you to stop by, Stevie," she mocked, swinging on her heel and heading down the alley for the car. "Give me a call sometime and we'll do lunch."

He hurried after her, and grabbing her elbow, jerked her to a halt. Maya shot his encroaching hand a withering look, and he hastily released his grip.

"Look, Maya, I'm sorry, all right? Life's a bitch sometimes, you know that. But I've got that recording contract," he continued excitedly. "I can take you and the baby back to L.A. Where is she? Does she look like me? Where are you staying?"

Maya stared at him as if he were Peter Pan offering to fly her to Never-Never Land. How had she ever thought this irresponsible idiot was the man of her dreams?

She hadn't, she realized. Stephen was fun, energetic, and talented. She'd once had hopes they could eventually make something of their relationship, but Cleo's arrest had prematurely ended any chance of that. Her pregnancy had just been an unexpected result.

She could blame him for his shameless irresponsibility, but the truth was, she hadn't been much better.

With a sigh, she released her temper. "You'll have to overcome one or two preconceived notions, Stephen," she said dryly. "One being that you ever have a remote chance of imitating fatherhood."

"C'mon, Maya! I've been busy. How can I support a baby unless I'm making money? I'm on the brink now. The studio's talking multi-albums, my agent's lined up a tour, and we're getting a percentage of gate. I can do it."

She really didn't want to take him to Alexa, but what choice did she have? She'd never lied to him. It was a little late to start now. She fought back a familiar bubble of panic.

"Look, I've got people waiting for me. Why don't you go back to your hotel and new girlfriend and I'll call you later, all right?"

"Zita? Is that what this is all about? Don't worry about her. She's just some jealous bitch who hung around the band and screwed things up a lot. I flew into Charlotte from Nashville and hitched a ride from the airport. I figured I could bunk with you until you packed things up. C'mon, let's go to your place and I'll baby-sit. How's that?" He steered her eagerly from the alley toward the glass-plated storefronts lining Main Street.

This was going to look real good. Word would be all over town in hours. Axell was probably watching from his office windows. What the *hell* was she supposed to do?

"I don't expect you to remember these little details, Stevie," she replied acidly, pulling out of his grasp again. Giving up on the car, she hurried toward the new shop. "But my sister got herself locked up, remember? And I flew out here because she has a little boy? None of that has changed."

"I'll ask my agent if he knows a good lawyer. We can make it work. C'mon, Maya . . ." He halted in front of her, forcing her to look at him. "What are you telling me? You picked up a new boyfriend while toting around my baby in your belly?"

He seemed to find the idea so ridiculous she briefly considered punching him for the insult. But remembering how ridiculous the idea really was, she let him off with a smirk and a verbal punch. "No, I picked up a husband, a word with which you're not familiar." Swinging around, she crossed the street and continued her progress toward the haven of company in the new store.

"A husband!" he screamed as he raced up behind her. "You're insane! You can't do that. That's my kid. I've got my rights!"

"We'll see about that, I guess. As far as I'm concerned, a minute's worth of genetic material does not make you a father." This was getting entirely out of hand. She hadn't meant to expel all this bile in public, alienate Stephen, or create a scene of any sort. She'd hoped to have a reasonable conversation and settle matters quietly. She should have known she was incapable of any such rational behavior.

Stephen grabbed her elbow again. Beyond reason now, Maya swung around and slammed her fist into his belly. He had a damned hard belly and didn't flinch an inch.

"Maya, dammit . . ."

"Having trouble, love? Next time, I'll get you a pager with an alarm so you don't have to break your fingers." Axell strolled down the street in their direction, no hurry in his stride, but his eyes were that steely gray Maya recognized instantly.

Stephen dropped her arm and swung to confront the man in business suit and tie. Not completely unintelligent, Stephen relaxed his belligerent stance and stuck out his hand.

"I'm Stephen James, an old friend of Maya's." He said that with enough emphasis even a fool could take his meaning.

Axell was no fool. He didn't take the extended hand. "I'm Axell Holm, Maya's husband." He turned to Maya and gently examined her bare elbow where Stephen had gripped it. "You bruise easily," he commented without inflection.

She didn't need auras or tarot or astrology to recognize the intense vibrations ricocheting between the two men. She'd suffer from testosterone inhalation if she stood between them too long.

"Redheads have thin skin," she responded ambiguously. "I'm taking Stephen to see Alexa, but I really need to go pick up Constance and get over to the school. I don't have time for discussions."

"Arguments," Axell corrected. "And you're very good at weaseling out of them. I'll get Constance and come back for you." He nodded at Stephen. "We'll talk later."

Axell didn't raise his voice, but the warning was clear. He might as well have posted a sign reading, "Private Property. No Trespassing." Maya bit back an inappropriate urge to giggle. Grown women didn't giggle.

She stood on her toes and kissed Axell's cheek, just to

watch both men flinch. "Don't slay any dragons on the way. You know how the scales litter the road."

She thought he almost grinned. Instead, he caught her waist, planted a much sounder kiss on her lips, and when she almost went limp, he set her back down again. "I'll just rip out his tongue and you can serve it for dinner. Don't tell Matty, though, or he'll turn vegetarian."

"That'll be the day." Last night, Matty had managed to pick every pea out of the casserole she'd disguised them in.

As Axell calmly walked away, Stephen growled in disgust. "You couldn't wait, could you? You had to go for the money."

Maya fisted her fingers and waved them in his face. "He doesn't like me to break my fingers, Stevie. Do you want to see Alexa or take me to the hospital?"

"You're a ditz, you know? A first-class ditz. You've probably got the kid singing 'Aquarius.' " As she swung open the door to the new shop, he caught and held it for her.

"No, I'm into country now. We sing in the sunshine." Grateful for the wispy dress Axell had bought for her, Maya flaunted her newly slender figure past Stephen and into the chaos of the cleaning and unpacking of Cleo's stock. They were immediately swamped with a thousand questions, but she was determined to get through this as quickly and painlessly as possible. With a wave of her hand, she walked past the crew and headed for the stairs and the kids.

"What are you doing, taking up shopkeeping? I thought you wanted to be a teacher." Stephen followed close on her heels.

"I am a teacher. I'm part owner of a day school. This is Cleo's. I'm just helping out while she's away."

"Away, yeah. That's a polite way of putting it. C'mon, Maya. We know each other too well. You weren't cut out for this small-town shopkeeper thing. Why'd you do it? If it's money, I'll have money. I don't want my kid growing up to be a country hick."

If she were the confrontational type, she'd shove him down the stairs, Maya mused. Normally, aggression wasn't her style. Maybe she'd absorbed a little of that loose testosterone.

She didn't even bother looking at him. She couldn't imagine why she'd enjoyed looking at him before. Nordic gods were infinitely more appealing than skinny musicians with long hair. The adolescent tingle at the base of her belly threatened to ignite at the thought of Axell calmly stalking to her rescue.

"This is scarcely country. We're minutes from one of the fastest growing cities in the south. If you'd open your narrow mind, you'd see this is an ideal place for a child to grow up, with all the benefits of city and country and none of the disadvantages of the artificial life in L.A. I'm never going back."

Stephen didn't reply. Teresa appeared with Alexa in her arms, and his attention was focused entirely on his daughter.

Maya bit her lower lip and wondered how she'd thought this would be easy. Or if she'd thought at all.

❧ TWENTY-TWO ❧

Out of my mind, back in five minutes.

Axell gritted his teeth and tried to pleasantly question Constance about her day as they drove into town. He'd learned from Maya how to be a little more subtle. If he asked, "How's your day?" which made sense to him, Constance would only grunt and shrug. If he asked, "Did the teacher judge your essay today?" he got a more direct response. But today, she seemed to pick up on his tension and did little more than cross her arms and glare out the window in unconscious imitation of him.

Being a parent was damned hard, harder even than persuading the town council to talk sense. Kids picked up on all the wrong signals and ignored the right ones. With a sigh, Axell tried the Maya approach. "All right, I'm upset, but not with you. Grown-ups get mad at lots of things that don't have anything to do with kids."

Steering the car around a particularly treacherous curve, Axell felt more than saw his daughter's curious look.

"Maya gives me a code word to let me know when she's angry with me."

That was a new one. "You don't mind if Maya gets mad?"

Constance shrugged. "Everybody gets mad. She says 'we'll talk' is a good code word, 'cause that's what most people say when they're mad and trying not to show it."

Amazed, Axell absorbed this tidbit. How many times had he said "we'll talk" and meant he'd like to verbally chop someone into sushi? He'd probably said it to Maya. The damned woman was entirely too perceptive, and that seemingly open smile of hers hid a mind with more twists and turns than he'd ever explore in a million years. She was downright dangerous. And he'd left her back in that apartment with her lover. Shit.

"All right, then I'll say 'we'll talk' if I'm mad at you," he forced his thoughts back to Constance, "but it still means I just want to talk so we can work things out, okay?"

Constance considered that briefly, then nodded. "Okay. Are you mad at Maya?"

Realizing they were actually having a conversation, Axell was almost disappointed that they had reached town. Communicating with his daughter could have some real benefits. "Yeah, I'm probably mad at Maya, but it's not her fault. And I'm madder because I got mad, and I don't like to lose my temper."

Constance grinned. "That's what Maya said. She says you get mad at yourself and not me."

"I'm beginning to think Maya is a witch," he muttered as he parked in front of Cleo's shop.

"Like Glinda, the Good Witch." Constance nodded knowingly. "Their hair is a lot alike."

Axell chuckled. "Except Maya's is red."

"I wish my hair was red," Constance said wistfully as she unbuckled her seat belt.

"Your hair is just right the way it is. It matches your eyes. You'll be beautiful like your mother one of these days."

"I want to be pretty like Maya," Constance replied with an almost rebellious tone as they entered the store.

"Well, Maya being a witch and all, she might manage that." Axell prayed Maya had set a spell on her ex while he'd been gone, or he'd have to throw his ass out a window. He didn't think a charge of assault would help him maintain his liquor license. The drug charge rumors were only just settling down.

"The Impossible Dream" blared from the speakers as they reached the top of the stairs. One of these days he'd figure out if Maya's choice of music reflected her mood. Maybe what he needed was more code words. Figuring out women was worse than untangling a Rubik's cube. How the hell was he supposed to tell where they stood?

The first thing he saw as he walked into the front room was the skinny musician in tight jeans cradling Alexa in his arms. Axell wasn't prepared for the fury and possessiveness punching him in the gut at the sight of another man holding his daughter. His daughter. He hadn't fully realized how he'd come to think of her. Alexa was his. And so was Maya. Primitive jungle instincts would have him circling the intruder shortly, waiting to rip out his throat.

Axell automatically swung to the corner where Maya stood, hoping her serenity would civilize his unexpected surge of violence. He knew instinctively where she was at any given moment, just as he'd known to look out his office window when she walked down the street with Stephen.

She wore her fey smile as she rocked with Matty on her lap, but Axell had the gut feeling that she was anything but happy. Gravitating in her direction, he introduced Stephen to Constance, then placed a reassuring hand on Maya's shoulder. She didn't relax, but she threw him a grin that trembled only a little.

"I can take you and the kids out to the school, if you'd like," he offered. "Why don't you invite Stephen to supper?"

"You have the lawyer, and the kids have the doctor's . . ." She gestured helplessly.

Stephen frowned at both of them. "We have to talk."

Axell grinned. He couldn't help it. The situation had reached the limits of absurdity and Maya's code phrase pushed him over. With the ease he used in escorting drunken bar patrons to a taxi, he crossed the room and appropriated Alexa from Stephen's arms. He'd learned a lot about holding babies these past weeks, and he handled her with expertise now. "We'll talk, but not now," he told the startled young musician as he shifted Alexa to his shoulder. "Maya's not strong enough yet for major battles. This apartment is empty for the moment. Make yourself at home and we'll get back to you."

Oddly, Axell had the feeling Maya bristled like her cat as

he took the reins, but that's what he did—took charge. She might as well get used to it.

"I'm not a weak, helpless idiot," she whispered in protest as the kids ran down the stairs ahead of them a minute later.

"No, but you're supposed to pretend you are so I can feel like Amazon Man. This is the south. Learn the culture." Axell lifted the squirming baby from his shoulder and dropped her in Maya's arms. "She's wet."

"Amazon Man." She shook her head in disbelief. "Why do I do this to myself? You'd think by now I'd have learned."

"You're a quick study," he reassured her. Then before she could climb into the car and escape into the protection of the children, Axell caught her by her pointy little chin and made her look at him. "And you're doing it because you're as curious as I am to see what we'll be like in bed."

That shocked her into speechlessness, he noted with satisfaction. He'd damned well never said anything so blatantly suggestive to any woman in his life, but with Maya, he felt free to say or do anything he pleased without frightening her. He could really get into that kind of understanding.

But first, he had to eliminate the competition.

"All right, Chickadees, what do *you* think Madeline should have told the teacher?"

"She should have told the truth!" two of the Chickadee girls chirped.

"That she's full of dog poop," the outnumbered male Chickadee answered sullenly.

Silently, Maya had to agree with the boy. Sometimes, honesty just didn't pay and dog poop was much more satisfying. She didn't think the children's parents would agree.

She held up the book she'd been reading to them. "Well, let's see if Madeline chooses truth or dog poop."

The children laughed and giggled, and she relaxed into the story. She loved the Madeline books. Maybe she would run away to New York and sell children's book illustrations. Anything was better than a town with both Axell and Stephen in it.

Or maybe even the whole state wasn't wide enough to hold

her and all her troubles, she decided a little later as Selene flagged her down before she could escape for the day.

"Did you know that miniskirted bitch of Axell's is working for the mayor now?" Selene demanded as soon as Maya shut the office door.

"I do believe three or four people may have mentioned it," she said, dropping onto the couch. "People do seem to have an interest in Katherine the Long-Legged." She looked at Selene with curiosity. Her partner didn't use words like "bitch" lightly.

Selene ignored her sarcasm. "The Scorned Woman and the Bought Mayor are a bad combination, girl. I oughta know. I went to school with Ralph Arnold back when I bothered going. That man isn't a skirt chaser. He's a manipulator. And so's she."

Selene and the mayor in the same school? A private one, no doubt. Wealthy families around here supported an abundance of them. She didn't follow Selene's train of thought, however.

Sighing with impatience, Selene pointed out the obvious. "Now that we've nailed the school license inspection, those two are pushing for the highway condemnation route, and there ain't a man on that DOT board who's going to see anything but Katherine's legs when she makes her spiel."

"Well, we could always get one of the secretaries to substitute the bill with one favoring us, and hope their minds are so addled they won't notice the difference," Maya suggested brightly.

Selene glared. "That's weak, even for you. All right, spill, girlfriend. Is that Viking of yours giving you grief?"

Maya worked her shoulders edgily beneath the gauzy layers of her dress. "The world's giving me grief. It's nothing new. Alexa's father showed up today."

"And you didn't tell me?" Selene shrieked. "Girl, what did you do?"

"Nothing, yet." Maya stood and reached for the door. "Look, I've got to get the kids to the doctor. I'll tell Axell about the road condemnation thing, though right about now, I'd say he ought to be sick and tired of all my problems."

"Does that musician fellow want you back?" Selene demanded shrewdly. "Is that the problem? You're regretting playing yuppie lady already?"

Maya tilted her head and thought about it. "No, I'm not exactly regretting it. Axell will be a much better father, if only because he'll be there and Stephen wouldn't. I'm just wondering if I should have steered clear of men altogether. They mess up my mind."

"Your mind's already messed, but I agree, men don't help it none. Maybe you should go back to living at the store until you work it out."

"Repay Axell for all his hard work by moving out? I don't think so. Besides, he's installed Stephen in the apartment."

"One round for the white boy." Selene whistled appreciatively. "I thought the place was still closed for repairs."

"Axell thinks we'll get a clean inspection next week. I suppose, if Stephen isn't paying rent, maybe his staying there doesn't count. If I dawdle around long enough, perhaps he'll get tired of waiting and leave me alone. Stephen never hangs around long."

"Oh, no doubt you'll wiggle your way out of this, too, but someday, you're going to hit that wall, girl, and you'll have to face a few realities."

"Yeah, thanks, I needed that reminder on a day like today." With a wry twist of her lips, Maya went to collect the kids.

And with her luck, she supposed she wouldn't see the wall until she ran slap bang into it.

Axell walked into the kitchen as Maya was clearing the table after supper. She caught Matty's glass as he threw it at the dishwasher in his haste to get a hug before Constance did.

"I thought you were eating at the restaurant," she said as noncommittally as she could with her heart banging through her rib cage. Axell didn't exactly have his "happy" face on, but he bent and hugged Matty, as if he were an old hand at dispensing hugs.

"I thought maybe we should talk," he said in the same offhand manner.

Maya glanced up sharply at Constance's snicker, but Axell's expression remained bland. She waved a dirty fork at her stepdaughter. Stepdaughter. She'd never thought to have such a thing, but that was the right legal term, she was certain. "You need to pick out your clothes for tomorrow. Matty, you, too."

Prepared to protest, Constance caught her father's eye, thought better of it, and grabbed Matty's hand. "We'll both wear dragons tomorrow," she said defiantly, dragging Matty after her.

"You never did tell me how you got Constance to dress on her own." Voice still neutral, Axell helped clear the rest of the table.

Baby Alexa was awake but not protesting yet. Maya straightened her in the infant seat rather than face Axell. "It was just her means of getting your attention for a few extra minutes a day. Kids have weird ways of striking back when all's not well in their universe. After she picks out her clothes, I go in and compliment her choice, find a barrette or ribbon that matches, discuss what the other kids are wearing, and she's happy."

"Are you telling me this now so I'll know how to handle the problem after you leave?" he asked quietly.

The glass in Maya's hand smashed to the floor with the same effect as the bombshell Axell had dropped. She stared at it stupidly for all of a minute before bending over to clean it up while furtively glancing up to her husband. Her husband. She was having a hard time adjusting to these labels. This one diminished her somehow, as if she weren't a whole person in her own right any longer.

"What on *earth* made you ask that?" she demanded, almost angrily. She'd had enough confusion from her own head for one day. She didn't need his.

Axell grabbed the infant-seat handle and Maya's elbow with almost the same motion. "You look beat. Let's sit down first."

She shook off his hand. "Fine time to think of that. It's a wonder I didn't fall flat on my face." But the familiar messiness of the family room beckoned, and she escaped to the haven it offered, wrapping herself in the throw as she hit the sofa. Remembering the last time they'd had a heated discussion in here, he'd kicked shoes like footballs, she braced herself. "Explain."

Setting the baby seat on the table, Axell paced the room, straightening picture frames and knickknacks. "Just because a man is a lousy father doesn't mean you can't love him. Stephen's young and good-looking, and from what he says, he probably has an exciting future ahead of him, a much more exciting one than I can offer."

Maya thought if she had the energy, she'd laugh. "You think I crave excitement? If I want excitement, I've got collapsing buildings and road condemnations and Matty's social worker and my sister for excitement. Stephen's brand doesn't begin to compare."

She saw Axell's mouth tighten in disbelief, but she didn't have the power to drive his doubts away. They didn't have that kind of relationship.

"I know I pushed you into this marriage at a time you were vulnerable and didn't have a lot of options," he insisted. "I thought two intelligent people could work it out. But I know women don't think like I do, that they want things I can't always give, and I don't want to be the cause of your unhappiness. If you want out, better say it now, before our lives get any more entangled and the kids get hurt too badly."

Maya shivered. She'd been shoved aside so often in her life, she knew when it was time to pack up and leave. Had it just been her, she would be out the door right now. But she had the kids to think of, and she knew damned well that kids didn't need to be shoved from pillar to post like so much furniture. For them, she would learn to dig in and hold her ground.

If she fought him, would she drive him away even faster?

Uncertainty swamped her. Since the age of ten she'd been misunderstood, unloved, unwanted. . . .

Was it too much to ask for just one person to see that she was perfectly rational, and as capable of doing the right thing as everyone else? What the hell did he think she would do, hop Stephen's concert bus with infant in arms and play groupie?

She was afraid to look at him, afraid to see disapproval in the eyes of a man she'd come to respect and rely on. She'd hoped . . . But she knew all about the uselessness of hope.

"Unless you're telling me that you're tired of my problems and want me gone, I'm not going anywhere, Axell." She might as well throw down the oars and start bailing. "You knew I was a disaster waiting to happen when we married. Are you chickening out at the first rough spot in the road?"

He stiffened, and crumpled the discarded newspaper in his hand. "I'm not chickening out of anything. I just don't want you running off in the middle of the night, leaving Constance brokenhearted."

If she wasn't feeling so battered, she'd slide into his arms and kiss him. This wasn't about her! This was about his late wife, Angela, and maybe his parents, and all the other people in his life who'd left him. Relief overwhelmed her, and she had to fight back a smile as she reassured him instead of the other way around. "There's no thunderstorm, there's no sports car in the garage, and I think I'd like a gardenia bush outside that bay window. Can I order gardenia bushes planted? Or do I have to dig the hole myself?"

Axell stared at her as he slowly processed her leaps of logic, blinked, then shoved his hand across his hair and shook his head. "I'll dig the hole. Just tell me where you want it." His hands relaxed their tense grip on the newspaper as he watched her quizzically. "You really are planning to stay, aren't you?"

Maya beamed and reached over to pat his arm. "I like men with both feet on the ground who know how to deliver babies."

"Even if I am as boring as yesterday's news and not the latest rock singing sensation?"

"Stevie can write lullabies," she answered dryly, climbing to her feet with his assistance. "But you'll be there to rock the cradle. Don't ever underestimate me like that again, Holm, or I'll whip your head off so fast you won't know what hit you."

Axell watched her go with a burgeoning feeling of dread

deep in his heart. Maya was so beautiful, so talented, so wise in so many ways, and so damned ephemeral, that one of these days she would have to sprout wings and fly like a butterfly.

And he had the perishing feeling that her departure would kill him.

January 1946

I saw Helen in town today. She looked pale but more beautiful than ever. She looked right through me as if I didn't exist. She must regret sending that letter, but I can't get it off my mind. My "wicked, sinful lips" ache for hers. I've not dared to so much as brush Dolly's cheeks with them.

I'm not a sentimental man. I thought what we shared was of the flesh only, but may the Lord have mercy on me, I crave Helen with all my body and soul.

The town calls her a fallen woman, but she's not. She's warmhearted and fun-loving and in desperate search of what her cold and calculating uncle cannot give. Had her parents lived . . . There's no point in speculating. She needs rescuing, but I don't know if I have what it takes to do it.

If I lose my job, I'll lose the land and the house my grandfather built and my sister will go homeless. Can I choose love over honor and respectability?

I look in the mirror and see a coward.

❧ TWENTY-THREE ❧

Always remember, you're unique,
just like everybody else.

Chimes tinkled a musical scale as Axell opened the door to the Curiosity Shoppe. The powerful thunder of waves rushing to shore roared over the chimes. May sunshine poured through the plate windows, and the breeze that followed him in stirred dancing rainbows from the crystals sparkling overhead. The kiosk of brightly hued bumper stickers swayed as he brushed past, and he noticed Maya had stuck still another quote on the sticker collage forming between the shelves.

Her cheerful "I'm up here" was a startling reversal of his first entrance into his wife's wonderful wacky world, and curiosity escalating, Axell scanned the ceiling.

Maya sat on a high stepladder, carefully hooking what appeared to be multicolored ribbons of a hanging mobile to an emerald green papier-mâché dragon. Among the streamers hung grinning gnomes, surly trolls, and crystal treasures. In the nearly seven weeks since their marriage, Axell had discovered his wife's creative mind had a few more twists than he'd suspected.

"I think you're supposed to put a mobile together before you hang it," he said cautiously, watching her lean from the ladder to reach the hook she wanted. With the warmer weather, she had taken to wearing short tight tank tops beneath loose blouses, but he'd noticed she usually shed the blouses when she was alone, which was probably why he was here. He'd known she'd be alone.

He admired the bounce of Maya's unfettered breasts as she

climbed down. She'd been forced to give up trying to nurse Alexa, but her breasts were still as full as a man could desire, not to mention high and firm and easily discerned beneath that damned tight knit. Sometimes he thought she wore those shirts to taunt him. His restraint was dangerously near the cracking point. Maintaining any semblance of equanimity in her presence was a challenge that might eventually break him.

"But I didn't know where the streamers belonged until I hung it."

She stood on tiptoe and kissed his cheek, and Axell responded to the scent of hyacinths wrapping around him. Maya wore the damnedest perfumes. If he was a man of any less restraint, he'd have her down on the floor by now.

As it was, he had to ball his fingers into fists to prevent grabbing her by the waist and swallowing her tongue. He knew he could kiss any resistance good-bye if he so much as touched her, and he didn't think making love to his wife in full view of the public would enhance either of their reputations. He almost had the Alcoholic Beverage Control board believing in his sterling character.

He glanced warily at the enormous laughing dragon flying high above his head. "And I suppose the dragon told you where he wanted his streamers?"

"Of course." She crossed to the counter and produced her carafe. "Tea?"

"Not now." He watched as she poured hot water into unfamiliar china. "Where are your teacups?"

She looked briefly embarrassed before she threw up her usual defenses and shrugged. "They're still at the school in a box. I haven't remembered to bring them back."

He wouldn't have thought anything of it except for that brief embarrassment. Those teacups meant something special to her. He didn't like the idea of them still in their packing box, ready to be moved at a moment's notice. They were all Maya had that were truly hers, he realized.

He'd learned that confronting Maya wasn't any easier than getting direct answers from Constance. Instead, he took the indirect route. "Stephen's band took that show at the club in Charlotte?"

She pulled a bottle of water from beneath the counter and threw it in his direction. "The album's done and the tour won't start for months. They have to do something."

Axell caught the bottle and unscrewed the top. It gave him something to do while he quelled the imps wreaking havoc with his stomach. He couldn't object to a father wanting to be near his daughter, not with any rationality anyway. It was Stephen's proximity to Maya that was driving him crazy. He glanced upward. "He's back, then?"

Maya grinned and sat cross-legged on the cushion of one of the giant high-backed wicker chairs she'd added to the inventory. "If I know Stevie, he's sawing logs. He doesn't come awake until the owls do. Sit down, Axell. You make me nervous prowling around like that."

Instead, he crossed the room to examine the row of painted sneakers behind the counter. "You're still taking orders for these things?"

"They're fun, and almost pure profit. I'm working up a book of different characters people can choose from. I took in fifty dollars yesterday," she added defensively.

At fifty dollars a day, the shop could scarcely pay the utilities, but it was better than where they'd started. He hadn't come in here to criticize. Axell swung around and took the chair beside her. Thank heaven she'd sold those hideous wrought-iron things.

"The transportation board is going ahead with land condemnation proceedings. They're calling for a public meeting next month." He hadn't wanted to tell her. The school had just had their first full summer session this week, and Maya had been so excited, she'd almost closed Cleo's shop in celebration. Only a curt note from her sister had dimmed her exuberance and forced her to agree to teaching afternoon classes only. It seemed Cleo might be getting time off for good behavior. She hadn't been very polite in her inquiries about Matty and the store. He was having grave doubts about the sister.

He didn't know which was harder on Maya, the shop or the school, but he loved having her close at hand for breaks like this. Usually, she had the kids with her, but today Matty and Constance were on a field trip, leaving just Alexa to coo in her cradle. If it weren't for his unhappy news, he could be using the time to woo her a little.

At his warning, Maya bit her bottom lip and turned troubled eyes toward the dancing prisms in the window. The speakers blared a mournful Gaelic folk song, and Axell had the urge to smash them into plastic grounds. He had a lot of explosive urges lately, but fortunately, he'd curbed them.

"Well, I suppose we'll have to see to it that the public supports us," she finally responded with her usual cheer. "The Pfeiffer property is practically a historic monument. How could they want an ugly old road in its place?"

Very easily, Axell wanted to remind her. People preferred shortcuts to the grocery store over historic monuments. But he didn't have the heart to shoot down her cloud. By now, he realized Maya knew when she was ignoring reality. She did it deliberately. It saved a storm of tears and rage and avoided the confrontations she so thoroughly disliked. He couldn't argue with that attitude, since it saved him tons of grief, too.

"We'll start a campaign," he replied gently. He didn't have much hope of it working, but he didn't want to let her down either. They were still at that awkward stage of courtship where they skirted around all the issues while warily testing each other's boundaries. Well, he was wary. Maya had a habit of treading his toes whenever it occurred to her. The purple larkspur on his dining room walls had grown six-feet tall.

"Won't it be costly to build a road in a flood zone?" she asked, wrinkling her brow as she sipped her tea.

Pow! Right between the eyes. Axell stared at his amazing wife in incredulity. "Sometimes, you're a lot more connected than I realize," he declared before his brain kicked in, and he gave a mental groan at his unintended insult.

She beamed her understanding gypsy smile over the rim of her cup. "Gotcha."

Oh, God, that look struck him with the full force of an arrow through the heart. Rattled, he set down his water and stood. The mayor would kill him if he approached the city council with this new tactic. Asking for a cost study would delay everything. He could be certain the ABC inspectors would return. But Maya's beaming smile bestowed him with invincibility. Or lust was infecting his brain. "I'll look into it. People understand taxes and money more than historic monuments."

"Thought so," Maya murmured, lowering her cup and watching him hurry to the door. She didn't think civilization was healthy for Viking gods. Axell looked as if he needed a broadax and helmet as he stalked into the sunlight, his square jaw set for war. He really needed some violent physical outlet besides pens and legal posturing.

She thought she knew what he really needed, but he didn't seem willing to commit to the physical side of their marriage yet. She hadn't decided whether that was a relief or not. She was physically more than ready. Just watching Axell bare-chested and sweating as he'd dug the hole for her gardenia bush had almost boiled her blood and melted her resistance. But emotionally, she was a basket case, and sex could easily upset the basket.

Having a life steeped in irony instead of disaster was a pleasant change, she reflected as she finished her tea and watched Alexa waving her fingers at dust motes. Or maybe the continually looming disasters were cushioned by the distance and comfort Axell provided. She was still in danger of losing her school and all the dreams it represented. Stephen was overhead, scheming to separate her from her daughter.

And Axell wasn't exactly offering her passion or love.

Well, as she'd decided long before, she didn't need either. She could survive, knowing the children were happy. They could give her the love she missed.

Only, sometimes, in her dreams maybe, she really, really wished she could have something deeper and more satisfying than sex and safety with Axell.

The door chimed and Katherine the Long-Legged intruded on Maya's reverie. Relaxed on the high of jasmine tea, Maya merely smiled and lifted her cup in greeting. "Come to buy a love potion to bind our favorite mayor into matrimony?" she asked without resentment.

Katherine's smooth blond hair bobbed as she swung to find Maya nearly hidden by the huge chair. "What the devil do you mean by that?"

"Leos can't tolerate loneliness," Maya replied calmly, pouring more tea. "And they love the center of attention. The mayor is a perfect choice for you. You'd make a good politician's wife."

Looking shell-shocked, Katherine dropped into the chair across from her and accepted the cup of tea Maya pushed toward her. "You're spooky, you know that?"

Maya shrugged. "Nah, I've just learned survival. I'm better at astrology than tarot, but I can read your cards if you'd like."

"I don't believe in that mumbo-jumbo," Katherine said. "I've just come to tell you that Ralph's willing to cut a deal with you over the Pfeiffer property so we can speed up proceedings rather than waiting on DOT."

Maya handed Katherine the tarot deck. "Shuffle," she insisted. "Humor me."

Katherine grabbed the deck and shuffled half-heartedly. "There's no reason we can't come to some suitable compromise without dragging this into the hostilities of a public meeting." She smacked the deck down on the intricately carved wooden table Maya had discovered in the storeroom.

Laying out the cards, Maya raised her eyebrows as Death appeared, but she didn't interpret the possibilities out loud. "Oh, I imagine the hostilities will come from the taxpayers who discover how much a bridge over that creek will cost, not from me. The direct route is not always the best one." She tapped a card in front of her. "Take love, for instance. Coupled with the Fool over here," she tapped another card, "it doesn't stand a chance in the normal run of things." She tapped another card. "But if you subvert the Fool with power, sort of do an end run around the goal, as Axell puts it, then you can tackle the unsuspecting object of your interest."

Tearing her gaze away from the horrifying Death card that

Maya ignored, Katherine looked at her with disbelief. "You're crazier than a bedbug."

Maya shrugged and smiled. "I've never seen a bedbug, but I've never seen a crazy insect either. They know exactly what they're doing. Wish the mayor well for me."

For a moment, Katherine cast the scattered cards a hesitant look. Then she shook her head and pushed her chair back. "I take it that means you're going to drag this into a legal battle."

"Oh, Axell will hire lawyers, I'm sure." Maya curled up in her chair and insouciantly sipped her tea. "Me, I'll just take it to the people. Did you know the Garden Club asked me to join them? It seems they're aching to get their green thumbs on some of those old-fashioned roses out at the school."

That topic wasn't as irrelevant as it sounded. The Garden Club was an old southern tradition. It included the wives of some of the richest and most influential men in town. Maya benevolently refrained from grinning as Katherine absorbed that blow. Maybe she would learn how to fight back from a position of power. It sure beat running.

"You don't own that property," Katherine warned. "The lease can still be challenged. And if Axell's not careful, he could be too busy with the ABC board to care." She slammed out with a violent tinkling of chimes.

Well, two points to the lady in the red suit—she'd hit the school and Axell's major weak spots. Maya glanced at the tarot layout and frowned. She wished she was a little better at actually reading the cards instead of playing with people's minds. She didn't like the looks of that Death card in Katherine's pack. Generally, it meant some form of transformation, not something so literal as death. But she very definitely did not like the threat in the lady's voice. Did Axell's kindnesses have a cost—her school for his license?

"You look like you need a drink, honey," the woman at the bar murmured as she leaned over and pushed a glass toward Axell, bending just enough to expose an astounding expanse of cleavage for his benefit.

Her heavy perfume soaked his senses more than a bottle of

rum. Fascinated by the deep shadow between the heavy platform of her breasts, Axell wondered how she held up all that weight. Without thinking, he sipped the drink she shoved at him. He sputtered and almost spat out the whiskey. Knowing his preferences, Maya always handed him water.

The perfume and the whiskey and thoughts of Maya stirred baser interests, and Axell shifted uncomfortably on the stool. The woman beside him could pull local political strings, and he'd thought it circumspect to garner her interest, but not this kind of interest. He frowned at the bloodred fingernails tapping the sleeve of his suit. Maya had said he didn't notice women, but there was a reason for that. He didn't want to get involved.

He pushed her hand away and stood up. "My wife's waiting and I have to go."

He liked the freedom that one little sentence offered. The minute some barracuda closed in for the kill, he could wave Maya like a harpoon. They didn't have to know she was harmless.

Almost harmless. She had the power to stir sexual images he'd thought he'd left behind with adolescence, but Axell figured that was a result of prolonged abstinence. He rather enjoyed idling a spare minute or three conjuring up the moment when he confirmed his memory that she was a natural redhead. He hadn't found the perfect opportunity yet. He was always home late and didn't want to disturb her or the kids by trespassing on their side of the house. Maybe he should hire a sitter and take Maya out on a formal date of some sort. Constance would probably hunt them down afterward, but his bedroom door had locks. He'd have to figure out how to know when Maya was ready. He hated trying to read a woman's mind. Had he missed her signals already?

Thinking the evening was fairly quiet and maybe he could escape early, Axell sighed in frustration as Headley strode through the front door, looking primed for bear. He thought the damned man had decided to retire, but he knew that look. The metropolis of Wadeville had just suffered a newsworthy act of violence.

Axell didn't try to hide as Headley stalked toward him. The old man was as close to a father figure as he'd had since his own father had died. He cleared a stool at the end of the bar and Headley signaled the bartender for his usual.

"I don't suppose I can be so lucky as to hope Katherine murdered the mayor?" Axell inquired facetiously as the reporter threw back his requested drink.

The older man turned his shaggy white head and glared at him. "Almost as good. Old Man Pfeiffer died tonight. The coroner doesn't think it was from natural causes."

Pfeiffer. Maya's landlord. The school would now be owned by a motley lot of scattered relatives who would all demand its sale.

The cops wouldn't have to look far for motives for murder. The problem would be deciding which one of all those cockroach relatives would be the most likely suspect.

And the clamor for Maya to give up her dream would escalate.

January 1946
I proposed marriage to Dolly today. She accepted. Her father promoted me to general manager as of the first of the month.
I will have to tell Helen.

❧ TWENTY-FOUR ❧

Lead me not into temptation.
I can find it myself.

Bending over to reach the strawberries in the fruit drawer of the refrigerator, Maya nearly jumped out of her nightie as the kitchen door slammed behind her. It was ten o'clock at night and Axell never slammed doors.

She swung around to face a man shredding the last black thread of his temper—a far cry from the calm, self-assured character she'd married. As his steely gaze slid to the garbage heaps of crumpled newspapers on his once pristine kitchen floor to the clutter of paint pots, paste, and streamers across the antique kitchen table, Maya thought he'd lose his grip for certain.

The dangerous flare of his nostrils and the sensual narrowing of his eyes as his gaze finally settled on her—or her scanty nightshirt—warned that the disintegration of Axell's personal Berlin Wall had begun on all fronts.

Maya shivered in anticipation as he looked from the rather revealing neckline of her silky shirt to the length of her legs exposed by the high hem, and back again to focus on her breasts. She had the urge to cross her arms to protect herself, but the imp inside her head took command. Maybe she hadn't deliberately planned this scene, but subconsciously, she was capable of anything. She propped her hands on the table behind her and struck a seductive pose.

"Finally broke you, did I?" she taunted.

She should have remembered Norse gods were dangerous and unpredictable when provoked. The hank of golden hair cascading over Axell's brow nearly quivered with intensity. He'd thrown off his suit coat and tie in the humidity of the May night, and his shoulders strained at the tailored cut of his blue silk shirt. Fixated on the V of his open shirt collar, Maya didn't dare drop her gaze lower. She didn't generally inspire men to unbridled passion—unless it was fury—but she sensed Axell had gone past the point of reason.

He struggled gamely to regain control, but when she deliberately rested her weight on her hands, flaunting her breasts in his face, he threw restraint to the winds. Dropping his coat on a kitchen chair, he narrowed the distance between them in a single step.

Maya gasped as Axell swung her against him as easily as he did Matty. Slammed against his broad chest, her feet dangling inches from the floor, she nearly succumbed to heart failure as she grabbed for his shoulders. When Axell's mouth covered hers, she stopped functioning on any rational level at all.

She tasted the whiskey on his breath as his mouth crushed hers. His hand cupped her bottom through the thin nightshirt, and she knew the strength with which he held her was far greater than her own. Experience had taught her to fear the combination of power and alcohol. But Axell's breath was sweet with the taste of desire, and she'd wanted to sample it for so long, she couldn't resist now. The reassuring heat of his hand through her shirt melted any resistance that remained. She trusted him—in this, at least.

Wrapping her arms around his neck, Maya surrendered to the heady bliss of Axell's kiss. If this was a sample of the passionate nature he so successfully penned inside, she'd have to drive him to the brink more often. Arching her breasts against his chest, crooking one leg around his knee, Maya opened her mouth beneath his, until all the air expelled from his lungs, and he drank desperately of hers. She gave without protest or complaint, not only accepting his devouring kiss, but meeting it with an equal hunger.

Greedily, Axell set her on the table and molded her breasts with his palms. Lifting his head long enough to admire the treasure he had captured, he murmured, "I never thought I could be jealous of a baby. Alexa doesn't know what's good for her."

Maya nearly swooned as Axell's capable hands swooped inside the loose neckline of her shirt and bared her breasts. She was scarcely in any condition to comprehend his words. When his mouth fastened over her nipple and suckled to show what he meant, she cried out in delight and near panic at the sudden, insistent urges swamping her.

Grabbing his shirt, she jerked at the buttons, instinctively seeking the heat of his skin to share the flames of her own. The slippery silk practically flew apart, and Axell groaned deep in his throat as her hands spread across his chest. Frantically, she tugged the shirttails from his trousers so she could unfasten the whole placket and shove it aside.

Lifting his head, he looked directly into her eyes as if he wanted to say something. She didn't want words. Finally, at long last, she could run her fingers over all those lovely muscles.

Axell nibbled her lips as she spread her palms across his broad chest, igniting the flames in more places than one. He cupped her breasts in return, taunting them into readiness.

She arched higher, and at the pressure of his leg against her knee, she gladly parted her thighs.

Maya shuddered as Axell's fingers slid downward, discovering she wore no panties. He growled in appreciation and caressed her with his thumb, while his mouth drove her senseless. Raising her legs, she wrapped them around his hips, pulling him closer until she could feel the heat of his arousal through the layers of his clothing.

"I hope you've taken care of birth control," he muttered thickly as his kisses melted her into tingling nerve endings, "because I don't think I can stop."

"The pill," she gasped, just before Axell's hot mouth greedily covered hers in an excess of gratitude. She'd sworn never to leave herself unprotected again, but she'd never thought to need protection from this man. She moaned as he spread her thighs wider and only their clothing prevented their joining.

The phone rang.

Axell jerked, but his mouth didn't release hers and his hands cupped her tighter.

The phone rang again.

"They may need you at the . . ." Maya's voice trailed off as Axell's fingers caressed the aching peak of her breast.

"They can handle it." He slid his kisses toward her earlobe.

The phone shrilled louder.

Nervously, Maya thought she heard Alexa cry. They were making love in the middle of the kitchen with three children only a few thin walls away. She was the one losing it.

"What if it's Cleo?" she asked weakly as Axell's teeth nibbled at her ear and his hand slid beneath her nightie again. It wasn't an unreasonable question. Cleo had said she had a probation hearing coming up. She just couldn't think straight enough to recall the importance of such a call.

"She and Stephen can entertain each other," Axell answered without rancor, sliding his mouth back to hers.

That would have shut her up, but the wavering cry of an infant stopped them both before their mouths connected.

Maya could feel Axell shudder as he stroked her where she'd opened for him. Just a minute more . . .

The phone rang insistently. Alexa increased her wails. And a sleepy voice calling, "Maya," from the back bedrooms finally broke the spell.

Maya flushed as she looked up and read the regret behind the heat in Axell's eyes.

He glanced down to where his tanned hand cupped her pale breast. "Damn," he muttered. "Damn, damn, and double damn."

"Point taken," she said wryly, squirming backward, hoping to escape his reach.

Refusing to let her go, Axell leaned over and grabbed the phone. "What do you want?" he yelled into the receiver.

"My, my, the lion isn't sleeping tonight," Selene's voice

purred from the other end of the line. "Did the fish slip away from you again?"

Axell grimaced in defeat as Maya did just that—slipped backward over the table and out of his hands, straightening her nightshirt in the process.

"You got a telescope?" he asked in irritation.

"No, but I've seen our girl in action. You can catch her later. Right now, we've got a problem. Put her on."

Maya had already fled the kitchen to quiet Alexa and reassure whichever of the kids the noise had disturbed. He could still feel the heat of her bare skin on his hands. The ache in his groin pounded with the need for release.

He'd forgotten the kids, the bar, Pfeiffer, and everything else in his degenerate need to plow his maddening wife until she screamed surrender. He was a sick man.

Wiping the sweat off his brow, Axell spoke abruptly. "If it's about Pfeiffer, I've already heard. There isn't a damned thing we can do at this hour. Go back to your party, Selene."

"My source says it's murder, Holm. How far is your mayor friend willing to go to get his damned road?" The phone slammed in his ear.

Axell stared blankly at the receiver until the warning signal shrilled, then hung it up. Ralph Arnold, a murderer? No man could be that desperate for a road, could he? Murders around here tended to be drug related, but that didn't make sense either. Old Man Pfeiffer wasn't exactly the sort to deal in drugs.

Glancing at the knee-deep clutter surrounding him, Axell took a deep breath and ordered the pounding in his pants to cool. Remembering Maya's willingness, he couldn't summon much eagerness for the effort. Maybe once she got the kids quieted . . .

Cursing Selene, phones, and his rotten timing, he stalked upstairs to the part of the house Maya had claimed for her own.

She wouldn't buy a damned thing for herself, but he noticed she had no such compunction about buying for the kids. A six-foot Big Bird greeted him as he turned the corner, buttoning his shirt. Brilliantly colored art prints from the Madeline books and others of knights and dragons adorned simple frames in between the bedrooms. He'd stumbled over enough stacks of books in previous ventures into this territory to know to tread warily. He couldn't imagine how he'd once thought these rooms empty and without life. They scarcely seemed big enough to contain all the energy bouncing around in them.

Not knowing whether to be irritated or happy at the discovery, Axell sought the sound of Maya's voice. No one had ever driven him over the brink of sexual frustration as she had. His loss of control frightened him, heightening his irascibility. She'd damned well taunted him into that scene—in the *kitchen*, for pity's sake! The kids could have walked in at any time.

He flushed at the thought of literally being caught with his pants down. The only other time in his life he'd ever been so incautious was to believe Angela when she'd told him she had used protection. He'd almost made the same mistake again. Although, if he was being rational about this, he'd have to figure Maya wasn't in any hurry to get pregnant. She didn't need to. They were already married.

His head hurt with all the conflicting issues rampaging around inside. Discovering Maya in her room, rocking a whimpering infant and reassuring Matty in a low voice, Axell leaned against the doorjamb and just let it all go for a moment. He couldn't do anything about Old Man Pfeiffer or Mayor Arnold or the Mid-East crisis at this hour. His concern now was getting Maya into his bed so he could release some of this tension. *Then* he'd worry about getting to the bottom of their problems.

"I think Alexa has a fever," Maya whispered over Matty's head.

That shot his ship down fast enough.

"Even *I* know that's ridiculous," Axell shouted. He never shouted. Resting his head in his hands, he propped his elbows on his desk and wondered when his life had taken this bent direction. He didn't have to wonder. He knew.

"It's either the mayor or that New York developer he's connected with," Headley replied with assurance, appropriating a seat on the couch without being asked. "I've done my homework. Ralph's invested heavily in that real estate corporation owned by the Yankees. This is their first big project. They've got some condos near town in the blueprint stage, and they've acquired land for town-house apartments. They need the cash flow from that shopping center."

"Shit." Axell sat back and stared out his window. He really didn't want the mayor's job. He'd just thrown out the threat to smack Ralph into line. But apartments and condos weren't the kind of lifestyle he wanted for Wadeville. The bastard.

He took a deep breath to clear the cobwebs. "That doesn't make Ralph a murderer. That's preposterous. Pfeiffer has a hundred and one relatives waiting with bated breath for his demise. Any one of them could have been desperate enough to hurry him on."

"They've not determined the cause of death yet," Headley reminded him. "That noxious brood of Pfeiffer's are the gun- and knife-toting sort. The sheriff would damned well know the cause if they were involved."

Axell pinched the bridge of his nose. "Speculation will get us nowhere. I've got lawyers reading over the terms of Maya's lease, but we've got to start considering alternatives. No place else is as convenient to the houses out there, and land prices are too exorbitant to consider buying anything. She'll be turning my house into a home school if I don't do something soon." Maybe the best thing was for her to give up the school. Men desperate enough to murder over land wouldn't let the little complication of a lease stop them. Besides, he liked coming home at night to the sound of Maya's laughter and the kids' giggles. He was even beginning to enjoy the purple monstrosities growing in his dining room. He liked even better the idea of slipping home when the kids weren't—

"That little girl of yours sure has you wrapped around her little finger, doesn't she?" Headley broke into his reverie. "You know, there used to be a kid from Texas named Alyssum who came into the grill in your father's time. Married a local girl. You think it's some relation?"

Axell glowered at the old man. "Maya's parents are dead." He returned to staring at the building next door—the one Maya and her former lover occupied, though on separate floors and for different reasons. It still drove him nuts thinking about it.

Headley was right. Maya had him wrapped around her finger and it had almost nothing to do with Constance's welfare, or protective instincts, or any of the other crap he'd been rationalizing.

He'd do a damned lot for his daughter, admittedly. She hadn't asked to be brought into this world. He accepted the responsibility for that. But he didn't think it was for Constance's sake that he worried about Maya and her school. He'd already provided a permanent solution for Constance by marrying her teacher.

No, the hell of it was, now he was worrying about the damned teacher.

Instead of solving several problems with his marriage, he'd multiplied them into hordes the likes of which Genghis Khan had never known—because of a wisp of a female with big blue-green eyes and hair the color of sunset.

Maya wasn't just a challenge. Maya was the moon and stars and planets all rolled into one, and he sure the hell wasn't NASA.

Reaching for the phone, he started to call to see if Alexa was any better.

Instead, he dropped his hand and got up. He'd go next door and see for himself.

He ignored Headley's laughter as he strode out.

❧ TWENTY-FIVE ❧

Give pizza chants.

Maya barely looked up as the shop chimes rang and Axell entered. She was furious and embarrassed with herself, and not entirely happy with him. This morning he'd grabbed a cup of coffee, kissed the kids on the head, and escaped before they could exchange two words. She didn't like being given a taste of her own medicine. Axell was a Virgo, dammit, not a Pisces. He wasn't supposed to slip away like that.

His cautious approach warned he was treading as warily as she. He glanced down at Alexa sleeping in her cradle. "How is she?" he whispered.

Damn, he set every one of her nerve endings on fire just by his presence. Maya glanced up from the shoe she was painting and studied him from beneath her lashes. Axell never looked uncertain. He always looked self-confident and in charge. But today . . . Did she detect just a hint of nervousness in the way he loosened his tie? He'd apparently left his coat in his office. Even that was a sign of something. She just didn't know what.

"The doctor says I should expect fevers with colds and allergies. If I'd been able to breast-feed, she'd have had more immunity. I'm not supposed to worry unless the fever lingers or gets worse."

"*We're* not supposed to worry," he corrected, not looking up from the cradle. "We're in this together."

"We" was a hard concept for Maya to wrap her mind

around. She'd never really been part of a "we" and wasn't entirely sure how it worked. Axell was trying to teach her, and she appreciated his efforts, she really did, but she'd had the supports pulled out from under her once too many times in the past. She'd taught herself to be smarter than Charlie Brown with his football.

She painted the dragon's breath a brighter orange and didn't reply.

Axell leaned his hip against the counter beside her, and Maya could smell his shaving lotion. Last night, she'd gone to bed with that scent on her hands. Tonight, she could easily go to bed with the scent of the whole man on her. The quivering in her lower abdomen warned that was a path she shouldn't take with Axell standing this close. She didn't like being dominated by macho men, she reminded herself. His size alone could diminish her. His superior attitude would wipe her up off the floor.

"I thought maybe I should take you out to dinner tonight."

Out of the corner of her eye, Maya could see Axell confidently crossing his arms as he leaned against the counter. For whatever reason, the combination of his tentative statement and confident pose struck her funny bone.

"You thought maybe a bed would be more comfortable than a kitchen table," she translated for him, biting back a giggle.

That shut him up briefly. Then he grunted. "It's a damned good thing that table weighs a ton or I would have slammed it against the wall."

Maya grinned in relief. So, maybe they'd both come a little unglued. "I vote we reserve the table for special, nonkid occasions," she replied noncommittally.

"Dinner?" he persisted, not letting her off the hook.

A cautious step on the stairs prevented Maya's immediate reply. She'd heard the shower earlier. Stephen never got up this early. Nervously, she glanced at Axell. He was watching whoever descended with that narrow, Norse god look, as if he'd shoot thunderbolts at any person who dared invade his cloud.

His expression turned from anger to wariness. A few months ago, Maya would have sworn Axell had no expressions, but she recognized the signs now. She glanced over her shoulder.

"Cleo!" she shouted with joy.

Axell caught the paint pot as Maya leaped from her seat and ran to embrace her sister. He should never have allowed Maya to leave a key out for an unknown factor like her sister. Although he could see the resemblance between them in the redhead coloring and delicate bone structure, the similarities ended there.

Maya's sister exhibited a tough, sharp edge that would cut a man in two if applied deliberately. She wore her dark red hair in a clipped, rough cut that emphasized the harshness of her cheekbones and the thinness of her lips. Partially tinted glasses hid her eyes, preventing any comparison with Maya's open, honest turquoise. Even as Maya enveloped her in a hug, Axell could sense Cleo's cold gaze on him. This was not a woman he'd like to meet in a dark alley.

"Come meet Axell," Maya said eagerly, urging her sister forward. "Axell, this is my sister, Cleo." She didn't give either of them a chance to respond but leapt to the next question. "Why didn't you call? I wanted to come and get you. How did you get here?"

"I've got friends." Cleo dismissed the question curtly.

"You didn't have trouble finding the key where I told you it would be? And I fixed everything just like you had it before."

"It's fine, I found it just fine." She glanced down at Alexa. "This your kid?"

"Isn't she beautiful? Would you like to hold her?" Without waiting for an answer, Maya lifted Alexa from the cradle and offered her to Cleo.

Axell wanted to grab his daughter and shield her from this hard-eyed woman. He had to start remembering that Maya had more in common with this ex-convict than she did with him. Alexa didn't belong to him in any form. Stephen had refused to sign any release papers allowing Axell to adopt her.

He bunched his fists at his sides and watched as Maya's sister inspected Alexa but refused to hold her.

"Where's Matty?" Cleo demanded, pulling back from her niece's ruffled pink blanket.

Axell thought he ought to leave the sisters to their reunion, but his stubborn protective instincts wouldn't surrender to logic or politeness. He wouldn't see Maya hurt.

"At the school," Maya replied happily, apparently not aware of her sister's icy distance. "I think kids benefit from year-round school, and he loves it, so I enrolled him in summer sessions." At Cleo's silence, Maya continued defensively, "It's my school. It doesn't cost anything."

Cleo nodded, and eyed Axell with suspicion. "Who's the turd who tried to climb in my bed last night?"

"Stephen! Oh my gosh, I forgot Stephen!" Anxiously, Maya handed Alexa to Axell. "What did you do, Cleo? It's my fault. I didn't know you were—"

Cleo cut her off. "He's in Matty's bed." She continued staring at Axell. "I want my son back."

Axell shifted Alexa to a more comfortable position. The more tense the situation became, the more he relaxed. It was an old defensive technique he'd learned long ago for defusing situations in the bar.

"That's up to Social Services," he replied blandly.

Cleo turned her glare on Maya. "He's got your daughter and my son. What's he doing, holding them hostage?"

Axell thought it might be time to take his leave, but a shout from above aroused his curiosity.

"Maya! Maya, are you down there? That bitch stole my best flannel shirt!"

This could very well turn out better than a Three Stooges farce, Axell concluded with glee, as he wiped baby dribble from Alexa's chin and waited for the next scene in the drama. He used to hate emotional scenes, but since Maya's arrival in his life, he'd learned to observe them with a measure of appreciation for her talent in manipulating them. He let Alexa wrap her chubby fist around his finger and returned Maya's harried look with equanimity. Her sister was very definitely wearing a man's checkered flannel shirt.

Cleo shrugged. "He's sleeping in my shop. It is still my shop?" she demanded, narrowing her eyes at Axell.

"The lease papers are ready for your signature." He was having second and third thoughts about signing them, but he'd promised Maya.

That seemed to satisfy Cleo for the moment. She turned her attention to the man clattering down the stairs, half-naked. "You want your damned shirt?" she yelled. "Come and get it!"

Lifting an eyebrow, Axell watched Maya for some signal as to what she wanted him to do now. He shook his head at her irrepressible grin and dumped Alexa into her arms. "Shall I hire a baby-sitter or a lunatic keeper for tonight?"

Maya brightened. "That's ideal! Cleo, you can come over this evening and stay with the kids so Axell and I can go out for a while. Social Services can't object to that."

That wasn't ideal in Axell's book. He didn't want a drug addict looking after his kids. Their kids. Whatever. He opened his mouth to protest, but the blasted musician leapt into the fray instead.

"I'll not have this pervert looking after my daughter!" Stephen shouted. "She nearly took my balls off last night. Why didn't you warn me she was coming so I could have bought a gun?"

Maya's grin faltered, but Axell thought he really might get into this scene if he hung around long enough. Watching Stephen and Cleo duke it out could provide amusing entertainment. Some other time.

"I've got a friend on the police force we can hire for the evening," he informed them dryly. "I'll instruct him to shoot the first one who yells in front of the kids. I want to take Maya out around seven. Suit yourselves."

Giving Maya a peck on the cheek, Axell strode out, confident Stephen and Cleo would kill each other before they intruded on his safe, sane world. He'd call the baby-sitter and arrange for her to watch the kids just in case either of the idiots took Maya seriously.

"California is too close," Maya muttered as she paced Selene's office at the school. "I'm considering Alaska. Whatever made me think having a family was a good thing?"

"You didn't think," Selene replied bluntly, hitting the computer key that sent the monthly invoices to the printer. "You just have this weird idea that because you breathe love and laughter, everyone does. Well, it's not so, girlfriend. Grow up."

"I'm not naive," Maya responded sharply, then took a calming breath before continuing. "I know Cleo has problems. Part of her probation requires she get counseling. What I need is some fairy dust to send Stephen back to Never-Never Land."

"He's not half-bad looking," Selene mused, watching Maya's pacing with a foxy grin. "Want me to adopt him?"

"Your own personal boy toy?" Maya inquired dryly. "He's not quite that malleable. He's moody, irritating, and bad-tempered. I don't know what I ever saw in him."

"He's talented, sexy, and you hadn't developed a taste for hot-blooded Vikings at the time," Selene concluded.

Maya shrugged. "I always thought Vikings were cold."

Selene laughed out loud. "That's because you know nothing about men. Axell's been hot after your bod since the day you met. The man's practically slavering. You want to get rid of Stephen, just mention it to Axell. He'll have him transported to Siberia before you can take it back."

"Stephen's my problem," Maya replied sulkily. She didn't know when her life had become everyone else's business. She was feeling trapped again. The footloose life had some definite advantages she hadn't appreciated when she had them.

But even the fleeting thought of losing Axell caused a full-scale panic attack.

"Pfeiffer's death is a bigger problem," Selene pointed out. "I've contacted his lawyers for confirmation that our lease is still valid, but they haven't got back to me."

Diverted, Maya pursued this new path. "How do the police know he didn't die a natural death? I can't believe anyone would kill that nice old man." She shook her head in disbelief. "I was going to visit and ask him about my grandmother. Now I'll never know."

"You said he knew Cleo. Maybe he told her." Selene gathered up the printed invoices and handed half to Maya. "Start folding and stuffing. Until we hear otherwise, this is your bread and butter."

No topic would distract her for long from the knowledge that her "date" tonight with her husband could only have one outcome. Maya wriggled in nervous anticipation as she stuffed envelopes.

Religious ceremonies had little meaning to her, but after tonight . . . Axell would probably expect her to share his bed on a regular basis. She didn't know if she was prepared for that kind of commitment. Between the kids, the school, and the shop, she barely had time for herself. How would she find time for a husband?

She had to. She'd promised. Maybe he'd be satisfied with one night a week.

Maybe she wouldn't.

"You didn't really mean it about the policeman, did you?" Maya asked anxiously as Axell came home after she'd finished feeding the kids. "I called Dorothy and she said you'd already called her. She can look after Constance and Alexa while Matty and Cleo get reacquainted." She nodded toward the bedroom wing. "Cleo's reading him a book."

Axell set his briefcase down on the table and glanced around the miraculously spotless kitchen. "Why am I getting premonitions of disaster?"

Maya dried her hands and surreptitiously watched him. He looked perfectly calm and reasonable tonight. No slamming doors, no wild looks melting her like candle wax. He'd combed the wayward strand of hair back from his forehead and apparently shaved before coming home. She could smell his aftershave as he approached. Nervously, she eyed his impeccable blue suit.

"I didn't know how to dress." She backed away. "I thought we'd be going somewhere casual. It's a weeknight. . . ." That was a stupid thing to say. Did she imagine the flare of heat in his eyes?

"I'll order pizza and you can wear nothing," he answered calmly, in that bland tone she knew concealed the workings of his mind.

The suggestion shot a shiver of arousal down Maya's spine.

"But I thought we ought to attempt something civilized like a date first. There's a place in Charlotte with good jazz. Do you like jazz?"

That offer fished her thoughts out of the gutter. A date. She could handle a date. "I don't know anything about jazz, but I'll learn. What do I wear?"

"Black is traditional," he said solemnly. At her look of horror, a twinkle developed in his eye. "Anything that makes you happy is fine."

Apparently his ability to push her buttons incited sufficient confidence for him to reach out and brush a recalcitrant curl from her forehead.

Just his touch ignited smoldering fires. Maya backed off.

Smacking him would make her happy. Getting this over with would make her happy. Even the spontaneity of last night was vastly preferable to his pragmatic approach. If it weren't for the kids, she'd be tempted to walk into his bedroom and tear her clothes off and have done with it.

"I'll only be a minute." Scooping up Muldoon for reassurance, Maya fled.

Taking a deep breath to calm his rocky nerves, Axell wandered into the family room. In these last weeks he'd grown accustomed to finding Matty and Constance bent over some game together. It felt odd to see just Constance sitting in front of the TV. He hadn't realized how much he'd miss Matty once Cleo took him. Would Maya be interested in giving him a son?

That was definitely not the direction to follow right now.

Constance threw him one of those suspicious looks he recognized as one of his own.

"Why can't I go with you?" she demanded.

Well, at least she was talking to him. "Because sometimes married people like to do things alone."

"You and Mama never did."

He and Angela had few interests in common. Hell, he and Maya had few interests in common, but this time, he meant to develop some. He was capable of learning from his mistakes.

"We did sometimes, you just don't remember," he said quietly. "You get Maya all to yourself all the time. It's my turn tonight, okay?"

She wrinkled her nose in disapproval and looked away. "Will the mean lady take Matty away?"

Maybe they shouldn't go out tonight. Her whole world had been in a tumult for so long. . . .

It wasn't likely to get better soon. With a sigh, Axell stroked her hair as he'd seen Maya do. "Cleo is Matty's mama, and Maya's sister. She's really sad right now, so maybe she says mean things. Try to be nice, will you?"

Constance shrugged, and he figured that was the best he could hope for.

Standing, Axell wondered for the millionth time if he'd done the right thing in marrying a woman like Maya, a woman a decade younger and a universe apart from his stodgy, conservative background. Maybe he should have tried harder with Constance on his own. Maybe he should have married someone like Katherine, with the same background as his. Maybe he—

Maya appeared in the doorway wearing some kind of slinky blue-green dress he knew he'd never seen before. The hem hit just above her knees but the slit in the side shot clear up her thigh, revealing a silky, sparkly glimpse of stockinged leg so tempting his eyes nearly fell out. He could scarcely tear his gaze away to observe the rest of the . . .

One look at the peekaboo bodice and Maya's bare shoulders rendered him incapable of walking across the room without crippling a vital part.

He thought maybe he'd take her to the nearest motel first.

❧ TWENTY-SIX ❧

WANTED: Meaningful overnight relationship.

"Will this do?" Maya asked uncertainly.

She'd piled all those glorious curls into a tumbling mop atop her head, so she was all naked neck and shoulders, except for the thin strip of material at the top of the gown which drew the eye to the very nice cleavage displayed below. He'd gratefully pay any amount that showed on his credit card for this view. Or was this another of her thrift shop bargains?

"Depends on what you wanted to do," Axell replied skeptically. "Bring me to my knees?" He glanced at Constance, who watched with interest. He wouldn't complete his thought. He couldn't think with all his blood concentrated well south of his brain. He had thought himself immune to women. No man in his right libido could be immune to Maya.

The front doorbell rang. No one ever used the front door. Sidewalks weren't a part of the landscape here. Maya blanched a shade whiter and Axell knew at once who their caller was.

He returned a few minutes later trailing the musician, who—with his gold earring and long ponytail—looked decidedly out of place in this family setting.

"Stephen! I thought you worked at the club in the evenings." She cupped her elbows in her palms and drifted nervously toward the doorway where Axell stood.

"Even God got a day off," Stephen grumbled, searching the room until he discovered the baby-sitter returning a wide-eyed Alexa to her infant seat. "I figured I could take care of my daughter for one night."

Like hell, he would. Axell draped his arm proprietarily around Maya's shoulders. Her bare shoulders. His ability to concentrate on Stephen's declaration and not the electricity shooting up his arm revealed the extent of his anger. "Have you ever changed a diaper? Mixed formula? Heated a bottle? Those are the essentials of infant care."

Stephen looked angry and confused, and Maya apparently took pity on him. Axell hoped it was pity. Any minute now and he'd be growling and baring his teeth at the intruder. He damned well hoped she understood that because he didn't.

"Dorothy is here. She can teach you what Alexa needs," Maya said reassuringly. "Or you can just kick back and relax and watch some television. You don't have to be doing something every minute."

Cleo appeared in the hall doorway, holding Matty's hand. "What's he doing here?" she demanded, glaring at Stephen.

"Time to go!" Maya cried cheerfully, swinging toward the doorway into the kitchen. "We're late. Kids, behave yourselves. We'll be back to see you're tucked in, so you'd better be in bed and sound asleep when we return."

Axell smothered a grin as Maya executed another of her graceful exits. Behind her back, he raised a reproving eyebrow at the glowering combatants. "Dorothy is in charge," he announced in a tone that brooked no interference. Stephen looked relieved. Axell pinned a mutinous Cleo with a glare. "Remember those guys at Social Services? Do you suppose it's a coincidence that their initials are 'SS'?"

Cleo's glare wavered uncertainly. Axell accepted that as surrender. He was exposing Constance to unhealthy influences, his conscience warned. But Dorothy was here, and Stephen and Cleo were adults—of a sort. And Constance had a sensible head on her shoulders. She could always leave the room if the hostilities escalated. She'd probably take Matty with her. She'd inherited a few of his instincts.

He caught up with Maya and practically shoved her out the door and into the garage.

Wrapping her arms around herself, Maya slipped into the

BMW. "It's awful late." The grim set of Axell's jaw rang all her warning bells. "Maybe we should put this off to another time. I'm starving."

Axell reached into the backseat, grabbed a lap throw, and wrapped it around her shoulders, grazing her arm in the process. Heat immediately combusted where he'd touched her. Biting her lower lip, Maya stared out the windshield as he backed out of the garage at a speed that should have taken them through the trees at the rear of the yard.

"I should have hired a zookeeper. How long do you think we dare leave them alone?"

"That depends on the amount of destruction you can tolerate." With the blanket wrapped around her shoulders, Maya relaxed a little into its warmth. She should never have worn this dress. She'd been challenging him again. Although, it had been fun watching Axell nearly crumple when she flashed her leg. Men didn't generally look at her as if she were a sex symbol. She was too short, too red-haired, too weird looking. But her husband looked at her as if she were the only female on the planet. She really, really liked that feeling. It gave her warm butterflies in her middle.

"You know them better than I do. How much destruction can they wreak? I don't want the kids involved in a war zone."

She even liked the worried timbre of his voice in the velvet darkness of the expensive car. She liked so many things about him, it scared her to death.

"I haven't seen Cleo in years. I barely know her anymore. But she's always been more self-destructive than hurtful. Stephen, well, Stephen has tantrums. But they're usually harmless," she replied brightly. She didn't know what she was saying. Was she trying to make him turn around and go back? She'd never have left the kids with Stephen and Cleo if she'd had any doubts about their welfare.

"We'll get home early," he said evenly.

Early. Did that mean they'd just eat and not stop anywhere on the way home? Or that they'd eat and go home and climb into Axell's bed? She wished the damned man wasn't so enigmatic. She'd never been this nervous in her lifetime.

"It's too late to drive all the way into Charlotte," she answered cautiously. As much as she would have liked an evening of dinner and dancing, she knew when she had to be practical. The kids weren't used to their absence. Stephen and Cleo would entertain them for a while, but they couldn't be trusted for long. Dorothy was a good sitter, but she couldn't control adults.

"I'm all for reducing driving time," he said solemnly, staring straight ahead, but Maya thought she detected a teasing note to the comment.

"You want to tell me just what you have planned?" she demanded. He *always* had everything planned, even sex, she figured.

"Fine wine, dancing, and good music." Glancing at the slit baring her thigh, he admitted in all honesty, "Followed by hot sex."

The covetous glance, his seductive tone, and the promise of his words shot straight through Maya's sex-deprived hormones. She'd never made love with a man half so handsome, half so downright *masculine* as her husband, and she wanted it right now.

Clearing her suddenly dry throat, she tugged at the gap in her skirt. "Feed me, and we can skip the first three."

He almost drove the car straight into the ditch.

"Fast food." He swung the car off the main road and roared down a secondary one.

"They have chicken in town," she offered. Axell's restaurant was the only other alternative in Wadeville, and that definitely wouldn't be fast.

"I feel like a cheap jerk taking you for fast food chicken."

Axell's hold on the steering wheel was pretty tight, Maya noticed. She wondered if it was because of the kids or her and started to inquire, but as they approached the main street of town, he cursed and veered the car into a parking lot.

Holm's Bar and Grill took up the entire end of one of Wadeville's blocks, so that the rear of the restaurant could be seen from this side street. Startled, Maya glanced up to see what had caught Axell's attention.

"I'm sorry." He jumped from the car without explanation and stalked toward the kitchen.

All she saw was two men entering the rear door. The employees often stepped outside to have a smoke. She didn't see anything unusual about that. The furious expression on Axell's face in the light of the security lamp warned otherwise, not that anyone else would read that tightened jaw as easily as she did. A stranger would just think him more stern than usual.

Hurrying in her high heels wasn't easy, but Maya managed to cross the gravel lot and enter the back door just after Axell. Men in a fury were often unpredictable. With Axell's concealed Scorpio, he was capable of anything, including paranoia. She didn't know why she should worry, but she did.

She heard the angry shouts as soon as she walked in. In front of her, some of the kitchen staff edged toward the back door where she stood, and the rest, toward the exit into the restaurant. Axell stood in the center of the kitchen, speaking in a low, taut voice to a couple of surly-looking young men. One of them was shouting and shaking his fist. In horror, Maya watched as the other grabbed a meat cleaver from the butcher-block counter.

She wanted to scream, but sound froze in her throat as the punk swung the weapon toward Axell. Gory images of gushing arteries and bloody hearts from every horror movie she'd ever watched flashed before her eyes. The idea of losing Axell in such a catastrophic manner barely had time to lodge in her brain before Axell's hand shot out.

Grabbing the wrist holding the swinging weapon, Axell twisted until the guy shrieked and dropped the cleaver. Then with the same efficient movement, Axell wrapped the punk's arm behind his back and propelled him toward the door. Maya jumped out of his way, her heart thudding in relief.

The man sailed out, landing palms down in the parking lot. Not even noticing Maya's presence, Axell swung around and pointed at the other one, jerking his head toward the exit. The young man hastened to follow his friend.

One of the waitresses whistled her approval. The others returned to their work as if this were a daily routine. The chef winked at Maya before returning to his stove. Still weak-kneed and starting to shake, she took in the staff's calm reaction with astonishment and stared at Axell as he casually ordered someone to call the police. She'd thought him a safe, sane family man, a respectable guy who wore business suits and ties, like the kind of family men she'd seen on television. No one had warned her he had the manners of a five-hundred-pound gorilla when angered, or that his job entailed cleaver-waving madmen.

Axell expressed no emotion as he spotted her hiding behind the door. "I'm sorry you had to see that. I can't afford to jeopardize my liquor license by having those two hanging around here. They're out on bail awaiting trial on drug charges. I've just got the ABC board off my back over that incident."

"He could have killed you!" Maya couldn't shake the image of that cleaver swinging at his chest. She stared at him in wide-eyed horror. It had never occurred to her to worry about Axell's safety. He was just there, like North Carolina's ever-present jungle of trees. Discovering he was as human and vulnerable as Matty and Constance and Alexa turned her version of the world on its head.

A glitter of amusement lit his eyes as she gripped his arm. "Bigger men than that have tried. I grew up in a *bar*, Maya. I can take care of myself."

"You lifted him off the floor! He was nearly as big as you. He had a meat cleaver!"

A waitress returned with glasses of wine. Axell shoved one into Maya's fingers. "Settle down. I have to wait for the police and make a report. I want it perfectly clear that they weren't here at my request." Regret puckered his brow. "I'm sorry, Maya. I wanted to have you to myself for a little while, but I know you're hungry. Shall I have Alphonso fix you something to eat?"

The question was moot. The chef had already dished up

plates of pasta and one of the busboys was carrying them in their direction.

"It's my new recipe," Alphonso shouted over the noise of the kitchen. "Taste it." He turned to snap at one of the waitresses scurrying to keep out of his way. "Bring them a Caesar salad, and don't bruise the lettuce this time!"

Still amazed, if not as shaken, Maya shook her head at Axell. "The pasta will be fine. Will you sit and eat it with me or do you have to check on the bar?" She was slowly understanding that she had married not just a man, but his business, too. They were part and parcel of each other. She hadn't decided how she felt about that, no more than she was certain about his violent streak, or the electrical excitement leaping between them.

In reply, Axell gripped her elbow and steered her toward the employee break room, away from the staff and his patrons and any other interference. "The evening isn't over," he warned as he seated her in the same booth they had used the night the shop collapsed.

Anticipation shivered up Maya's arm as Axell squeezed it. He wouldn't kiss her in front of others; he wasn't a publicly demonstrative man, but she could see the heat in his eyes as he looked down at her. The man definitely intended for the evening to have a more intimate end.

"We found them smoking in the alley, both higher than kites," the patrol officer announced as he accepted the soft drink a waitress handed him. "Claimed they came after their back pay, but the drugs blow the terms of their bond. They won't be out again."

The detective in charge snapped his ballpoint shut and shoved his notepad back in his pocket. "Until we find the dealer and where he stashes his stuff, the problem will only get worse." He glanced in Maya's direction. "Heard your sister is back in town."

"My sister has absolutely . . ." Maya started out of her seat as if prepared to scratch the cop's eyes out.

Axell grabbed her shoulder and shoved her back down. She turned her glare in his direction and spiked his foot with her heel so hard, he grimaced, but ignored her fury. He calmly answered for her. "Cleo is out at my place tonight, reading books to her kid. That was a cheap, lazy shot. And I'd already paid the bastards. This is a setup. Ask them where they got the stuff."

"Those kind never give straight answers." Undeterred by Axell's insult, the detective got in his parting remark. "Heard that musician staying at the shop is working at a club downtown that got raided. You might wanta be more careful who you associate with, Mr. Holm. Tar sticks."

For a woman who detested confrontation, Maya certainly put up a struggle as Axell grabbed her arms and physically held her in her seat, clapping a hand over her mouth as the detective walked off. She bit his fingers as savagely as she could and dug her fingers into his arm. He was damned glad he wasn't wearing just a T-shirt. She'd had her nails done, and they cut like miniature knives.

"You have no right—" she sputtered as the door closed behind the police and Axell released her.

"I have every right," he returned coldly, dragging her from the booth and toward the door. "This is my place, and I'll not have the local cops on my back. They just don't like outsiders, and Cleo and Stephen," he glanced down at her briefly, "and even you, are outsiders. It's much easier to pin bad things on people they don't know. They're human. Hell, I've met your sister and Stephen, and I still don't trust them. So let it go."

"You don't trust them?" she asked incredulously as he pushed her into the alley. "You think I would leave the kids with anyone I didn't trust? What kind of person are you? Would you leave Constance with someone you think deals drugs?"

"I'm trusting your judgment in leaving them there, and that's all I'm trusting. And there are times I wonder why the hell I'm doing that." Axell could see all his plans for the evening going up in a tower of flame. If he'd thought Maya capable of planning anything, he'd blame *her* for the evening's fiasco. He was in dire need and she was no less attractive for being furious. He had to hold on to her arm to prevent her from slapping him. He could think of a lot better things his hand could be doing right now.

"Right. I'm an airheaded idiot too naive and too stupid to know if someone's doing drugs. What do I know about people, anyway? They all look alike to me."

She was on a real roll, Axell realized as he tried to steer her toward the car. He'd married a spacy pacifist, and she'd emerged from her cocoon as a Valkyrie, prepared to defend those she loved. He'd always detested scenes like this, but the earlier adrenaline rush had combined with too much testosterone, and his lust not only took on new proportions, but entirely new perspectives. The heat of her in his arms baked his brains.

"Why don't you take away my license and keys and keep me at home, where I can't hurt myself?" she taunted as he tried to drag her toward the car. "That's what you'd really like, isn't it? Complete control. Well, dammit, I'm not one of your little tin soldiers."

To Axell's surprise, she jerked her arm from his grasp and ran down the alley in those ridiculous strapped high heels. He'd never seen Maya in high heels. She had ankles halfway up to her knees. Shaking his head at his wayward thoughts, he waited for her to discover she had nowhere to run.

He figured she'd give it up before she crossed the street to the next block, but she didn't. Cursing at making a spectacle of himself, Axell chased her across the street and down the alley behind the town's oldest stores. Stumbling over a garbage can, he caught up with her before they could both break their necks. Grabbing her arm, he pulled her hard against him, despite her twisting protest. To hell with arguing. He was ready for the next part. Past ready. "Yell at me if you want, but don't run away, dammit!" Holding Maya's squirming curves tight with both arms wrapped around her, he dived down to claim the lips he'd coveted for too long.

In seconds, they were both going up in flames. Gasping for air, Axell leaned back against the door of Cleo's old shop.

The door opened, and they fell in.

❧ TWENTY-SEVEN ❧

If you smoke after sex, you're doing it too fast.

"You forgot to lock the damned door!" Axell muttered as he staggered backward into the musty darkness and righted both of them before they could collapse into the chaos of old boxes left from the move.

"It's a condemned building, let someone else lock it," Maya sniped, more disgruntled by having the fieriest kiss of her entire life interrupted than worrying about whether or not she'd locked a door. Still, she shouldn't have let him manipulate her like that. She was angry at him. Furious. She just couldn't completely remember why.

"Proper civic attitude." Slamming the door closed and casting them into total night, Axell backed her against the wall. "Now, where were we?"

"If you think you can—" she started to protest, but Axell's mouth cut her off. His tongue took advantage of her parted lips and initiated an intoxicating foray that had her gripping his shoulders for support. Virgos avoided spontaneity. Surely he didn't . . .

"Axell, we can't—"

"We can." He propped his hands on either side of her head and deepened the kiss.

The heated, masculine aroma of Axell's skin and shaving lotion surged through Maya's senses as his weight pressed her against the wall. She was piercingly aware of all the places they touched, of the way her breasts in their thin silk crushed against his suit coat, of the way his zipper ground into her belly beneath the pressure of his arousal. With what remained of her mind, she knew this was insane, but the insistent hollow in her lower parts had no mind, only needs, and her hips pushed up to find his.

"I'd meant to take you to a hotel and buy champagne," he muttered in frustration as his hands located the curves of her breasts and crushed them in a desperate caress.

"The nearest hotel is in Charlotte and I hate champagne," she protested without thinking, sinking her fingers into Axell's glorious golden hair and pulling his mouth back to hers.

"Oh, God, yes," he muttered hungrily against her mouth. "No kids, no cats, no interruptions . . ."

She couldn't argue with any of that, especially with his hands unfastening the thin collar holding the top of her dress in place. She could see nothing in the darkness, but the lack of vision heightened her other senses. Axell's fingers slid caressingly beneath the fabric of her dress, slipping the neckline down until he cupped her breasts with those big firm hands she'd admired from the start. She sucked in a breath as the callused roughness stroked her skin.

The urgent mouth plundering her lips suddenly lowered to suckle at her breast.

Given the freedom to scream, she did. The moisture of Axell's mouth connected with the electric current already surging through her, jolting her into a different dimension. Maya arched higher, grasping his broad shoulders for support, pushing into him and demanding more. Axell obliged. With a haste she'd never seen in him, he drank her deeper, harder, until she thought he'd sucked her inside of him and swirled her somewhere in the dark vortex of his soul. His other hand plucked the nipple of the breast his mouth had yet to claim. The twin sensations spun her into a spiral from which there was no return. Only the crush of his hips against her belly prevented her from elevating entirely from the floor.

Somewhere in the back of her mind, Maya knew what they were doing was ridiculous for two grown, married people, but she didn't care. Releasing Axell's shoulders, she wriggled her hands between them and sought his belt.

He groaned deep in his throat as her knuckles brushed his fly. "I've been wondering what you wore under this piece of nothing," he muttered, lowering one hand to pull at her skirt while his mouth traveled from one breast to the other, via the hollow of her throat and by means of kisses so hot they left scorch marks.

Maya got his belt unfastened and started on his zipper. "Keep your romantic fantasies a little longer. Just help me with this damned . . ."

He obliged readily. Before she could exclaim over the size of the erection she brushed against, Axell had her skirt hiked to her waist, and his hot palm seared her flesh.

"Garters. Damn, you wore garters. I want to see. . . ." He uttered a guttural groan as she stroked him. "Maya-a-a-a . . . ah-h."

She thought he tore her panties in two—her stoic businessman reverted to uncivilized Norse god.

She wasn't in any shape for thinking. She only knew the moment when Axell's fingers probed higher, stroking her to the brink with a rough caress. His fingers weren't enough. Clutching his shoulders again, she shoved against him, demanding more, demanding what now rubbed against her belly, heavy and aroused.

A keening cry of ecstasy escaped her lips as Axell stroked her deeper, in just the right spot, instantly carrying her to the precipice and . . . over. . . .

Maya shuddered and wept and fell against him as she lost control. It had never been this way before. Never. Men used her. She used men. Nothing like this had ever happened. She couldn't stop. She needed more, needed it more urgently than ever. The tension spiraled up inside her so quickly, she gasped. It wasn't enough.

Axell understood. Lifting her hips in his hands, he raised her to his height. Instinctively—because she was incapable of thought—Maya wrapped her legs around him and arched outward, demanding what she knew he could give.

He drove into her with a stroke so deep, he should have

struck her backbone. Crying now, she rocked against him, taking him deeper, until he rubbed the mouth of her womb and the shudders rocked all the way through her.

He withdrew and plunged again, took her all the way up, then teased her by drawing back some more. Maya screamed, then cursed, then buried his throat in kisses. He didn't even have his shirt off. She pawed at the cotton, but she couldn't reach his chest. He pounded her against the wall again, protecting her hips with his hands, driving her back into that spiraling vortex that swept them both into its center like leaves in the wind.

"Now, Maya, now . . ."

And at his command, she broke, splintered into so many pieces she'd never recover them all. She was aware of Axell's shout of release, of his powerful surge deep within her, of the rush of hot liquid filling her as he shattered along with her. All their atoms and particles twinkled and twirled in a cosmic dance in the darkness, combining them as no piece of paper or human words could ever do.

Speechless, they panted in each other's arms, ignoring their surroundings, wrapped up in the physical bond they'd just forged. Anything else would be an intrusion, and they'd had far too many intrusions in the past.

"My God, Maya, I never thought . . ." Axell lowered her carefully to the floor, not releasing the smooth skin of her buttocks. She had such delectably soft skin, skin that wafted a scent of roses as he stroked, skin he couldn't stop touching if his life depended on it. Maybe if she would let him, just one more time . . .

He must be mad. They were in a condemned building, no doubt surrounded by rats. He'd meant to give her champagne and a honeymoon suite.

"Could we do that again?" she whispered breathlessly somewhere just below his ear. "So I could know it wasn't just a fluke?"

Axell laughed helplessly against her fallen stack of curls. Even her hair smelled of roses. No complicated chemical scents for his Maya. The ache inside him right now was all her.

He lifted his head, and finally releasing her tempting skin, smoothed her hair. "Let's test it out in bed, all right? I'm afraid that next time, the walls will tumble down with the vibrations."

"I'm still furious at you," she reminded him.

"I want to see what you look like with all the lights on," he countered, pulling up the neck of her dress and reluctantly trying to fasten it.

She wriggled beneath him, inflaming his senses instantly. He didn't do things like this. He never lost control of a situation. He'd never tried to control Maya. His palm filled with plump breast as he tried to hold her still.

"Gotcha," she whispered. Then, as suddenly as she'd wriggled, she went stock still. "Did you hear that?"

His mind wasn't thinking clearly. His hearing wasn't working at all. "Hear what?" he murmured without paying attention to anything other than the warm squeezable places his fingers explored.

"Mice?" she offered tentatively. "Really big rats?"

She wasn't cooperating here. Forcing his muddled mind back to her words, Axell tried to listen. There was a definite rattle of trash, and a footstep where there shouldn't be any. Every protective instinct he'd ever possessed leaped into action.

"Stay here," he ordered, shoving his shirt back into his pants and quickly fastening them. He couldn't believe he'd just behaved like some freaking adolescent. He hadn't done this kind of thing even as an adolescent. Sex in a public place. He had more sense than that.

"Let's just get out," Maya whispered, shimmying her dress back in place. "We can call the police from the restaurant."

"Whoever it is will be gone by the time the cops show."

He didn't give her time to protest again but moved deeper into the storeroom. Maya should never have left the back door unlocked. Vagrants could take up occupancy and burn the place down. It wouldn't be the first time an old building had gone up in smoke.

"Chill man, I hear something."

Axell dived for the source of the voice, but it was too far ahead of him. A door slammed and feet clattered on what sounded like stone steps. Shoving boxes aside, he tried to locate any sign of a door in the darkness. He vaguely remembered one back here in the storage space Maya hadn't used.

"Axell! Axell, where are you?" Maya's anxious voice called from nearby.

"I thought I told you to stay put." He needed a flashlight. All he was getting out of this was bruised shins. "Isn't there another door back here?"

"To the furnace room."

He almost heard the shrug in her voice. "Furnace room? Below here?" In a building this old, that could mean almost anything. "What kind of furnace?"

"The kind that heats things," she said dryly, catching his arm. "The enormously expensive kind, if the bills we received last winter were any indication. I don't know why steam heat ever went out of favor. There are radiators all over that would have done a better job than whatever the modern version is. Why are you suddenly concerned by the heating system?"

Axell gave up the search and steered her toward the door they'd entered. With Maya beside him, he could probably generate enough steam to fuel every radiator in here. "Coal is scarce," he reminded her. "Steam requires coal. Chances are, your furnace room has a coal cellar."

She thought about that a minute as they worked their way back to the door. "Coal cellars have coal chutes, don't they?" she asked reflectively.

"You got it. I can't imagine how they get up and down it without a ladder, but chances are, that's what they're doing right now."

"Who?" she demanded. "What who's doing? This is a condemned building, for pity's sake. There's nothing here to steal."

"Tell me something I don't know." Axell jerked open the alley door and pushed Maya through. Then he firmly turned the lock and pulled the door shut. He wished he had the dead-bolt key. "But the cops are looking for the place the dealer stashes his drugs. Empty buildings are ideal crack houses."

"Let's get back to the restaurant." Nervously, Maya tugged his arm.

He wanted to look for the coal chute. He wanted to know who was using Cleo's old building. And had they been doing so even while Maya lived here? That idea gave him cold chills. Maybe he'd better take Maya home first. They had some unfinished business, and he doubted if he'd catch the intruders at this late date.

Reason warred with lust and lust won. He wanted to see Maya spread-eagled across his bed, wearing nothing but garters. He wanted to see if he could control the situation a little better next time, or maybe not. There was something exhilarating about utter mindlessness.

"We'll call the police from home." With sudden urgency, Axell hurried Maya up the street, toward the car. To hell with intruders. It wasn't his building anyway.

"Your place or mine?" she murmured provocatively as he helped her in.

Her room, with the possibility of kids and cats running in and out, or his, a million light-years distant from Alexa or childhood nightmares. Cursing as he started the engine, Axell decided not to think about that either. They still had to get through the twin tempests of Cleo and Stephen. Why had he ever thought life with Maya could be handled in a rational manner?

"Told you so," she mocked through the darkness, apparently reading his mind. "Ready to throw me out yet?"

"You're just waiting for that, aren't you?" He understood her that much, anyway. "One wrong word, and you'll be gone. You're not a kid anymore, Maya. You can stand up to the grown-ups on equal terms now."

"Equal." She snorted inelegantly. "Like you don't have it all. There's nothing equal about this relationship. Once the sex grows boring, what will you do? Run for governor and live in Raleigh?"

"Don't start, Maya," Axell warned. "I'm not in any humor to handle your baggage right now. I've got enough of my own to deal with. Just concentrate on how quickly we can get Cleo and Stephen out of the house."

"One thing at a time," she said, her humor restored if the amusement in her voice was any indication. "Sometimes life doesn't let you do things the way you like them done."

"Well, until that happens, I'll do things my way, thank you." He already had the plan formulated. Get rid of nuisances, check on kids, seduce Maya. Worked for him.

Every light in the house blazed as they turned up the driveway. Axell cursed under his breath. Maya remained blessedly silent. The kids should be asleep by now. Lights were not indicative of sleep.

"It's still sort of early," Maya said carefully as they pulled into the garage. "The kids were probably just overexcited."

"If hyperactive kids are all I have to handle, I wouldn't be worried."

The instant they walked through the door into the kitchen, a babble of excited voices greeted them.

"Muldoon scared Kitty!" Matty shouted.

Looking more like a harassed mother and less like a dispassionate murderess, Cleo grabbed his pajama shirt. "Matty, get back to bed. I told you we'd take—"

"Right, like pulling down the drapes helped. The damned cat will come down when it's ready." Obviously steaming, Stephen strolled into the kitchen pressing a wet cloth to cat scratches on his bare arm.

"Daddy, he's been saying dirty words. And Alexa spit up all over Mommy's rug."

Taking a deep breath and counting to ten, Axell thanked God there were no police or fire engines involved, fixed a glassy gaze on Maya's beaming, expectant face, and exhaled. He could deal with this. Months of sexual frustration had finally found a divine source of release, and he hadn't had his fill yet. He could move the Great Wall of China right now if it meant landing in Maya's bed. He'd been rude, crude, and uncouth the first time, and he desperately needed to make it up to her. He didn't want her getting any more strange ideas than she already had. He didn't *do* things like that.

"Constance, back to bed! Matty, take your cat and get back to your room." Axell swept the rest of the room with a look that he used to clear brawlers from the bar. "Out! The lot of you. Visiting hours at the asylum are over."

Belatedly, as everyone scrambled, Axell wondered what they'd done with his reliable baby-sitter.

July 1946

   As you may have heard, I have been visiting in the country with cousins. I wish you well with your new bride, although I do hope you've developed a taste for sheep since sticking it up her ass is about the best you can hope from her. Her type certainly would never welcome you with open arms.

   Be that as it may, your daughter was born July first. She will stay with my cousins, where she cannot cause you undue embarrassment, or I cause her the same. Should you wish to contribute to her upbringing, you may send what you will to my cousins at the enclosed address. As she reaches the age of understanding, I will refrain from telling her of her origins for fear she will recognize how very small a man her father is.

❧ TWENTY-EIGHT ❧

Diplomacy is the art of saying "Nice doggie" until you can find a stick.

"Your mommy will see you after school tomorrow," Maya reassured the tearful five-year-old as she led him back to bed.

Axell had all but thrown Cleo and Stephen into his car and driven them to town when the local cab couldn't arrive soon enough to suit him.

"Don' wanna go to school," Matty replied sullenly.

Oh, great. Loving, obedient Matty had turned on her, too. Sometimes she had to wonder if she'd started down the wrong path somewhere and if she should turn back and see where she'd lost her way.

"Mr. Pig would miss you." She used her best no-nonsense voice as she tucked him in. "And you wouldn't get to play Duck, Duck, Goose with Peggy and Billy," naming his two favorite friends of the moment. "Now off to sleep." She pressed a kiss to his forehead and slipped out the door.

Matty had stayed in his own room several nights in a row this past week. Maya had the distinct feeling tonight would not be one of those nights.

Oh, well. She checked on Constance and got a rundown on the evening's events. Poor Dorothy had apparently put up a valiant front, but she'd been called away on a family emergency, reassured by the so-called adults in the house that everything was under control. Maya couldn't really blame the woman. Cleo and Stephen looked old enough to handle three little kids and a few cats.

"Well, learn from example, love," she warned Constance. "Never swing Alexa in the air after she's had her bottle."

Constance giggled and snuggled beneath the covers. "Aunt Cleo yelled at Mr. James for saying those words. What does 'bugger it all' mean?"

With the whole scene vividly clear in her mind, Maya chuckled. "It means Alexa's daddy was very, very angry. Now go to sleep. I'll take care of the carpet."

By the time she'd checked on Alexa and made certain the other two were settled, Axell had apparently returned from town and rescued the kitten from the drapery rod in the family room.

"I'm thinking tile and throwaway rugs in here," he said in disgruntlement as he surveyed the interestingly stained carpet.

"Don't you mean 'throw' rugs?"

"No, in this case, I mean exactly what I said." He didn't explain but looked at her instead.

She was still wearing her evening gown, and Maya shivered at the focus of his gaze. Making love in total darkness the first time seemed somehow symbolic. She didn't know if she could do it again, in the light, in a bed. Commitment was not something she understood, but "bed" and "husband" seemed irretrievably linked with "commitment," and it scared the hell out of her. A condemned building just seemed more her style. She bit back a grin, remembering just how completely her dignified husband had lost his cool.

"My bed, or yours?" he asked when she didn't answer his rather pointed silence.

"Matty will come looking for me," she murmured, fretting at a loose thread. "And Alexa usually wakes in the night. And Constance has nightmares."

"Fine, your room, then," he said confidently, steering her in the right direction. "Matty will have to learn to knock."

Maya gulped. She didn't know why this was so difficult for her. She was a grown woman. Men had slept in her bed before. Not many, admittedly. She'd never had much time or patience or interest before. And none of them had erased all thought of sleep. She didn't know why Axell should be different. He was just a man. An arrogant Virgo. With a strong streak of passionate Scorpio.

The labels didn't help. Her heart still fluttered and her breath did a little raspy number as Axell loomed large and strong beside her bedroom door, waiting for her to enter. Labels didn't make the man.

"We've done this before," he said gravely as she hesitated, but Maya could see the twinkle behind his placid expression. Add "impossible" to her list of labels.

She swept past his imposing frame. "I want to shower first."

Axell closed the door and propped a chair beneath the knob. "You showered before we left. You can shower later. Right now, everything is quiet. We might not have another chance."

He didn't even look at the chaos that was her bedroom. With his gaze focused totally on her, Axell began unfastening the buttons of his shirt. He'd discarded the fancy jacket and tie before climbing after the kitten.

Maya bit her bottom lip as Axell's spectacular chest emerged from his starched shirt. Tanned, muscled flesh rippled temptingly as he flung the shirt over a chair. Golden brown hair formed an inverted triangle between flat brown nipples. Stephen didn't have chest hair. Heck, compared to this, Stephen didn't have a chest.

"Need help?" he taunted, moving closer.

The muscles of his shoulders bulged. His biceps flexed as he reached for her. Underneath those expensive business suits, he was all animal muscle. Her gaze dropped to below his buckle. All muscle.

"Your turn," he whispered challengingly.

Wits fled, she didn't slip away in time as he closed the distance between them. For the second time that night, Axell popped the tiny hook holding up her dress.

"If the cat's got your tongue, I want it back," he murmured beside her ear as her dress fell to the floor.

Axell's kiss was as devastating as she remembered. Maya

tasted traces of the wine they'd consumed earlier before her mind hit sensory overload.

Her palms stroked over rock-hard solid muscles which rippled and surged beneath her caress. The heat between them was intense enough to ignite spontaneous combustion. His mouth savored hers as his hands explored, and his touch brought the realization that except for garters and stockings, she was completely naked. Somewhere in the trash of the storeroom, she'd left behind what remained of her panties.

He stroked between her thighs and she almost crawled up his leg. Axell stepped back to study what he'd bared. Maya had known the intensity of his concentration could be a dangerous thing. She melted beneath the heat of it now.

"You're so . . . so . . . petite," he said, struggling for the words as he stared.

Maya saw the worried frown form between his eyes as Axell fingered her nipple. She knew she wasn't anything to write home about. "Disappointed?" she asked lightly, as if the bottom hadn't fallen out of her stomach. People had rejected her all her life.

He looked startled at her question. "Disappointed? Are you kidding? You're so perfect, you scare me. Did I hurt you earlier? I didn't realize . . ." He gestured helplessly, but his hungry gaze dropped to the dainty blue garters on her thighs.

Maya didn't know if it was his words, or his gesture, or his gaze, but suddenly it was all just right. He wasn't rejecting her. He wanted her. She was woman to his man, and all their other differences disappeared.

She reached for his belt buckle. "Do I look hurt?" she asked in a sultry voice she scarcely recognized.

"You look glorious." He unfastened the buckle on his own, stripping off trousers and briefs faster than she could think of it. "I'm thinking that I got the best of this deal."

Without any warning, Axell caught her waist and dropped her on the bed, falling down on top of her so that his knees splayed her thighs wide. "Were the garters for my benefit?" he whispered as he nibbled her ear.

Yeah, they were, but she didn't think she'd inflate his ego

further by admitting it. "I just thought I'd make things easier, in case you'd forgotten how," she taunted.

"The basic principles don't seem to have changed any." He teased her breast into a pucker and kissed her until time stood still. Then, lifting his head, he finished thoughtfully, "It goes in like this, right?"

Maya squealed as Axell drove home with a thrust so powerful it lifted her from the bed.

Amazingly perceptive was this business-suit husband of hers, she reflected wryly in those few seconds left in which she could think at all. It went in just like that.

He breathed the heady aroma of roses. Air-conditioning cooled his backside, but the warmth of summer snuggled against his morning arousal. How long had it been since he'd held a woman in his arms when he woke? Not even Angela . . .

He didn't need to take that path. For the first time in his life, he held a woman who caused him to forget the bar and all the demands of his day. He didn't want to just make love to her, although the physical pressure to do so was strong. But the urge to see Maya's eyes when she woke was stronger. He wanted to watch her wakening interest, hear the humor in her voice, longed to see the affection. . . .

Hell, he wanted a lot more than the same affection she gave to her students, but he wouldn't dwell on that now either. Maya's generous nature encompassed one and all. He just happened to be the lucky recipient of her physical favors, too. That's all he'd wanted when they entered into this arrangement, wasn't it? He had no right to demand more.

Axell cupped his hand around a full, firm breast. He'd take his pleasure where he found it, and he found it in the warm curve of buttocks pressed against his arousal, and the enticing moan his caress elicited from the woman snuggling into his arms. His woman. He really, really liked the idea of this wonderfully imaginative, inherently passionate woman belonging to him alone. If that was disgustingly prehistoric, then so be it.

"Do you like mornings?" He leaned over her, admiring the

tousled spill of colorful hair across the pillow. He pulled the purple strand, discovered gray at its roots, and smiled as he realized Maya didn't believe in dyeing her hair in any normal manner.

"I do now," she murmured sleepily. "No one's pounding on the door?"

"Not yet." Even as he said it, Axell heard his namesake cooing in her cradle and a pair of feet hit the floor running in the room next door. "I don't suppose even a quickie—"

Small fists thrashed the door. "Maya! Maya! It's late. Wake up. Why is Matty sleeping in front of your door? We gotta get to school."

"You've taught her to murder the English language," Axell complained as he pulled his aching loins away from temptation. Self-denial did not improve his humor.

"Constance can speak properly when she likes. Slang just means she's comfortable with us." Maya groped under her pillow and produced a long purple football jersey.

"If comfortable equates lazy," he grumbled.

The sudden silence on the other side of the door seemed ominous. Axell grabbed his clothes.

"Did I hear Daddy?" a timid voice squeaked.

"Now we're in for it," Maya said cheerfully, wriggling into the jersey. "You may be sorry she's talking again."

"Women and children should be seen and not heard." He jerked on his trousers. Only Maya's admiring glance over her shoulder restored some of his humor. Maybe she was right. Maybe he didn't notice women when they looked at him. He sure as hell noticed when Maya did it, though. It made him wish his pants weren't so damned tight.

Assured that he was at least decent, Maya opened the bedroom door to a silent Matty sucking his thumb and a wary Constance. "All right, I'm running late," she admitted. "Why don't the two of you fix cereal? I'll be out to help in a few minutes."

Axell could see Constance straining to peer past Maya as he pulled on his shirt, and dread filled his soul. He didn't know how to handle these awkward situations.

"Did Daddy sleep with you?" Constance asked, half-accusingly.

"That's what daddies and mommies do. Now hurry up. Alexa will be hollering for her bottle soon. You can pour your milk, can't you?"

Not entirely accepting this new arrangement, the kids reluctantly reacted to the command in Maya's voice. Some people talked to animals. Maya spoke to kids. By the time Constance and Matty hit the kitchen, Axell could hear their giggles.

He looked at her wonderingly and with definite admiration. The jersey emphasized all the right curves and almost matched her purple streak as she turned around. "I can see why you teach school."

And he could. All this time, he'd thought her teacher act was just something she did for the money because she couldn't do anything else. He'd known the kids liked her, that the school was clean and decent and had the kind of teacher/student ratio he preferred for Constance. Other than that, he'd thought the school a duplicate of every other school of its kind. He was just beginning to grasp what the kids understood instinctively: with Maya on board, the Impossible Dream was unique.

He didn't want it to be that way. He wanted the school to be dispensable. He wanted Maya for Constance. He didn't care about the other kids.

But Maya did. Maya cared for those kids as much as she cared for her own.

Someone may have murdered for that school. He didn't want Maya or the kids in their path. How the hell would he talk her into closing?

"Why are you looking at me like that?" Maya slid her arms around his waist and stood on tiptoe to kiss him.

Groaning, he kissed her back, then firmly set her away. "There's only so much denial I can handle in one day. And I was looking to see if you wore wings and a halo or sported a magic wand. How do you do that?"

"What?" she teased, slipping her hand beneath his partially buttoned shirt and teasing at the curl of hair above his waistband. "You don't know how sex works?"

"Not with two kids and a whimpering infant underfoot," he said dryly, removing her hand from temptation. "I think I'll hire a nanny."

She snickered and headed for the shower. "You had three of them here last night. Just let me know when you want your peace back."

An icy breeze washed over Axell as the bathroom door closed between them. She was still thinking of their marriage as a temporary arrangement that would end the minute he tired of it.

She still kept her teacups packed in a box at the school, ready to move at a moment's notice. Maya didn't know the meaning of permanence, didn't share his ability to ride out life's storms.

The druggies in his restaurant last night were probably the opening volley of the mayor's new war against his license. What would happen to their marriage if he was forced to trade Maya's school to protect their livelihood—and maybe even his family's safety?

❧ TWENTY-NINE ❧

I tried sniffing Coke once, but the ice kept bumping my nose.

The chimes tinkled as Maya entered the Curiosity Shoppe. It wasn't her store anymore, but she needed to clue Cleo in on some of the changes she'd made at the instigation of Axell and Selene. She was rather proud that the place was finally making a small profit. She prayed Cleo would appreciate what they'd done. Her big sister was the only real "home" she'd known growing up. She wanted that connection back—another impossible dream, she supposed.

"What are you doing here?" a raspy voice asked from the dark interior. "Isn't it enough you've got my kid, you want my store, too?"

Well, so much for prayer. Maya was beginning to remember why she and Cleo hadn't parted on the best of terms. "You wanted me to leave Matty with Social Services?" She probably ought to just turn around and leave. She didn't have the stamina for Cleo's anger this morning. Axell had left her limp and so confused she didn't know whether she was coming or going. She had to be doing one or the other. She'd never stayed still in her life.

"That's not what that legal paper you sent was all about. You want my kid." Cleo emerged from the back of the shop, coffee cup in hand. She looked as if she hadn't slept all night. Her short hair stood on end, and her T-shirt looked as if she'd wrung it out and put it on wet. She was so thin, the shirt outlined her rib cage.

Maya searched for some sign of drugs, but Cleo's eyes

255

were clear and snapping. "That's a legal maneuver. Axell's lawyer says if we have guardianship, then Social Services can't do anything if we let you take care of Matty as much as you like. Otherwise, you can't have Matty until the social worker says you can."

"Where's my teapot?" Cleo reached for her pockets as if hunting for a cigarette, cursed, then shoved her hands in her jeans waistband.

Maya didn't need an explanation. Cleo had always smoked, for as long as she could remember. Cutting out cigarettes and drugs both must be driving her crazy. "It's at the school. We almost lost everything when the other building collapsed, so I packed it up and stored it somewhere safe. I'll get it for you."

Cleo dropped into the wicker chair and curled her legs under her, not looking at Maya. "I want my life back. You've got my kid, my store, my damned teapot. Hell, you've got my town. You married Wadeville's golden boy. What am I supposed to do, crawl off in a hole somewhere and let you have it all?"

This was the point where Maya was supposed to slink off into the sunset and let everyone do their own thing. She didn't have answers. Never had. But she'd made some decisions that got her in this position, and she didn't see any immediate way out.

Maya dropped into the other chair. "Why did you move to Wadeville?" Maya kicked herself, but the question was out there and she couldn't think of a better one.

Cleo shrugged and rested her head against the high back of the chair. "When I left the Creep, I had to go somewhere. I thought maybe I could make it in our hometown, find our roots. I should have known better."

The Creep, Cleo's husband, the one who'd hooked her on drugs. Maya knew all that from garbled phone conversations over the years. But the Creep hadn't been in Wadeville. Whatever Cleo had done here, she had done to herself.

"I kind of like it here." Maya was surprised to hear herself say that. She didn't like places. They changed too often. But she'd had her first opportunity of building her dream here.

The people of Wadeville had offered her more opportunities than anywhere else. "Wouldn't it be nice if we could be a real family, raise our kids in a real town?" she asked with a tinge of hope.

"It ain't gonna happen," Cleo said callously. "I can't keep this place running. The only job I qualify for is waitressing. The rent around here is too expensive to live on tips. Old Man Pfeiffer cut me a break on the other building, but I'm not living off your husband's charity."

"Pfeiffer? Mr. Pfeiffer owned the other building? I paid the rent to some corporation." There was a topic she could sink her teeth into without disturbing old arguments.

"Yeah, but he must have owned it. I think the old goat owns all kinds of stuff around here. He says he's our grandfather, isn't that a hoot? He has more relatives than Adam has apples, owns half these doddering buildings, and he wants to own us, too."

"Grandfather?" Maya couldn't take that in. They had aunts and uncles and cousins all over creation, she knew that. But the blood between them had been damned thin. She didn't remember any grandfathers. He'd said he knew their grandmother. Did that fit?

"He's dead, you know," Maya said. "He owned the property the school is on, and now Axell says the court will sell it since he didn't leave a will."

Cleo's head shot up. "Dead? Well, shit, that cinches it. He gave me some cock-and-bull story about how he'd met our grandmother before he married, but he didn't do right by her and he was going to make it all up to us now that his wife was gone and he could admit what he'd done. I figured the old goat was just lonely and wanted someone to talk to. He has nieces and nephews and cousins who never visited unless they wanted something. I kinda felt sorry for him."

"So did I, but he definitely had a muddy aura. Maybe that's why he gave us such a good deal on the school. We could never have afforded it without his help." Maya dug her fingers into her hair and tried to sort it all out, but she didn't have much confidence in ancient history—although with the names their mother had given them, she supposed she should at least show some interest.

"Muddy aura." Cleo snorted. "You're as crazy as I am." She shifted uncomfortably. "But he wasn't above muddy deals. It's probably good that he's gone." She sank into glum thought.

Maya didn't want to hear about muddy deals. She didn't want to know what Cleo had done in her former life. But for Matty's sake, she had to know. "He didn't get you mixed up in anything, did he?"

Cleo spiked her hair worse than it was. "Anything I did, I did to myself. Pfeiffer might have blamed himself, but it wasn't his fault."

"Cleo?" Maya asked uncertainly when she didn't continue.

Cleo sighed. "He let some slimeballs use some of his old buildings. I know dealers when I see them. When things got bad, I sought them out, not vice versa. But if Pfeiffer's gone, they'll have moved on. You don't have to worry. I'm clean, and I'm staying that way."

Maya nodded in relief. "That's hard to believe of that nice old man. Maybe he didn't know they were dealing."

Cleo grunted in disbelief but didn't argue. "Your turn to spill. Since you were already knocked up when you came out here, how the hell did you get Superman to marry you?"

Superman. Maya smiled. "I was thinking in terms of Norse gods myself. Thor, maybe? It's a long story. You really don't want to hear it. But Axell's good with lawyers. Do you think if we could prove Mr. Pfeiffer was our grandfather, we might get part of his estate?" She wasn't really interested for herself, but for Cleo . . . it might give her a reason for hanging out awhile longer.

"If a collapsed building and a run-down old house is the extent of it, we wouldn't get enough to pay the lawyers." Cleo sipped her coffee and stared around at the sparkling shop inventory. "I kind of liked the stuff dusty and moldy. It had a certain flavor to it."

"Yeah, it was called Eau de Rat. The store made a profit

last month," Maya offered tentatively. "Axell said with all the new growth around here, this town would be seeing a lot of new business, that with the right planning, your shop could be a major asset."

"If I stay off dope and out of the clutches of idiots," Cleo answered gloomily. "It's not that easy. I owe a lot of favors." She sat up and glared at Maya. "I want Matty back."

"You want to run," Maya accused her. "I'll be damned if I let you do that to him."

"He's my kid."

"He's your responsibility. There's a difference." Maya dug her fingers into the chair arms. She'd never learned to stand up for herself or anyone else, but Cleo was her sister. If she couldn't stand up to her, she couldn't help anybody.

"You don't understand. Nobody understands. It's just better if I leave." Cleo slumped back in the chair and glared at the glass counter.

"You can't leave. You're on probation. You've got to stick it out and fight whatever it is you're running from. You've got family behind you now. It can work. We're not alone anymore."

"Oh, yeah, and Beaver and his mom will bake cookies and serve lemonade." Cleo struggled silently with her inner demons for a minute more, then narrowed her eyes and turned her glare back to Maya. "I'll do whatever it takes to get Matty."

All right. Step one. That's all she could handle right now. "Talk to Social Services. See if they'll give him over to you. If they won't, we'll talk about alternatives." Maya got up. "I'll finish up those shoe paintings. You talk to the system."

Miraculously, Cleo seemed to accept this order of things. She wandered off to clean up while Maya took her usual place behind the counter. It had been a very confusing few days. She needed the security of her paint and brushes.

Maya glanced up as the door chimes rang. The shop had just opened for the day and nobody came in at ten in the morning. If it was Axell, she didn't know if she was ready to speak to him. They had some issues they needed to sort out, and not the way they had done it last night. Making love was a lot more dangerous to her equilibrium than she had imagined.

Her eyes widened as Katherine and the mayor walked in. They stared around as if they'd never been inside a store before. She bit back a grin as they ran into the bumper sticker rack. Nobody could get by that rack without looking and chuckling, even these two starched-up yuppies.

Ralph Arnold brought a sticker saying FORGET WORLD PEACE—VISUALIZE USING YOUR TURN SIGNAL to the counter. "Maybe we could put one of these on every car in town," he said dryly, laying it down and reaching for his wallet.

Maya shrugged and waved away his money. "It's on the house." She studied the man on the other side of the counter, looking for the devious aura that would nail him as up to no good, but she could see nothing more than his narrow-minded conservatism. At least they agreed on the poor driving habits of the local townspeople. "Maybe I could sell you a crystal ball? They're supposed to be real handy in telling the future."

The mayor looked at her suspiciously, but Katherine sauntered up and distracted him. She was wearing red, as usual, but a little more modestly tailored for a change. The skirt only rode halfway up her thighs.

"Pfeiffer's heirs want to sell the school property." Katherine dived right into the issue at hand. "We thought we could offer alternative properties to expedite the sale."

Axell had taught her one or two things over these last months, and one of them was to beware wiggling bait. Maya gestured toward her high-backed chairs. "Have a seat, if you like. Dazzle me with your knowledge. But remember, the house and the lease are in the court's hands, and there isn't a lawyer or judge in the state that will break my lease. I've got three years."

She watched the mayor's complexion turn purple and Katherine's eyes narrow to slits. Maya settled on her stool behind the counter and picked up her paintbrush.

"I thought Axell had explained to you that we need that

property *now*. We can get a judgment from the court allowing the road to go through there while the estate is pending. We just need your release."

"Axell explains lots of things to me. I don't remember him telling me I had to move or sign anything. Actually, if I remember correctly, someone mentioned that if anyone wanted me out of there early, they'd have to buy off my lease." Selene had actually mentioned that. Maya wasn't entirely clear on what it meant, but it had sounded good. Not that she had any intention of giving up the lease, but she liked shocking people.

"Axell promised!" Katherine all but shouted. "He said if we scratched his back, he'd scratch ours. He's supposed to help you find a new place."

Well, that was an entirely new perspective. Add one more issue to discuss with Mr. Axell Holm. But Maya was accustomed to keeping her mouth shut in the presence of civil servants. She smiled patiently. "So, scratch your own itches. They have nothing to do with mine. I have a lease and the school stays. There's an old depleted tobacco field just down the way. Why don't you buy it if you have to have a new road?"

"It's two miles out of the way!" the mayor argued. "It would cost a fortune to run that road through there. The Pfeiffer property will save the state hundreds of thousands. If you won't cooperate, we'll have to proceed with the land condemnation."

Maya shrugged. "Aside from the cost of building a bridge over the flood zone, moving the school should make you real popular with the parents of my students. They like the school where it is. And the ladies of the Garden Club are planning a fall tour of the landscaping. They've been working hard at it. Apparently, Pfeiffer has some plants in there that date back to the settling of the colony. Come to think of it, the Historic Society might get interested. There aren't many sites like that left."

"It's just a damned piece of land!" Arnold exploded. "You can't deprive the public of their right of access or the heirs to their rightful inheritance. We'll take it to court. Axell will be damned sorry he let you get into this."

Probably, but Axell would be damned sorry about a lot of things, and the Pfeiffer property was the least of them. Maya shrugged. "Whatever. I'll give you a good price on the crystal ball."

"There's no point arguing with her," Katherine pointed out, taking the mayor's arm. "She'll be reading your cards next."

"Remember the Fool in yours?" Maya called out as they hurried toward the door. "Keep him in mind when you think of me!"

Katherine was too literal to catch the reference. As the pair hurried out, Maya sighed and stared at the unhappy dragon she'd just created. The cards played tricks with the mind, but she could tell she was the Fool in Katherine's woodpile. Even the Death card had been literal. Pfeiffer had been a relative of Katherine's, she remembered Axell saying.

August 1946

I have taken my savings and purchased a lucrative rental property. I cannot tell Dolly of my child or use her money for the child's support. She does not know about the property. I have found a lawyer who will send the proceeds to Helen's cousins. I will pray they will raise my daughter to be stronger than I am.

❧ THIRTY ❧

Change is inevitable, except
from a vending machine.

"Shit." Swinging his chair to face the window as he hung up the phone, Axell glanced out in time to see Katherine and Ralph Arnold scurrying from the building next door. He couldn't think of anything good coming from a conversation between Maya and the mayor.

He was probably better off letting Maya simmer in peace until she'd had time to cool off. But he'd held her naked in his arms just hours before and the memory of that closeness still warmed the long-empty hollows of his heart. He didn't want to lose the tentative ties they'd begun to form. If marriage was anything like a business, it had to be tended carefully. With that kind of rational outlook instead of a sentimental one, he should be able to make this marriage work.

Not knowing whether he'd meet the newly confrontational Maya or the fey one, Axell took the stairs two at a time. If nothing else, life with Maya would never be boring. He'd never realized he had such a strong streak of curiosity in him, or that it thrived on constant nourishment.

The sound system was ominously silent as he entered the shop. Belatedly, he realized Cleo was in charge now, but he'd seen Maya arrive earlier. The mayor wouldn't have gotten far with Cleo.

Fog still hid the sunshine this morning, and no one had turned on lights in the back of the shop. Axell smacked the switch and discovered Maya curled up in her wicker chair, cuddling a cooing Alexa in her arms. The empty chambers of his heart clanged hollow as he read her look.

"All right, what did the mayor have to say?" Axell asked in resignation as he took the other chair. He wished she would offer him a cup of tea. She still hadn't brought the damned cups back.

"I'll scratch my own back, thank you very much," she said coldly.

That should make no sense at all, but he'd learned to look past Maya's words to the convoluted path of her mind. He didn't have far to go for this one. "I never said that, and at the time the mayor suggested it, I had to get him and the alcohol board off my back," he reminded her. "I figured I could find you another property if I had to."

"I don't want another property." Stubbornly, she refused to look at him. "The school is mine and you have nothing to do with it."

Definitely not the tack he'd hoped to take. "Maya, I hate to say this," he began cautiously, "but it's possible Mr. Pfeiffer died over that land. The mayor and the developer are pretty heavily involved in that shopping center. I'm not laying any blame, just pointing out the danger. I don't want anything happening to you or the kids."

"You think someone murdered poor Mr. Pfeiffer over that old house? That's crazy! You're more paranoid Scorpio than I thought. He didn't even have a will."

"That just means the land goes into escrow until the court sells it and divides the proceeds between the heirs, which is what the mayor wants. If you produce that lease and fight the sale, you're in his way." The more Axell thought about it, the more nervous he became. He couldn't believe the mayor guilty of murder, but he knew little or nothing about the heirs and the developer.

"It's still a stupid place to put a road." Maya set her small chin at a determined tilt. "It's a flood zone. It's historic property. If it's sold, they'll turn the land into tacky boxes and condiments."

"Condominiums," Axell corrected with a grin.

"Cheap condiments for hiding bad taste," she insisted. "The tobacco field down the road is a better alternative."

"Look, Maya, I don't want to argue with you."

Her eyes flashed with pleasure. "I am arguing, aren't I? Are you mad at me yet?"

She peered at him from beneath thick long lashes and Axell almost forgot the question. The knowing slant of her lips returned him to the moment. He kept forgetting that even if she looked like somebody's fairy godchild, Maya was no damned innocent.

"I'm not mad at you. I just want you to see sense."

"Then don't call my sister names. I'm still furious at you for that one," she responded irrelevantly. "Cleo's made mistakes. She's had a rough time of it. But with a little help—"

"Dammit, Maya!" Axell tried not to shout but he didn't think he was succeeding. "Drug addiction is not something that goes away. Your sister will always be an addict. I was just stating facts. Maybe she's reformed. I don't know. That's not the point—"

"It is the point!" she said loudly enough to startle Alexa into a surprised cry. Calming her voice, Maya continued. "You want to control our lives, and I won't let you. They're *our* lives, to mess up as we will. The school is *mine*, Axell. It's my dream. You can't tell me what to do with it."

There was something wrong with this argument, but Maya had his mind twisted in so many directions, he couldn't pinpoint where they'd strayed from the path. If she weren't holding Alexa like a shield, he'd lean over and kiss her until their heads spun in the same direction. Axell derived some satisfaction in knowing he had that much influence.

"The kids are my concern as well as yours," he warned. "If I think they're in danger, I'll act on it. Right now, there isn't much anyone can do with the property tied up in escrow. The minute that changes . . ."

Maya returned to rocking Alexa. "You're a worrywart, Axell. I heard Mr. Pfeiffer died with a whiskey glass in his hand, and his nieces just got all atwitter because they claim he never drank alcohol." Her eyes lit. "You know what Cleo told me this morning?"

Axell was afraid to find out. He suspected Cleo was capable of saying almost anything. "What?"

"She said Old Man Pfeiffer claimed to be our grandfather."

"Shit." Axell closed his eyes and sank back in his chair. He was accustomed to an orderly process of thought, but Maya kept knocking him into tailspins. "If *that* turns out to be true," he ground out, "the mayor will be accusing the two of you of murder. Pfeiffer had no children by his wife. If you could prove that tall tale, you could stand to inherit a substantial share of the property over distant relatives."

"Oh."

Maya sounded mildly interested, and Axell winced. Obviously he'd just handed her another weapon for her arsenal. "Don't even think about it," he warned.

She shrugged and beamed her Maya smile. "My mother never knew who her father was. I just thought it might be interesting for Alexa to know her heritage. Maybe not," she concluded hastily at his glare.

"We can do the genealogy after the murderer's caught." Axell pried himself from the chair before he got too comfortable. It was getting harder and harder to remember he had a business to run.

"Cleo will do what's best for Matty," she called after him.

As if that reassured him any. Squaring his shoulders, Axell marched out.

Women were for motherhood and sex, he repeated mentally as the sound system blared on behind him. Sex—sex—sex . . .

"This is what I wanted, Kitty," Maya muttered as she ripped the sheets from her bed, crumpled them in a ball, and flung them into the hall. It was nearly midnight, and Axell wasn't home.

The tangerine kitten—one of several named "Kitty" because Matty couldn't tell one from the other—peered down from his perch on the dresser and licked his paw.

"You're a fat lot of help. If you're so tidy, why haven't you cleaned this room by now?" She shook out a fresh pillowcase and jammed a pillow into it. "I'm not waiting up for him any longer," she warned the kitten. "We don't have that kind of marriage. He'll probably go straight to his room rather than risk life and limb coming in here."

Maya studied the explosion of clothing strewn over every surface and spilling from drawers. She'd never owned so many clothes in her life, and she wasn't entirely certain what to do with them. Sorting between dry cleaning and laundry alone required a Ph.D. in household maintenance which she didn't possess. She wasn't even certain where all the clothes had come from.

She supposed she could put away the card table with the remains of the dragon mobile, but if she didn't use up the rest of those paints soon, they'd dry out. And she had this idea for . . .

She heard the garage door open. Double-D bad word, she grumbled to herself, punching the pillow deeper into the case. If Axell came back here, he'd probably think all this excess energy was for him.

She'd never known sexual frustration, and she wasn't about to admit to it now. Axell Holm could go directly to his own bed, Do Not Pass Go, Do Not Collect Maya. The kids would be up at the crack of dawn, and she needed her sleep.

She heard his step in the kitchen below as she punched the second pillow into its case. She should have turned out the light. She shouldn't have stayed up in the first place. She was still mad at him for thinking her school expendable and Cleo unreliable. He obviously thought her a real ditz who couldn't get her head out of a bucket. She could have gone for the Ph.D. if she'd had any money—or if she'd thought it necessary. She wasn't a ditz.

She knew the instant Axell appeared in her doorway, even though she deliberately kept her back to the door. His subtle aftershave wafted on the currents she was stirring. She glanced up at the mirror and saw him prop his shoulder against the doorjamb. His tie was unknotted, his golden hair rumpled, and his suit coat hung over his arm as he watched her. His eyes looked tired, but damn, he looked too sexy for words.

He threw the coat over a chair already decorated with two dresses. Silently, he crossed to the other side of the bed and helped to pull the bottom sheet across the mattress.

"Matty's in his room?" he asked cautiously.

"Matty's with Cleo. Social Services said she could have him for the weekend." She sounded stiff, even to herself. Matty with his forlorn waif eyes and puckish grin had wormed so deep in her heart, he would always be a part of her.

"Is Stephen still over there?" Axell asked with lingering wariness, smoothing a sheet corner at the bottom of the bed.

He shouldn't look so damned handsome and masculine making a bed. Maya's wormy heart pounded a little louder. "He skipped out for Nashville yesterday, something about fixing a track on the new album."

"That figures," he said dryly.

"It's not as if working is irresponsible," Maya snapped.

The kitten pounced on the fresh pillowcase. As casually as if she were stripping a sheet, Maya scooped the cat up, tossed him into the laundry in the hall, and shut the door.

"I didn't say otherwise," Axell protested. "Why are you mad now?"

"Because you want to tuck us into little boxes," she retorted without thinking. Because she'd wanted him home hours ago. Because she wanted to be on this bed with him right now. Because he'd taught her to want things she knew she couldn't have or wouldn't last. "Mad" didn't even begin to touch her mood.

"All right," Axell replied warily, taking the corner of the top sheet she tossed him. "I like things organized," he admitted. "Structure makes it easier to choose priorities and get things done."

Now he was even trying to *understand* her, damn the man. "We're not *things*!" Maya tossed a freshly made-up pillow at him. "And fish don't nest, and trees don't bend, and we must have been insane to believe this would work."

Axell grappled with her words as he untangled the sheet.

Talking to Maya was like working a crossword puzzle. He just needed to understand the references. He understood her last declaration well enough for fear to grip his stomach. He'd walked into this marriage with eyes wide open—any failure would be all his fault.

"Some fish don't swim far from their spawning grounds," he offered tentatively. He didn't know a hell of a lot about fish, but he figured she was talking about herself, so he could improvise.

Maya shot him a dark look. "There won't be any spawning around here at this hour."

He almost grinned at that, but he thought she'd throw him out on his ear like the cat. "It's Friday," he pointed out patiently. "I'm lucky to get home before two A.M. The new trainee doesn't know the clientele yet." He folded a hospital corner on his side of the bed while she shoved her sheet under the mattress without looking at it. "If that's all you're mad about, I'm sorry, but I warned you."

"That's *not* what I'm mad about." She flung the comforter across the bed. "I'm mad because you think my school is less important than your damned bar. School—bar," she spat out, "Just listen to the words! Think, Axell. What's more important, teaching kids or feeding drunks?"

This was going a little too far. Grabbing the comforter she was flinging on sideways, Axell shook it out straight. "That bar paid for this house, bought the building your sister's damned shop is in, and pays for the food we eat. Intellectual exercise is very nice, but not of much use on an empty stomach."

"I was keeping food in our stomachs, that's not the *point*." Maya tugged the comforter farther to her side. "The point is, all my *life*, ever since grade school, I've wanted to build a school that was like *family*."

Axell halted his straightening and let her tug the comforter where she wanted. Maya was arguing, so this had to be important. He just wished she'd speak in terms he understood: goals and touchdowns, invoices and assets. "Life" and "family" were too broad to translate.

"I wanted a school where the teachers treated each child like their own, whether they were wearing hundred-dollar Nikes or Goodwill Keds. Do you have any idea how much more attention the polite, well-dressed, country club kids receive than the unruly, or the poorly dressed, or the misfits? The child who can do math gets heaped with praise but the one who can only build block castles gets ignored. It's not *right*. Every child has something he's good at, even if it's not recognized as one of the three R's." She flung the lacy pillow shams on top of the comforter.

Axell eyed the decorative pillows skeptically, but didn't argue with their placement. He didn't know why they were making a bed at midnight when they should be unmaking it, anyway.

He could hear the creative child she'd been crying out in protest and figured she knew what she was talking about. He'd been one of the country club kids by the time he was in his teens. Before that . . . Well, he'd always played sports well. He'd never felt unaccepted. Maya had.

"You want a school where the poor kids and the creative kids and the kids who can work with their hands better than their brains can all be equal," he translated. "That's not possible. You're dreaming."

"Damned right, I'm dreaming. Somebody has to." She scowled at him. "It's obvious you quit long ago, if you ever dreamed at all."

She was heading for emotional meltdown, and Axell was at a loss as to how to handle it. He'd gone this route with Angela. She'd scream and he'd stare at her in bewilderment. He could see it happening all over again. The cliff's edge he walked on crumbled a little more with each step.

"Dreaming doesn't pay," he answered guardedly. "But you're entitled to try it your way. I wish you'd give me straight answers, though. I told you, I don't do well at reading between the lines."

To his surprise, Maya's scowl vanished. She finished straightening the bottom of the bed and sauntered to his side with a definitely wicked gleam in her eye. Axell wondered if it was too late to run. Glancing at the sway of her hips, he decided running wasn't an option he wanted to take.

"Actually, you've been doing exceptionally well," she murmured, sliding her hands behind his neck until soft curves brushed him in tempting places, backing him up against the bed. "Let's see if you understand this."

Standing on tiptoes, she gyrated her hips against his zipper until Axell thought his pants would explode. She was right. This, he understood.

Falling backward onto the mattress, he pulled her with him. Before she could scramble away, Axell flipped over, pinning her beneath him. Capturing Maya's flailing arms, he proceeded to kiss her into a different form of passion. Maya did passion exceptionally well.

Tomorrow night, maybe they'd make it to his room.

May 1970
  I cannot tell anyone but my journal, so I have dug it out after all these years to record my tears and joy—my daughter was married today to a fine, upstanding young man. I don't know whether her mother is watching from heaven or hell, but I'm sure she is smiling with the same teary-eyed happiness as I am.

❦ THIRTY-ONE ❦

The more people I meet,
the more I like my cat.

Maya gaped at the shiny black Cadillac in front of Cleo's shop. If the rich discovered some of her sister's eccentric artists, business would definitely boom.

Cheerfully, she shoved open the shop door.

"The same arrangement as before," the bald black man at the counter was saying as the door chimed. "You owe us," he finished, glancing dismissively at Maya and turning to leave.

The man had an aura the same color as his Cadillac, Maya decided as he shoved past her. She didn't think she was a bigot, but the nasty snarl on the man's face made her think in terms of pit bulls, semiautomatics, and gang colors. This man wore a suit and tie and cuff links.

As the door closed behind him, Maya searched her sister's weary, resigned expression.

"Matty's upstairs watching TV," Cleo said coldly at Maya's look. "I have to work on Saturdays. It's our busiest day."

Several teenagers lingered near the inexpensive pewter fantasy figurines. No one appeared interested in the two magnificent paintings of a medieval sorcerer and his lady, on the high walls. Maya had really thought they'd sell quickly. Maybe she had no business sense after all. Maybe Cleo couldn't make a living here.

"That man who just left was pure evil," she hissed quietly so the kids couldn't hear.

"Bigot," Cleo countered.

272

"Don't give me that. Evil comes in all colors." Terrified, Maya looked closely at her sister but couldn't see any sign of drug use. "Cleo, if you've got trouble, share it. You can endanger yourself if you like, but not Matty. He's too young."

Cleo's expression shuttered. "You don't know what you're talking about. That man is a customer who likes to use mystical party favors. I supply them."

"That man never showed his face the entire time I ran this store," Maya retorted. "Cleo, I'm your sister. We can fight this."

Cleo shook her head. "You always were a dreamer." Forcing a smile, she emerged from behind the counter and spoke to one of the teenagers. "That's a crystal from Nepal. It's supposed to have the power to heal. . . ."

Maya marched up the stairs and retrieved Matty. As she held the boy's hand through the shop, he tugged and dragged his feet. "Don' wanna go," he protested.

Furious with Cleo, Maya marched on.

"Mama needs me!" Matty whined, fighting her hold.

Arrows of pain piercing her heart, Maya halted and kneeled beside him. "Of course your mama needs you, sugar. She loves you. But she needs to be by herself right now."

Wiping his eyes, Matty shook his head. "The bad man was here. I'm gonna *kill* him!"

Shocked to the core, Maya glanced up to see Cleo hovering in the background, her expression stony but her eyes blurred with tears.

Maya hugged her nephew and lifted him in her arms. "Bad men can't hurt people if they stay away from them," she said loudly enough for her sister to hear. "We'll chase him away, like the Boogie Monster."

Swiveling on her heel, she walked out of the shop, carrying Matty to safety.

"It's drugs, Selene, I know it is," Maya sighed into the phone. "How can I repay all of Axell's kindnesses by letting my sister smear his reputation? Axell *owns* that building. The cops will be all over him. He'll lose the building and maybe his license. How can Cleo be so damned *stupid*?"

Selene never argued over Maya's leaps of logic. She accepted them at face value and worked from there. Maya wished Axell could be so understanding.

Remembering just how much Axell had understood when he'd come to her room last night, Maya brushed her hand over her wet cheek. She'd always known how to spurn the attention of men, even when she wanted it. Axell knew how to climb right over all her defensive barriers, straight into her bed. Just remembering what he'd done to her last night made her blush. Maybe "domineering" wasn't entirely a bad thing when coupled with understanding. She didn't want to lose him because of Cleo.

"Look, girlfriend," Selene's voice jarred Maya back to the moment, "I'm not into that scene, but I know a few people who are. I'll sound them out, see if I can get the dude's name. If we turn her over to the cops—"

"The whole story will hit the paper and Axell's name will be tarred in print. I may have to give up the school, Selene." Maya bit her quivering lip as she expressed the fear nagging at the back of her mind.

"Say *what*?" Selene screamed.

"If I give up the school, the mayor will get off Axell's back, and even if Cleo gets busted again, no one will make the connection without the mayor's instigation. He'll scratch Axell's back if Axell scratches his, is the way he put it."

"That's blackmail," Selene snapped. "You swim out of this school, Miss Fish, and you swim out for good. I've got too much invested here, and I don't mean just money. This is my dream, too, you'll remember."

Maya pinched the bridge of her nose as she'd seen Axell do. It didn't help. Any way she looked at it, she risked losing her husband, her sister, her best friend, and the dream of a lifetime.

Life had been much easier when she could just swim along on her own.

"The lawyers promised to call back Monday," Selene continued. "If our lease is bona fide, the mayor has to go the condemnation route. You got your Garden Club lined up?"

"Teamed with the Historic Society," Maya agreed numbly. What difference did saving the school make if she lost Axell and Constance because of it?

She'd never fully realized the high price of a dream.

"How much do you know about drugs in this town, Headley?" Axell asked as he kicked aside the fallen police tape surrounding Cleo's condemned building and unlocked the alley door.

"I'm semiretired, remember?" Headley glanced around the alley with interest. "I don't know nuthin' 'bout nuthin'."

Axell switched on his flashlight and scanned the nearly empty storeroom. "Don't give me that. You're a sponge. You absorb information without trying. I've got two crackheads haunting my kitchen and this alley, and someone's using this storeroom. What are the chances drugs are involved?"

"Drugs are involved in every crime in the country." Headley snorted. "It's worse than Prohibition. Government ought to tax the damned stuff and use the proceeds to build crack houses where the morons can fry their brains without hurting the innocent. You're better off messing with the mayor than these guys, kid."

"They chose my restaurant for their crimes." Axell shoved aside old boxes and searched the walls for the cellar door. "The police don't have time to find out why, so I guess I will."

"That's ridiculous. You make it sound like a personal vendetta. Kids do drugs. They do it wherever they are. They happened to be in your kitchen when they did." Headley gingerly followed him into the vacant interior.

"I fired their asses. They had no business back there. Someone was setting me up. And I think that someone was in here that night. How much more have you found out about our Yankee developers and their cash flow problems?"

"You don't really think there's a connection, do you?"

Headley inspected a box of trash as Axell tried the knob of a door in the far wall. "Real estate is booming. They'll cover their cash flow with a few loans."

"Headley, you're not helping here." Axell tried the back door key in the cellar lock. "The mayor's risking his career by approving a road through the school grounds. If a loan would solve the problem, he wouldn't be after Maya." The key didn't fit. Axell jiggled it in irritation.

"Drugs are to the nineties what alcohol was to the fifties and sixties." Headley gingerly removed an old hypodermic from the trash and wielded it for Axell to see. "Only kids are more involved today, so they don't have fancy nightclubs. They have places like this. The city is spilling into suburbia, Holm. We're smack in its path."

Axell grimaced at the evidence that someone was using the place for drugs. He'd have the council expedite condemnation proceedings and get the place torn down. He ought to find out who owned it. Maybe Maya would know.

"You know, I've been thinking about that kid named Alyssum," Headley replied irrelevantly, returning the needle to the trash. "He was working construction with some crew out of Texas about thirty years ago. Nice kid, ambitious."

Axell tried every key on his ring, but none worked on the cellar door. He pulled out a credit card and tried jimmying the lock. "Maya said she was born here. Probably her father. You should be telling her this. I doubt she knows much about her parents."

"The kid quit sharing my bottle after he got married. Seems his bride had an alcoholic mother and wouldn't tolerate drinking."

The credit card trick didn't work on old doors. Giving up in disgust, Axell jammed the card back in his wallet and picked his way around trash bags toward Headley. He had the sneaking suspicion the reporter was leading up to the connection between Pfeiffer and Maya and her sister.

"Don't take that route, old friend," Axell warned. "Maya isn't interested."

"I just thought you ought to know," Headley replied calmly, leaning on his cane as he opened the alley door. "The bride's maiden name was Arnold, if I remember rightly. Her mother was the black sheep of the family, a little too free-wheeling for the postwar years. She ran a seamy nightclub during the fifties when the county was dry and had a daughter out of wedlock. Scandal, even if it was before my time."

Before his time, Axell snorted to himself. Headley had probably helped build the nightclub. As they hit the sunshine outside, the name "Arnold" hit him smack between the eyes.

Maya could be related to the mayor, from the wrong side of the blanket.

Oh, hell, first Pfeiffer, now the mayor. He must have been out of his mind that day he'd walked into the Curiosity Shoppe to speak with Constance's teacher. Maybe that "Fate" Maya kept talking about had switched sides from her to him. Maybe he just ought to stand here and hope a bolt of lightning struck him.

"I suppose you're going to tell me next that the mayor's family ran Maya's family out of town?" Axell asked in resignation as they wended their way through the alley and back across the street to the restaurant. This was a small southern town. The mayor's family wouldn't like evidence of any scandal around once they took up politics. Ralph's father had been mayor back in the seventies.

"Actually, I hadn't thought about that, but the chances are pretty good." Headley beamed at him with approval. "Want me to find out?"

"I think I'd rather not know," Axell said gloomily.

He needed to get his life back in order again, he decided as he drove toward home later. Maya had been right. He liked all his soldiers in a row, and he didn't see why he couldn't have them that way just because marriage had added a few extra complications.

Constance was safe and happy; that was the important thing. She was blooming like a wildflower under Maya's attentions. So the marriage was definitely not a mistake. It had accomplished just what he'd hoped.

And then some. Axell ruthlessly shoved aside all thoughts of Maya sprawled across her bed in the morning sunshine, her hair an auburn tangle across the pillow, her breasts taunting creamy cones awaiting his taste. He wasn't a sensual man, he told himself. The sex was convenient, but he didn't need to dwell on it.

So, if Constance and sex were in order, what else needed reorganizing? What were his priorities here?

His license. He had to protect his liquor license. It was his livelihood, his means of taking care of his family. He'd prefer to err on the side of paranoia and believe someone was up to sneaky tricks by sending those druggies into his place. This was a small town—not so rural any longer, but small. The cops should be able to spot a dealer from a mile away. They'd know where he lived. Something was not right with this picture.

He didn't want to believe that flaw was Maya's sister. For Matty and Maya's sake, he prayed she was clean and could stay that way. For the sake of his license and reputation, she'd damned well better be. Maybe he could hire someone to work in the store and keep an eye on her. Cleo would pitch a fit. Maybe he could say he was renting out that unused corner. . . .

He pulled into the driveway behind an unfamiliar car blocking access to the garage. Now what? The damn thing looked like a rental.

Climbing out of the Rover, Axell heard the musical chimes of childish laughter. Rolling his shoulders and relaxing some of the tension his morning's detective work had generated, he sauntered in the direction of the backyard, past the cascade of petunias Maya had planted in pots on the driveway wall.

An obscene blue plastic pool jarred the sedate view of landscaped lawn. He'd intended to eventually build a real pool, but he'd wanted to wait until the kids were older.

The kids . . .

Axell swallowed past the lump in his throat at the thought of the children he'd once intended to have. He still had Constance, and now Alexa, and it looked as if he had Matty again.

He frowned at that as he strolled over to watch the horseplay in the pool. He'd thought Cleo had taken her son for the weekend.

Maya looked up from where she was happily planting colorful banks of impatiens around the spindly boxwood. He hated to tell her, but those plants would croak in the noon sun. He'd already figured out she knew diddle-all about flowers but chose them for their colors. He had to admit, they cheered up the boring yard.

"Axell, there you are!"

That wasn't the musical greeting he'd anticipated. Maya's sunny smile froze as she raised her eyebrows and jerked her head in the direction of the deck.

Oh, shit. Sandra. The chalkboard-scratching tones finally registered. Axell checked the deck, recognized the plastic bubble of hair, and grimacing, bent over and kissed Maya. "I'm getting that beeper," he whispered against her welcoming lips. "I want to know when to run next time."

"Forget that, mister. She's your problem. Just be lucky I haven't roped her to the deck and planted petunias between her teeth."

With that enchanting image to contemplate, Axell headed for the deck. The kids were apparently too engrossed in a watery battle to greet him. Alexa slept in her shaded basket. All was well with his world except for the blond fly in his suntan oil.

"I told her you wouldn't appreciate that trailer park trash in your yard," Sandra complained as he reached the stairs. "But she wouldn't listen. Constance will be wearing tattoos and those dreadful pink plastic shoes before long. Whatever could you have been thinking?"

Biting his tongue, Axell vowed to buy Constance the first pair of pink plastic shoes he found.

Wearing a pressed linen shorts set and oversized sunglasses, Sandra sat beneath the patio umbrella sipping an iced drink. With her manicured fingers, she gestured at Maya. "Just look. She's planting impatiens in the sun. They'll be dead by morning."

Axell thought he recognized the grim determination in the set of Maya's chin as she shoved her trowel into the loose mulch beneath the shrubs. The yard wasn't so large that she couldn't hear every word of Sandra's shrill complaint.

"And what brings you back to our part of the country?" he asked calmly, checking the cooler Maya had brilliantly provided to prevent the kids from running in and out in their wet suits. He smiled as he discovered a bottle of spring water.

"I came to check on Constance," Sandra replied.

Translation: she'd had a fight with her family in Texas and had hastily repaired to her North Carolina friends for sympathy. When her husband had been alive, it had worked in reverse.

"Well, I'm certain Constance is delighted to see you." Unscrewing the bottle top, Axell settled into a lounge chair. He was aware of Maya out of the corner of his eye, but strangely enough, he didn't feel compelled to shield her from Sandra's venom. He thought Maya had his former mother-in-law's number and could take care of herself better than he could. His gypsy had backbone. It was a rather relaxing revelation.

"What are you going to do about that pool?" Sandra demanded. "The neighbors will be incensed."

Axell agreed the pool was an abomination, but it was a practical solution for the moment, even if it did kill the manicured lawn. "What neighbors?" he asked mildly. "They'd have to walk through the woods to see it. Surely you didn't come all the way from Texas to complain about a little pool."

"No, I've decided I'm moving back here. If you won't take care of Constance properly, I will. My suitcases are still in the car. If you'll get them out, I'll begin house hunting on Monday."

Je-humping-hosaphat. Axell pinched his eyes shut and tried to mute more virulent swear words as he pictured the immediate consequences of this decision.

The kids and Maya currently occupied one wing. He had the choice of installing Sandra in Maya's room, or in the sanctity of his wing of the house—the only island of serenity in this chaotic world he could call his own.

Opening his eyes and glancing at the pale curve of Maya's shoulders above her halter top, Axell knew damned well Sandra wasn't the one he'd be introducing to his inner sanctum.

❧ THIRTY-TWO ❧

Reality is a crutch for people
who can't handle drugs.

"They're all asleep. Are you sure this will work?" Maya asked worriedly as she slipped into the family room carrying the last of Alexa's blankets. She didn't know how she'd accumulated so much stuff in a few short months. She used to be able to pack everything she owned into a suitcase. Those days were over.

"I'm not sure of anything," Axell replied a trifle grimly, taking the blankets from her. "I just couldn't find a polite way of throwing the woman out on her ear."

The urge to reach out and kiss him bubbled deep in her belly. Her Norse god looked so bewildered and beleaguered that she wanted to cuddle him and tell him everything would be all right, even if it meant sacrificing his holy privacy. But he wasn't a child to be cuddled. She could tell that by the fire igniting in Axell's eyes the instant she tucked her hand between the buttons of his shirt.

"Well, just pretend I'm a wanton woman come to share your bed for the evening. You can throw me out in the morning."

"And keep Alexa?" he inquired in a deep, low drawl that chased shivers through her midsection.

"Well, there is that," she admitted as she followed him down the hall to his room. Rooms.

They passed a comfortable den/office complete with bar and television, where he could retreat to watch football while the kids watched cartoons. The next room had been turned into a home gym, with all the latest paraphernalia. No wonder the damned man looked like a pinup model beneath those suits. He probably worked off a lot of frustration.

She supposed the smaller room next to it could have been anything when the house was designed, but Axell had installed clothes racks and used it for a dressing room. Alexa's cradle and toys added a splash of color to the rows of dark suits all hanging in the same direction. He dropped the stack of blankets on a dresser and leaned over to adjust the covers around Alexa's defiantly upturned rear end. Ever since she'd learned to roll over, she'd insisted on sleeping on her stomach. Or her knees.

Watching Axell's big body tenderly leaning over the tiny cradle brought tears to Maya's eyes and a painful longing to her heart. She'd gone and done it now, she realized. She supposed it had been inevitable. She'd been in love with the intelligent curiosity peering from behind his smoky eyes from the day he'd walked into the shop. She'd fallen in love with his strength of character and competence the day he'd delivered Alexa. And the night he'd slammed her against the wall and taken her to heaven . . .

She was lost. Hopeless. Done for. She loved the big dope so much it hurt in every cell and pore of her body. She had shit for brains.

She'd never felt so alone in her life as she did when Axell held out his hand to lead her into the chamber he called his.

His. The room was his. The house was his. *She* was his. And now he even owned her heart, while she had nothing. She'd been terrified before, but nothing to compare with the sinking sensation of total vulnerability. She'd learned at an early age not to care—not to care when she got yelled at for something she didn't do, or for something she did do but didn't know was wrong. She'd learned not to care when no one hung her pictures on their walls or hugged her for making A's. She hadn't even cared when Stephen hadn't bothered to call after she told him she was pregnant. Not for long, anyway.

But now she cared so much she'd do almost anything Axell

asked in hopes he'd love her back and want to keep her. She thought she'd killed that futile dream when she was ten years old. As Axell drew her into his darkened room and pulled her shirt over her head, Maya shivered at the possessive caress of his big hands over her bare breasts.

"I didn't think this day would ever end," he whispered near her ear as he stroked her breasts, arousing them to aching tenderness.

If she could just remember this was only sex to him . . . Forcing her mind to focus on the physical, Maya fumbled at his shirt buttons until her palms lay flat against his heated chest. Axell was always warm, and strong, and hard. . . .

Dammit, she couldn't think straight. She wanted to whisper love words and kiss him all over, but then he'd know he had her, that he'd won, that he could do with her as he wished. She couldn't allow that. Somehow, she had to retain her independence, so when the day came that he threw her out, she could walk away without looking back.

"Your new manager is learning so fast you didn't need to keep him company tonight?" she asked, deliberately licking at his nipple and feeling his shudder with triumph.

"The crowd was light when I left. He knows how to reach me if there's—" He groaned deep in his throat as she unfastened his belt and brushed her knuckles against the coarse hair there. "It's not supposed to be this way," he muttered, finishing the task she'd started and stepping out of his trousers.

Maya wanted to question him, but Axell swept her from the floor and flung her on the bed and she forgot everything else.

"Axell . . ." She breathed his name as he stripped off her shorts and underwear in a single stroke. The cool air and his hot hand caressed her intimately at the same time.

"I'll make this up to you later," he murmured, pressing his hand against her mound, teasing her. "But I've been thinking about this all day and can't stop now."

Maya grabbed Axell's arms and choked back a scream as he slammed into her, sending her spiraling over the edge before she knew what hit her. Even as her blood boiled and her brain melted to putty, her soul reacted to the matching desperation in his and reached out with all the power she possessed.

Their rhythm pounded a steady "yes, yes, yes!" until tears of joy slipped from the corners of her eyes and all the atoms of her body surrendered to the sweet oblivion of Axell's obsession. As he drove up inside her and shuddered with the force of a raging river crashing through a dam, Maya surrendered to the bliss of physical satisfaction.

This was enough, for now.

"Let her watch cartoons," Axell grumbled as Alexa's coos threatened to become squalls in the early dawn.

With her nose buried in thick feather pillows and Axell's heavy, muscled arm holding her down, Maya woke from hazy dreams of being twenty-months pregnant again. Only, this time, the child was Axell's.

Shivering at this premonition, she shoved awkwardly at his hand. He merely curled his arm around her chest and dragged her backward against him, plucking her nipple into instant readiness.

"I didn't know you were going to be insatiable," she yawned, snuggling her posterior into the masculine angle of his hips, waking rapidly at the rod probing between her thighs—the hot rod, she giggled to herself.

"In a few months, you'll be staggering around in a ratty bathrobe, yelling at the kids," Axell warned as his fingers did wonderful, marvelous things to her awakening body. "Let's enjoy the honeymoon while it lasts."

While it lasts. Those prophetic words rang in Maya's heart even as Axell held her hips and her body opened wide at his command. She buried her cries of ecstasy and protest in her pillow with his thrust.

She'd forgotten to take her pill last night, she remembered in panic as Axell stroked her deep from the inside. Damned dreams had a way of infiltrating the brain to become self-fulfilling. As his rhythm became wilder, she vowed to take two today to compensate.

In another few months, Cleo could be back in jail, the state could be condemning her school, and Axell could be sorry he'd ever met her. She certainly didn't need another baby tying her down when it all collapsed around her again.

As her womb shivered in joy and accepted the hot flow from her husband's body, Maya wished it could be otherwise.

Her insides still aching with the force and promise of Axell's lovemaking all weekend, Maya added the final touches to the dining room mural. She was still furious with Cleo. She didn't dare step inside the store until she calmed down. The peace of the empty house—Sandra had gone out house shopping—appealed to the turmoil inside her. The roar and grind of a heavy truck outside shattered any illusion of peace.

Holding her paintbrush and glancing out the bay window, she frowned in bewilderment as a huge tree backed into the yard.

A heavy construction truck stopped near a stake someone had driven into the lawn. Even as she gaped in astonishment, the wide drill on the back of the truck lowered and began to dig.

In awe, Maya watched the process of a full-grown tree miraculously sprouting in the barren backyard—a tree that would shade her tender plants, cool the kitchen, provide branches for the children to play in and the birds to sing from. She could hang feeders from those limbs and watch the goldfinches and cardinals. A tree was life.

A tree was promise.

Tears welled, then spilled as Maya clutched her paintbrush and watched the lovely maple tucked into the ground and mulched. Axell was incapable of expressing emotion in any verbal manner. She was starting to understand that.

That didn't mean Axell couldn't *feel* emotion.

Maya stood transfixed in front of the window until the very last particle of dirt was tapped down and every last needle of pine mulch was in place. The maple rustled its fat green leaves in contentment as the trucks drove away.

She wanted to fly to Axell's side, fling her arms around his marvelous shoulders, and scream "I love you!" to the world while covering him in kisses. She would embarrass him to death if she did.

Excitement zipping through her soul but brain shouting "Whoa!" Maya dithered in indecision. Slipping outside and turning on the garden hose, she stood beneath shady leaves and welcomed the tree with water. Her wilting flowers had already perked up by the time she turned the hose on them. Maybe she could tuck some more around the tree.

She was doing it again: swimming back and forth rather than striking out in a determined direction. Maya shut off the hose and advanced into the house. Maybe the tree wasn't a declaration of love. Maybe Axell's practical streak had recognized the need for shade and he'd just dialed the phone and ordered the tree plunked down. Maybe he had ordered it months ago, even before they'd met.

Racing into the house, Maya came to a screeching halt as she turned down the wrong hallway. She didn't have her own room anymore. Sandra had it.

Stalking down the hall past her husband's playthings, Maya ground her teeth. She was Axell's *wife*. She had no room, no house, no life of her own except as an extension of his. What had she been thinking?

She hadn't, as usual. She'd just jumped right in and gone with the flow because it was easiest.

Well, she'd damned well better stop and think now. She could love Axell and even trust him—and Lord knew, she did, with every fiber of her being. Her heart ached with the depth of it, and she wanted to explode with the joy of knowing a man as steady and trustworthy and intelligent and sexy as Axell could conceivably want someone as unwantable as her.

But life happened. It had happened to her one too many times, and she was never prepared. This time, she couldn't afford to go with the flow. She had Alexa to consider. If—when—Axell realized life with her was too impossible to go on, she had to be able to walk away.

The phone rang.

Staring gloomily at the rumpled bed she'd shared with

Axell last night, Maya ignored the intrusion. Axell had left her sleeping this morning, or this room would never look like this. Axell didn't leave beds unmade or clothes hanging on chairs. Remembering the round of lovemaking that had left her satiated and curled in a cocoon of contentment, she grimaced. It was too damned easy to make babies and she was too damned careless.

The phone rang again.

She picked up the clothes they'd scattered in haste last night. She'd have to get Sandra out of here so she could move back to her old room before this became habit. If she just thought of herself as a boarder . . .

She grabbed the phone on the third ring rather than follow that thought. The city council had a meeting tonight. If it was one of Axell's damned constituents, she'd personally ram the receiver down their throats. Axell better believe she'd make a lousy mayor's wife.

"Miss Alyssum?" the voice inquired on the other end.

"Alyssum-Holm," she corrected determinedly. She hadn't bothered changing the name on her legal documents. She'd better start considering how much of her identity she wanted to sacrifice.

"Mrs. Holm," the deep voice continued with more assurance. "This is Philip MacGregor with MacGregor and Blythe in Raleigh."

Lawyers. Mr. Pfeiffer's lawyers. Maya remembered them well. She wrinkled her nose and wondered why they weren't calling Selene. She remembered they were supposed to. Panic immediately ripped through her. What if they were calling to say the lease was invalid?

The lawyer had continued talking while her thoughts spun out of control. She'd missed the first part of his spiel. Frantically, she tried to tune in now.

"We've filed the will with the court here in Raleigh. As executors, we're free to begin proceedings on the deed transfers. If you prefer, we can send someone down there with the documents. We're having the property appraised for estate-tax purposes. The appraisal value will be your basis at the time of transfer, so you may wish your attorney or accountant . . ."

Maya choked the receiver and stared blankly at the window. Deed? Not lease?

"Mr. MacGregor," she interrupted tentatively. He'd think her a nutcase. She *was* a nutcase. She didn't care. "Could you please start all over? I don't understand. . . ."

"I should have realized this came as a surprise to you," the voice replied soothingly. "Perhaps I should drive down and explain in more detail. Would your sister be available? I'm not certain how to reach her."

"Cleo's at the shop," she said absently. "I'll call her. I just don't understand. . . ."

"Mr. Pfeiffer acknowledged you and your sister as his granddaughters in his will, Mrs. Holm. He came to us a few years ago, after his wife's death, to have it drawn up. I think it would be best if I drove down and explained it to you and your sister in person."

"Yes. Yes, I think that's best."

Maya sank to the floor and stared into space, dimly aware of Alexa's crying in the background.

The lawyer had mentioned deeds.

Did the school belong to her now?

November 1976

   Some rumormonger has told Dolly of my daughter's existence. I cannot even correspond with my lawyers for fear she will discover what I have been doing without her knowledge. If Dolly should go to the Arnolds to verify this damned story, there will be hell to pay. I'm not as wealthy as they are, but by damn, I'll do what it takes to look after the ones I love.

❧ THIRTY-THREE ❧

I used to have a handle on life, but it broke.

Glancing out his office window, Axell saw the unmarked police car parked in front of the building next door and cursed. He didn't need this now. The police had been all over the bar Saturday night after he'd gone home. One of the local yokels had pulled a knife on a city salesman, and his new manager hadn't realized the seriousness of the situation. He'd been too scared to call Axell.

So now he had police reports scattered across his desk, lawyers and insurance companies calling about liability, and a curt message from someone at the ABC board to deal with. The damned mayor had made certain they'd heard about it. He didn't need more police at Cleo's shop—his shop. He was a damned partner, thanks to Maya.

Flinging down his pen and striding out, Axell faced a fleeting regret for the days when a leggy Katherine in her red suit used to greet him in the mornings with nothing more noxious than gossip about the latest backyard panther sighting. Now he had cops and knifings and drugs and a skinny college graduate assistant in too-narrow ties anxiously waiting to be thrown out on his ass. Life had been so much simpler. . . .

Before Maya.

Axell rubbed his brow. He couldn't reasonably blame any of this on Maya. True, Katherine had quit because he'd married Maya, but he couldn't blame anyone but Katherine for that. And Maya had nothing to do with the knifing, other than luring him home when he should have been here. Maya had nothing to do with her sister's drug habits, either. She was completely innocent of everything except existing. Maya just needed to exist to attract trouble like honey draws bees.

As Axell threw open the Curiosity Shoppe door, evil laughter erupted over his head. Startled, he stopped in the doorway and glanced upward for the chimes he'd personally installed himself. A grinning demon lit from within beamed down on him. Swell, now Cleo was probably into demonology, or worse.

With images of satanic rituals ballooning in his mind, Axell scanned the interior where a plainclothes detective had stopped talking and turned to stare. Cleo, looking rattier and more tired than usual, glared in his direction. So much for the once cheerful atmosphere of the playful shop Maya had created.

"I haven't done the weekend's receipts yet," Cleo declared, as if Axell normally came in every day and demanded them. "And tell your wife I want my teapot back."

"You tell her. She's your sister." Determined not to be shoved aside by Cleo's machinations—he knew enough about human nature to know her rudeness had a purpose—Axell nodded at the detective. "Morning, Rick. Anything I can do for you?" Calm and controlled. He could do that. That's how he functioned.

The detective's expression remained unreadable. "Morning, Axell. Just having a word with the lady."

"I'm no lady and never will be," Cleo retorted. "You've had your say. You can find your own way out." She glared at Axell. "That goes for you, too."

It struck Axell that Maya's sister was in need of a good spanking, but that didn't fall in his line of duty. He walked out with the detective.

"All right, Rick, now tell me what that's all about. That's my building, my wife's sister, and I own half the shop. I've a right to know."

The detective looked uncomfortable. Axell was a council member and on the police oversight committee. His vote was one of many, but his influence in the town was considerable. Axell didn't normally use his influence for the purpose of intimidation, but he was tired of being on the defensive.

"She had a known dealer in the shop the instant she hit town." The detective shrugged. "That's all I'm free to say, and I shouldn't have said that. Forget where you heard it."

Axell waited for the pain to grip his stomach, but miraculously, it only twisted a little. With a nod, he acknowledged the detective's request. "She wants her kid back. She'll stay clean, if she can. We've got to get the dealer off the street."

"That's what I intend to do." The detective slammed into his car and drove off.

Axell took a deep breath and prepared to beard the lion in her den. This gladiator intended to rip the lion's damned head off.

"Selene, you've got to be there," Maya yelled at her friend's skeptical silence. "You're the only one I can trust. Axell will be *furious*, absolutely furious. He didn't want anyone to know about our relationship to Pfieffer, and now we're actually *heirs*. . . . Heirs! Can you imagine? I'm an heiress." Dizzily, Maya paced up and down with the cordless, ramming her hand through her hair and almost giggling at the absurdity, except its implications were too enormous.

"People will think we *murdered* that poor old man. You know how they've been whispering about the mayor and Mr. Pfeiffer's nieces and nephews. Now they'll accuse *us*. I think I'll throw up." She glanced out the window at the new maple for reassurance. If she could only believe it meant love. . . .

"Hurling is one alternative," Selene said dryly through the phone. "Calling Axell and a lawyer is another. Your choice, girl."

"I want it all to go away," she whispered, sinking down beside Alexa, who was resting in her infant seat, and stroking her daughter's petal-soft cheek. "I just want to live my life and love my kids and make the world go away."

"Seems to me, that's why you married Axell. Call him."

Maya was terrified the world would make Axell go away.

"What happens if we own the school free and clear?" she whispered.

"We have a bonfire, whoop war cries, and circle the wagons, 'cause the rednecks will be after us with a vengeance," Selene replied grimly. "You call Axell. I'll call my attorney. And then we'd better consider a security fence and armed guards, or selling out."

Maya would rather throw up. Hanging up the receiver, she crooned a silly love song to Alexa. Maybe she could call Stephen and he would agree to send her back to California. Maybe she could take Axell's credit cards and book passage to Australia.

Maybe she could call Axell.

Cradling Alexa in her arms, changing her diaper, and watching her kick with sheer exuberance, Maya remembered the moment Axell had delivered her, the astonishment and wonder on his face as he brought this living, breathing human being into the world, and she knew she couldn't run anymore.

She'd reached the destination Fate had intended for her. She could let the current carry her away on a slow and lonely journey through life, or she could fight to stay here—in her spawning grounds. She grinned at the reference. Axell had said fish have spawning grounds, not nests. That was probably true. She'd spawn with him any day. But first, she had to find a way to anchor herself.

The demon screamed as Maya opened the shop door. She almost dropped Alexa in surprise, but the furious shouting match at the counter distracted her sufficiently from the demon to keep her grip.

"I'll not have Maya—"

"Don't give me that crap, you—"

"Don't interrupt me!"

Maya blinked in surprise at this last roar. Axell. Axell never shouted. Axell never raised his voice. Axell looked as if he were about to murder Cleo.

Both of them ignored the screaming demon and her arrival. Well, she was an heiress now. She expected a little attention.

Wickedly, she leaned over the counter and plugged in the current to the dragon mobile.

The multihued dragon began to rotate slowly. Small trolls and elves orbited around him. The duo at the counter continued shouting nonsensically. The dragon spun faster and swung in wider arcs.

Maya hummed a little tune, set Alexa's seat on the counter, and pushed the button wired to the mobile motor.

The dragon's trapdoor flew open and his treasure exploded in a bright swirl of glittering confetti, hard candy, and dried rose petals. She hadn't been able to make up her mind about the contents, and she'd never tested the results. The effect was quite as amazing to her as to the others.

Cleo screamed and dodged ricocheting peppermints. Sparkling metallic confetti drifted, caught in the air currents from the overhead fans, and scattered in rainbow flurries across the contents of the store.

Axell merely turned and arched a questioning eyebrow in her direction, before gathering up Alexa and stepping out of the hail of destruction.

"Party pooper," she pouted as Axell caught her elbow and pulled her toward the door where the confetti didn't reach.

"Too bad there's no way it could shoot out helium balloons," Axell replied reflectively, examining the spinning dragon.

Looking mildly abashed, Cleo warily stood up, and in wonder watched the cloud of confetti settle and swirl in dying eddies. She picked up a peppermint and absently unwrapped it as a small tornado of petals pirouetted over the wicker chairs.

"You're not happy unless you're blowing things up, are you?" she asked.

Maya smiled and wrapped an auburn curl around her finger. A rose petal drifted to the floor. "I showered you with treasures, Cleo. You never learned to appreciate them."

Beside her, Axell choked. She couldn't tell if it was from laughter or not. Axell didn't laugh often, but she knew he had a sense of humor.

"Well, it's more colorful than dust," Cleo acknowledged, blowing purple and red stars off her cash register. "You had a point?"

"I'm celebrating."

Axell watched as Maya sailed into the center of the room with all flags flying. He knew that airy look. The ditzier Maya got, the worse the situation. She was swimming so fast downstream right now, she'd be over the falls before she knew it.

"People commonly do that with champagne. Are you going to enlighten us?"

He didn't dare approach Maya when she had that dangerous glint in her eye. He didn't know if the tree had been delivered yet. He didn't know if she'd seen it or understood. For all he knew, she considered it an insult, and she was here to smack him in the face.

Now that she had everyone's attention, she slipped into full Maya mode, curled up in the high-backed chair, and beamed. Axell wouldn't be surprised if rainbows formed over her head. Blissfully stricken by the power of her smile, he didn't even have to look lower to recall every sensual detail of her bare breast against his palm, her lithe body arching into his. Her siren call . . .

"We're heiresses," she announced sweetly.

Black clouds obliterated any rainbows. Axell groaned and covered his eyes.

Cleo ignored him and waited patiently for Maya to explain. Instead, Axell had the distinct feeling Maya was waiting for him. It was frightening how easily he read her sometimes, as if there were some unspoken current of understanding between them. He'd never known anything like it before. The responsibility was not only frightening, but overwhelming.

He could handle responsibility. With a sigh, Axell uncovered his eyes and glared at his wife. She didn't flinch, just waited expectantly. Damn, but he loved the way she did that.

"Pfeiffer?" he asked wearily.

She nodded. Cleo turned to Axell for explanation.

"He named you and Cleo and the relationship?" Axell

clarified. At Maya's nod, he pinched the bridge of his nose. "The school?"

"Don't know," she finally replied. "The lawyer blathered on about deeds. He's driving down this afternoon to explain." She looked a little less certain. "They've already filed the will at the courthouse. There's nothing we can do."

"A vacation in the Bahamas until this blows over would be nice." Leaning against the counter, Axell wished escape was an alternative.

Idly, Cleo fished another petal from her hair. "Inheriting is good, isn't it? Why the long faces?"

"Mr. Pfeiffer was *murdered*," Maya emphasized. "Who do you think are the prime suspects now?"

Silence.

Axell looked up. Cleo didn't have to look guilty. He wagered she looked guilty sleeping. He turned to Maya.

"Cleo got out the day Mr. Pfeiffer died, remember?" she reminded him.

Axell summoned the unpleasant memory of Cleo walking down the shop stairs on them one morning—the day after the murder. He didn't think prisons let people out in the middle of the night. She must have been released the day of the murder. Shit.

"I didn't know anything about any damned will," Cleo responded defensively at Axell's look. "He said he'd take care of us, but I figured it was an old man talking. He was my damned *landlord*," she shouted beneath the force of their stares. "I paid him rent. I figured he gave me a discount because I listened to him talk."

"Where were you the night you were released?" Axell asked as calmly as he could. For Maya's sake, he wanted to believe her sister. But the circumstances definitely looked questionable.

"I was *here*!" Cleo gestured at the stairs. "I got a ride, found the key over the sill, like Maya said, and came in and inspected the place. I went upstairs and went to bed. Stevieboy came in around three and woke me. He can verify I was in bed."

"At three. News of the murder was all over town before midnight," Axell replied with resignation. "I don't suppose you know the name of the person who drove you here? I don't know the exact time of death. There might be a chance . . ."

He saw the exchange of looks between the sisters and knew that alley was a dead end.

Cleo shrugged. "He's not a reliable witness."

Axell cringed at the defeat in her voice. He thought he understood something of how a person could be used for a doormat for so long, they began to think that's all there was to life. Beaten down by circumstances all their lives, with no money, no resources, no friends or family for support, the doormats of the world existed to take the blame for others.

He turned to Maya and recognized the gleam of confidence in her eyes as she watched him. She thought he could solve her sister's problems.

Logically, he should run the other way.

Insanely, Maya's faith pumped new energy through Axell's blood, inflated his heart—and probably his head, not to mention other parts of his anatomy—and released something previously fettered and downtrodden in his soul.

He thought it was hope.

❧ THIRTY-FOUR ❧

It IS as bad as you think,
and they ARE out to get you!

"You'll understand that we haven't talked with Mr. Pfeiffer since the will was signed. He gave us this list of his properties at the time, but they could have changed since then. All except his house are in the name of his corporation, so it's merely a matter of listing you as the new stockholders of the corporation, and filing a deed on the house."

The lawyer sipped his martini and sampled one of the stuffed mushroom appetizers Axell's chef had brought back to the meeting room. Maya clung to the seat of her chair and tried not to squirm as he chewed. She couldn't label her emotion. She'd lost a *grandfather*. She hadn't even known she had one. Didn't know if she wanted one. But the choice had been taken from her. And now she was staring at the immense responsibility of his properties and wondering if she could give them away.

She glanced at Cleo. Her sister had flattened her hair into something that almost looked normal and Peter Pannish. She still had tired circles under her eyes and looked brittle enough to crack, but she seemed more connected to this conversation than Maya was. Maya couldn't get beyond the grandfather part. Cleo had already nailed the lawyer for a list of properties. The list wasn't long. Maya had no clue if any of the places listed were valuable. She simply understood that her school was one of them.

Cleo had passed the list to Axell, who scanned it with more

knowledge than the others. He'd grown up here, and most of the places listed were in the area.

"Does the corporation have a bank account?" Selene inquired.

Maya had insisted that Selene be part of the meeting. Axell would have the best interest of his family in mind. Selene would favor the school. Maya didn't know which way to turn.

"We have a list of bank accounts, and we've notified the banks of the death and change of ownership. The court will issue releases when the paperwork is complete. We asked for account balances for estate-tax purposes." The lawyer slid a paper to Cleo, who sat next to him.

Cleo's eyes narrowed as she scanned the list. Shrugging, she handed it to Maya. "The properties better be in good condition. He didn't leave enough to pay the electricity."

"One of them is the condemned shop," Axell pointed out. "It will cost to have it demolished." He took the bank list Maya handed him and grimaced.

"Mr. Pfeiffer said he'd given his cousins and his wife's nieces and nephews countless loans over the years that had never been paid back. He left his sister the small house he lived in the last few years." The lawyer popped a mushroom in his mouth and savored it before shuffling through his notes again.

"I understand the rents have decreased as the properties deteriorated, so there may not be much cash. Most of the Pfeiffer family possessions were apparently divided among the family when he moved out of the big house, with the exception of the few he took with him, and that his sister inherits. He considered that inheritance enough for the extended family." The lawyer sipped his drink and sat back. "We're still looking to see if any accounts have been overlooked. The relatives haven't been very cooperative."

"The relatives know about the will?" Maya asked with a tremor of fear.

"We've told them we're executors of his estate. I'm not entirely certain they understand the meaning of that. We did not give them the terms of the will until it was officially accepted by the court."

Maya glanced at Axell, who was beginning to look exceedingly grim. Maybe she should go check on the children. She'd left Constance and Matty eating supper in the restaurant kitchen. She glanced at Alexa sitting contentedly in her chair, sucking her fist. She never cried when Maya needed a disturbance.

"There are some old papers and junk in the attic of the school," she said tentatively. "Should we turn them over to the family?"

The lawyer shrugged. "The house and its contents belong to you. You might want to check and see if there are any bank statements that could lead us to other accounts."

"I can get on that tonight if there's electricity up there." Cleo glanced at Maya.

"There's just one of those old work lights hanging from a beam. We need to carry the stuff down and go through it."

The lawyer shoved back his chair. "I really should be going. If you have any questions . . ."

Axell rose with him. "You'll need to eat. My chef will prepare you something. Relax and enjoy before you drive back."

MacGregor smiled and patted his rounded stomach. "If the entrees are as good as the appetizers, I'll be delighted to take you up on that offer."

The women watched as the two men wandered into the restaurant. Selene was the first to speak.

"Well, ladies, looks like you got a corner on the market of the hottest real estate in the state. How does it feel to be slumlords?"

"Slumlords?" Maya bit back a giggle and glanced at the list. They were just addresses to her.

Cleo leaned back in her chair and crossed her arms over her chest. "We'd better choose which ones we're going to sell. We'll need the cash for lawyers' fees when the family finds out."

Selene beamed approvingly. "You got your head on right. Maybe instead of rooting through attics, you ought to be finding a good Realtor. You'll need cash to maintain these places, cash to tear down that junk heap . . . Pfeiffer didn't do you any favors by draining the corporation."

Maya listened in amazement as her sister and Selene dived into an animated conversation on real estate economics. All she wanted to know was if she could keep her school. It wasn't in the corporation. It was a separate property. The lawyer had said it belonged to her and Cleo now.

An awful thought occurred to her. What if Cleo wanted to sell the school? All that acreage was outrageously valuable. It would provide the cash needed for all the things Cleo and Selene were discussing right now.

Maybe selling the school was the best solution. Maybe she was the only one who thought it special. What did it matter if that land had been in the Pfeiffer family for generations? The Pfeiffer family had never considered her and Cleo as members. Its historical value was meaningless. It wasn't as if George Washington had slept there or anything. Just because she thought it an ideal location for her school, that the children loved the yard and the huge rooms and all the nifty secrets old houses and gardens concealed—none of that mattered when it came down to the almighty dollar. How long would it take before Selene and Cleo reached that conclusion? Maya figured Axell had reached it the minute he'd seen the nonexistent bank accounts. He was just being polite and letting someone else say it out loud.

She'd quit following the flow of conversation but a sudden silence drew her back in. She looked up to see both Cleo and Selene watching her. Well, that didn't take long.

"I don't want to sell," she said firmly.

"You're a pigheaded jackass, Maya," Cleo complained as she rifled through a trunk of old photos Axell had carried down from the school's attic. They were working beneath the bare bulbs of the upstairs bedrooms, and she squinted at the spidery handwriting on some of the letters.

"A jackass, a moron, a ditz, whatever," Maya replied with

unconcern as she flipped through an ancient ledger. "I don't want to sell."

"When was the last time Maya behaved like a jackass?" Axell inquired as he carried in another box.

Cleo halted, stared at him, stared at Maya, then shrugged. "All right, you got me. Stubborn, she's not. Stupid, she is."

Maya ignored both of them. "You realize this is our family history in here," she marveled, glancing at entries dating back to the 1800s. "These things belong in a museum."

"Charlotte is full of attics with this kind of stuff. Unless you come across a reference to Robert E. Lee, no one's interested." Axell opened a carton that looked slightly newer than the rest. "I don't think you're going to find what you're looking for in here."

"Yeah, the recent stuff is probably in the house the sister inherited. She won't be too happy to hand it over. This moldering mansion is her family home." Cleo reached in the new box and removed what appeared to be a black-bound journal. A yellowed, much-folded letter fell from its pages.

"The sister doesn't have kids," Maya pointed out. "She's an old lady without the resources to maintain a place this size. She would have sold it. Mr. Pfeiffer knew that."

"Says who?" Cleo replied belligerently. "He never mentioned it to me. I don't remember you saying you had any long heart-to-hearts with him."

Maya glared at her sister. "Don't you have any understanding of human nature? He—"

"Ladies," Axell interrupted, blowing dust off his hands, "I think we can give up any hope of finding anything tonight. We need to get the kids home and look for other options in the morning."

"It's early yet. I'll stay here," Cleo declared, flipping through the journal.

Maya intercepted Axell's look and shut her mouth. Cleo was probably safer out here in the rural isolation of the school than at the shop with drug dealers running loose. "It feels odd having ancestors." She stood and brushed herself off.

"You want ancestors, start with the living ones," Cleo

called, carefully opening the crumpled letter. "Our father has aunts and uncles and cousins out the wazoo back in Texas and Tennessee. You can have a family reunion."

Maya didn't comment. Her sister remembered their early days of traveling from place to place much better than she did, and even she remembered all the long-boned, harsh faces of distant aunts and uncles frowning at them. She didn't think she wanted to get better acquainted with all those grim relatives.

"All right, so we fell from a lousy family tree. It makes a good excuse for our faults and foibles," she replied airily, skirting around boxes toward the door. "Maybe the one we really ought to dig into is our mother's maternal side of the family. Someone had to pass on good sense."

"I promise you, you don't want to go there," Axell muttered, opening the door and pointing to the hall. "Believe me when I say you came by your eccentric genes naturally."

Cleo shot Maya a look of disgust. "Homeboy knows something."

Maya grinned back. "Homeboy has connections." She smiled sweetly at her husband. "Headley's been at it again, hasn't he? Spill."

"It's hearsay," he warned. As both women watched him expectantly, he sighed. "According to Headley, your mother's mother was the black sheep of the Arnold family."

Cleo looked blank. Maya grinned wider.

"The mayor's family? We're the black sheep of the mayor's family? Can we call him up and tell him now?"

Axell caught the nape of her neck and shoved her out the door. "Don't you dare. And if you greet him in church as 'cousin,' I'll disown you."

"Won't be the first time," Cleo called airily as they departed.

"Daddy! *Daddy!*" Constance shouted in alarm from the floor below.

"Mr. Axell, Mr. Axell! Fire!" Matty yelled in excitement.

Exchanging looks of panic, Maya and Axell dashed down the stairs.

Flames licked at the walls of the woodshed behind the

kitchen. They could see it the instant they hit the bottom of the stairs and the uncurtained window popped into view.

Axell slammed his cell phone into Maya's hands. "Get the kids out and call 911. I'll look for a hose."

"There's a connection on the right," she shouted as he raced toward the kitchen door. "Cleo!" she yelled up the stairs. "Get down here now! Fire!"

Pounding the cell phone, gathering up Alexa, and shooing the two excited children toward the front door, away from the fire, Maya didn't even consider what valuables might be left behind. She'd never learned appreciation for material things, but she knew the value of human life.

Shouting directions into the phone, she listened for Cleo's feet on the stairs, and satisfied she heard them, herded everyone out the door.

She couldn't leave the children to help Axell. Anxiously, she sought a place in the side yard where they could keep an eye on him. The old shed contained nothing more than spiders and snakes, as far as she was aware. It was the proximity to the house and Axell's determination to stand between it and the fire that scared her. She heard the hiss of the hose and smelled the smoke the instant he turned the water on the flames.

Cleo ran out carrying an armful of old books and letters. Frantically, she glanced up at the house, then back to where Axell fought the flames. She dropped the papers at Maya's feet. "It's not at the house yet. Are there blankets in there?" Apparently remembering the stack of cots and blankets in the back room they'd passed, she darted back up to the porch.

"Cleo! Wait!" Maya screamed after her, but bent on helping, Cleo dashed inside.

"Mr. Pig!" Matty wailed. "The fire will hurt Mr. Pig!"

Oh, Lord, please don't . . . Maya couldn't phrase the petitions she wanted most. Save Axell, save Cleo, save the school, save the animals. . . . The list was too endless for debate, and she wafted wordless prayers heavenward as she crouched beside Matty, and hugging him as well as Alexa, watched the flames leap higher.

Constance gnawed on her bottom lip and clenched her little hands as she watched the shadows illuminated by the growing fire. Axell attacked the highest flames with the hose. Cleo ran out the back door with a stack of blankets and began beating at the sparks leaping to the dry grass and dead brush of the uncleared lawn between shed and kitchen.

As sirens wailed in the distance, Maya wondered what could possibly have set off a fire in an unused shed. There was no wiring, no cans of gasoline, no gas lines, no heaps of chemical-laded rags, no nothing but old wood and spiders.

And spiders didn't light fires.

🦎 THIRTY-FIVE 🦎

I'm not a complete idiot.
Some parts are missing.

Soot-coated, soaked, and sweating, Axell wearily trudged past the charred embers of the woodshed and the storage building containing all the school's yard maintenance equipment. Volunteer firefighters continued dousing the back of the house and the smoking ruins of the outbuildings with water pumped from the school's well. They'd managed to protect the school building from all damage except for a few charred boards of the kitchen porch. They hadn't managed to protect Axell's sense of security.

Floodlights illuminated the overhanging shrubbery and trees of the front yard, where neighbors had gathered in the balmy Carolina night. Mosquitoes buzzed and fireflies flickered in the shadows of the fence rows. Normality was slowly returning, but not for him. He'd never be the same again.

He could see Maya relentlessly hugging Alexa, her other arm around Constance's shoulders, while Cleo sat on the ground with Matty clinging to her neck. Neighbors had brought pots of coffee for the firefighters, people milled about the lawn, but Maya and the children formed an island of their own, an island he'd almost lost.

Insides wrenching, Axell strode briskly past firemen rolling up their hoses and hauling down their ladders. The damned school wasn't worth it. Maya could start one somewhere else. He should have let the thing burn to the ground. That would have ended the debate once and for all.

The fire chief had confirmed arson.

Axell wanted to believe that whoever had set the fire didn't know anyone was inside. Normally, no one would be at this hour. He just couldn't imagine how anyone could miss the lights upstairs and the car in the drive. Someone had tried to kill his family.

He couldn't face that kind of loss again. He'd survived the deaths of his parents, his wife, and his son, but he didn't think he could accept the loss of Constance, or Maya or Alexa or Matty. He didn't want to remember the blank, lonely existence he'd led before their arrival. He didn't want to admit his failure to protect them. It was his job to see them safe, and he hadn't done his job when he'd bowed to Maya's wishes to keep the damned school. It was time he started listening to his head instead of the mindless muscle below his belt—which stirred uncontrollably the instant Maya flung herself into his arms and buried her face against his filthy shirt, unheeding of his stench and grime.

Axell gathered her up for a brief moment of thanksgiving. Then, ignoring the turmoil of his heart, he kissed her hair, checked Alexa's serene expression, and set Maya back on the ground. "Take the kids home. I need to talk to the officers. They'll give me a ride later."

Maya stared at him with eyes wide with hurt. She was so damned transparent sometimes, it scared him. She'd have to learn to live with him as he was. She could create all the happy illusions she liked, but it was his duty to beat reality into submission when it threatened life as he knew it. She wasn't going to like what he was about to do. The knowledge cut like a scalpel through some vital part, but he was strong. He would endure whatever it took to see her safe.

He hadn't known what he was doing when he got mixed up with her. Maya filled his life like the joyous balloons he'd loved as a kid. She made life sparkle, decorated it with laughter and surprise, and gave him the kind of chest-pounding hope he'd never thought to know.

He loved her.

The realization was too huge to swallow all at once. Off-kilter, Axell reached for Constance and hugged her against him. She wrapped her skinny arms around his waist and more love welled inside him. He didn't dare express the emotion spilling through him—not in front of a crowd. His father's training was ingrained.

"Cleo can take the kids home," Maya said quietly. "I'll stay with you."

Oh, God, that's just what he didn't need. He'd rather keep Cleo here. At least her cynicism was on his side. But he couldn't tell Maya that. He couldn't puncture her dream-spun rainbows right now.

"Axell!" The shout over the murmurs of the crowd jerked Axell's head in the direction of the drive.

The mayor.

Ralph Arnold hurried over the trampled grass, not a blow-dried hair out of place, not an inch of his immaculate suit revealing a wrinkle. Axell groaned inwardly, then with a definite Maya twist, offered his grimy hand as the mayor stopped in front of them.

Ralph looked at Axell's filthy palm, glanced at his sooty face, then nervously smiled at the women and children. "Everyone's safe!" he said with relief, pretending Axell's outstretched hand didn't exist.

Maya apparently caught the byplay and offered a half grin to Axell before donning her usual vague expression when confronted with someone she couldn't relate to. He was learning all her tricks, it seemed.

"No thanks to the arsonist," she replied sweetly. "We could have all been roasted alive. Would you have put a marker beside the new road in remembrance?"

Ralph looked rattled and turned to Axell for guidance. No matter how much he despised the man and his politics, Axell couldn't believe the mayor capable of arson. He shrugged. "It's been an unpleasant evening, but I think I have news you'll want to hear. We need to get together in the morning."

Maya shot him a suspicious look. "I'm still not selling."

Damning her perceptiveness, Axell calmly met her gaze. "Cleo is ready to sell, aren't you?" He glanced in his sister-in-law's direction. His sister-in-law. Damn, he'd exchanged a busybody mother-in-law for an ex-con sister-in-law. It didn't matter. Protecting his wife and kids was what mattered.

Cleo glanced suspiciously from him to the mayor and shrugged. "No skin off my nose. It's Maya's dream, not mine."

Maya's dream. Axell wanted to stop the discussion for now. "We'll talk in the morning, Ralph. Everyone's nerves are shot tonight."

"I won't sell, and that's final." Maya gathered up Alexa, caught Constance's arm, and glowered at her sister. "We're going. Have a good chat."

Axell recognized the sinking feeling in his stomach as she walked away, but he was prepared for that, much more than he was prepared for the sudden urge to shout at her to come back. He didn't want to be divided from Maya in any manner, physical or emotional or in their hopes for the future. For a little while, he'd almost felt as if they were one whole, as if their physical joining had truly brought them together in heart and soul. But that was patently ridiculous. Grown men did what they had to do, and usually got yelled at for it.

Maya had always declared she went with the flow. Maybe she would drop the scheme for a school now that she had Cleo and those rental properties to occupy her mind.

Axell ruthlessly blocked out the memory of Maya painting the picture of misfits and poor children standing on the outside, looking in, yearning for the love and understanding she could provide. Schools were for learning, not sentimental claptrap.

If only he could block out the fear that Constance could easily have become one of those misfits.

February 1977
 It's over. She's left, taking her babies with her, not even knowing why the storm broke over her innocent head. Perhaps she'll be happier with her husband's family, away from the stench of her father's cowardice and the cruelty of her mother's kin.

 What difference does anything make now? I have an offer of easy money, money that can someday go to my

*daughter and her babies. They'll be too far away to be
affected by anything I do here. Why not paint the whole
damned town with tar? Helen would have loved the
irony.*

*The Arnolds deserve to have their faces rubbed in the
dirt they strive so desperately to pretend doesn't exist in
their pretty little town.*

Axell followed the light in the family room as he entered
the house well after midnight. He hadn't expected Maya to
wait up for him. She must be totally wiped by now. He certainly was.

He needed a hot shower, and a long soak, and clean sheets
with Maya's sweet-smelling curves in his arms, and then he
thought he could sleep for a week. Heaven was having Maya
to come home to. He was aroused just thinking of her sleepy
kisses. She'd forgive him for his plans to sell the school.
Maya simply didn't have it in her to hold a grudge.

Prepared to scold her for waiting up, Axell stopped dead in
the doorway at the sight of Sandra flipping pages of a magazine.

"Well, it's about time," she said huffily, standing up. "Constance has been crying for hours. What do you intend to do
about it?"

Constance? Axell blinked and tried to rearrange his relaxing thoughts of showers and bed to this new perspective.
"Where's Maya?" he asked cautiously.

"Gone, of course." Sandra threw the magazine down. "You
really didn't think she'd hang around once she came into a
little money of her own, did you? Those kind only think of
one thing."

Gone? Axell dragged his hand through his hair, realized he
was smearing soot, and grimaced. "Where did she go?" he
asked in genuine puzzlement, although his stomach was
telling him exactly where she'd gone and why.

"How should I know?" Sandra asked arrogantly. "I'm not a
mind reader. She dropped Constance off, packed up Matty's
toys and the baby's diapers, and left. She'll probably be back

for the rest sometime. You can ask her then. I'm going to bed."

Icy cold numbed him as Sandra swept past. Maya would never have left Constance behind if she'd simply meant to spend the night with Cleo. He hadn't believed she would leave Constance at all. She loved Constance.

Maya had a heart full of love for everyone.

Clutching his grinding gut, Axell sank to the couch, oblivious to what his filthy clothes did to the upholstery. She'd left him. She'd walked away. Over the damned school. He knew better than to think she'd left him because of money. Maya didn't have any idea whatsoever how much those properties were worth and wouldn't care. But she was completely capable of leaving him over a principle.

Let her, dammit. She was so frigging determined to swim away at the first sign of trouble, then he'd damned well let her go. He didn't need this hassle, worrying about Constance and Alexa and Matty and Maya and that damned school and an arsonist and how the ex-con sister and her drug dealer friends mixed in.

What if she'd gone back to Stephen?

Oh shit. Oh hell and shit and damn them all, there and back again.

Wanting to shout his agony and confusion from the rooftop, Axell bit back his moan as he heard the pitter-patter of bare feet in the hall.

Constance. How the hell would he explain it all to Constance?

"He looks like hell warmed over. You're crazy to do this to him." Cleo collapsed in the dilapidated wooden chair Maya had retrieved from some junkyard. It now adorned the upstairs room of the school where Maya had taken up residence. Cleo glanced around at the sheets draped over stripped wallpaper and broken plaster, and wrinkled her nose. "This place looks worse than that apartment Mama rented."

"I don't remember that," Maya answered absently, feeding Alexa a spoonful of milky cereal. She didn't want to be told

Axell looked terrible. She wanted to hear that he was going on happily without her. He hadn't let Constance return to school.

"Leaving him was stupid," Cleo admonished. "All you had to do was refuse to sign the papers if you didn't want to sell. He would never have thrown you out for that."

"Remember that family we stayed with in L.A.? The ones with the lovely pink-frilled bedroom?"

Cleo glowered. "Yeah, the ones that had a holy cow when you painted purple roses on the walls. So what?"

Maya glanced at her in disapproval. "What do you mean, so what? They threw us out, didn't they? I tried to make the room prettier to show them how much I loved them, and they threw us out. Is it so hard to make the comparison?"

Cleo stared at her sister in disbelief. "Is that what this is all about? You left so he couldn't throw you out? Are you *crazy*? That man's blind-deaf in love with you. He worships the ground you walk on. He's a damned Don Quixote who would have walked into a burning building for you. And you threw him away so he couldn't do it to you first? I can't believe we had the same parents!"

"You don't understand anything." Maya wiped Alexa's chin. She'd thought of all people, Cleo would understand. Selene was barely speaking to her for leaving Axell, but he hadn't even called. That was proof enough in her mind. She'd finally pushed him too far and he was relieved that she'd left without forcing him into a fight. Now he only had Constance to protect, and he didn't need to worry about arsonists and drug dealers. She knew how his mind worked. He wanted to keep everything in his world in neat little compartments where he could take care of them. The school didn't fit, so he wanted to get rid of it. She understood that. She simply couldn't live with it.

"I understand this blamed building is sitting on a multi-million-dollar piece of property and that someone tried to burn it down and will probably try again." Cleo bit into the cold piece of toast Maya had left uneaten beside her cup of tea. "Axell isn't stupid. You're the jackass here."

Maybe she was. For the first time in her life, she'd chosen to take a stand, and maybe it was the wrong one. Heaven only knew, she had doubts enough to build a mountain. She'd always had doubts. She'd never had enough confidence in herself to finish anything except college. She supposed it was ironic that Axell had been the one to feed her the confidence she needed to fight for what she wanted. If she backed down now, she might never be able to stand up to anyone ever again.

"The concept of this school is more important than anyone's hurt feelings," she said quietly, trying to convince herself as well as Cleo. "If I fail, then no one will ever try again. I can't fail. Look at how much Matty has changed over these last few months." She concentrated on her known accomplishments. "He wouldn't even smile when I first got here. Now he bounces up and down with eagerness. He's marvelous with animals, and tells the younger kids wonderful stories. *That's* what I want to do here."

Cleo ripped off another mouthful of bread and chewed it jerkily before replying. "He's still lousy at reading and writing. He's got the books memorized, but he doesn't know the words."

"He's only five. His motor skills aren't as strong as others at that age. But don't you see?" Maya pleaded, looking up at her sister. "He shouldn't be judged on his undeveloped skills. Maybe he'll never be great at reading and writing. The world's full of people who can do those things just fine. But how many people can nurture animals and tell stories and make children laugh? It takes all *kinds*. That's what I want people to understand."

Cleo looked uncertain. "You're dreaming. You can't raise kids to tell stories instead of reading and writing. That's ridiculous."

Maya patiently wiped Alexa's face again. "You need to have him tested to see if he has any learning disabilities, or if he's just immature in that area, but don't you see? If I hadn't given him confidence in his ability to take care of the animals, he wouldn't have had the confidence to learn as much as he has. He used to throw his pencils against the wall rather than try to write his ABC's."

"Shit, now you'll have me believing this garbage." Cleo stood up. "I've got to get back to the store. I still think you're crazy about not selling this place."

She probably was. Maya watched her sister go, then picked up Alexa to give her the rest of her bottle. Alexa breathed a gassy grin, and Maya's heart twisted. She wanted Axell to see his daughter's first smile. She wanted him to see her crawl and walk and to hear her say her first words.

Tears sprang to her eyes, and she tried to concentrate on the principles that had brought them to this impasse.

Axell had pushed her away as deliberately as every foster parent who'd given up on her. He'd known what he was doing when he told the mayor he was willing to talk about selling. Maybe she'd demanded too much, invaded his space, and made him uncomfortable. But Maya knew better.

Axell loved her, and he was proving it by shoving her away because he was afraid of losing those he loved. And because she loved him, she was obediently swimming downstream.

She wanted to laugh hysterically at the mismatch they'd made of their lives.

Instead, she lay a sleeping Alexa into her cradle, cleaned out her teacups, and looked for their box.

❧ THIRTY-SIX ❧

Some people are alive only because it's illegal to kill them.

Axell rolled out of bed the minute he was conscious of
birds singing. He didn't want to lie there remembering the
mornings he'd woke with Maya in his arms, because then he'd
start remembering her seductive chuckles and playful fingers
and his already unassuaged arousal would reach painful proportions. A cold shower helped prepare him for another
empty day of approving invoices and listening to idle chatter.

Why had he ever thought the damned restaurant so important? He'd spent the better part of his life appearing there
every day like some automaton, but it ran like clockwork
even if he disappeared for hours at a time. Once he got rid of
this little problem with the mayor, he wouldn't need to worry
over losing his license. He could take Constance to the beach.
He couldn't remember the last time he'd taken her to the
ocean.

He was beginning to think like Maya.

Groaning, he scrubbed his hair, dried off, dressed, and
staggered into the kitchen. Sandra wasn't up yet. Constance
was preparing her own breakfast. She gave him a haunted
look, then drifted into the family room to watch cartoons.
Sandra's idea of taking care of Constance was an electronic
baby-sitter.

Remembering his daughter giggling and decorating pan-
cakes with blueberries under Maya's instructions, Axell
gulped down a glass of milk and called it breakfast. Maybe
tomorrow he'd go to the grocery and buy some pancake mix

and blueberries and Constance could show him how to fix clown faces in the batter.

Maybe tomorrow the sun would orbit the earth.

He refused to wallow in self-pity. He could do this. It was simpler this way, without women in his life. He'd never learned to deal with them anyway. He could reach out to Constance without Maya's intervention. He could quit spending eighteen-hour days at the restaurant. He wouldn't swear he'd learn to cook or plant colorful flowers around the yard, but he could find a hobby of some sort to fill the empty hours.

He glanced out at the maple he'd had planted to shade Maya's garden. A cardinal sang "pretty-pretty" from one of the branches. The pink and purple impatiens beneath the canopy of leaves needed watering. The great gaping vacancy of his insides whistled hollow as if a cold wind swept through.

He had to be the biggest jerk of all time. He couldn't force Maya to sell her dream. She was living out there in that slum with Alexa, as unprotected as before their marriage. What the hell had he thought he'd accomplished? He'd succeeded only in placing them in worse danger.

Selling the school was the sensible thing to do. The old house needed too much expensive work, the shopping center would destroy the rural atmosphere, the mayor would leave them all alone if they agreed to a right of way for the road, and whoever was behind all these disasters would presumably go away and leave them safe. The sale would create considerable cash flow to aid Cleo and her shop and give Maya a chance to open a new, more modern facility elsewhere. Keeping the school where it stood was stupid.

Keeping the school was Maya's dream. She'd never owned a home of her own, never had something that was completely hers. He'd installed her in a house his late wife had built, and expected her to be happy. She had been. Axell could swear Maya had been happy here. Maya could be happy in a cardboard box. That didn't mean she didn't dream of a place of her own.

Damn.

Axell wandered into the family room to check on Constance. "I'm going in to the office. Give me a hug?" He didn't want to sound plaintive, but it sure had that ring.

Constance glanced at him, then huddled her shoulders so she looked like a possum playing dead. "Can I go to school for just a little while?"

Well, if he sounded plaintive, she sounded just plain pitiful. He'd have to get used to it. This was for her own good. "It's not safe, honey. We'll find you a new school."

"Is Maya not safe?"

His daughter was too quick for her own good. Axell massaged his forehead and sought an easy answer. There was none. "Maya's a grown-up. She can take care of herself."

He heard his own words with amazement. Maya could take care of herself. He didn't have to do it for her. He'd known that. It just hadn't sunk in. If she wanted to risk life and limb fighting for a falling-down building, that was her responsibility. Not his. He could offer to lend a hand, or stand in her way, or keep his nose out entirely, but it was her fight.

She had thought they'd approached marriage as equals. He had thought he was taking on more responsibilities. He should have felt relief when she left. Instead, he felt as if the weight of the entire world had fallen on his shoulders. He hadn't realized how much of his burden Maya had cheerfully carried.

He didn't like to admit he was wrong. He was never wrong. That's how he'd gotten where he was today.

Alone.

Shit.

Axell bent over and kissed his daughter's hair, then ruffled it. "I'll see what I can do, honey. We'll get Maya back."

She beamed in relief and happiness. At least someone needed his help.

With that one little grain of confidence to carry him forward, Axell aimed for the garage. He just didn't know where he was going yet.

* * *

September 1981

My lawyers have lost track of her. I'm frantic. She's left her husband and disappeared with the babies. How will she live? How can she take care of them?

Damn you and your temper, Helen. You've passed on the worst of both of us. And the best.

I'll find her, Helen. I'm a tainted old man now, too tired to fight. You're gone, Dolly's dying, our daughter doesn't know I exist, and nothing seems worth the effort anymore. But I'll spend every ill-earned dollar to find them.

At the crossroad, Axell glanced to his left, in the direction of the school, then back to the right, in the direction of town. He wanted to see Maya. He wanted to set things straight with her.

He couldn't set things straight until he'd straightened out a few things in town first. Acting against the strong urge to turn left, he steered the Rover toward Wadeville.

The first thing he saw when he hit town was a huge black Cadillac in front of Cleo's shop.

Swearing violently, he screeched the Rover into a U-turn, slammed to a halt in a loading zone past the Curiosity Shoppe, and jerked the key from the ignition. The first thing he would straighten out was Maya's damned sister. He was in just the right mood for flinging her up against a wall, and smacking some sense into her.

A tall bald-headed black man in an expensive pin-striped suit loomed over the counter, pushing his face into Cleo's. As usual, Cleo wasn't giving any ground, but Axell thought he saw fear flicker across her face.

Not in any humor for diplomacy, Axell jerked the front door wide open and held it. "OUT!" he shouted. "Get your ass off my property before I throw you out!"

The black man turned his head and gave him a glassy stare. "You and how many others?" he asked coldly.

All that unleashed testosterone slam-dunked straight into Axell's bloodstream.

Releasing the door, Axell grabbed the heavy metal kaleidoscope off its tripod. "Out," he repeated with more calm than earlier.

Cleo emitted an "eep" of dismay, whether for the kaleidoscope's fate or his, he couldn't ascertain. The black man sniggered and reached for his inside pocket—one of two moves Axell had anticipated. He hadn't been an All-State quarterback because he was dumb, or slow.

Before the other man could produce his gun, Axell swung. He had enough fury behind the swing to crack something. Unfortunately, it was the kaleidoscope and not the dealer's brick-hard head.

The man staggered but remained upright and groping for his weapon.

Well, he hadn't spent his adolescence in a bar without learning to fight dirty. Feinting with the remains of his weapon, Axell waited for his opponent to dodge, kicked high and hard, and almost winced in sympathy as his foot connected with its soft target.

The other man screamed in mortal pain and crumpled.

"My God, Axell," Cleo whispered prayerfully, leaning over the counter to watch her tormentor squirm in agony. "Can you kill him now?"

"Call the cops and give me something to tie him with." Axell glanced around and found an extension cord plugged into Maya's mobile collection. He snapped it out of the socket, then glanced warily at Cleo, who hadn't moved.

"I can't call the cops," she murmured. "They'll revoke my probation. I can't go back to jail."

"He's a dealer, you can't protect him," he said coldly.

"He'll hurt Matty if I don't," she whispered.

"Not after I'm done with him." Axell jerked an expensively cuffed wrist away from the source of his prisoner's pain and wrapped the cord around it. "Call the cops."

"You gonna pay for this," the man on the floor muttered from between clenched teeth. "Nobody messes with me, man."

Axell ignored the empty threat and pinned his gaze on Cleo. "Where's the dope?"

He gave her credit for not being stupid enough to deny the obvious. She glanced nervously toward the back of the shop. "In the boxes labeled 'china.' " She still didn't reach for the phone. "Take him out of here, please," she begged. "I'm straight. I promise. But I owe him a lot of money, and he's got friends—"

"Damn straight," the dealer shouted. "And you're gonna pay, like I make all double-dealers pay."

"Go find that box," Axell ordered. He'd be damned if he let the drug cops claim his building for illegal possession, and he'd be damned if he let a dealer go free.

"You don't touch my stuff, man!" the dealer screamed. "You got no right—"

Axell jerked the extension cord tighter around cuffed wrists, then searched the pockets of the pin-striped suit, locating the gun and car keys. "And call the cops or I'll turn you in with this animal."

Terrified, Cleo ran toward the back and returned with a couple of small cardboard boxes. "This is all I could find."

"Don't you dare!" The dealer struggled against his bonds as Axell stood up. "That's high-quality stuff. Look, I'll cut you a deal, same one I had with the old man. . . ."

Axell halted and stared down at the panicky dealer, his brain finally kicking in. "What kind of deal?" This man threatened kids. This man could kill people.

"You just give me a key to this place, like I had to the old one. I need a new place to stash my stuff. I'll cut you a piece of the take, just like I did with the old dude. You don't have to get your fingers dirty a'tall."

"How much of the take?" Axell demanded, grasping for clues.

"Depends. The old man had lotsa places to meet so the cops wouldn't get suspicious. This one piddly building ain't much." More confident now, he negotiated.

"What if I have lots of buildings?" Axell asked quietly.

"Then we're talking." His eyes narrowed warily. "But you ditch on me, and you end up like Pfeiffer. He owed me big-time, and I made him pay, and I got my own back, too." He looked up at Cleo who had picked up the receiver again. "You'd better not finish that call, girl."

While the dealer was looking away, Axell shook his head slightly at her. Cleo hovered with her hand above the phone, watching both of them uncertainly.

"You got your own back?" Axell asked calmly. "How?"

When Cleo didn't hang up, the dealer turned over and glared at Axell. "I ain't sayin' nuthin' more."

Axell jerked his head at Cleo and threw her the car keys. "Put the stuff in his trunk where it belongs, then set the car on fire."

"Wait!" the dealer screamed.

Cleo halted with her hand on the door.

"I got connections," the man threatened. "They'll do most anything for a price. They take care of things for me. They'll take care of *her*," he warned, jerking his chin in Cleo's direction, "if you don't let me go."

"What if I want something taken care of?" Axell asked quietly, afraid to hear the answer but too close to the truth to stop now.

The prisoner sensed the danger in his captor's voice. Narrowing his eyes, he watched Axell carefully. "I get a piece of the action," he warned, "so it costs."

"If I want one of my places burned?" Axell suggested. Hiring arsonists to scam Yankee insurance companies was almost a southern tradition.

"Untie me, and we'll discuss it."

Axell considered him. "What do you do if someone botches the job? Take him out, like Pfeiffer?"

"Do it myself," his prisoner exclaimed with disgust. "You know all about it, don't you? All you white boys stick together. Well, I took care of the problem. That crack head messed up, but I fixed it last night. You're working with a real professional. No one sees smoke at night. That heat just been smoldering until by now; the whole place is so hot, it will go up all at once. Even if it's daylight, the place will be in cinders before they can stop it."

Axell thought his lungs would collapse and his heart stop. If he understood right . . .

Heart beating wildly, he turned to Cleo. "Report a bomb threat at the school. Get the whole damned county out there." He kicked the thug on the floor. "Where did you plant it? You'll fry right now if you don't tell me." He reached to plug the extension cord into the socket—a useless maneuver, but he figured he could cut the wires and intimidate the hell out of the bastard if he didn't get the answer he wanted.

"Don't do that!" the dealer screamed, eyeing the cord and the socket. "The old man's dead. It ain't as if I'm hurtin' anyone."

"There's a house full of children out there!" Axell shouted back. "Now tell me where you planted it or you'll go to hell right here and now, without appeal."

Cleo was already yelling into the phone. The man looked terrified, then beaten. "Under the back porch, man. I didn't mean to hurt no kids. The place seemed empty last night."

Dropping the cord, Axell dashed out the door.

Before Axell could reach the Rover, Ralph Arnold stepped in his path, blocking his way. "You said we'd talk about the school, Holm."

Wrapping both hands in the mayor's lapels, Axell lifted him from the sidewalk and dropped him to one side. "You can have the bar, Ralph. You can have the restaurant and the whole damned town. But you'll fry in hell before I'll let you have Maya's school."

Maya would have kicked his shins if she'd seen him roughing up the mayor. *Maya*. Axell's soul screamed in agony as he bent over the steering wheel and roared the engine to life.

He could almost smell the flames from here.

❧ THIRTY-SEVEN ❦

We are born naked, wet, and hungry. Then things get worse.

Axell saw the smoke billowing over the forest of trees long before he reached the school. His gut clenched and a cold chill spread through him. If he didn't think about it, he wouldn't feel it. *Don't think, Axell. Do.* That always worked. Keep moving, keep an eye on the road ahead, don't feel, don't imagine life without Maya. . . .

God. *Maya.* His insides cracked and memories poured out of him despite his best efforts. Maya grinning proudly over a spinning dragon treasure. Maya frustrated, with baby Alexa beating at her breast. *Alexa!* Damn and triple damn. Shudders rippled through him. He couldn't bear it. Couldn't think of another tiny infant . . .

He couldn't do this. He couldn't lose any more people he loved. He must be a jinx. There must be something wrong with him. He should never have dared bring Maya into his home, to open up to her, to love her. . . .

To love her. Oh, God, how he loved her. He'd never known it hurt so much. Agony crawled around under his skin. He should have told her. He might never get the chance to tell her.

A Buick pulled in front of him and slowed to a crawl as its driver gaped at the black clouds of smoke spewing into the cloudless blue sky. Axell cursed. He slammed his horn. The smoke billowed higher. Was that a flame shooting up?

"Lord, give me a giant bat to swat these damn Yankees off the road," Axell growled as the Buick continued its crawl on the winding back road.

Abruptly, Axell shot the Rover off the road, slammed across a drainage ditch, and plowed through an old tobacco field. Ahead rose the fence line of trees with black smoke mushrooming higher. The utility vehicle bucked and swayed as it hit erosion ruts and old furrows, but Axell concentrated on doing and not thinking. Mercifully, cold numbness replaced rampaging panic.

Flames shot through the smoke.

Thoroughly focused now, he swung the Rover between tall Georgia pines, over sumac and willow oak saplings, through thick beds of brown pine needles, screeching to a halt only when he reached the row of sycamores and azaleas on the outskirts of the property. The tires skidded in the debris and the Rover's front bumper crumpled against a sweetgum trunk. He shot out of the car before the tires stopped spinning, and the air bag exploded.

Children milled in the front yard, and as he ran toward them, Axell strained to count heads, searching for the faces etched on his heart. Maya had an entire school full of children on her hands this time. How many teachers did she have? Three? Could they get all the kids out?

And baby Alexa, who couldn't walk on her own. Who had Alexa?

Mind screaming in anguish, Axell burst through the forest of trees and shrubs into the swarm of terrified, crying children in the drive. He finally located Matty, clutching a squirming guinea pig and staring with huge dark eyes at the flames leaping from the back of the house. One of the teachers held a wailing Alexa, and Axell's stomach dropped to his feet. If Maya wasn't holding Alexa . . .

Two of the older children stumbled out the front door, one carrying a rabbit cage and the other a fishbowl. Axell didn't even have to question the teachers shepherding the children down the stairs—he knew at once who was inside, organizing the retreat, looking after everyone but her own damned self.

All the icy shards of his frozen insides splintered and crumbled as another spurt of flame erupted on the back roof and children shrieked. *Maya is inside.* Not stopping to think, to calculate logistics, or use any rationale whatsoever, Axell dashed up the stairs. As he hit the smoke-filled hall, his only thought was that the children needed Maya. He was expendable, but he had to save Maya. The world didn't need another yuppie bar. The world needed Maya. Constance needed her.

He would die without her.

Saying his prayers and screaming her name in the murky dimness, he fought his way down the wide hall—and nearly crashed into her.

"Axell!" she screamed in joy, before shoving a cage into his arms. "Thank God. Muldoon ran back in here, and I can't find him." She sounded frantic.

With relief so bone deep tears formed in his eyes, Axell crushed her in his grip, cage and all. Smoke poured from the back of the house as he hauled her toward the door. If he was expendable, so was the damned cat. Maya was not.

"Muldoon!" she wept, nonsensically. The whole damned building was going up in flames, and she cried over a cat.

Attacked by a snaking sensation around his ankles and refusing to release Maya, Axell shoved the cage at her and leaned down to scoop up a terrified ball of fur. Hero of the year, he'd saved the life of a cat with a father fixation.

"I'll kill you for this, but not now. Where are your damned teacups?" he shouted, coughing on smoke, shoving her toward the door while the cat clung to his shirt. He damned well wouldn't have her running back in there for china. She might do what she wanted the rest of the time, but he was still bigger than she right now, and he wasn't letting her out of his grip.

"They're in the car." Exchanging crying cat for cage, Maya fought through the smoke toward the front door. "All my stuff is in the car."

In the car. The words chimed like church bells in his ears as Axell finally saw daylight ahead. In the car. She'd already packed her teacups in the car. She wouldn't have done that because of the fire. Maya would never have carried out material things first. Had she been coming home to him?

Or leaving forever?

Maybe those chiming bells tolled doom.

They gasped as they fell through the front door and stumbled down the steps to the lawn. Fire trucks screamed up the drive as the teachers steered the children to safety, away from trees and shrubs that might ignite. Maya hurried toward them, her arms full of yowling cat. Axell followed. This time, the damned school could burn. He'd rebuild it personally. He wasn't letting her out of his sight, not even for Cleo and her damned dealer. Let Cleo figure out what to do with him.

Shoving the rabbit cage into the outstretched arms of one of Constance's playmates, Axell grabbed Muldoon from Maya, plunked the cat into Matty's arms, and caught his wife by the elbow. As the fire engines slammed to a halt near the porch steps and rubber-coated men leapt out to swarm over the lawn for the second time that week, he steered Maya to the outskirts of the crowd and wrapped her securely in his arms so she couldn't bolt. He wasn't surprised to discover she was sobbing with huge gulps of air.

"It's all right," he murmured, stroking her back, wishing he knew something, anything, about comforting women in moments of disaster. "No one's hurt."

That wasn't enough. He had more to say, but didn't know how to say it.

She nodded against his chest, hiccups shaking her through the sobs. "I can't look, Axell. Tell me they're all okay."

"Muldoon's on Matty's head, yowling. There's a teenager rocking Alexa. Your teachers are explaining to the kids what the firemen are doing. They're all fine. You're the one who scared me out of my wits. So help me, Maya, if you ever do anything like that again . . ." He still shook with fear. That wasn't what he'd meant to say. The words pounded at his chest and screamed in his heart, needing release.

"The school is a loss," she whispered what they both already knew.

"I'll build you another," he promised. "We'll make it look just like this one, if you like. I know contractors, architects. . . ."

He couldn't help it, her quiet hiccups tore at his already shredded insides. Axell pulled her into his arms, for all the world to see. As she buried her face against his shirt, the fear of never being able to say the words caused them to pour out in a rush. "I love you, Maya. I love you, and I don't want to lose you, too."

She looked up at him through tear-glazed eyes. All the wonder and excitement he so prized shone back at him now. "You love me?" she whispered, then hiccuped again. Embarrassed, she buried her head against his shirt. "No one's ever told me they loved me before."

"I do. I love everything about you. I love your purple hair and purple flowers and kaleidoscope eyes. I don't want to live without you, Maya. It's been driving me crazy, trying to pretend I don't care when it's tearing me apart. I couldn't bear it if I lost you."

"If you love me, you can't lose me," she said insensibly, her words muffled as she swung her head back and forth. "You can't lose the ones you love, Axell," she announced more emphatically, lifting her head and defying him to argue. "Haven't you learned that?"

She rubbed her eyes and tried to speak firmly, but her voice cracked. "I was only ten when I lost my mother, but I can remember how her hair bobbed up and down when she laughed, how she loved pushing us on the swings, how the wind felt blowing through my hair as I swung higher and higher and she laughed with such joy. . . ."

She gulped on a sob and Axell crushed her closer. Just to hear her voice was Beethoven's Fifth and a child's laughter all wrapped into one. He understood joy again. Ice shards of his heart melted into warm, rainbowed puddles.

"And my father," she continued brokenly. "He used to wear ten-gallon hats and cowboy boots and swing me up in his arms and call me his cowgirl. He'd put his hat on my head and it would cover me up to the shoulders and we'd laugh and laugh. He bought me cowboy boots of my own. God, I loved him so much. And he's still here. He *is*," she insisted when he didn't respond soon enough.

"What happened to them?" Axell asked quietly, slowly absorbing her words, working them around inside himself to see how they fit, pulling out memories of his own parents and trying to put them into the picture.

She wiped her eyes on his shirt. "My mother died of appendicitis. We were poor. We didn't have insurance. She figured it was just a stomachache. By the time she collapsed and the neighbors called an ambulance, it was too late."

Axell clutched her tighter as she wept. She had so much love inside her, and now he saw where it came from. Her mother had died to save the pennies for food on their table. He could see it because that was what Maya would do. "And your father?"

She hiccuped. "When he lost his job here and we started drifting, he started drinking. My mother had a thing about alcohol, so she started nagging. That made him drink more. They broke up when I was pretty little, but I remember the arguments. I never saw him again. We never knew what happened to him until the social workers went looking for him after Mom died. They found out he died in a drunk-driving accident in Texas. Some days, I could never forgive him, but I can't forget him either."

She was weeping quietly now, a torrent of tears and heartaches Axell couldn't bear as his own memories flooded through him. He knew love. Maybe it wasn't a loud and joyous love filled with laughter and tears like Maya's, but it was strong and solid and he could offer it to her, if she would accept it.

"Come home with me, please," he pleaded. "I'll do whatever it takes to make you love me, Maya. I'm sorry, so sorry I'm such an ass. I'll never tell you what to do again. You can have cowboy hats and swings and the school and anything you like. You were right and I was wrong and I'll get down on my damned knees and beg if I have to. . . ."

Her sobs began to shake suspiciously like laughter. Warily, Axell lifted his head from hers and tried to see her face. She buried it in his shoulder and clutched his shirt tighter. He'd ruined more shirts this way. He'd have to start buying wash-and-wear.

"Don't b-beg," she stuttered into his shirt between sobs and laughter. "Please don't beg, then I'd have to grovel and I'm really no good at it. God, Axell, just hold me. Tell me you love me some more. I love you so much it scares the hell out of me and I don't know what to do about it, and running just seemed simplest, but it's not really."

She practically disappeared into his arms when he held her this close. He'd hold her closer if he could, pull her inside of him, where she could never be hurt again. Pain and joy ripped at what remained of his insides. Or his heart, or whatever it was Maya had gotten into and claimed for her own. She could have it. He didn't need it anymore. He just needed her—and the dreams she made possible.

"I love you, Maya, I need you. We all need you. Don't ever do this to me again."

She nodded against his chest. Her sobs had lessened somewhat. She hiccuped. "I was coming home, honest. I decided if I meant to learn to fight, it ought to be for something more important than a building. It's all right about the school. It's just boards and walls. I shouldn't have hurt you, though, or Constance. I won't do it again, I promise."

Something tight and hard unfurled inside Axell's chest, and he relaxed and loosened his grip enough to rub her back. "It's all right if you need a time-out every once in a while. You can swim to some safe place and come back again when you're ready. We'll understand, just as long as we know you're coming back."

She lifted her head, and red-rimmed eyes shimmered with tears as she gazed at him worshipfully. "Loving you is the scariest thing I've ever done, Axell Holm. If you understand me any better, I'll feel like a walking, talking crystal ball."

He grinned. "Don't worry. You're more like a kaleidoscope. I can see through you, but boy, is it confusing. Not to mention colorful." He glanced over her shoulder. "And speaking of colorful . . ." He sighed in expectation of the walking, talking disaster climbing out of the police car at the end of the drive. "Here comes your sister."

Staying solidly within the circle of Axell's arms, Maya turned to watch as Cleo gathered up Matty and cat and purposefully strode in their direction. She couldn't bear watching the school go up in flames, so she focused on what was important. Cleo trailing a policeman was important. She wiped her tears on the back of her hand and waited. Axell's arms made everything all right. He'd said he loved her. Axell loved her for herself, just as she was, without any compromises. The words smiled in her heart and the world glowed brighter. She could handle anything right now.

"I used up all your honey," Cleo declared harshly as she came within speaking distance.

Puzzled, Maya blinked. "That's okay, I'll buy more. Your teapot's safe. I've got it in the car."

Hugging Matty against her, Cleo nodded and looked past Maya to Axell. "Cueball is puking his guts all over the police station."

Axell's arms tightened around Maya. She had the feeling she wasn't catching something here. "Who's Cueball? Does he have food poisoning?"

Axell stroked her reassuringly as if she were a darned cat, and she glared over her shoulder at him. He was looking worried but that curious light gleamed in his eyes.

He watched her carefully as he answered. "The fires weren't accidental."

"Tell me something I don't know," she practically spat out. "And if I ever get my hands on the slimeball . . ." Her eyes widened as she read their expressions in a different light. "You know who did it!" And then the honey statement kicked in.

Maya stared at her sister with disbelief. "You didn't? Tell me you didn't, Cleo?"

Cleo shrugged. "The shop had a little ant problem. I'll call the exterminator when I get back."

Maya could sense Axell struggling to follow, but she couldn't explain. She still didn't believe. "They have fire ants down here, Cleo," she said in horror. "Tell me they weren't fire ants."

Cleo scratched her son's head and didn't offer any expression at all. "He sells dope to kids, Maya. He offs old men for refusing to help him hide the stuff. He sets fire to buildings, little sis. I made sure they were fire ants, just like the last time."

The policeman was almost grinning, even if Cleo didn't crack a muscle. "We had to take a hose to him. Any time he doesn't answer a question, we turn the water off. Mr. Holm, we need to ask you some questions when you have a chance."

Maya heard Axell choking behind her. She wasn't certain if it was laughter or not, and she refused to turn and find out. She didn't have a violent bone in her body. She remembered the time Cleo had dumped honey over one of her tormentors and left him for the ants to find. It hadn't been funny then. It wasn't funny now.

Smelling the smoke as her dream and a century of history burned to ashes, Maya thought that maybe it wasn't funny, but it sure the hell was justified.

She watched as Headley limped through the crowd of onlookers. Parents had started arriving to take their children home. Several of the matrons from the Garden Club were shaking their heads and checking the roses on the boundaries to see if they'd survived the intense heat, and the flood from the fire hoses. The plants near the house would be a total loss. Maya couldn't turn and look. She could still hear the hiss of hoses and steam. Even if they saved part of the structure, it couldn't be rebuilt. She leaned into Axell's embrace. She could stand on her own if she wanted. She just didn't want to right now.

"I'm sorry, Maya," Headley said with complete sincerity as he reached them. "I'm getting old and not as quick as I used to be. If I'd put two and two together a little faster . . ."

"The pusher killed Pfeiffer," Axell interrupted coldly. "But someone paid him to burn the school. Who?"

"It's not what you're thinking, Axell," the reporter said warningly. "There isn't any way you could . . ."

Maya watched with interest as a silver Mercedes halted in the driveway and the mayor leapt out, searching the crowd frantically. As soon as he saw them, he hurried in their direction. Amazingly enough, Selene slipped elegantly from the passenger side and sauntered in his wake.

Headley caught the object of Maya's interest and stopped what he was about to say until the newcomers arrived.

"Hello, cousin," Maya said dryly as Mayor Arnold approached. Behind her, Axell groaned and squeezed her shoulder warningly, but she wasn't afraid of Ralph Arnold.

The mayor shot Maya a dubious look but turned his full attention on the elderly reporter. "Headley, damn you, if you report this, I'll rip your head off and stuff it down the toilet."

Headley shrugged his sloping shoulders and tut-tutted.

"Admit it, Ralph," Selene said in a bored voice, "You picked the wrong investment this time. I warned you, but you wouldn't listen. There are plenty of entrepreneurs right here who could make you money hand over fist, but no, you had to go hunting down Yankee strangers."

"Selene, so help me," Arnold glared at his companion, "I'll paddle your rear end if you don't shut up and let me handle this myself."

Selene beamed and tousled his moussed hair. "Promise?"

Maya stared at her partner in astonishment but didn't manage a word. The byplay looked entirely sexual to her, but what did she know? Selene was perfectly capable of consorting with the enemy for her own purposes. But what about Katherine?

The mayor gripped Selene's wrist and pulled her hand out of his hair as he faced Maya and Axell. "I know what everyone is saying, but I didn't have anything to do with this," he declared. "I have the connections to get that road through here without taking such drastic measures. But I won't," he added hastily. "I'm recalling the petition for a through road. The shopping center operation is defunct until new investment money is found."

It was a little late for that, Maya thought, but she merely

snuggled into Axell's arms and pretended this was all a movie. She kind of liked being a hooked fish. She would face the disaster of the school when she was stronger.

"Tell it all, Mayor," Headley prompted. "The whole town will know it, sooner or later."

Ralph gritted his teeth and glanced helplessly at the small crowd of people around them. "Let me just talk to Axell."

At any other time, Maya would have objected, but she read something in the mayor's face that spoke of desperation, and she thought she was beginning to understand. Squeezing Axell's hand as he started to protest, she stood on tiptoe and pressed a kiss to his cheek. "Cleo and I will see to the kids. I can't bear watching the place burn to ashes. Come home and tell me about it later."

Axell caught her head, and kissed her fiercely, then let her walk off beside Cleo, with Matty between them. Both red heads held proudly, they swam through the crowd as easily as fish. He happened to think that Maya wore a rainbow-hued halo as she gathered Alexa into her arms and turned to offer reassurances to anxious parents and teachers. But then, he was crazy in love and capable of seeing sunshine and roses in a rainstorm—she gave him hope, so much hope and joy the future glowed with the brilliance of it.

He returned his glare to Ralph. "Spill."

Ralph glared at Selene and Headley and the policeman. The policeman hurried after Cleo. Headley crossed his arms stubbornly. Selene patted the mayor's cheek and strolled off to check the fire damage. Axell lifted an eyebrow in her direction but didn't question. Selene was as unpredictable as a summer storm.

"Well?" he asked.

"She only meant to help," Ralph insisted, before Headley could speak. "She didn't know the moron thought it was just an insurance scam for a derelict building. I just said I wished the flood had washed it away, and she took it a little too far."

Axell lifted his eyebrows in Headley's direction, but he already knew the answer. A part of him should have known it from the beginning. She'd always been too eager to please, too eager for acceptance, too eager to be someone. And Maya and the school had stood in her way.

"It's Katherine," Headley confirmed. "Katherine hired the arsonist."

❧ THIRTY-EIGHT ❧

If at first you do succeed,
try not to look astonished.

November 1999

I've seen them, Helen, our granddaughters. We're great-grandparents. Can you believe we're that old? Not you. You'll be forever young in that place in my mind where I see you, but I'm a senile old man now, weak and rotting at the core, as you discovered for yourself. It's so damned difficult watching them make the same mistakes we made, but I'm no example for them to follow, so I stay out of their way. Maybe they're forged of sterner stuff than you and me. Our dreams died for lack of trying, but they don't give up as easily as we did.

For their sake, I'm mending my ways, Helen. I can see now as you saw then that love and not money fulfills dreams and hopes. I've been hoping to impress them with my wealth, hoping to make a difference in their lives, but they're carving their own paths without need of my help. I can cut out the rottenness without fear now. If that means I'll be joining you soon, I won't complain. I'd rather hope that, if I do this right, someday our daughter's children will be proud to call me granddad.

Maya propped her elbows on the step behind her and admired the newly restored wood and glass of the foyer below them. The building was the first of her grandfather's properties to be renovated—an old Victorian on the residential outskirts of town.

Axell slid his arm behind her and idly stroked the small of her back. She loved the way he was always touching her. She'd missed that desperately growing up. Perhaps Cleo had forgiven the people they knew now as their grandparents, but she couldn't, not entirely. How could anyone, with any huge stretch of the imagination, believe cold hard cash or nasty alcohol could replace the warmth and love of someone's arms? She felt sorry for those broken people in the papers Cleo had saved, but she regretted more all the years wasted because no one cared to give her grandparents a hug, and they, in turn, had never passed their hugs to their daughter.

Perhaps they'd passed on their lesson anyway. Those papers were an eternal reminder of the love she shared, the love she felt compelled to pass along to all around her.

"I've never known anyone who could actually make dreams come true," Axell murmured with an undertone of amazement as he gazed at the new school created in just three months. "You must be a fairy godmother."

"Don't be silly. I didn't do all this. I just nagged a lot."

His hand rose higher to stroke the underside of her breast, but she could tell by his voice that his thoughts were elsewhere, following their own curious paths.

"No, you dreamed the impossible, and you persevered through everything this town and fate and whatever threw at you. You never gave up, Maya. And this school isn't the only dream you've made come true."

Glancing at the big man sprawling on the stairs with her, Maya felt the love welling up within her. Once, she would have sworn he didn't know how to relax enough to sprawl. Shrugging off his philosophical fantasies, she followed the path of Axell's long legs to the crumpled cuff of his expensive trousers, and grinned. The chaos of their life had diminished the importance of his immaculate attire, along with some of his uptight habits. She caught him in shirtsleeves more often now, although she noticed he'd carefully hung his coat over the newel post today.

"I still don't know what you're going to do with this place

here in town once the school is rebuilt out in the county," he continued idly, not expecting a response to his wilder theories.

She knew he wasn't criticizing her. All summer, he hadn't told her what to do unless asked, and he had accepted her eccentric, impractical ideas without question, because he actually believed she knew what she was doing. Maya beamed at him for that.

"The church across the street will need a new Sunday school building if it continues growing as it has. In two years, when my school is finished, Selene will persuade the church that this is the perfect property. If they don't think so"—she shrugged—"maybe we'll be big enough to need two schools by then."

Axell shot her a skeptical look but didn't comment on the likelihood of that. He couldn't, she knew. Their enrollment had tripled for the fall semester.

"Well, it's better than letting this old building sit here and rot, I suppose. Still, Selene and Cleo are taking a lot of chances by renovating all these old buildings instead of ripping them down. The land alone is worth a fortune."

They'd had this argument before and both knew the routine. Axell didn't like taking risks, but it wasn't his inheritance. Working with Selene had given Cleo a new lease on life, a reason to get up in the mornings, a life without the ceaseless worry of finding the next meal. Maya would exchange her entire inheritance just to see her sister drug-free. She didn't mind the risk.

"Our grandfather took from the community and never gave anything back," she replied complacently, watching the sun sparkle over the prisms hanging from the old chandelier they'd rescued from the fire remains. "He took drug money to buy some of these buildings. Maybe he tried to make up for his wrongs by renting the school and shop to us cheaply and telling the dealer to take a hike, but that doesn't right the wrongs he committed. But we can see downtown restored, see that the tenants have decent places to live, offer their children an education they wouldn't get elsewhere. It's a start."

Axell was watching her, and Maya wanted to bask in the

warmth of his approval and the stirring awareness between them, but she continued staring at the prisms. The opening ceremonies for the fall session of the Impossible Dream in its new location were about to start in half an hour. They didn't have time for what he was thinking, what they both were thinking. On some subjects, they were perfectly attuned. Her breasts tingled beneath his lightest touch.

"That's a nice thick carpet you had installed in the office," he murmured.

Maya darted him a hasty look. "We can't," she whispered. "There isn't time. Cleo and Selene . . ."

"Will be running late, as usual. Do you realize this is the first time in months we haven't had the kids underfoot?"

Oh, dear Lord, he was such a beautiful man. Maya gazed up into dreamy gray eyes and got lost in them. When Axell lowered his head and scorched her lips with his, she melted bonelessly and would have flowed down the stairs like hot molasses if he hadn't caught her waist and dragged her up.

"I hope you have ocean tides in the CD player." He hit the stereo button as he hauled her into the office and the crashing waves exploded from the speakers overhead.

"Axell, this is insane," Maya protested as he laid her down on the thick carpet and pinned her with his weight. He had his necktie on, for pity's sake, and his best white shirt.

Anyone could walk in downstairs. She forgot her objections as he slid his hand down the scooped neck of her summer dress. "Ummm, Axell, don't . . ." Her voice trailed off as his lips found a more interesting place to play and she arched upward for more.

"Don't what?" he murmured, trailing kisses up her throat. "Don't kiss my wife in the middle of the morning? We're perfectly respectable, you know."

No, they weren't. He had his big hand up her dress and she was frantically loosening his tie and looking for his buttons. There was nothing respectable about this. But it was wonderful, just the same.

"We're an old married couple," she whispered. "We should have grown out of this by now."

Axell snorted as he nibbled her ear. "We've been married all of five months and two don't count. I figure we've got another five good years at least." His fingers found her panties and stroked. "Maybe ten. Then I'll be over the hill and what will you do?"

She laughed with a trill blending with the ebb tides on the sound system. "Follow you over to see what's on the other side. You'll never be old, Axell Holm, you have too much curiosity in you."

A hank of golden hair fell across his brow as his smile gleamed down at her, and Maya's heart pounded as it always did when he looked at her like that. Nordic gods weren't meant to be possessed, but she thought maybe she owned just a little piece of him, or maybe more. She cried out in delight as he finally unsnarled their hampering clothing and sank into her.

Afterward, they lay in disarray upon the thick carpet, listening to the sounds of birdsong emanating from the speakers.

"I forgot to take my pill again last night," Maya worried out loud.

"You always forget to take it," Axell replied calmly, pulling her tighter against him. "One of these days, you're going to get caught." He tickled her breast as he adjusted her head more comfortably against his shoulder.

"You wouldn't mind?" she asked breathlessly as the sensations he generated swept through her.

Axell propped himself up on one elbow. "Are you trying to tell me something?"

She shook her head until her hair tumbled around her ears, but she smiled. "No, I just wanted to know you wouldn't mind. Alexa is a handful already."

He gazed speculatively at her still unbuttoned dress. "Maybe breast-feeding makes them quieter?" he suggested with a gleam of hope.

Hot waves of desire crashed through her at his words and look and implication. She wanted more babies, Axell's babies, and he seemed equally interested. She breathed a sigh of relief. She wasn't certain, after that last episode. . . .

"Shall I deliver them for you?" he inquired with a mischievous curve to his smile as he followed the path of her thoughts.

Maya smacked his arm and struggled to sit up. "I want sedation next time. Now we've got to get up from here. Selene and Cleo will be here any minute, then half the town will arrive."

"You're missing Matty," he declared as he helped her button her dress.

"He belongs with Cleo. She needs him." Maya shooed Axell's hand away when it did more stroking than buttoning. "But Constance misses him. There's a boy in our summer class, one of the scholarship kids who's in a foster home. . . ."

Axell sat up and straightened his tie while watching her warily. "Maya . . ."

She hastened on. "He's up for adoption but his foster parents can't afford another kid. He and Constance play well together. He's only six, Axell."

He sighed with resignation and fastened his belt as the door chimes rang below. "What's one more?" he agreed.

Maya flung her arms around his neck and buried his cheek in kisses. "I knew you'd say that. Thank you, thank you . . ." She was so blessed. She only wished everyone could have a man like Axell in their lives.

"Maya? Axell? You up there?"

"We're coming, we're coming!" Maya called joyfully as she brushed down her skirt and raced toward the hall.

That was an understatement, Axell reflected as he watched his wife flit from view. He shouldn't still be thinking about sex after just having it, but Maya did that to his mind. He wanted to pull her back down on the rug and put babies in her. He was deranged. In a wild spurt of caveman hunger to see his wife carrying his child, he'd agreed to take on another six-year-old. Given a chance, she'd populate his house with strangers.

And why not? They had room for them, and Maya had enough love in her heart for entire schools of children. With her help, he could learn to love them all, too. Tightening the knot in his tie, Axell wandered out to greet Maya's sister and partner. Hell, with Maya around, he wouldn't just accumulate kids, he'd have relatives and friends crawling all over the damned place. The house would never be empty again.

Spirits decidedly high, he stood at the top of the stairs and watched as Maya gesticulated wildly over whatever topic had popped into her head now. Selene caught sight of him and blew him a kiss. Cleo frowned, but Cleo always frowned. "Cool dress," Axell called down to his sister-in-law, and she brightened perceptibly. Like a kid, Cleo just needed attention.

As he sauntered down the stairs and all three women turned to welcome him, Axell realized something else: For the first time in his life, he was a participant and not an observer. He belonged in the world Maya created around them. Reaching Maya and hugging her shoulders, he savored the moment.

"The psychiatrist has declared Katherine competent to stand trial," Selene declared without prelude. "The lawyer will probably plead temporary insanity."

Axell was aware of Maya watching him with sympathy. Him. Katherine was a distant cousin of Maya's, had hired an arsonist and tried to destroy Maya's school, and Maya was looking at *him* with sympathy. He shook his head in disbelief and chucked her chin. "Don't look at me that way, honey. I didn't encourage her obsession any more than Ralph did. The lawyer's right, she was delusional." He didn't mention that the Pfeiffer side of the family seemed to have more than its fair share of quirks.

He chuckled as he looked down at the currently crimson streak in Maya's hair. It contrasted nicely with turquoise eyes and a pink flowered dress that only Maya could make sexy. And he'd thought Maya was delusional. He shook his head all over again.

"She was your *friend*," Maya reminded him. "She probably thought she was saving you from my clutches."

"Or making Ralph so happy he'd marry her," Selene replied dryly. "Which makes her truly delusional. Ralph will never marry anyone his mama doesn't approve of, and so long as he's taking care of her, his mama will never approve."

"Want me to put a contract out on his mama?" Cleo asked cynically. "Where are the twin disasters today anyway? I thought they'd be leading a protest march down Main Street against allowing riffraff into their community."

Axell grinned. "Mrs. Arnold and Sandra have gone up to Cherokee to break the bank at the casino. I think they're planning on buying the town back with Indian money."

Beside him, Maya snorted. "They're looking for men," she countered. "I wish them well with any they find up there."

Axell raised his eyebrows at the idea of his former mother-in-law picking up strangers, but the speculative look on Selene's face caught his eye. He'd wager Selene's father would be introducing a wealthy, unattached banker into the Arnold household before week's end.

The high-pitched whine of an electric guitar screamed through an amplifier, rattling the windows. For a minute, Axell thought the sound system had gone berserk. Then he remembered, and groaned. Stephen.

"Don't look that way," Maya reprimanded, hurrying toward the front door. "The advance sales on his School-Aid concert have brought in twice the scholarship money we'd hoped to have. We may not even have to mortgage the property to rebuild the school. So come outside and be polite."

The mayor had closed off all the streets around the school for the concert and ribbon-cutting ceremony. Crowds already poured through the early-September morning, carrying lawn chairs and coolers, elbowing for the shady seats beneath the spreading oaks, greeting friends and neighbors, seeing and being seen. It was the next best thing to a three-ring circus, Axell decided, and grinned. Maya had finally succeeded in turning the town into a circus.

His restaurant and Cleo's shop would be doing a booming business. He wasn't about to complain.

"Hey, cuz!" Ralph Arnold emerged from the business-suited knot of men near the stage to wrap an arm around Maya's shoulders. "Gonna save a dance for me?"

Grabbing the mayor's necktie, Selene hauled him sideways and branded his cheek with her lipstick. Ralph flushed, hurriedly removed his arm from Maya, and with an embarrassed grin, wrapped it around Selene's waist and kissed her cheek. Ralph would damned well ruin his career in politics with Selene at his side, but he'd be one wealthy former mayor. Who was he to stand in the way of true love and improbable matches? Maybe Maya ought to hand Ralph her granddaddy's journal for a lesson in life and love.

Proudly, Axell watched as Maya swam through the crowd, hugging all and sundry, mother and child alike. She was practically walking on air, and her happiness bubbled through him with a joy he'd never quite known. She'd unlocked something inside him that allowed the sun to shine in and the music to ring as it never had before. The entire street had become one of her kaleidoscopes, swirling with colors and shapes, but this kaleidoscope had sound, too—the sound of laughter and love and music.

"Got you by the balls, doesn't she?" Headley asked dryly, coming up behind him.

"Among other things." Axell didn't take offense. Headley was a lonely old man. He wouldn't understand.

He watched as Stephen helped Constance onto the stage. Constance had been bubbling with excitement for weeks. She was becoming the outgoing child he'd never been.

"I hear the shopping center project is back on."

Axell shrugged, brought back to the moment. "Maya and Cleo sold the developer a right of way through the field down the road in exchange for an access road through the back of the property so they don't have to worry about floods anymore. The Garden Club is overseeing the removal of any plants in the way of construction. Maya has a way of working things out."

Maya had a way of making impossible dreams happen. If only more people would ignore the word "impossible," mankind could visit Mars and Jupiter, abolish prejudice and poverty, and create utopia. He'd settle for the sunshine of her love.

"Yeah." Headley sighed in contentment as Maya swam

back in their direction, her smile a brilliant sunbeam as she spotted them. "Maybe she should run for mayor."

"Over my dead body," Axell declared boldly, reaching for his flashy wife and dragging her close.

Tipping her head back, she gazed at him through dangerously long lashes. "Is Cleo putting out a contract on your body?" she asked laughingly, wrapping her arms around his waist without an ounce of shyness. "I'll take care of her."

And Axell realized with the freedom of love that she would, that she would take care of him and his daughter and everyone around her, and would make a damned good mayor should she ever put her scattered mind to it. He didn't have to do it all himself any longer.

He hugged her tight against him and whispered against her hair. "You take care of everyone else. I'll take care of you. Fair enough?"

"Yeah." She snuggled blissfully against him as Stephen's band, with Constance in accompaniment, roared into a rousing rendition of an electronic "Carolina in My Mind," and the crowd cheered wildly.

*Read on for a sneak peek
at the next thrilling romance
from Patricia Rice*

NOBODY'S ANGEL

Coming in December 2000

Published by Ivy Books

After all the vengeful years of plotting and planning, and weeks of searching, he thought he'd found her.

Adrian's stomach rumbled as he ordered a beer and clenched his fingers into his sweaty palms. In his haste to get there after work, he hadn't stopped to eat. He couldn't eat. His stomach was twisted in knots so tight he wasn't certain if even the beer would pass through.

His hand clutched the bottle the waiter brought, but Adrian's gaze never left the stage. The shaved-head waiter shoved his tip in his pocket and sauntered off. The kid looked too young to work in a bar, but Adrian wasn't in any position to card him. He sank lower in the cracked vinyl seat of the booth and tried drinking the beer, barely noticing the taste. He hadn't touched the stuff in years, but in these last few weeks of hunting his prey, he'd guzzled enough brew to dull any desire he might have had to drown in it.

The noise level in the barroom had already reached rocket-launch proportions. Tearing his gaze from the unlit platform of the stage, Adrian scanned the almost all-male gathering, gauging the crowd as he had learned to do during these last years in confinement, surrounded by repressed male hostility.

The red and blue bar lights illuminated the smoky haze just enough for him to catch glimpses of weather-seasoned faces. Despite the peanut shells crunching beneath boots and heels, this wasn't a polite yuppie hangout where the constant murmur of networking laced through the entertainment. This was a very large, noisy, drinking, brawling, pickup crowd. How the hell had Miss La-De-Da wound up here?

She was a "miss" now, he remembered. Before, she'd been *Mrs.* SOB.

For the most part, the crowd left him alone. Herd instinct warned them to steer clear of loners, and his naturally brown coloring marked him as alien in their all-white world. He knew how to downplay his mother's Hispanic origins when he wanted to, but he wasn't in the mood for that game anymore. He had only one purpose here—to find the woman who had ruined his life and return the favor.

Adrian cracked a peanut shell between tense fingers and sought the stage again. The band was moving about, setting up instruments. The last singer had left to a chorus of boos and catcalls. The audience didn't care for melancholy love songs, it seemed.

He hadn't even known Tony's wife could sing. Hell, what he knew about her could fit in a thimble. If it hadn't been for that conniving old reporter Headley, Adrian could have spent the rest of his life searching for her.

Or he could have bought a gun on the street and rapped a few skulls until he got what he wanted.

First time around, he would try the peaceful approach. He wasn't in a hurry to spend any more time behind bars. The black hole of the last four years had already sucked him dry.

The audience stirred restlessly. The tinny noise from the jukebox didn't provide sufficient vibration to animate more than a tapping toe or two. Two couples in the booth across from him erupted in a name-calling argument. The burly bouncer edged his way through the throng at the horseshoe bar, coming in their direction.

Adrian sank lower in his seat. He was out of his territory. Hell, he was out of his state, violating probation. No one knew him here, but he had no wish to be identified later.

The band began tuning up. The crowd's roar lessened perceptibly, and all eyes turned toward the stage. Obviously, the performer wasn't a newcomer.

He propped his snakeskin boots on the far seat and sipped from his bottle. Those boots had caused him some ribbing years ago, back in Charlotte, in the good ol' days. But boots were the order of the day here in Knoxville, in this end of town. Maybe he should have a hat, too.

He couldn't afford one.

He didn't go down that depressing trail. He'd been broke before. He knew how to persevere against all odds. Hope was what mattered. As long as he had a smidgen of hope to cling to, he would survive.

Hope came in the form of Faith this time. Faith Hope.

Adrian snorted at the incongruous appellation. He assumed it was a stage name. He'd known her as Faith Nicholls back in the days of yore. Even that name hadn't fit. Faith Dollars might have made sense. Faith Fatbucks. Faith Moneybags. Her kind didn't deal in nickels and dimes.

Curiosity curled the edges of his mind as the spotlight blinked on. Maybe the beer was working on his empty stomach. He threw another peanut in his mouth and wrapped his fingers around the neck of the bottle. What the hell was Faith Moneybags doing in a dive like this?

Headley had broken the story that had ended in Adrian's arrest all those years ago. The old reporter had felt responsible or guilty enough to keep in touch ever since. Headley had been the one to tell him that Ms. Moneybags had walked out on her SOB of a husband long before the trial. Adrian hadn't known that at the time. Nicholls hadn't said a word, and once the shit hit, Adrian had been too busy trying to save his own hide to care what his partner's wife did.

The spotlight changed colors, and Adrian popped another peanut as his gut clenched. Would he recognize her after all this time? Last time he'd seen her, she'd looked like the proper SouthPark matron she was—her flaxen hair smoothed into a chignon, her red suit screaming "designer," her nails neatly buffed and polished as she swore on a Bible to tell the truth, the whole truth, and nothing but the truth.

She'd lied.

The band struck a fast chord with a heavy bass beat. The crowd roared, probably more in gratitude at not having to make more small talk than in appreciation for the music. If that was her signature tune, it wasn't very original.

Adrian had his doubts that he'd found the right woman, but Headley had sworn she was in Knoxville and that he'd heard reports she'd been singing in bars. That meant some of Headley's drunken cronies had seen someone who looked like her. But if she used the name Faith . . .

The cymbals crashed, the guitar hit a screeching crescendo, and the spotlight burned red.

Adrian nearly crushed the bottle neck as Faith Hope strolled on stage, belting out a familiar country refrain.

He didn't hear the song. He strained to see the Stepford Wife he knew behind the white leather miniskirt, sequined vest, bouncing blond locks, and red knee-high boots. Only the red silk shirt hinted at the woman he wanted to see. He didn't recognize her, but he'd never really met Faith Nicholls. He'd seen her in the office occasionally, saw her once at the trial. This couldn't be her.

Disappointment washed over him as the singer crooned a song of love, her blond shoulder-length hair swinging with the beat. She already had toes tapping and heels stomping. She didn't look any older than the damned waiter.

He signaled for another beer and continued staring. Maybe she was the right size. It was hard to tell. There was a difference in perspective between a witness stand and a spotlighted stage. He remembered her as small-boned, but the boxy suit she'd worn the last time he'd seen her didn't superimpose well over the curves in tight white leather on the stage.

How in hell did that enormous voice exist in such a delicate package?

Adrian would have ripped the cap off the bottle with his teeth if the waiter hadn't already removed it. His blood simmered and settled in his groin as he studied the slender bundle of energy on the stage. She probably wasn't being deliberately seductive. She'd covered nearly every inch of her body but the long legs, and she wore boots to de-emphasize those.

He'd planned to bang the first whore he found as soon as the prison gates opened, but life had got in the way. That had been a mistake. As Faith Hope's voice lowered into a sultry refrain, he practically sizzled in his own juices.

It couldn't be her. Nothing he had seen of Faith Nicholls had ever caused him to so much as blink an eyelash, and not just because she'd been his partner's wife. He didn't like dainty blonds. People shorter than him made him feel like a gangly youth, and he didn't like blonds.

But the woman on stage was an irresistible ball of fire. She shouted, she crooned, she laughed and sweet-talked her way into the heart of every damned man in there. And she wasn't that great a singer.

Adrian scowled as even that realization didn't cool his lust. He wasn't a musician, but he recognized most of the songs because he'd grown up hearing them blaring out of the radio. She had most of the words right and didn't mangle the notes badly enough to jar, but a skilled musician she was not. She captured the audience with sheer passion alone.

He watched in awe as she not only silenced the testosterone-laden crowd with the haunting refrains of "Blue Bayou," but had them weeping in their beers for lost loves and lost places as her voice broke with tears on the chorus. Without missing a beat, she swung into a rocking version of "Rocky Top," and the crowd stampeded to the dance floor, with or without partners. The woman might not be a musical genius, but she knew her audience.

He couldn't tolerate the doubt any longer. This couldn't be Faith Nicholls. Every cell in his brain screamed the impossibility. Respectable society matrons did not descend to stinking, smoky dives to sing for truck drivers and hog farmers. But he couldn't bear hitting another dead end, either. It had to be her. He didn't know where else to look, and the rest of his life depended on finding Faith Nicholls.

Leaving the bottle on the table, Adrian edged around the foot-stomping crowd on the floor. Sticking to the shadows outside the circle of light, he leaned against a massive, vibrating amplifier at the edge of the stage and watched her from a few yards away.

She was all sparkle and light, flashing sequins, flying golden hair, and shimmering stockings over tanned legs. She stroked the microphone and crooned into it in a way that probably aroused every prick in the place. It certainly did wonders for his own.

Wryly, Adrian noted she had a run in her stocking that snaked a thin trail along a leg so shapely a man's hand could mold it like clay. He wanted to cling to that small evidence of imperfection, to prove to his straining groin that she was a woman just like any other and no goddess capable of restoring his life with a wave of a wand.

But if she was Faith Nicholls, she had that power.

Normally, Faith wouldn't have noticed a stranger standing in the darkness. She tried not to really see any of the men avidly following her every move. She hated the stares and concentrated on the words and the music. But the intensity of the stranger's gaze drew her like a magnet. Alone in a crowd, he collected shadows.

Did she know him? Was that why he was staring at her? Faith swung to the other side of the stage, away from him, but the spotlight allowed only so much leeway. She preferred not to be recognized, but she'd always known the chance was out there.

Damn, why didn't he at least move? Out of the corner of her eye, she caught the coiled tension in the muscled arms folded tightly over a wide chest, giving the lie to his casual pose against the amp. Had he worn a cowboy hat or a work shirt or anything normal, she might have disregarded him entirely, but in a black long-sleeved shirt and jeans he was a silhouette of sharp edges. She caught a glimpse of silver at his ear and the swing of coal-dark hair slicked back in a long ponytail. He had DANGER imprinted on his forehead as clearly as any flashing road sign.

A beer bottle crashed somewhere in the rear of the bar, jarring her attention back to where she was. On Friday and Saturday nights the place could explode like a powder keg if not controlled. She could see Egghead elbowing his way to the shouting combatants, and she eased into a laughing song. The man in the shadows didn't break a smile at the sexual innuendos and puns that had the rest of the audience howling.

She'd break after the next set and hope the stranger would leave. The regulars there treated her with respect and had a habit of removing hecklers without Egghead's help. But the stranger wasn't heckling. Maybe no one noticed him but her.

She shivered as the altercation in the rear escalated. She needed to concentrate on the songs, soothe the savage beasts, give her audience the kick they came for, not obsess over possibly lethal strangers. Keeping the crowd from igniting into warfare was in her job description.

Even the stranger turned at the sharp report of gunfire. A woman screamed, men shouted, and the crowd broke in two directions at once.

It took only seconds, too fast to entirely follow. The dancers on the floor surged toward the stage as the crowd at the bar retreated from the brawl onto the dance floor. Someone took a dive over the sound and light booth, tilting it precariously. Beer spilled, amplifiers crashed, and the house lights shorted out just as a mass of bodies rammed into the plywood stage.

Faith tripped on a wire in the dark and started to tumble into the sweat-and-beer stench of the crowd.

Taut-muscled arms caught her by the waist and hauled her out of the melee with no more effort than that of a shopper heaving a bag of flour into a cart.

She gasped as she sailed over sprawling bodies and swinging fists into the relative safety of the harbor at stage right, sheltered by heavy equipment. The amp the stranger had been leaning against shifted as someone slammed into it, but the stage behind it held. She gulped a deep breath the instant the hard arms released her.

"Some party you throw here," a whiskey-velvet voice spoke through the darkness.

She knew that voice, but she couldn't place it. The mellow drawl shivered down her spine, reminding her of ages past, long-ago emotions, times won and lost and better not sought again. Though she searched for the memory, the connection eluded her. Maybe, in the chaos of the moment, she imagined the voice's self-assurance.

"We hand out balloons to everyone still standing when the lights come on," she answered lightly, trying to ignore the electric vibrations generated by his proximity. His tension ignited shock waves in her bloodstream, making her wonder if she could short out the lights by touching them.

"Faith, hey, you all right?" the drummer called from the stage.

"I'm fine, Tommy. I don't know about the mike.

Maybe Artie ought to unplug the amps before the electricity returns. They may short the place out again."

"Hell, let's electrocute a few of the assholes first," the bass guitarist replied from the edge of the stage near them. "Where you at, Faith? Want me to get you outta here?"

"Go pull the plug, Artie, and stick your finger in the socket."

Tommy hooted, and apparently ungrudgingly, Artie stood up and sauntered back to the sound and light booth.

"Speak softly and carry a big whip," the stranger quipped dryly from behind her, nearly startling her to death. He was as still and silent as a phantom until he had a notion to make his presence known.

"They're good guys; they just don't think it's macho to give up." Faith didn't turn around to look at him. Intuition told her it would be as dangerous as gazing at Medusa, even through the veil of darkness. "I appreciate your help, but I'll be all right now. They'll have the lights back shortly."

"It has to be you," he whispered.

Startled, she froze.

He hesitated. Even though she couldn't see him, she knew he wanted to say something.

To her surprise, he didn't.

As the lights flickered on, she turned, and he was gone.

By Patricia Rice

GARDEN OF DREAMS

JD Marshall is a computer programming genius on the run to protect his company, his teenage son, and his life. When JD's truck flips over near the tiny backwoods town of Madrid, Kentucky, Miss Nina Toon comes to his rescue and offers him and his son shelter. Opening her home and her heart and her most precious dreams to JD, Nina decides to take a chance on love. But it will be the biggest gamble of her life. . . .

BLUE CLOUDS

Around the small California town where Pippa Cochran has fled to escape an abusive boyfriend, Seth Wyatt is called the Grim Reaper—and not just because he is a bestselling author of horror novels. He's an imposing presence, battling more inner demons than even an indefatigable woman like Pippa can handle. Yet, while in his employ, she can't resist the emotional pull of his damaged son or the chance to hide in the fortress he calls a home.

VOLCANO

After landing in gorgeous St. Lucia on business, Penelope Albright receives the shock of her life: She is accused of smuggling drugs. Then a sexy stranger appears, claiming to be her husband, "kidnapping" her before trouble begins. Or so she thinks. Trouble and Charlie Smith have met. He needs a wife—temporarily—to help him keep a low profile while snooping into the mysterious disappearance of his partner. And like it or not, Penny is already involved.

Published by The Ballantine Publishing Group.
Available at bookstores everywhere.

Sometimes you have to lose
everything to find what really
matters. . . .

ON MYSTIC
LAKE
by
Kristin Hannah

Published by Ivy Books.
Available in bookstores
everywhere.

BODYGUARD
by Suzanne Brockmann

Threatened by underworld boss Michael Trotta, Alessandra Lamont is nearly blown to pieces in a mob hit. The last thing she wants is to put what's left of her life into the hands of the sexy, loose-cannon federal agent who seems to look right through her yet won't let her out of his sight.

FBI agent Harry O'Dell's ex-wife and son were tragic casualties in his ongoing war against organized crime. He'll do whatever it takes to bring Trotta down— even if it means sticking like glue to this blonde bombshell. But the explosive attraction that threatens to consume them both puts them into the greatest danger of all . . . falling in love.

Published by The Ballantine Publishing Group.
Available in bookstores everywhere.

HEARTTHROB
by Suzanne Brockmann

Once voted the "Sexiest Man Alive," Jericho Beaumont had dominated the box office before his fall from grace. Now poised for a comeback, he wants the role of Laramie bad enough to sign an outrageous contract with top producer Kate O'Laughlin—one that gives her authority to supervise JB's every move, twenty-four hours a day, seven days a week.

The last thing Kate wants to do is baby-sit her leading man, and Jericho Beaumont may be more than she can handle. A player in every sense of the word, he is an actor of incredible talent—and a man with a darkly haunted past. Despite her better judgment, Kate's attraction flares into explosive passion, and she is falling fast. But is she being charmed by the real Jericho or the superstar who dazzles the world?

Published by The Ballantine Publishing Group.

Available wherever books are sold.